Falling Through

Falling Through

Into the Void: Book One

Ben Pick

To my family and friends, who turn every day into an adventure worth living.

CONTENTS

CONTENTS

CONTENTS

1

Party Tricks

Derek

Derek Fen struggled to keep up with Tracy Wayfield. He wheezed and clutched the stitch in his side as he hurried after her.

I could almost kick myself for letting her in on my secret. When someone develops superpowers, secrecy is paramount.

Tracy led them on a snaking course through the lush, green forest of his backyard, following some wayward internal compass.

She stopped and pointed at a small, gray rock on the ground. "Prove I'm right. Try to move that stone without touching it."

Her chosen target was one among many. Derek looked around to ensure they were out of sight of his neighbors' homes. They were alone.

"Why can't you believe me?"

"Because you're being ridiculous. You're not psychic. How do I know you didn't set up another trick like that floating pen illusion in your den? I'm controlling your tests to prove you're messing with me, and this is all a joke."

Derek took a deep breath to scrub his mind of distractions. He stood several feet away and imagined an invisible third hand reaching for the stone, lifting it free.

It didn't budge.

He stared at the stone a while longer, feeling the hot September air bake his skin and make his shirt stick to his chest. The brutal Maryland summer held Autumn in a stranglehold and showed no signs of relinquishing until every flower had wilted.

But suffering on this lazy Sunday afternoon was worth it if he convinced Tracy his skills weren't figments of an overactive imagination.

Tracy brushed away her chestnut bangs, which clung to her forehead. "Okay, Derek the Magnificent. Can we go back inside? Your neighbors must have thousands of turkeys. You want to show me an impossible power, how about making me not gag on their sulfuric shits from a mile out? I bet they can smell this all the way in Washington, D.C., and that's a thirty-minute drive. Forty, if you're at the wheel."

Power sparked within Derek's trembling fingertips like a buildup of static electricity. "Give me a minute. I almost had it."

"Fine. One minute." Tracy dug in her small purse for her phone.

A rock ballad's intro blasted from the device, destroying his train of thought. "Knock it off!"

"What?" Tracy drummed her fingers against her phone's plastic case. "This soundtrack inspires me when I need to concentrate."

"Lifting stones with my mind isn't easy and your musical choice from three decades ago isn't helping."

Tracy stopped her music, returning the woods to relative silence, which gave Derek a chance to think.

He focused on the gray stone partially buried under soil and moss, and concentrated his thoughts on lifting it. As if a gate unlocked inside of him, power flooded along the canals of his veins. Lingering energy charged his unruly head of hair, making less obedient strands stand upright.

Tall pine trees swished under an overdue breeze. Every inhale brought scents of sap and pine needles. Each exhale felt as though he might unleash a breath of fire from the power building inside him.

His telekinetic hand pried Tracy's chosen rock loose. It spun, flinging a thin layer of moss onto his shoe. The rock wavered in the air. Derek poured out more power to keep it airborne. Squeezing too hard with his mental muscle, the rock flew at his arm, breaking skin before plunging into the ground. He flexed to make the accidental slip seem intentional.

One side of Derek's lips curled. Much like other rules, he found the laws of last year's physics class to be little more than suggestions. He toed the line between the believable and the unexplained for a few weeks since he began moving objects with his thoughts. At some point, the line faded into the distance until it was no more than a dot.

Tracy's oval face softened. "Hmm. I know there's a trick. Move that stick so I can see how you hid the string."

"Seriously? You still don't believe me?"

She shook her head, her finger still extended, pointing at the stick.

Using his power was much easier this time. A slight tremor rattled the stick, lifting it a few feet above the ground. He pushed it away with enough force to snap in half against the trunk of a thick oak.

"In-ter-es-ting." Tracy's voice dragged over each syllable.

Derek put his hands behind his back and bumped the side of her hand with his mental fist. Tracy jumped, giving a small yelp.

Her cinnamon eyes settled on Derek, looking him up and down. She moved in close and jabbed his chest with a finger. "You—aren't —lying?"

"Nope."

Tracy settled against a log, speechless, regarding Derek with awe.

Derek's smug grin stretched across his face. "See, this was the reaction I was expecting back in my house."

"This is too much," Tracy said into her hands. "We need the rest of our friends here."

The excitement building in Derek came crashing down around him. "They were all busy. At least they let me know this time."

"Then it's up to me."

She leaped to her feet and grabbed Derek's arm. "This is incredible! Let's see how far you can take this."

"You're not scared? I am. You skipped the three or four emotions I went through when I first discovered these powers."

"I'm well past panicking and want to know what you can do. I'll be here to spot so you don't hurt yourself." Tracy's eyes reflected the light filtering through the trees. "Move that branch."

The forest was littered with potential targets. Derek doubted Tracy cared which object he used his mind to throw. He launched a branch out of sight. Tracy responded with enthusiastic applause.

Though he only intended to raise the branch to waist height, Derek still brushed his shoulder as a sign of triumph. "Anything else you'd like me to move?"

Tracy retrieved a plump, green pawpaw fruit from her purse. "Juggle this."

"Thanks for stealing my family's crops."

She had the decency to flash a sheepish grin while inspecting the prize. "I figured it was payment for braving this sauna of a day."

Derek's mind carried the fruit into his outstretched hand. Not much for juggling, he used the telekinetic third hand to toss the fruit back to Tracy.

His delighted friend kept finding more rocks to throw or leaves to make dance. Luckily, accuracy wasn't a concern. They dodged his misfired projectiles when he got overzealous, ever pushing himself to do more. A couple of rocks bounced off his head and left tiny welts.

Eventually, he collapsed when his telekinetic fingers failed to raise a pebble off the ground.

Tracy loomed over him, offering her hand to help him up. "Feel like calling it a day and heading back inside?"

Derek's head swam and his eyes drooped. "I got one more in me."

"In that case, enough of these warm-ups. Push that tree."

Her finger settled on a fifty-foot oak, which must have sprouted when his parents were kids. The tree was wider than his outstretched arms, and thousands of times heavier than the sticks and stones he'd been tossing.

Rot had eaten its insides, causing it to fall and wedge against another upright elm, giving him a chance. Derek placed his heavyset arms against it and pushed for all he was worth.

The leaning tree didn't budge.

Derek clenched his teeth; his pride was on the line. "I got this."

Cobwebs flushed from his thoughts. He threw his mental prowess against the might of the forest. Pushing against the immobile tree with telekinesis pushed him back, his power proving to be too weak. Losing inches, Derek dug his shoes into the dirt. Anything to hold him in place.

Tracy stepped away from his tree-focused fury as he let loose an impressive string of curses.

"I have it. Give me one more shot." Derek went deeper and deeper inside until he felt as though he was dropping into a bottomless pit.

The edges of his vision dimmed. A prickling sensation spread from the base of his neck along his spine like glacial melt dripping down his back. The fringes of his mind recognized the sound of a low growl. He pressed on.

I'm passing Tracy's test.

Seven points of light shone from the darkness inside his mind. Blazing lines formed in the space between the lights. These connected the dots to create the ends of a star, which seared into Derek's thoughts and obliterated all others.

On the other side of the star in his mind's eye, a large bear-like creature stared back at him with pale eyes. Undaunted by the odd creature inside his head, Derek reached out and touched the barrier separating them. Pockets of power blistered on the shimmering surface around his fingertips.

He pushed his hand through the cold liquid substance, reaching for the immense lake of power beyond. Nausea riled his stomach, as though he had plunged his hand into his chest to rip out his still-beating heart.

Pressing through the pain, he felt like he inhaled lightning as his lungs sent supercharged energy to lift lethargic limbs.

Derek shaped a giant fist of air above his right hand and aimed at the tree.

When the raw power could no longer be contained without ripping him apart, he hurled the giant fist at the ancient oak. It struck with enough force to make him wince at the booming sound.

In a slow-motion domino effect, the elm tree bracing the fallen oak bent under the shifted weight until it gave out entirely. Thundering cracks echoed over the forest. An uneven splintering break skewed the larger elm in a new, unexpected direction—toward Tracy.

She was sluggish to react, likely thinking herself safe and out of the way. She leaped to the side to escape the falling bulk but fell short of clearing the tons of wood falling on top of her.

Derek ignored his agonizing muscles and pulled in more power, scalding his insides with its journey from his stomach to his arms. He punched the air, desperate to save Tracy.

A blue ball of light emerged from his fist, searing his skin from the inside out. In desperation, he trusted in his powers, throwing the ball at the falling tree, splitting the tree into smaller pieces.

Splinters showered the forest floor, followed by faint trails of smoke. An afterimage of the light scorched his sight, leaving a streak across his vision. The ball continued to decimate everything in its path. It plowed through several trees before fizzling to nothing.

The ground shook as two solid tree limbs landed safely on either side of Tracy.

She stared up at him from her crouched position, unharmed and stunned at his display of power.

Derek's chest heaved. Pink, flaky bits of flesh peeled from his knuckles. His fist looked as though he had spent a week at the beach without suntan lotion. Tingling pain ran across his exposed inner layers of flesh. He stared at his hand, spinning it about, expecting to find it belonged to someone else.

Wrong. This is all wrong.

Derek shuddered, uncomfortable in his own skin. He dug his fingernails into his arms to get rid of the sensation of heavy sludge caked over them.

The sounds of knives carving wood yanked him back to reality.

The bear-like figure Derek had seen in his head paced between trees. Its white fur stood out against the brown and green of the forest, and its long claws scraped over a fallen log. Tiny horns protruded from behind its ears and sharp teeth extended from its open mouth.

Derek strained to move, to run, to do anything. His feet were anchored in place, ignoring his brain's pleas to budge.

The creature's pale, milky eyes tracked him hungrily.

2

Burned Remains

Tracy

Charred bark rained down on Tracy. The tree that was moments away from squishing her had blown to pieces. Embers burned pin-prick holes through her clothes. Her nose stung with the crisp, acrid odor.

Tracy relished the relief at still being among the living and not flattened by a tree. She wobbled across the littered forest floor to reach Derek, nervous laughter uncontrollably escaping her lips. Branches and leaves crunched beneath her boots, a haunting sound amid the absolute stillness.

Blood dripped from Derek's flayed hand. The incredible power he'd hurled carved new exit paths through his skin. He was planted in the same spot from before his feats of mental strength, like an immobile statue. Sweat-soaked hair clung to his forehead, leaving unkempt brown strands stuck at odd angles. Derek's fair-colored cheeks were flushed with exertion. His mouth hung open in a stupefied cavern.

Tracy sucked in a deep breath. "That looks bad. Let's get you home so I can wrap your hands."

Derek didn't respond. His dark brown eyes stared into the woods.

"Did you hear me?" Tracy tapped his shoulder.

Derek's hefty arms encircled her in a crushing embrace. "Thank you for being okay."

Tracy extracted herself from his grip. She laughed, but it sounded hollow. "Come on, you're not able to get rid of me that easily."

"We have to get inside," he hissed, pushing her behind him. His fists lifted to chin height in some ill-conceived fighting stance. "We aren't alone."

Chomping sounds, which resembled a crumbling house, brought her attention to a large bear-like creature. Easily ten feet high, it gnashed the tree trunks Derek had exploded with his power. The creature's large muscles rolled the smoldering logs.

Tracy held in a scream.

Derek's legs gave out. He dropped to his knees onto a bed of leaves. Tracy winced at the crunching leaves, worried it might catch the creature's attention. She let out a breath as it ignored Derek, continuing its meal.

Even though he outweighed her by a good sixty pounds, adrenaline fueled Tracy, giving her the strength to pull Derek to his feet. They took off for Derek's house, his arm draped over her shoulder for support.

Derek's thick legs stumbled over roots, putting more of his weight onto Tracy's shoulders. She'd gained half a head on him since her seventeenth birthday this past summer. Thanks to the awkwardly late growth spurt, she was forced to hunch over to drag him along.

Branches nicked her skin and thickets snagged her shirt, pulling her to either side as she broke free. The woods didn't want to let them go. Tracy refused to turn around or slow down to check if the creature was chasing them.

She pushed her legs harder, afraid the creature would hunt them once it finished eating the logs.

They broke from the tree line, greeted by Derek's renovated barn-turned-family-style house. Large windows allowed a perfect view from most of the first floor, but they would do little to stave off the huge bear. The outer shell was made of burgundy wooden boards, meant to look impressive and not intended for defense.

Tracy hobbled with Derek to the side entrance of the home's addition, ready to barricade the doors. Once inside, she lowered him to the floor and checked all the windows for signs of the creature. Relief flushed through her; it hadn't followed them.

She threw down a towel on the couch in the den under Derek's sweaty body. Tracy angled his body to not ruin the world's most comfortable royal blue couch with blood.

If need be, the couch, along with the furniture in the den, could be useful to barricade the windows and doors. Unlike Derek's messy room upstairs, this den had a sense of order. Full bookshelves lined the walls. Although she normally preferred her Kindle because it contained twice the content, right now she appreciated the extra furniture. She planned how best to drag the heavy pieces around if she needed to reinforce the windows and entrances.

She peeked out the windows again, scared of what might be gazing back at her. She saw no signs of the creature.

She hurried to the medicine cabinet to get bandages and ointment. In closing the mirrored door, she stole a quick look at her reflection. She looked a little better than Derek. Smudges of dirt marred her creamy, light complexion, and she desperately needed a fresh shirt as this one was riddled with singed spots. Minor cuts ran along her arms, tingling in the cool, indoor air.

Tracy returned to Derek, applying liberal amounts of antiseptic to his knuckles. He tried and failed to hide his wince at the contact. When finished, she wrapped his hands in gauze.

"What the hell was that bear doing here?"

Derek lifted his head to look out the window. "I think I created it or summoned it from somewhere else."

Tracy sank into a chair. "What makes you say that?"

"I saw it in my head before it appeared in the forest."

"That's odd." Tracy shifted her thoughts to the bigger problem. "How do we stop it?"

"Want to try the police or animal control?"

"They won't take us seriously if we tell the truth." She shifted in her seat for a position where her damp clothes didn't cling to her skin. "We seem safe for now, so tell me, how did you get your powers? Maybe there's something we can use to give us an advantage if that thing comes back."

"About two weeks ago—"

"Pause right there. You waited *two weeks* to tell me about this?"

"I didn't know what to say and look what it took for you to believe me."

"Fair enough. Promise you won't keep any more secrets."

"Deal. So, two weeks ago, I felt strangely connected to the objects in the den. It felt like static electricity building in my fingertips. The next thing I knew, my video game controller soared from the couch into my hands. That scared the crap out of me, and I dropped it. I thought I was studying too much and had gone crazy. Then, I willed the controller to leap back into my hands without touching it. I've been struggling to make sense of where these powers came from since that day."

"Until we piece it together, I'd suggest you practice using your powers so you can toss cars instead of sticks."

"That's not a good idea. You almost died when I cut loose with my powers. Besides, we still have that monster to worry about. Training may bring more of them here."

Tracy shook her head. "If you learn to control these powers, you won't erupt like you did earlier. You might even be able to handle that creature and not create any more. We don't know what caused it to come to life and we need to make sure you don't do it again."

A roaring yawn escaped Derek. "Fine, fine. You make valid points. Mind if I get some rest? I'm wiped from your experiments."

She examined his injuries to ensure none were bleeding through the bandages. "Rest up. I'll make sure you don't get hurt the next time you practice."

"Thanks."

Tracy peered out the window hesitantly.

"Do you want to stay here? It might be safer to stay put."

She sighed. "Nah. I don't see anything unusual out there. If I leave now, I think I'll be fine to get home. Call me if you spot that thing."

"Sure. Stay safe." Clearly unable to keep his eyes open, Derek drifted into a nap.

"See you tomorrow at school," she whispered.

Tracy carefully left his house as quietly as possible, in case the creature was nearby. Tiptoeing to her car, she was ready to sprint back into Derek's house at the first sign she wasn't alone.

She drove off in silence, wary of what might hop out from behind any tree along the driveway.

3

Guidance

Derek

Early Monday morning, Derek arrived at Highland View High School. He sat in his guidance counselor's office, waiting to plan his college-bound future. His fingers fidgeted and he tapped his feet, his thoughts still not having settled since yesterday.

Thanks to Tracy, he had taken his powers further than he knew was possible. There was nothing more incredible than moving the world with a thought. Even spotting that strange bear monster couldn't bring his mood down. Thankfully, he hadn't seen it since he and Tracy left the woods.

His guidance counselor's office lacked any family photos or a generic portrait of a calming, picturesque forest.

The stress ball emblazoned with the school's name and plastic labyrinth cube on Mr. Marshal's desk begged to be played with. Derek resisted the urge. Instead, he rubbed the scabs covering his knuckles. Despite the blast of energy, which ripped his skin apart, he had healed considerably overnight.

Derek waited for his guidance counselor to look at him, unwilling to interrupt Mr. Marshal banging on his computer's keyboard.

"Save, you outdated pile of scrap!"

Wrinkles filled Mr. Marshal's forehead beneath a full, silver mane that grew atop his head. Mr. Marshal's argyle, long-sleeved shirt stretched over his muscular upper body.

Derek struggled to not stare at what was missing. The right arm of Mr. Marshal's shirt was tied in a knot, dangling freely. Rumors varied as to what happened to Mr. Marshal, each as colorful as the next. The most popular one was he lost his arm defusing bombs on foreign shores. Derek hoped that wasn't true.

Derek couldn't venture a guess at Mr. Marshal's age. He seemed both too young and too old. More than anything else, his eyes carried too much weight.

Unwilling to remain idle, Derek said, "I followed your advice and confided in someone I trust to work through my issues."

Mr. Marshal looked up from his computer at Derek. "When I said that, I was implying you should reach out to me."

This old man was too far out of touch with anything in this century. Tracy had proved to be an excellent alternative to reveal his secret to, even if she was overzealous.

"I'm here because I need your help in getting into my dream college. I'm not looking for life advice."

Mr. Marshal cleared his throat. "The two are one and the same."

"I haven't decided what I truly want, so how can you know what's best for me?"

"I remember our discussions. You're going to change the world with a degree in microbiology, right?"

"It's the fastest path to discovering a cure for pancreatic cancer. Every day, I watch how that particular monster turns my dad's body against itself." Derek's face flushed, his hands forming fists at his sides.

Mr. Marshal's mouth twisted as though he was fighting for the right words to say. "I'm sorry for what your father's going through."

"Sorry doesn't come close to fixing how my dad's cancer spun our lives around."

Unbidden power sprang into existence against Derek's will, rolling the stress ball across the desk, with no one touching it. He buried his emotions and regained control of his powers, stopping the ball. Derek held his breath, not knowing how to hide this slip of his mental prowess.

Mr. Marshal stared at Derek, unaware of Derek's overflowing powers acting on their own.

"Derek, put your hardships into the essays you submit with the applications. Along with that, you need balance in your life. Your grades are high, but there's a clear lack of extracurricular activities."

"It's too late to join a sports team to pad my college applications."

"Nevertheless, your senior year is a critical one for the man you're becoming, and pre-med colleges look favorably on being well-rounded."

A lion-sized yawn escaped Derek's lips. "I don't suppose speed-running video games are assets for college applications?"

"Doubtful for your goals." Mr. Marshal retrieved a wrapped chocolate bar from a desk drawer and presented it to Derek. "Have a pick-me-up to start the day. You need to concentrate in your classes."

Derek ate the candy. His body woke up like he had inhaled a cup of pure caffeine, leaving him ready to run for miles.

"Did you happen to see anything unusual yesterday?" Mr. Marshal pressed.

Derek tested the water, his voice intentionally rife with sarcasm. "What, like a monster in my backyard?"

All of Mr. Marshal's focus zeroed in on Derek, and his piercing eyes seemed to search for any secrets. "Was there a monster?"

Under Mr. Marshal's hungry gaze, Derek fidgeted and let the lie flow. "No. That's impossible."

Derek checked his phone to pass the moment where he didn't know what else to say. There were three minutes to get to AP Chem. His teacher was unforgiving of those who arrived late to the first class of the day.

"Shit, I have to run."

Derek sprinted out of the office and down the hall. He dashed around gathering students and passed countless green and gold falcon cutouts taped to the walls.

At three-foot intervals, these displays of school spirit were excessive for their second week back from summer break. The falcon mascot images blended, making the calculated hunter appear to spring to life and fly alongside him.

The oncoming sugar rush from the chocolate allowed Derek to sprint the length of the building. He skidded to a halt at a choke point of merging hallways. Two thousand students attended this school built for twelve hundred. Half of them had to be idling *here*, blocking his way.

He bit down the urge to push everyone aside using his powers and wove through the people ahead.

Derek slid into his classroom as the bell rang and took his seat next to Tracy, noticing the one to her left was empty. He looked at her for a hint of where their other friend, John, might be. She shrugged.

"Any monster sightings?"

Letting out a tiny sigh, Derek said, "Nope. Today is a monster-free day."

Elaborate drawings and equations were displayed at the front of the room, as the newest addition to this year's staff made finishing touches. Mr. Sprog flooded life into Advanced Placement Chemistry, which in less capable hands was dry and monotonous.

He was dressed in a red-striped, button-down shirt with an orange tie and a suit covered in various molecules. Mr. Sprog was particularly eccentric, even compared to the other teachers in the science department.

What started as concise notes on the projected screen expanded into a kaleidoscope of details. Diagrams and arrows were jumbled over the color-coordinated equation for calculating the solution's saturation limit.

One student, a few desks over, raised his hand the second Mr. Sprog turned to regard the class. Tracy made an exasperated groan.

Derek smiled at Tracy. Four years of suffering through classes with Tony taught them what to expect. He possessed the astounding ability to ask teachers inane questions the moment following the class starting bell or immediately before the bell to leave.

Before Mr. Sprog called on Tony, John walked through the open doorway. A few inches shorter than Derek, John's well-toned body was wiry, giving him a presence much larger than his actual size. His warm, hazel eyes flicked to Derek and Tracy.

Mr. Sprog extended his arms forward with his palms facing up and his eyes emanating the utmost disappointment. "Class started already, Mr. Brooks."

Drops of water fell from John's peppered blond hair. "This is from Coach," John muttered, handing Mr. Sprog a folded note. "Our morning workout ran long."

John's arm, evenly bronzed from a summer outside, remained outstretched. Over the next few months, his skin's tone would fade to its regular tan hues when his preseason training switched to the windowless wrestling room.

With a deadpan glare, Mr. Sprog accepted John's excuse. "Next time when choosing between being prompt and taking a shower, skip the latter." John opened his mouth to object, but Mr. Sprog cut him off. "This is your one warning for the year not to be late to my class."

John slunk into his seat, managing a quick fist bump with Derek and Tracy before copying the on-screen notes.

John leaned across Tracy to whisper to Derek. "You'll never guess what I found on our street halfway to your house. I was walking my dog last night and stumbled onto a half-eaten deer carcass with some nasty slashes."

Derek's body clenched. Images of the monster's pale eyes ran rampant in his head until sweat broke out across his forehead. He checked outside the window for the monster, but saw only the empty football field.

Tracy sucked in air and spoke for him. "We saw a bear in Derek's woods, so be careful."

"Are you sure? That seems unlikely," John replied, one eyebrow raised. "I assumed it was a hunting dog on the loose. I'll pay attention when I'm outside."

Mr. Sprog addressed the class, preventing further debate. "Your first exam is a week from this Friday. I will ensure you are all well prepared for it."

Nearly an hour later, Derek's hand muscles cramped. Mr. Sprog proceeded with the lecture at a breakneck pace to cram as much knowledge into their minds during the limited class period as possible. The bell rang at the end of class, and Mr. Sprog rushed to gather last week's assignment, delaying Derek's freedom.

He caught up with Tracy and John in the hallway. Before they got to the split where they each went to their separate classes, John said, "Sorry I missed your big, life-changing surprise yesterday. What was it?"

Derek was left with the taste of bitter disappointment as though a tiny part of his chest was being carved out. All his closest friends, except Tracy, had found other ways to occupy their Sunday.

"I—" Derek froze. "I'll tell you some other time."

John looked like he wanted to press for more details, yet changed the subject. "My pre-season wrestling conditioning is on track, so Coach told me to get some rest this weekend. Feel like supporting our football team's first home game on Saturday and watching Rachel perform at halftime? We can get gelato at Louis's family's place after the game."

"We have a side project to work on all day," Tracy interjected.

"Have fun," John said, his gaze shifting between Derek and Tracy. "Louis and I will save you seats if you change your mind."

As John headed to his next class, Derek whispered, "Thanks for giving John an excuse. I'd rather see what I can do with these powers."

Tracy gave him a quizzical look. "Why didn't you tell him about yesterday?"

"It's too complicated to explain between classes. I had a big plan to tell all our friends yesterday. You're the one person who showed up, and that means a lot in terms of who I can depend on."

"At least John knows about the monster. Even if he's skeptical of a bear on the loose, he'll be careful on your street."

"Once I have a better idea of what I'm capable of, we can decide how to tell John, Louis, and Rachel."

Tracy leaned in close. "Feel like practicing your powers tonight? We'll track how many rocks you can throw with your mind at the same time."

Thinking of another round of training in his woods reminded Derek of yesterday and the creature's pale eyes. An involuntary shudder ran through him. He needed to get stronger to protect himself if it returned.

"I have to work at the gym tonight, front desk duty. I'll stop by your house after."

4

One Thousand Paper Cuts

Tracy

Tracy's deft hand motions wielded her toothbrush, comb, and palms over the bathroom sink and faucet, playing a melody which caught her fancy.

Dum. Dig-it-a-dum. Dig-it-a-dum-tat-tir-r-r-a-tat.

She imagined she was in a stadium playing music to enthrall tens of thousands of people and she couldn't help but grin. Derek's powers were the first step in following her dream, so much so she had quit her band to devote more time to training him.

She had no idea how Derek mentally throwing rocks or punching progressively larger craters in trees would lead to her performing at a sold-out stadium, but it was going to help somehow.

In the two short weeks since Derek showed her his powers, his abilities had grown considerably. Better yet, neither of them had seen the bear creature. She made a mental note to figure out if Derek's powers could induce nightmare hallucinations to trick them into *believing* a monster had appeared in his backyard.

Her younger brother, Victor, interrupted her musing by banging against the door. "Get out of the bathroom. I need to use it."

She placed her instruments in the cup holder and hollered, "Use the downstairs one."

"It doesn't have a shower."

"I'm almost done. Can you give me another minute?"

Jangling the lock, he shouted through the thin door. "I overslept. Someone kept me up all night clobbering on those drums."

"My worst song is better than the best pop trash coming from your room."

As soon as she opened the door, her little brother dashed around her. He pushed her out and slammed the door in her face. "You better not have used all the hot water."

Back in the safety of her room, she worked the towel through her hair. She checked her phone, and groaned. There wasn't enough time to fully dry off. Her damp head would keep her company through at least two morning classes.

Tracy grabbed a S'mores Pop-Tart to tide her over until lunch and left with her freshman brother in tow. Her Hyundai Sonata came to life with the push of a button. Though reliable, this red, midsize four-door vehicle was in no way flashy.

A sappy song started from her synced playlist. The intro notes burrowed deep in her chest, filling her eyes with tears.

I thought I'd scorched this from my music on the day Nicole and her family moved to Colorado.

Tracy checked her phone. All the texts, app messages, and—because she was desperate—emails she had sent to her friend Nicole to recap the first month of school had gone unanswered.

"What were you saying about good musical tastes?" her brother asked, settling into his seat.

Tracy shifted to a new playlist and kept her voice from wavering. "Don't knock the classics."

Heavy metal blasted from her sound system.

* * *

A giant 81% marked the top of Tracy's disappointing AP Chemistry exam, a kick in the shins considering her outstanding performance in the class's prerequisite.

Derek's bandaged hands clasped his results, bending the edges. "Sixty-six percent? I told you I needed more time for studying and less on—" Derek stopped himself, seeming to remember they weren't alone, eventually adding, "—other things."

"More time?" John asked. "You told me you've been too busy with schoolwork for anything else." His eyes moved from the graded test to Derek's hands. "Have you taken up martial arts or brawling in the streets?"

Careful to follow Derek's wishes for secrecy, Tracy shifted the topic. "I can give you pointers to raise the score for next time, Derek."

A snort reached Tracy's ears, making her blood boil. Allerie Lorana flashed her exam with a 100% at the top. "You might do better with a smarter study partner."

Allerie's brown hair perfectly matched the warm undertone of her brown skin. Her tight braids met in a knot behind her head and flowed down her back in an impressive display Tracy couldn't help but be a little jealous of. Allerie inspected her fingernails, flashing haughty disdain at Tracy when she looked up.

Tracy shifted in her seat, fighting to find a comfortable position in chairs modeled after the stone slabs of an ancient dungeon. Leveling her voice, she challenged Allerie. "You got something to say?"

"Not at all. Aside from the fact it sucks to be you."

Liquid hatred simmered beneath Tracy's skin. She clenched her jaw, refusing to let Allerie's obnoxiousness bring her down.

"I'm good with Tracy's brilliance." Derek shifted his chair to turn as much from Allerie as his desk allowed.

Mr. Sprog finished passing the graded exams back to students and took his place at the front of the room, clearing his throat to silence the class.

"Some of you did not perform as well as I would have liked. We can discuss the answers to the exam later. For now, it's time to move on to the next chapter: covalent bonds."

Allerie raised her hand and spoke before being called on. "Is it possible for one atom's electrons to inject themselves in and take over a molecule's covalent bond?"

Allerie maintained eye contact while her scathing words crept into the recesses of Tracy's thoughts.

Mr. Sprog furrowed his brow. "No. That would be an impossible exception."

Allerie nudged Tony, who didn't look up from taking notes. Tracy had never been happier to not hear him speak. Allerie spoke again, firing her words directly at Tracy. "Are there certain molecules whose electrons bond to anything with a charge, even when previous bonds existed?"

Tracy hardly heard Allerie past the steam spewing from her ears. *How could Nicole have ever dated anyone this spiteful?* "You're not subtle, you one-hit-wonderful-bitch."

Mr. Sprog's breath caught. "Ms. Wayfield, you've earned de-tention."

"Uh, Sprog, that's not fair." Tracy crossed her arms and tilted her unbending chair back to a dangerous angle.

"Mr. Sprog, *Ms.* Wayfield. You are correct, though. Here is a consolation prize." Mr. Sprog dropped a similar slip of paper on Allerie's desk. "The instigator will join you for intentionally diverting the class's attention. There will be no more interruptions, or I will double the punishment."

Mr. Sprog returned to the board to teach about molecular bonds, and Tracy attempted to ignore Allerie's side of the room.

Derek passed a piece of wrapped chocolate into her hand. "Mr. Marshal gives me these when he knows I'm in for a tough morning. Want it?"

"Chocolate won't brighten my day." Tracy flicked it onto Derek's desk. "Is this from Europe? I've never seen a wrapper like that."

Tracy wanted to hurl it at the back of Allerie's head.

"Who knows? Who cares? Without this sweet treat, I'd be out cold right now because *someone* insists on late-night training sessions."

Careful not to draw Mr. Sprog's attention, Tracy said, "With all your practice you'd think you'd be better at punching trees."

When a minute remained until class ended, Mr. Sprog wrapped up the lecture. "In addition to this course, I'm substituting for freshman biology. They're having a field trip to the zoo in three weeks. For extra credit, we need mature student aides to manage the younger students."

Derek and John's hands rocketed to the ceiling. "We're in," they said in unison.

Mr. Sprog waved a sheet of paper and placed it on his desk. "Please use the volunteer sign-up form. Place your names there in an orderly fashion."

The bell rang like a starting signal for a race. Tracy ignored the mad dash. Her goofball friends were already at the front of the line.

"We're putting you on the list, too, Tracy," John shouted as she left the room.

Derek caught up with her on the way to her next class. "We need to talk."

Tracy playfully shoved his arm. "You can't dump someone you're not dating."

"That's not...this isn't one of those conversations. Look, training every night is making my grades slip."

She was careful to keep her voice down. "How can you be so worried about school? You have powers and there's a monster out there."

Bad lighting put the bags under Derek's eyes on full display. "We saw that monster once and my powers will be with me, no matter where I go to school. I need near-perfect grades to get into Johns Hopkins or Berkeley and training my abilities each night is messing that up."

Tracy stopped mid-stride. "What's so great about California? Do what I'm doing: take off a year. It's unfair to force seniors to decide our future without experiencing the world."

"College is one of the few acceptable reasons to leave Maryland. Traveling to find myself isn't. What about my family?"

"You have powers. Your dad's rising medical bills should be a thing of the past." Tracy regretted her words almost instantly. "I'm sorry," she blurted out. "That's not what I meant."

His shoulders slumped. "You're right. I have powers, and you don't. Tough."

Tracy's temples throbbed. The hallways grew warm under the press of hundreds of bodies. "If I could do what you can, I'd work my ass off each waking moment to discover every hidden gift."

Derek stopped moving. "Isn't that what we're doing?"

Over her shoulder, Tracy replied, "I'd do more. I left my band on the day you shared your secret with me because I knew this was more important."

"I had no idea." Derek paused, a curious expression crossing his face. "I never asked you to do that."

Her leg banged into something, and she stopped short, falling headlong against the hard floor.

"Watch it, slob!"

Tracy recognized the mocking voice. Allerie's leg withdrew as she pretended she didn't trip Tracy.

Derek offered Tracy a hand. "You okay?"

Tracy's fury boiled over, splashing onto the closest person, Derek. She brushed his hand aside, pissed at herself for letting Allerie get under her skin.

"I'm fine."

Allerie cackled. "Your boy toy isn't enough? Want to steal someone else's girlfriend instead?"

"Nicole wanted to break up with you anyway," Tracy said. "She was moving across the country the next day."

"Of course, that's what she told you. We had a long video chat last night. You didn't come up." Allerie's face twisted into a snarl, and her words stabbed into Tracy's chest.

Tracy stared at the gathering classmates. Too many faces. Tears welled in Tracy's eyes. *Not here.* She hurried away through the mass of swarming students, looking straight ahead without letting so much as a single tear fall.

Derek caught her a hallway over. "Want me to hit her with a mind punch?"

Tracy spun on her heels. "Don't fight my battles for me! Do you think I'm that much weaker than you?"

Derek's gaze dropped. "I'm trying to help. Don't worry, I won't make that mistake again."

Passing classmates stepped wide around them, though plenty turned their ears toward them, hoping for a juicy tidbit.

Tracy lowered her face. "Nicole is gone. I can't change how that ended. I have to change how I live now." Her voice faltered. A new idea sprang forward, one she couldn't ignore. "Maybe you can help... by giving me some of your gifts."

"What do you mean?"

Tracy leaned forward so no one else would hear. "Share your powers with me so I can fight the monster with you. You don't need to be afraid of it anymore with me by your side."

"I barely have a grasp on my abilities, and we have no idea if that's possible."

"We don't know where they came from. How do you know you can't share them?"

Derek opened his mouth to speak. No words formed.

Tracy's eyes met his. "Will you at least try?"

"You were there for me when I needed you. If there's a way, I promise I'll find it."

5

Cheaters Win

Derek

Sleepless weeks flitted by until Derek gave in to watch a Saturday football game with John and Louis. Tracy pushed the day's training, punching logs with his mind, to the last possible second and made them late. They were stuck parking in the farthest spot from their school's stadium. Derek hopped from Tracy's car before she shut off the engine.

"Why are you in such a hurry to get to this stupid game?" Tracy asked, stepping out of her car.

Derek slammed the car door, careful not to catch the bandages covering his knuckles. "We've bailed on plans with our friends for a month. I can't keep ditching them to train."

"So we've missed a few games."

A distant, sharp whistle from the football game made Derek walk faster. "John and Louis are getting suspicious."

Tracy matched his power-walk pace. "Then be a better liar."

"I'm too tired to think of good excuses on the spot. Thanks to you, I haven't slept four hours all week. The closest thing I get to a break is playing along with your impossible idea to transfer my power to you. I'm all for discovering my powers, but at this rate, I'll need to attach a coffee drip to my veins."

"It's not sunny skies and bed rest for me either. I'm with you every step of the way."

"For all we know, my powers are hereditary. We've been guessing at what to do and still don't know if I *can* transfer them."

"There has to be more than genetics."

"Wanting something to be true doesn't make it a fact."

Tracy stuck out her tongue. "You only think that because you aren't trying."

Derek thrust his wrapped hands in front of Tracy's face. "These look like the hands of hardcore weightlifters I see while I'm working at the gym. Except I'm not getting the bonus of gaining muscles or losing some pudge." Derek patted his stomach, frowning as it jiggled. "Trying has tanked my grades. Trying has caused my power to split open my skin. Trying has you pushing me to run on fumes."

"I'm sorry. I didn't realize. Tell me when I go too far."

"Deal." Anger drained from his voice, leaving exhaustion in its wake. "What makes you think I can transfer these powers?"

"You're past puberty, your birthday is a month away, and I can't think of another reason for you to spontaneously *get* powers."

"So?"

"If these powers showed up in you, then there's a chance I can catch them too."

"They aren't a cold, and I know what you're thinking. My powers have yet to solve all my problems."

"They'll solve a lot of mine."

A loud surge of cheers and boos rang out from Highland View's football stadium, saving him from second-guessing what he said. "We promised Rachel we'd watch her perform with the marching band's halftime show, and it's almost time. We'll figure out transferring my powers after."

The term "stadium" might have been giving it too much credit. The stadium itself was a chain-link fence surrounding the eight-lane synthetic track and the football field at the center. Three sets of raised bleachers sat behind either team's sidelines near the fifty-yard line. Together, each side formed metal leaf blades of a Venus flytrap that swallowed afternoons.

They hurried through the entrance, striding by the gauntlet of concession stands. Smells of fresh salty pretzels pulled from the oven caused his stomach to challenge the crowd to a loudness competition. Had the line of people not wrapped around the booth and down the hill, he would have stopped for a much-needed snack.

A sea of students filled the home stands. Parents and staff were adorned in green and gold.

On the opposite side, the visiting team reached a frenzied pitch thanks to four men painted in blue and silver chanting until their voices went hoarse. Sunny Creek High wasn't a rival school, but Derek hoped his team didn't lose the one game of the season he planned to watch.

John and Louis sat near the top of the bleachers. Their attention shifted from the game long enough to wave. Derek climbed to the last rows where they sat, careful to keep his head looking anywhere but down. His nausea wasn't bad, so long as he stared out at the distant players on the field.

Though, if he went up two more rows and looked over the ledge, the height would hit his gut. It was maybe a thirty-foot drop. Hell, that fall might not break anything. Reason meant nothing to his brain when it made the short fall feel like a death-defying ledge on a skyscraper's roof.

The whistle blew for a timeout and halted the dwindling time to single digits.

John gestured at the two empty seats next to him. "Sunny Creek scored when you arrived. Can't you turn around and take your bad luck with you?"

Derek sent a challenge right back. "Are you a real fan if you aren't covered in paint and screaming like your life depends on it?"

They fist bumped. John stared at the gauze wrappings for a second, then returned to watching the football game without another word.

Derek leaned over John to fist bump Louis Delfino, but his friend met him with a high five. Ignoring their mismatched greeting, Louis's sky-blue eyes never left the field as he spoke.

"We have to make a statement leading into halftime with at least a field goal. That will break up this rocky road ice cream of a tied game."

Louis's short, light-brown hair carried a wave, keeping his forehead free. His regular smile was missing from his olive-toned face. Every fiber of his being tensed, waiting for the next play.

The football snapped to Highland View's quarterback, who dropped back. Three receivers went into an all-out sprint.

Tracy nudged Derek in the ribs. "You should help us win."

"Not here," he whispered through gritted teeth.

"Go for it." Tracy inclined her head forward.

Louis arched an eyebrow. "Save whatever hijinks you're debating for later."

The defense closed in on their quarterback. A moment before being tackled, he sent the ball sailing on a current of hope. It spiraled perfectly, reaching its apex and descending toward the intended wide receiver. A single defender matched his pace.

The receiver juked to the sideline, then spun in the opposite direction of his coverage. He had an open field, but the ball was too fast, coming down too far ahead.

Screw it. I want to win.

Power built within Derek.

The football glided inches outside their receiver's outstretched arms. Stopping the ball in midair risked exposing himself. Instead, he sent a telekinetic gust at the football. It curved back into the receiver's outstretched arms. He hoped the receiver's body obscured the football's change in motion from anyone else.

"TOUCHDOOOOOWN!" The announcer must have blown a speaker.

Derek's side of the stadium erupted.

The kick was good, sending Derek's team into the half with a seven-point lead.

While the players ran off the field, Derek realized he could change the outcome of their school's season. His powers cost him any enjoyment at the spectacle of watching the game.

The marching band spread across the sidelines. They were dressed in matching green and gold jackets. One of them, Rachel Mason, strode to the center of the field with the demeanor of a much larger person, despite her petite stature. Her deep brown skin glowed under the waning afternoon light. The ends of her blue-tipped hair stuck out from the bottom of her hat, remaining as still as her hat's green plumage.

From the sidelines, the school's band conductor waved his hands in a diamond shape to set the time signature. Rachel raised her drum major baton over her head. Snare drums ran from the sidelines to form a line in front of her and unleashed an overlay of tight, rolling taps to merge with booming bass drums who followed into the line.

At Derek's side, Tracy repeated the main rhythm on her knees, nodding in approval.

Two rows of brass and wind instruments spanned the field. They marched and played, leaning their shoulders side-to-side to create the distinct illusion of flight.

The collective ensemble was put together so well, it left Derek unable to separate it into its parts. No amount of his power bestowed the ability to create such art.

The hairs on Derek's neck went upright, and he felt like a mouse snagged in a trap. The band's performance faded into the background. He scanned the opposite stands, finding nothing amiss. Dabbing sweat from his forehead with his shirt sleeve, he couldn't see anything unusual on the football field.

His eyes darted about until he saw the creature pacing back and forth on a far hill, well outside the stadium. It was the same one he'd last encountered in his backyard; its white fur covered four thick limbs of its bear-shaped frame.

Those around him were unaware of the monster prowling near the school grounds. Derek prodded Tracy's leg. "You see that?"

"Of course!" she cheered. "Our girl kicked ass. Thanks for convincing me to watch."

"No. Do you see the *thing* way over there?" Derek pointed to the hill, struggling to not alert John or Louis.

Tracy peeled her eyes from the performance. She wore an annoyed expression. "All I see is a farm that's going to be turned into houses by next year. Wait! I see something." Tracy threw her hands up to cover her face. "Oh, it's awful! He's sitting right next to me."

Derek ignored her antics. "That *animal* outside my house is back."

Tracy's sense of humor died. "What do we do?"

Derek wracked his mind for ways to escape, but when he looked back there was just an empty hill with no trace of the monster.

"It's gone now," he muttered. Perhaps his abilities were rending his mind apart in a downward spiral. Except, even now, he felt the need to hide coursing through his bones.

"You okay, man?" John studied Derek, concern covering his features. "It's a game. No reason to have a panic attack."

Derek forced his ragged breaths to settle. "I'm good."

"I'll keep an eye open for anything unusual," Tracy whispered.

Once the band's final note carried into silence, they marched off the field and were replaced by the football players.

Derek tried to shake the feeling the monster was watching him. He spent the third and fourth quarters ready to run to the steel cage of Tracy's car. Meanwhile, the game devolved into more of a tennis match as both teams struggled to gain yards. Three short plays, then a punt. Rinse and repeat, with no one scoring.

When there was less than a minute to go, the other team got the ball around midfield. Sunny Creek's fast running back took off as the ball was hiked, untouched in his sprint up the field while Sunny Creek's quarterback dropped back to throw.

The running back's cleats ripped soil, sending clumps of grass flying. He cut past the safety, Highland View's last defender.

The other team's quarterback threw the ball.

Getting a touchdown, along with the point after, meant going into overtime. Overtime meant less light as night approached, priming those in the stadium to become the monster's prey.

Derek gathered his power.

The running back turned to look over his shoulder at the oncoming football. He tripped over the telekinetic bump Derek formed on the ground and the ball bounced out of reach.

The running back lay at the ten yard line, clutching his ankle. Trainers and coaches rushed the field.

Derek dissolved his telekinetic barrier. His damn powers made the thing more solid than intended.

"What the hell happened?" John's confused voice called across the hushed stadium.

Louis leaned forward. "Did he hit a hole?"

"I hope he's okay," Derek gasped, barely willing to breathe.

"It looked like something took him out at the knees, but there's nothing there," John muttered.

Unable to look at what he'd caused, Derek's gaze settled back on the northern side of the stadium. There, he saw the monster approaching the stadium's fence, having descended around the back of the hill. His stomach lurched as though someone was wrenching it across the football field while the rest of him remained fastened in place.

The monster's proportions were wrong; its head could touch the top of the fence without standing on its hind legs. In the minutes since disappearing, the monster seemed to have grown larger.

Polite clapping surrounded Derek. While everyone in the stadium was watching the fallen player, Derek couldn't look away from the northern end of the stadium. His high seat offered a vantage point to see the monster others hadn't spotted. He forced himself to be calm. Panicking would cause a deadly stampede out of the stadium.

The monster sniffed the chain-link fence. With a swift motion, its claws sliced a hole in the metal.

Derek sought an escape, anything to get free of that monster. A bright, multi-sided star lit within his mind, then a tiny black ball appeared between his hands. Shock stole his will to cry out. The ball, smaller than his palm, was far too heavy to hold and dragged him to the edge of his seat. Power ebbed from Derek like fresh oil leaking out a hole in his car's engine.

The monster shoved its head through the slit fence.

Bitter, icy wind scraped across Derek's face, rising from the ball between his hands.

Tracy shivered, digging her fingernails into Derek's shoulder. In hushed tones, she said, "I see the animal, too. What do we do?"

"I don't know." Derek squeezed out the words as his power poured into the ball.

Sharp whistles sounded, and Derek's side of the stands exploded in deafening cheers. The loudspeakers cracked as they played booms for Highland View's victory. The game was over, and Derek no longer cared his school had won.

Halfway through the fence, the monster flinched. Its head jerked back and ripped more chain-links apart in its scramble to get free.

The band started a triumphant song, honoring the players for their undeserved win, thanks to Derek's assists. Music swelled over the monster's howls.

Abandoning the ruined fence, the monster fled.

The heavy black ball in Derek's hand evaporated, freeing him from its dragging pull. As his power dissipated, he gasped for air as though he had run for miles.

Classmates jumped in celebration, blocking his view of the monster.

Tracy stood on her seat, staring at the stadium's northern side. "The loud noise must have startled it."

"Then let's stay with the crowd," Derek said.

Tracy's wide eyes shifted between people exiting the stadium and the hole in the fence. "The band will be our best cover. We're congratulating our girl on an amazing show, then running to my car and blaring my music."

Louis injected into the conversation. "Our parking lot will be a chocolate fudge mess for the next thirty minutes. Feel like walking to get gelato from my family's shop instead of sitting in a car?"

Stuck in a car was exactly where Derek wished to be. "Sorry, not today."

Tracy, Louis, and John waded against the current of people leaving. Derek moved along the row of benches to gain a height advantage over those filing out. No monster lurked in sight. He forced air into his lungs to slow the rapid hammering of his heart and followed his friends.

They reached the far end of the bleachers in time for the band's collective held note to end. All at once, the music ceased, and the flurry of methodical cleanup began. Instruments were disassembled and stored safely in seconds.

Rachel ran up and kissed John.

Tracy swung an arm over Rachel's shoulder. Her happy personality was on display, and she didn't give a hint of their monster sighting. "Not bad today."

Derek followed Tracy's cue to not spread panic. "I'm impressed."

"Glad you made it," Rachel said, glancing over her shoulder at the progress of the band's disassembly. "Listen, I have to get our gear inside. Are you all coming to Lauren's party tonight to celebrate? It's down the street from me."

Louis snapped his fingers. "I've got an English report to write."

Rachel put on a fake pout. "Come on, today's a Saturday. Relax a little."

"It's due Monday, and it'll take the rest of the weekend."

John sighed. "I'm out. Wrestling preseason is ramping up, and I need my full rest."

Noise seemed to deter the monster. Gambling on that hypothesis, a loud party offered Derek protection and was a much better evening than barricading himself in his room. Unless John and Louis were going to the party, Rachel was unlikely to show. Without them, Derek would be bored and alone.

"It's been too long since we've all partied. John, I'll drive you there and back, so tonight's a freebie to relax."

Tracy's frustration was palpable. "What about our *side project*?"

"We can work on it for another hour, then take a break. We've been straining too much on it, right?"

Tracy looked ready to disagree, then turned to Louis. "English assignments are for Sunday at midnight. I write my best during crunch time. Are you in?"

Louis let out a fake sigh. "Fine, I'm in. I'll get there on my own so I can work until the last minute. We're already down by one since Nicole moved across the country, so the five of us need to party together as much as we can until senior year ends."

Tracy winced at the mention of their friend. Derek, too, was constantly aware of the absence of the glue that had held his friends together for years.

John's gaze passed over them. "Are you really guilt-tripping me to go tonight?"

Rachel leaned over and kissed John again. "Don't play hard to get. We know you're in. I'll be late because of my night rehearsal. Get the party started for me."

Classmates and their parents trickled out from the stadium. Derek and Tracy followed in the wake of the snare drums. The drummers were kind enough to play an outro, and he appreciated the noise.

Derek made it as far as the entrance gates on the opposite side of where he last saw the monster. There, he grabbed Tracy's arm and took off. They sprinted to her car like a pair of lost freshmen late for class, leaping into her car in under twenty seconds flat.

Derek's out-of-shape legs ached from the short sprint. Between heaving breaths, he gasped, "So much for keeping our dignity intact."

6

LOSS

Tracy

Tracy's red Hyundai purred to life. Her phone synced in seconds, encircling her and Derek with a proper driving mix. It bounced between alternative and R&B, with the occasional classical piece or Broadway hit. When her random shuffle came across the latter, she belted out its lyrics.

"There's no one else on this planet whose playlist jumps so abruptly," said her heathen passenger, still out of breath from their sprint to the car. "On the bright side, seems like the monster is scared of loud noises. We may have found its weakness."

"Say no more!" Tracy's car was pitiful compared to the others packed in this parking lot, but it damn well had the best sound system within a square mile.

She cranked up the volume to let the other cars inching forward learn what they were missing. Any passerby felt her music in their souls; her speakers brought them to a private concert. A full orchestra was stuffed in her car—strings, winds, percussion, and all.

A gold-colored BMW moved in the opposite direction to the end of the line leaving their school's lot and honked at Tracy. Louis's smile beamed as he drove his parents' car. John leaned across Louis to manage a sarcastic wave. Tracy couldn't help but wave back at her friends with a crooked salute.

Derek scanned the stadium and hills. "After that break to watch the game, I really am ready to get back to training. With the monster out there, I'll need all the help I can get. Still feel like working on new ways to share my powers today? My house's den is empty."

Tracy steadied her voice to hide her excitement. "I'm in."

She stopped at home to pick up clothes for the party, then headed to Derek's house. Derek's dad greeted them when they walked in. The skin on his bald head was paper white and equally delicate.

Bundled within a blanket, he leaned against the wall for support and placed a plate of carrot sticks, hummus, and Oreos on the coffee table. "How was the game?"

"The halftime show was superb, Mr. F!" Tracy took the plate of offered food. "Oh, and we won the game."

Derek glanced out the window. "Any word from animal control on large animals in the area?"

Derek's dad pressed a handkerchief against his nose. Bright red splotches showed through. "No. They still think it's a prank."

"It's not," Derek insisted. "I saw the bear again today."

"In our backyard?"

Derek rubbed the back of his neck. "Not exactly."

"Where then? The only way to get me to understand is to tell me."

"I think the bear caught my scent and followed me to the game."

Derek's dad heaved a loud sigh, looking at Derek and Tracy as though they were children caught in a lie.

"I'll call animal control again tomorrow and leave that part out so they believe me. I'm going to rest before dinner. Don't burn down the house with those fireworks you and Tracy launched a while back."

Derek scrambled to cover for his compounding lies. "One time. None of our neighbors noticed, and I haven't set any off since."

His dad left the room with murmurs that sounded awfully close to, "Your sister never gave us this much trouble."

"I can't wait to escape to college like she did," muttered Derek. As though remembering he wasn't alone, Derek glanced at Tracy and then down at his feet.

Tracy pretended to go momentarily deaf, opting to run to the kitchen for two glasses of water and a bag of chips. When she returned to the den, she lit a vanilla-scented candle on the table in the center of the room. There weren't any unpleasant smells hanging around, but the candle set the mood.

Whether Derek realized it, his power was erratic. Some days, he flung stones about when trying to hold them steady. Other days, his telekinetic grip crushed everything to dust. Far too often, he willingly trained until his stamina failed, leaving Tracy to drag him from the woods.

Derek checked his yard through the windows. After a minute of looking, he faced Tracy. "I'm ready."

"We're inside with lots of breakable furniture. Control is key. Work small amounts of power." Tracy ripped open the bag of chips and sprinkled the snack on the floor. "Clean this."

On the verge of arguing, Derek grabbed the chips. "Is this like those weird training methods to learn Kung Fu by completing daily chores?"

Tracy smacked the chips from his hands, knocking them back onto the floor. "No. Maybe. Lift the crumbs with your mind. You'll be as good as dead if your house isn't left standing, so we're working with small things. Remember, think control."

Ribbons of gauze streamed from his hands as he unwound the hasty wrappings from last night's training session punching trees. Scratching his knuckles, Derek looked ready to chew them off.

The spider web of connected cuts and tender flesh on Derek's hands made Tracy wince. "Do you want to take it easy today?"

"We saw the monster today, and it looked ready to tear people's limbs off. I can't slow down." He stood in the middle of the room and raised one hand in front of him parallel to the floor. Though he could use his gift without the motion, he once told her he used his hand as a focal point.

Wind spun around the room. Derek breathed as if in meditation. Flickering candlelight made him appear to be in motion. The handful of salty morsels lifted into the air, floating into the trash can as a delicious train.

Tracy noticed a problem. "You're holding back."

"Of course I'm holding back. These abilities are dangerous. Look at my hands."

"Your hands haven't gotten cut when using telekinesis. It was your energy blasts that did it, and you've been better about not opening those wounds with each punch."

Derek sighed. "Whenever I wield my powers, I balance on a razor-thin edge. It's taxing, and so, so easy to slip."

"Maybe give in."

"You don't understand. I changed the outcome of today's football game, not to mention the twisted ankle I gave that Sunny Creek guy."

Tracy grit her teeth. "If you're coasting through my training, then I don't stand a chance of getting your powers."

"Ah. Are you never not selfish?"

"That's ridiculous. I started this to help you."

"Your efforts have quadrupled since you decided to siphon my power."

"I'm sorry we aren't all as flawless as the great Derek Fen. Cut the crap. You're as self-serving as everyone else, except you won't admit it."

"You have no idea what you're talking about," Derek said in a strained voice. "When have you ever been the designated driver so we could have a good night like I'm doing tonight for you and John? You're always the obnoxious drunk we get home safely."

"Like you're any better? You'd rather be at home playing video games, except you're clutching to our group of friends by going to this party."

"I'm tired of watching us drift apart. Is it too much to ask for our friends to stick together, no matter the distance?"

Tracy thrust her index finger right at Derek's heart. "Nicole moved. She didn't die. I have much more reason to be upset about that than you do."

"Who cares about your crush? When Nicole left, cracks spread in our group of friends." Derek put his hands in his pockets, seeking comfort. "What happens next year? Everyone has their sights set on different colleges, and then we'll fade from each other's lives."

Tracy softened her glower. "Forcing us to be together is just that: forced. I can't see the future, but I can promise I'll fight to be in your life for as long as I'm able."

Derek rested a palm against her forehead. "I can't see the future, either." His hand grew warm and then hot. Through his clenched jaw, he continued, "I have no way of knowing if this will share my powers. All I can do is remember every time you supported me, placed your trust in me, and *believed* in me."

Spiraling winds encircled them. Goosebumps spread across Tracy's arms. Derek's hair swayed. Her own light-brown hair crossed sideways over her vision.

His nails dug into her scalp. His touch burned like being dunked headfirst into a boiling pot of water. Needles stabbed her shoulders and elbows, the pain traveling to her knees and every joint between. Cackling reached her ears, though she wasn't sure if it came from her or Derek.

The fiery sensation scalding Tracy fled. Derek's eyes rolled into the back of his head, and he teetered forward. He fell, dragging them both to the floor.

Tracy lay on the carpet, staring at the ceiling. Stars spun on the beige surface.

She struggled to get her bearings. Eventually, Tracy pulled herself into a seated position. More stars soared across her vision.

Trails of steam snaked from Derek's skin where he'd face-planted when he collapsed.

Heaving Derek onto his back, Tracy nudged him. "You alive?"

No response from his pale face.

Tracy leaned over Derek and shook his shoulder. "Say something, please."

He went into a coughing fit and curled into a ball. Tracy dripped water steadily into his mouth from her glass.

Eventually, his weak voice sounded. "Was I tackled by every football player, rammed by their cars, and then run over by the other team's bus?"

"Yup. That's exactly what happened."

Derek made no effort to move. "Got any powers?"

Tracy flexed her biceps, feeling nothing different about them. "No."

Derek hurled a stream of curses under his breath. "Are you sure?"

She tensed her muscles group by group, trying to sense any abilities. Everything felt the same and her body was devoid of the overflowing power Derek displayed.

"Zip. Zero. Zilch."

Derek sucked in air. He groaned and lifted his hand. It rose maybe an inch and shook. Strained grunts escaped his throat. "Damn. I can't pull in any power." His arm trembled even more. He pointed his clenched fist at the glass of water out of reach. It didn't move.

Tracy covered her mouth. "No."

After a minute of strained effort, the glass remained in the same spot.

Derek's arm fell to his side. While his will summoned a squall around them earlier, calm air now settled over the den. His muffled howl emerged as more of a whimper.

His powers were gone.

Needing to escape her guilt, Tracy went to his kitchen to get snacks, a measly offering for burning out Derek's power. She returned to a red-faced boy staring poison-tipped daggers in her direction. The peace offering of food and drink didn't last long. He downed the fresh water in one gulp, and the cookies disappeared so fast it warranted a choking hazard.

"I told you." Derek's voice quivered. "We shouldn't have messed with what we don't understand. In trying to force my power into you, I snuffed out my spark."

Tracy knew better than to apply a fake smile for his benefit, lying about how everything will be okay. "What do you want to do?"

Derek balled his hands into fists and pounded the ground. "Might as well go to the party like I promised so I can *force* our friends to be together. First, I'm going to rest here for another minute or two."

He slumped deeper into the carpet and closed his eyes, shutting her out.

7

Forced Fun

Derek

Sitting in his duct-taped box on wheels that loosely qualified as a car, Derek's mind reeled, clutching for the power he had lost.

Tracy exited the den's side door to join him. Her shoulders sagged under her casual orange dress, and she dragged her feet as she approached. All the excitement she exuded in the weeks since he revealed his powers to her had broken.

Plopping into his passenger seat, she fidgeted with the seat belt until it locked. "Mind if my car stays overnight? I'll get someone to drop me off tomorrow so I can pick it up."

"Sure," Derek said, searching for any way to undo the mistake which cost him his powers.

He coaxed his car to life. Dashboard lights flashed, then died. Derek smacked the steering wheel. He didn't know how his powers might have fixed his car, but since they were gone it was hopeless.

He turned the ignition again. The shuddering carried on. With a final spasm, his car started and settled into mild tremors. Derek pushed the gas pedal to the sounds of alternative hits on DC101.

Tracy interrupted his brooding. "Weren't you fixing this car?"

Erupting at Tracy would satisfy the nail driving into his empty chest over the failed attempt to transfer his powers and do little else. Instead, he drained all emotion from his voice to answer her.

"This month's paychecks from the gym went into my college fund. All my piece of crap needs to do is last me through the school year, so fixing it's a waste."

"If you need money, I'm sure my parents—"

Derek cut her off. "No. We're fine without handouts."

His driveway's gravel road accentuated every rattle and grind, sounds of his car's desperate pleas to be put out of its misery.

Once on the paved street, his mom's silver Mazda approached in the opposite direction, flashing its lights.

Derek's teeth clenched. He was in no mood to talk to anyone, let alone his mom. He wanted to slam his foot on the gas and accelerate to whatever speed his car allowed. Instead, he pulled alongside her car and rolled down the window.

Her blond highlighted hair was wrapped in a bun on the back of her head, keeping it out of her long face and angled nose she and Derek shared. The sweat on her workout clothes had dried, and her backseat was full of grocery bags that begged to be unpacked. His mom adjusted her sun-yellow rectangle glasses.

"I thought you were having dinner with us."

He deserved one night free of the world's burdens before spending all his time trying to recover his lost powers.

"My friends and I are heading out for the night. I'll be home late."

A tightness formed around her lips. "I bought groceries to make your tuna mac and cheese." She looked past Derek. "There's plenty for you too, Tracy."

Derek leaned forward to keep Tracy out of the conversation. He struggled to prevent anger over losing his powers from tinging his words.

"We have plans."

Like an injured puppy, his mom's face softened, her eyes pleading. "Are you sure?"

"Sorry. We have plans."

His mom let out a long, judgmental sigh. "Have fun then, and be safe."

Derek rolled the window up and drove.

Once his mom's car was out of sight, Tracy spoke. "You should be nicer to your mom."

As small as he felt without his powers, his mom made him feel more like a child. Attempting to bribe him with his favorite childhood meal didn't help.

"There's a lot I *should* do, like keep driving and not let Mom guilt-trip me into skipping a night out with friends. I'm too pissed at myself for losing these powers to want to stew with my thoughts at home. Plus, we had a monster sighting today, so going to a loud party seems like exactly what I should do."

"Yeah, but your mom doesn't know any of that. She was trying to help and snapping at her eats away at both of you."

Derek let out a long breath, doing his best to expunge a day's worth of anger and frustration. "You're right. I'll text her and apologize when we get to the party. I can make it up to mom tomorrow. We'll go to a park an hour away to bike for a bit, far from where the monster might be. She'd like that."

Derek drove around his street's next bend, stopping in front of John's house. John was already outside, leaning against his stone stacked mailbox. He wore jeans and a t-shirt with the words, "Wrestling Dept." emblazoned across the front. The clothes said he didn't care, but a delicate touch of gel applied to his hair said otherwise.

Out of habit, Derek pictured an invisible thumb flicking the car door's dull-gray lock to the open position. When nothing unlocked, he imagined an entire arm wrenching the tab. His former gifts failed, leaving him with the feeling of being punched in the gut for trying to draw on power he no longer had.

John tapped on the window. "Let me in. The sooner we go, the sooner I can get back."

Tracy clicked the unlock button from her side and John sank into the back seat. Derek's car jerked forward when he pressed the gas, like it had forgotten it was an automatic.

As he continued driving, Tracy tapped her foot along to music from the radio and threatened to dig a hole through the floor.

John leaned forward to hover next to Derek's shoulder. "Did you two hook up?"

Derek responded at the same time as Tracy, "Nope."

"Then why are you so weird right now, and what have you been working on together?"

Derek sought for the familiar sensation of drawing power. For an instant, he thought a flickering spark warmed his fingertips. Nothing happened when he tried to use his mind to twist the volume knob. Had it worked, he would gladly pretend his abilities were electrical issues for John's benefit.

"Nothing anymore," Derek grumbled.

John flicked the car's ceiling. "Fine, you don't want to tell me? I'll back off. Instead, do you want me to help you break from your dismal mood by finding someone to hook up with tonight?"

Stuck in his own head, Derek answered with, "We'll see."

"Come on," John pleaded. "Rachel's busy at band practice until late, so this was a perfect opportunity for me to work on major muscle gains. Instead, you're dragging me to this party. You owe me for sacrificing my workout. Feed me on your drama."

Tracy came to his rescue. "We're not your evening's entertainment."

"How about you, Tracy? Anybody catching your interest?" John leaned forward. "Homecoming is in a few weeks, so this is the perfect night to fish for a date. I could find you a girl or guy to have a fun night with, seeing how you aren't as hopeless as our designated driver."

"To get John off our backs," Derek began, "Tracy, do you want to go to Homecoming with me, as a friend?"

"Sounds like a plan."

Derek peeled his eyes from the road to glare in faux anger at John. "See? Problem solved."

John let out a long sigh. "You're both weird."

"The word you're looking for is awesome," Tracy said.

"This might be nothing," started John, "but did you really see a bear near our homes a few weeks back?"

Derek whipped his head around to face John, nearly swerving the car. Afraid of the answer, he asked, "Yeah. Why?"

John swore and pulled out his phone. "I'll tell my parents to stop letting my dog go out alone and call animal control. I found another deer carcass when I walked him down toward your house. Parts of it looked burned, though I can't explain that."

"My dad called too. Maybe now they'll listen."

Silence reigned, leaving Derek in the worst possible place, stuck in his head while he imagined all the ways an animal could have been burned.

Eventually, they turned into Rachel's neighborhood. Each house made it more difficult not to gawk. One was a certifiable castle, equipped with enough stone to sink a small nation. The only things missing were the moat and drawbridge.

He drove down a side street leading away from Rachel's house and toward the address she had sent. Parked cars occupied every space on the street, so he found a place to park one street over from Lauren's house.

Derek inched open the car door, ears straining to catch any sound. Without his powers, he and his friends were defenseless if the monster found them.

Clouds blocking the bright moon made the night darker. His phone's light cast a wide beam over the flowerbed next to where he parked.

"You okay?" John's eyes followed Derek's light, gazing around for a danger he didn't understand.

"Yeah." Derek strode toward the party, forcing his friends to hurry to keep pace. He held his breath to listen for the slightest growl or chomping teeth.

Lauren's house was a three-story mansion guarding the hill where it stood. A veranda wrapped around its sides. Several class-mates leaned over the railing, sipping from red cups. Lamp posts beside the walkway invited anyone with a pulse to enter.

Basking in the music loud enough to rattle the pavement, Derek uttered, "This is perfect."

The entrance led to a wide hall lined with paintings, one of which looked like paint randomly splattered on a white background. That this was considered art was baffling, but for a million dollars, he was willing to replicate the work.

He followed close-pressed bodies to the massive kitchen. Dozens of cheap liquor bottles rested on the marble countertop. Derek's stomach curdled when he saw the gin. After Tracy's summer birth-day celebration, the sight of it still made him sick.

John appeared in front of Derek and Tracy, magically producing two red Solo cups filled with beer. John and Tracy took mighty swigs from the shining, red goblets.

Odors of watered-down, bitter beer filled Derek's nostrils, which mixed with other less tasteful smells. Quite a few people must have come from the football game without a courtesy rinse.

Half of his classmates danced on one another, moving to heavy thumps of a techno beat pumping across the house. The other half stood idly holding drinks, weighing the decision to join in.

Tracy swung her arms and hips to the music like a beautiful cyclone. John smoothly moved in step to match, a dancing wonder in his own right. Derek bobbed his head, the last corner to the lop-sided triangle.

Yelling came from outside. Derek strained his neck to get a better view of the backyard. He relaxed once he realized the commotion was from someone splashing into the pool and not the monster. People standing around the pool raised their cups and cheered as the fully clothed idiot broke the surface.

"Anybody surprised Tony jumped in with his clothes on?" Tracy shouted to be heard over the music.

John took a long swig of his beer. "I'd consider throwing him in on principle."

"How soon until your better half gets here?" Tracy asked, chang-ing the subject.

John checked his phone. "Not for a while. In the meantime, why not tell me what you're hiding?"

Derek grasped inside for his missing piece, finding a dried chan-nel where a river of power once flowed. "There's nothing to tell."

"If you say so." John chugged his beer. "I'm going for another."

To John's back, Tracy called, "I'm empty, too. Wait up." After downing her beer, she muttered to Derek, "I'll throw him off the trail."

They dissolved into the shifting sway of students. Derek took an empty seat on the couch, occupying the moment by staring at a toppled rum bottle on the coffee table. He focused his thoughts to make it lift. The bottle wobbled and his heart leaped, sinking again when he realized someone bumped the table.

In a single motion, Derek's classmate, Brent, shifted from tripping over the table to drop next to Derek on the couch. Rubbing the top of his shoe, Brent winced and asked, "How's your sister doing?"

Derek thought about lying to end the conversation. "Olivia's making too many new friends at college to check in with me."

"Ah. Let her know the Cross Country team is suffering without her. No one's stepped up this season to fill her shoes and lead us all to train harder."

"Sure."

Derek stood, planning to search for his friends. Brent followed, so they wandered into the hallway together. Derek considered diving past a guy wearing a blue and silver shirt and into a side room to get free of Brent.

Studying Derek's gaze, Brent clicked his tongue and said, "I hope he wasn't one of those Sunny Creek dicks who tore apart our stadium's fence today."

All other noises stopped for Derek as he hung on Brent's words. "Did someone see them do it?"

Brent shook his head. "No, but it had to be them. One of the coaches sent a message to all teams asking for info about the vandalism. Imagine being that pissed at a loss."

Derek leaned in closer to listen for more of the rumor when a wet body collided into his back.

"Anyone have a towel?" Tony shouted, leaving a trail of pool water behind him, which was now on Derek's shirt.

Tony didn't wait for a response, funneling into the hallway to no small number of shouts and curses as he pushed people aside. In the scuffle, someone's cup knocked free from their hands, spraying the bright blue mixed drink at the canvas paintings.

Derek sought for his power to prevent the oncoming disaster. Power slipped through his fingers like trying to hold sand. Spiked punch spread over the wall from the painting to the floor, contaminating both in Rorschach patterns.

Derek suppressed a chuckle at the blue stain, which added to the chaotic brush strokes. "Seems like an improvement to me."

A short girl pushed Derek aside and screamed at everyone in sight. "Get out of my house!"

So that's Lauren.

She used one hand for balance and her other to trace the line of alcohol ruining the painting.

Blood flushed Derek's cheeks thinking about her overhearing what he'd said. Leaving Brent, he slipped deeper into the house to stay free of Lauren's wrath.

Although he left the makeshift dance floor, it did little to make the room vibrate less. He followed the vacuum of people, seeking relative quiet to think. The surrounding storm of noise offered a safe buffer from the monster. He went deeper in the house to the second open room.

Generations of video games stacked from floor-to-ceiling sent his pulse racing. Classics he knew simply by name and reputation were on display along with the ancient systems needed to play them. He could spend a lifetime here.

One piece of plastic caught his attention—the game controller that mimicked a guitar. Derek placed his fingers over the five colored buttons representing the frets of a real guitar. Beneath the other instrument controllers sat the game disc. A crushing weight flooded Derek with memories of staying up all night with his friends to get five stars on every song.

Louis's fake laugh rang out as he appeared in the doorway. "Figures I'd find you in the game room. Don't you check your phone? I've been looking for you, Tracy, and John."

Derek connected wires and turned on the system. "They went for more beer."

Louis grabbed the microphone and moved the drum set controller in front of a comfortable chair. He tapped on his phone. "Now this party's getting started. Give it a minute. Our top scorer is on the way. Tracy, at least, knows how to answer her phone."

Derek picked the song to play and waited. It didn't take long.

"Is this what you meant by a fun night?" John asked, entering the room with a glowering Tracy. "I guess this still beats planning Tracy's apology."

"There has to be a way to let Nicole know I'm sorry I forced a wedge between her and Allerie," Tracy said. "Though Nicole was as much of an active participant in our kiss as I was."

Derek held his tongue, not knowing how to offer his support.

John clinked his cup against hers and they drank. "Nicole will eventually realize how much better it is to have you in her life, even if it's only through a screen."

Tracy slumped into the chair in a loud huff. "That's the end of our extra shots and drinks, but thanks for listening."

"You know what might cheer you up?" Louis asked. "Checking out my amazing BMW."

"We've been in your car before," Derek said.

"Yes, except I don't have to borrow it from my parents anymore. It's all mine!" Louis scooped drumsticks from the cardboard box and gave them to Tracy. His grin never faltered. "I believe we were promised one hell of a night, and I see a game to be played. John, you're in for round two."

Derek, Tracy, and Louis started with an early 2000s song, which Tracy introduced them to years back. They clobbered the Expert mode's high score.

Tracy handed the drumsticks to John and stood. "I'm making another run to the keg."

"Want backup?" John asked.

"You've done your fair share of suffering through cheap piss water with me."

John took his place behind the drum set once Tracy left. "Any song requests?"

"Whatever you want, so long as it's not that scream-o music bleeding from the other room," Louis said.

Derek picked another classic and, four or six songs deep, they fell solidly into a groove. Without the push to improve his powers, Derek was simply living. John and Louis reminded him how being normal wasn't a travesty.

For the first time all night, Derek released a long breath from the bottom of his diaphragm. He missed nights like this. They were much better than exhausting himself by training his former powers.

Derek's phone vibrated in his pocket, causing his fingers to slip and break his combo. Preoccupied with the game, the message went unread.

Derek leaned into the microphone to help Louis, lowering their overall score without Nicole's vocal skills. A pang of longing reminded Derek of the Nicole-sized hole, and since Rachel had yet to arrive, their team felt less than half full. Derek's phone buzzed again, but he couldn't stop in the middle of a song to answer it.

Music in the other room died. Lights flicked on and off. Classmates in the hall ran by in either direction, their red cups dropped and kicked aside.

Approaching from the stampede came a woman in a navy-blue uniform.

As though trapped in a slow-motion dream or horror flick, the officer blocked the one exit out of the room. John shifted his drink behind his foot.

"You're in trouble now, kids," the policewoman said.

An hour later, Derek was one of a hundred unfortunate students forced to breathe into a plastic tube. Two of the worst offenders were deposited in a cop car and sent elsewhere, probably juvie. There, they'd need to make the embarrassing calls to have their parents come get them. Everyone else who was legally drunk got hit with underage possession citations. As quickly as the cops destroyed the party, they were gone.

Out of a sense of guilt for surviving unscathed, Derek scrubbed the more aggressive beer stains on the kitchen table.

Louis texted Rachel, warning her against arriving. Tracy reappeared from outside once the last cop left, citation-free.

Of the video gaming All-Stars, John was the only one to receive an alcohol citation. He was livid, and he fumed as he massaged his shoulder. "The cop didn't have to slam me to the ground." John's words carried enough venom to bring down an elephant.

Too tired to choose his words wisely, Derek spoke without a filter. "You didn't have to physically resist the breathalyzer. They were making an example of the most imposing person here. You. Considering they could have dragged you to a drunk tank, you got off light."

John's face alternated between ghostly white and eggplant purple. "'It's been too long,' you said. 'Tonight's a freebie.' Don't worry, Derek, I'll put my training on hold to satisfy our group-think."

"Obviously, I didn't plan on the cops making a guest appearance." Derek's words were a touch snider than intended.

"You pushed us to come to this party."

Derek dropped the cleaning rag, unable to think of a response to calm John.

Louis stepped between them both. "We can salvage the night. The cops poured out the booze, but we can go somewhere else without alcohol."

John stared at Derek as though measuring his soul. "I'm done with my allotted R and R. Let's get home."

They all left. Outside, Louis rested against the hood of a metallic gold colored car parked close enough to the house to be fully illuminated. Whoever had Louis's parking spot originally must have left early, missing the entire police incident.

He wiped the BMW emblem with his sleeve. "Last chance for part two of the night, thanks to this baby. That half sip of booze is out of my system by now. I can take us anywhere."

"This puts my rusted car to shame." Derek sighed.

"Mine, too. So, what's the plan for the night?" Tracy asked.

Louis opened the passenger side door. "I don't know. How about I give you a ride to wherever you parked, and we come up with one on the way?"

Derek was thankful for the offer. However, the second he took his first step, John spoke firmly to Louis, leaving no chance for rebuttal. "This car's full. Louis, can you take me home, please? I don't want to ride with shitty friends."

Offering an apologetic shrug, Louis left Derek and Tracy standing by the road.

Derek knew it was an illusion, yet as the BMW sped down the street, taking its high beams with it, darkness enveloped him.

8

LOCKUD

Tracy

Monday morning's AP Chemistry class moved like a heavy downpour, slogging over Tracy and stealing her warmth. She'd been part of the most incredible discovery in the history of history. Without grasping where it came from, Derek's gift had been ripped from him all because she wanted it.

Tracy blindly stared at the experiment instructions on the board and rubbed her face to stay awake. This was a basic lab, adding one liquid with red dye to another until the mixture changed permanently to red and then measuring the amount added. She should have followed Derek's example and skipped class. She should have been a better friend to him.

He lost everything because I pushed him.

John wrote answers to Mr. Sprog's pre-lab questions in silence and ignored her. Working alongside him was unbearable. John's compassion and optimism were two of those absurd constants of the universe, like the atomic weight of hydrogen. To find this version of John at her side was like watching a poorly paid body double.

John poured the red liquid from the graduated cylinder into a beaker containing water. The color dissolved, leaving no trace.

"Shouldn't you go slower?" Tracy asked.

Bloodshot eyes regarded her. "Since you know so much, how about you take over?"

Suddenly, the solution turned bright red. Slow to react, John stopped pouring and measured the volume remaining. "Forty-eight milliliters," he said gruffly.

Tracy recorded the value, knowing their calculations would be outside reasonable tolerance and hurt their scores for the lab.

"What I don't understand is how you escaped the cops," John hissed, keeping his voice low and controlled so the rest of the class couldn't hear. "You were as drunk as I was, yet I'm the one hit with a drinking citation."

"I lucked out by being near the side door. I ran when the cops entered from the front. Once Louis let me know the coast was clear, I came back."

"Of course, you Tracy-ed your way free of consequences."

"None of you responded to my messages. If you would have, you could have run, too."

"Maybe."

"Even if I stayed, the police were going down the hallway toward you when I sent my first text, so there was nothing else I could do to warn you."

Tracy was never happier to hear the bell at the end of class.

Except, Mr. Sprog didn't dismiss them. "For those student aide volunteers, our zoo field trip is next week. I need signed parent or guardian permission forms by Friday."

Tracy fished into her backpack for the signed paper. "Uh, Sprog, I got my form here and I'll get Derek to bring his tomorrow."

"*Mr.* Sprog," her teacher corrected. "Remind him the extra credit for student aides is for those in attendance."

Mr. Sprog extended his hands palm up like a valet expecting a tip. Tracy dropped her lab work in one of his hands and the permission form in the other.

She stole a moment for herself between classes. Alone in the back stairwell, her fingers tapped against concrete walls. Their sound echoed above and below her, and the melody eased her frayed nerves.

She was late to Music Appreciation, but Mrs. Kerlan reacted with little more than a head nod. Tracy hurried into her seat next to Rachel.

A saxophone played at a feverish pace from the room's speakers. Trapped by gloomy spirits, Tracy lacked the will to dissect the sounds.

Mrs. Kerlan spoke over the music. "Everyone who knows jazz knows the works of John Coltrane, such as this current piece. Few can identify Mary Lou Williams or Vi Redd. Please listen to the music at each station and rotate stations every ten minutes. Your next test will grade your ability to explain the influences of these groundbreaking artists on the genre and beyond."

Mrs. Kerlan glided about the room, queuing the devices for each pair of students.

Rachel offered Tracy the first turn to listen. Within seconds, Tracy was captivated by the drum solo, her heart rate refusing to settle, guided by its enthralling beats. The sounds allowed her to momentarily forget her regrets. She loathed to end the one thing bringing her joy today, but wanted to share the music with her friend.

Rachel held the headphones Tracy offered her in front of her, staring at them. "I'm sorry for everything that happened on Saturday."

"It wasn't your fault."

"It still sucks that the cops busted the party I told you about. I heard it got pretty fortissimo. No wonder the cops showed." Rachel took a moment before continuing. "I'll be better about balancing band rehearsals and show up more."

Tracy held up her hands. "Promise me you won't use us as an excuse to hold you back. I wasn't lying when I said your halftime show was incredible, but there's room for improvement. Now listen to this song before we're forced to move on."

Rachel pushed her blue-tipped hair aside and put on the headphones. Her head bobbed along in time with the music.

They rotated through the stations and took notes on each artist until the end of class.

Settling in her seat for Calculus II, Tracy planned to escape school once she found a believable excuse. Uniform, bland desks conditioned her for monotonous studies. The rigid, wood composite surface attached directly to the metal chairs, forcing students into a proper position. Any attempt at comfort was met with resistance and lower back pain.

She knew the remedy for days like today. Keeping her ear hidden by her hair, Tracy put an earbud in and listened to a song much more rewarding than the lecture. The next song began, an old sappy one. A pain formed in her chest.

The music brought a buzzing sensation inside her head that stung her ears and eyes like the world's worst migraine. It hurt too good to skip the song she played the last time she saw Nicole in person. When the song ended, the pain receded in a moment of sweet release.

Eventually, the bell rang. As she stood, Tracy was surprised to see her desk was thick plastic, the one surface like it in the room. All the others were cheap wooden frames. She never realized they used these nice desks outside the science wing. It was oddly placed, given she was near the back of the room. A nightmare to the order enforced by the school's design, this was as bad as a single floor tile facing the wrong direction.

* * *

Tracy walked to her afternoon class and took a seat near the back. Since she'd lasted through the first four classes plus lunch, she decided to stay the rest of the day.

Her routine of pretending to pay attention was second nature. She set her phone to play music in an earbud hidden beneath her hair.

The subject of Civilizations of the Ancient World was interesting when learning how those societies formed her present life, though Mr. Edsell's lesson was so grating that his voice turned her mind into shredded cheddar cheese. Staring at the large screen of notes, this sensation expanded into nausea, making it all but impossible to think.

Why can't Edsell teach something fun, like a famous joust or battle full of blood and fire?

She copied one fact out of every ten her teacher listed.

Her music changed to an old ska song. She covered her mouth so she wouldn't hum with the catchy, upbeat horn section and tapped her pen with the music when she wasn't occasionally taking notes.

A small twinge, little more than a disquieting urge, chimed in the back of her mind.

Muddled thoughts instantly locked onto her notes. Right-tilted fine script began at the top of her page and devolved into shaky scratches that were all written with generic black ink. Midway down the page, the ink changed to red. The only items on her desk were the sheet of notebook paper and the same black pen she used throughout the day. She checked the notes again. At the top, black ink. In the middle of dates to memorize, red ink.

Rolling the pen, she inspected it from multiple angles. It was a standard plastic tube with a removable black lid, indicating the ink inside was likewise black.

Tracy drew a line on her hand. Red. It smeared at her touch.

Fingers twitching, she did everything possible to remain seated. The glimmering hope of possessing a power needed to be proven beyond doubt. She didn't intend to make any false assumptions.

Her left hand continued tapping to the beats of the song. She had no idea if, or even how, she might change the color. Recalling every shred of a detail Derek used to describe how he harnessed his powers was unhelpful.

Turn the ink black. Turn the ink black.

That pure thought raged inside.

Turn the ink black.

Tracy peeked through squinting eyelids. She drew random lines at the bottom of the page. Fresh black marks colored it. She wanted to run through the rows of classmates, shouting for joy.

I have a power!

She drew another line on her finger. Black. Tracy licked it. Nothing tasted more beautiful or salty and gross. It seemed like normal ink, but as she never tasted it, there was no basis for comparison.

She made a game of changing the ink color back and forth, until her former notes on Caesar's conquests were covered with alternating colored scratches.

Time to get creative.

Green, purple, orange, and because she could, electric yellow shapes were strewn on the page in bright armies fighting across her paper.

Her breath came faster and faster. Tingling fingertips traced her sketches, smearing the inks. Looking around the room to ensure no one paid attention to her prowess, she willed the pen into a whole new form. Clear plastic morphed into a dull shade of yellow. Its innards were no longer liquid but solid layers of graphite inside of a wooden #2 pencil.

Thrilled at this discovery, Tracy changed it into iron. Without intending to, the hard object shrank considerably, leaving a small shape that felt about the same weight.

These escapades went unnoticed. Her classmates should have praised her for changing the meager utensil into the original pen. Though longer than the iron pencil, the new pen was shorter than its original form.

Tracy considered other abilities she might possess. She projected thoughts of dancing to her pen to figure out if she could move it like Derek's telekinesis. The pen didn't budge. She tried again. It didn't stir.

As she sought to create a new test for herself, a faint tremor from the clasped pen rattled her hand. She dropped it in pure shock.

The pen wasn't done moving. It flopped on her desk, then went upright. A shaking scrawl formed two wavy lines that might have been an "L". Tracy retrieved a clean sheet and placed it under the moving pen.

Maybe after changing inanimate objects enough times they become sentient?

Holding her breath, she agonized over slowly passing seconds for the pen with a mind of its own to finish each letter.

"L...O...C...K...U...D." The pen shook violently, then dropped, its job finished.

"Lockud?" she said out loud.

A head or two turned in her direction. Tracy peered closer at the letters. From a different angle, there was a small tail at the bottom of the D. It could be a sloppy attempt at a P. What she mistook for a C might be an unfinished O.

Look up.

Tracy's neck cracked as her head scanned the room. Her classmates' heads faced forward, all attentively copying notes. Glancing sideways past them, she caught Derek's bright face on the other side of the door's window.

Outside the teacher's view, Derek tilted his head backward slightly. Despite the twenty minutes left in class, Tracy clutched her precious colorful paper, packed her remaining things, and walked to the door. She barely moved a step when the teacher asked, "Where are you going?"

Tracy weighed her words. "I need to leave."

"And what, may I presume, is more important?"

"My future." Tracy couldn't believe her boldness.

She continued walking amid stunned silence. As she reached the door, Mr. Edsell stammered, "Leave and you've earned detention."

"I can live with that."

Once in the hallway, Tracy sped up, hoping Derek followed.

"That was uncalled for," Derek said. "You could have faked being sick."

She held her battle sketches high. "Who cares about class? I have a power! I changed the pen's color. This is going on the fridge."

"Oh, shit! Saturday's efforts to transfer my power paid off?" Derek looked over her paper. "Your art needs work, but you have an amazing skill. Ready to join me in training? My powers came back!"

"I noticed." Excitement brought a bell-like ring to Tracy's voice. "Your telekinetic handwriting needs work, too."

"My view of your paper was blocked by *someone's* big head. Be thankful I didn't launch the pen at the door."

When he put it that way, Tracy had to agree. "That might be hard to explain. Good thing you know my class schedule. I was looking for an excuse to ditch today."

"Let's wait until we're safe from any prying ears. I can't shake the feeling something's watching me."

The long hallway seemed to stretch forever, each juncture a hiding spot for an ambush. "Is it the monster?"

"I haven't seen it."

She raced ahead to face Derek. "Wait, how long did it take you to tell me your powers returned? I texted and considered knocking when I stopped by yesterday to get my car."

"I've been out cold since Saturday night. When I woke up about an hour ago, I was back to full strength. I guess I needed my beauty rest to recover. Now let's quit wasting time and go to my house. We can train a bit before I head to work. I owe you payback for weeks of working me so hard."

No power she possessed could dissuade Derek from his schedule. The universe might collapse, and he would still punch the clock to sign people into the gym.

She hurtled out of the lot, too excited to wait for Derek's turtle-paced car.

"Windows down, music up!" Tracy howled. Her car launched airborne over a speed bump thanks to the heavy bass flooding beneath her tires.

* * *

Derek's backyard woods appeared normal to Tracy. Under the cover of the thick trees, he kept them within sight of his house. They were ready to sprint to safety if they heard anything larger than a dog move.

Not knowing where to start, Tracy retrieved her practice drumsticks from her backpack and pictured one of them changing into gold. Nothing. The wood didn't even turn a more interesting shade of tan.

Derek never had these problems. Progressively deeper indents on unlucky trees marked how effective he had become at punching with his mind.

Tracy cursed. "My abilities are a little shy at the moment." Ecstatic to delve into her limitless possibilities, she had failed to consider they might not show.

Derek lifted stones without touching them. "What triggered them earlier?"

"My head started hurting, then, bam, red ink showed up on my paper."

"Why don't you dive a little more into the details of when you changed the pen?"

Tracy spoke hastily. "My history teacher was at the board reading from his slides while I was trying and failing to pay attention."

"You should give him more of a chance. His elective on Mesopotamian cultures is the reason I want to visit Italy, Greece, and Turkey."

Tracy raised her hand. "If I wanted a lecture, I'd go back to class."

"Do you want help or not?" Derek's curt voice cut the air.

"Fine. My capable history teacher was doing what he does best. I was in the back, taking some notes. Then the pen in my hands changed its black ink to red. No, transmuted. That's a better word for my abilities."

Derek lazily waved his hand in a circle. A sizable log flew. "What were you thinking about when you transmuted the pen?"

Tracy turned over each second from earlier in school. When the ink changed colors, her mind was occupied, but not by the lesson. "I was getting into a groove from an old song and daydreaming about bloody battles. In other words, red things."

"Sounds like a working theory. Lucky for you, I have my work-out mix." Derek pressed play on his phone. "Get inspired by your band's crappy music."

"Insult me all you want, but my band is off—" Her skin trembled at the flowing music.

A disorienting wave flashed across her vision. Instead of the wooden drumstick, she was clasping a golden rod that was shorter than it used to be.

"Nice work," Derek said. "Can you change it back?"

She envisioned the rod as it should be, not metal, but as her drumstick. It returned to its original form. Tracy's fingers traced the notches about midway down where she routinely struck the side of the snares. It felt off. On a hunch, she retrieved the drumstick's twin. Sure enough, her transmuted version had lost a quarter inch.

She transmuted tree limbs littering the ground into solid gold twigs. Soon Tracy was panting, surrounded by the vast riches, though she needed to rest for longer periods between each subsequently smaller transmutation.

"It's a shame I have to rely on music. What happens when I run out of battery life? You slip right into using your abilities."

Derek stopped tossing tree limbs and faced her. "Not quite. It takes effort to clear my mind and give up control as power ripples in my veins."

One of Tracy's Top 10 favorite songs started, hidden within the trash Derek listened to. A good chill coursed through her, forming goosebumps on her arms.

"You might want to step back. This is going to be very, *very* interesting."

Feeding on the song, she harnessed every inch of her power, placing a hand on the closest fallen log. Her mental image started with the round frame of a snare drum.

The outer layers of bark shifted according to her will, transmuting into various metallic and polyester pieces.

Her insides churned, and she faltered mid-transmutation. She leaned against a tree for support, fighting for air.

The creation was stuck as a half-snare drum, half-wooden disaster.

Derek helped Tracy to her feet. "Ready to call it for tonight and rest? I need to drive to work soon."

Tracy brushed the leaves clinging to her shirt, staring daggers at the drum-log on the ground. "I'm finishing this first."

"There's always tomorrow. I trained for weeks before consistently being able to use my powers."

"Then I'll train even harder to make up the difference." Tracy turned the music louder. Derek probably made a response, but she lost it beneath the deafening symphony.

Pouring all of herself through her spread fingers, inch by wretched inch, the log disappeared, changing into the drum. Sweat fell from her forehead, leaving blurry burns in her eyes. The snare's tension rod passed through the aluminum ring. Each long lug nut fit perfectly together until her snare drum was complete.

Gasping in short, quick breaths, she dropped to a knee.

Tracy hit the snare drum once with her drumstick. Like punching a pillow filled with rusted nails, the reverberating sounds were atrocious. That didn't matter.

This is mine. Transmuted with my power!

She brushed aside Derek's hand to help her up. It took longer than she liked to stand on her own. Wobbly, yet triumphant, Tracy spoke, "Okay. Now, you can go to work."

9

The Zoo

Derek

Between training sessions and schoolwork, days flowed together until Derek was left in charge of fifteen unruly freshmen for his school's field trip. Along with Tracy, he guided the students through the 160-some-odd acres of biodiversity at the Smithsonian's National Zoo.

Little had changed in the years since his last visit. When he was a kid, Derek thought the zoo was shaped like a bad rendition of a lung. It had the right overall shape, but drawn by someone who failed to stay within the lines. From top to bottom, it was a twenty-minute walk, assuming he didn't stop to view the animals.

Outside and under direct sunlight, the warmth made Derek forget it was mid-October. He stepped on an undone shoelace, catching himself before he tripped. With barely a thought, he gathered power and mentally tied the lace into a knotted loop.

He froze, holding his breath, worried someone saw his public display of abilities. Derek checked for the slightest signs of alarm on the faces of those around him, imagining scenarios of being discovered.

Underclassmen chatted loudly, ignoring his display of power. Children walked hand-in-hand with their parents, paying attention to animals. Derek glanced around to gauge if anyone was recording him, but no one was looking at him.

Mild, musty smells carried from the elephants' huge outdoor enclosure as Derek approached. Tracy leaned against the railing to watch the two elephants towering over the handlers feeding them. The ground quaked as tree-trunk-like legs covered in tough canvas skin lifted and fell. The nearest elephant's trunk slithered around the zookeeper's hand, entirely encompassing it and the stacks of grass she held. Loud munching made Derek glad this intelligent animal wasn't a carnivore.

Students shoved to get closer to the information displays lining the enclosure and answer the questions on their assignment sheets. Tracy's brother stood at the edge of the elephant pen next to her. He pressed his lips together and blew them out to make a sound like the animal's cry.

"I was never as much of a pain as these freshmen, right?" Derek asked Tracy.

Her raised eyebrow was ready to leap off her face. "Want me to be honest or lie?"

Derek sighed, watching the elephant wrap its trunk around a human-sized tire and flip it, creating a donut-shaped dust cloud. Though he watched it happen, Derek still jumped at the mighty thump.

"Why don't you impress the elephants by lifting one?" Tracy joked.

"No. They're playing. Besides, they're probably too heavy to lift."

"Fine." Tracy exhaled, forcing as much fake displeasure as her lungs could fit into the sound. "Has John spoken to you?"

"No. You?"

"A little. This is a pile of suck! We did nothing wrong."

"That's not entirely true." Derek kicked a loose brick. "I manipulated my closest friends so we'd go to that party together."

"Don't oversell yourself. We took little convincing."

"I chose to be in a place with a lot of noise to hide from the monster."

Tracy wagged her finger at him. "That has nothing to do with the party being busted. Well, maybe the noise part, but right now, John is being more thickheaded than you."

"We can't have that. It's one of my most charming qualities."

Tracy offered a flat stare.

Needing to fill the silence, Derek spoke. "I'm giving John space to sort out what he wants."

"That will only let your emotions fester. Talk to him so we can put this behind us. Besides, now's your chance. He's heading this way with Rachel and Louis."

John appeared from the crowd of students. His smile dropped when he noticed Derek.

John looked right at Derek, yet addressed the students around them. "The answer to number twenty-two is that elephants belong to the family Elephantidae. Now, we're moving to the next exhibit."

The students with Rachel, John, and Louis combined with the group Tracy and Derek were monitoring. The giant mass refused to separate. Derek knew it was a losing battle to try. Together, they walked with all their students downhill and into the Valley region.

Derek glanced at John, thinking of the right thing to say. He turned before John caught him staring.

Sleeping river otters sprawled across various rocks offered a convenient distraction. Their slick, brown fur glistened in sunlight filtering through the trees. These otters had the right idea. After days of grueling practice with Tracy's abilities, Derek wanted nothing more than to get a little shuteye.

Louis, on the other hand, was too excited to consider sleep. His mouth sprinted ahead, regardless of who listened.

"I set a flat-screen frame in the trunk of my BMW. Once I connect the electronics, we'll have a mobile gaming system. Next time we're sitting in a parking lot deciding where to go, all the entertainment anyone could hope for will be at our fingertips."

"Sweet," Derek said. "On the next warm night, that will be fun to play with outside your family's gelato shop."

John turned to Derek at the sound of his voice, then brushed past him to get a closer view of the sleeping otters.

Louis looked between them. "Why don't you two talk to each other?"

"That's what I said," Tracy muttered.

John spun to face them, fuming. "You want us to talk? Fine! Let's talk about how Tracy disappeared to save her own ass, and Derek stood by doing nothing when the cops showed up. A friend is someone to bail you out of jail. True friends are right there alongside you. On Saturday, Derek proved he isn't a true friend, and Tracy is only marginally better."

"Bail? You got a drinking citation. It's not the end of the world." Tracy's raised voice drew attention from other visitors.

Louis stepped in. "I didn't get a citation either."

"You would have if the cops arrived an hour later." John's shout sent spit flying. "Same with Rachel. We were all set for a carefree night, and yet, I'm the one who suffered."

Derek set his jaw. "What good are two metaphorical people in jail with no way out?"

"That's not the point."

Derek ignored the tiny voice inside telling him to stay quiet. "What is the point, then? Would you like an apology? In that case, I'm sorry. I'm sorry for convincing you that you earned one night to relax. I'm sorry the party got busted. More than anything else, I'm sorry I offered to drive you, so when you got a slap-on-the-wrist citation, I was sober and wasn't punished. We should have been side by side together until the bitter end."

"Sorry? What good is a sorry?" John's voice took on a hideous nasal quality. "I'm sorry *your* persuasion led to *me* being barred from joining the wrestling team this upcoming season."

Derek blinked, unable to form words.

John's shoulders slumped. "It's my senior year and this season's State Championships are over for me without a single match."

"Oh." Derek covered his eyes and rubbed his forehead. "I didn't know."

"You never asked. Hell, neither you nor Tracy asked why I've been so pissed at you."

As though physically struck, Derek cringed. "When? You've ignored me all week."

"A decade of punishing my body and I miss my last chance to dominate the competition because of one mistake. Colleges won't care how I did last year."

"You decided to drink."

Derek sensed John's fist hurling at him. He had half a thought to duck, but Derek's twisting innards clenched and refused to give. Wrapping his hand in telekinetic power, he caught John's fist, bringing it to an abrupt standstill.

John grunted, his feet sliding backward even as he threw more weight forward.

Crowding students widened into a circle, cheering for either side.

Derek mentally formed an invisible third arm, ready to knock John off his feet.

Rachel's hand smacked both their fists down, splitting them apart. Her stern tone interrupted the fight. "Boys! Set a good example for our students."

"You're supposed to be friends," came Louis's strained voice as he joined Rachel between Derek and John.

Derek didn't reply and John stood still, scowling at Derek. Rachel prodded John, moving him onto the Elephant Trail path and away from everyone.

"I need a breather," Derek told Tracy and Louis, striding in the opposite direction.

Tracy was at Derek's side. "Mind if I come with to help you vent whatever thorn you have stuck inside?"

Derek knew better than to trust his mouth with anyone trying to help. "No, thanks. Watch the students with Louis. I'll meet up later."

Derek trudged ahead. His power refused to flush from angry limbs. The otters bounded to the opposite side of their pen, scurrying from Derek's presence.

A father shielded his young daughter as they walked around Derek. Other visitors gave him a wide berth until he was alone on a side path. That suited him. He stomped bricks with each step to relieve frustration. Power soaked his clenched fists.

No one is within view. Good.

A tree stood outside the zoo's property line, taller and wider than the others nearby. Derek wound back his fist. He pictured his frustrations wrapping around his hand in a warm bubble. Stored power released, and he swung a telekinetic arm at the base of the trunk.

The impact shook the enormous tree down to its last leaf. Cracking noises broke the calm day as though the earth were shifting. In slow motion, the tree toppled, its long roots popping from beneath the ground. Thousands of pounds of wood slammed against the hillside in a crash so loud it reverberated through his body.

Rock Creek Park had one fewer tree standing, and its destruction was oddly soothing. He sat on the cool brick path to catch his breath. He wasn't ready to rejoin Tracy and the group.

A mountain of ice crushed Derek's lungs, halting his breath.

Beyond the zoo's outer fence, the large, bear-shaped creature appeared, sniffing the tree he had toppled. Easily double the size since Derek last saw it, the creature pawed the fallen tree, sniffing it from different angles. Long horns now protruded above its ears, setting the monster further apart from any known breed of bear.

The creature snorted every inch of the indentation where Derek's mental fist struck bark. The monster grew, its muscles bulging beneath its white fur.

The creature's nose lifted, testing the air for scents. No longer swelling in size, it lowered its face, settling its pale eyes on Derek while its long teeth bared through rippling lips.

Derek tried to swallow and found his mouth dry. Rational thoughts fled, leaving his mind a blank slate. A few hundred feet and a useless fence separated him from the monster.

His queasy stomach clenched as though hornets had made a nest inside him. Primal fear consumed Derek, holding him in place.

The thing stepped forward, then shifted, disappearing and reappearing lower on the hill, and coming much closer. Derek blinked. The distance between them halved.

A heavy, dark ball formed in Derek's hand. The ball grew, sapping his strength. He screamed at his legs to move, but they refused.

Bitter winds rose from the ball and wailed against his aching body.

Taking control of the one body part still under his control, Derek willed the trembling fingers on his free hand to pinch his thigh. Pain allowed him to move.

The heavy black ball faded to nothing, and the wind stilled.

He looked up to find the creature's fangs inches from his face. It opened its mouth wide.

Derek threw a mental shield in front of himself.

A beam of white light surged from the depths of the creature, plowing into his defenses.

Though his shield held, the blast knocked him back. His arms and legs scraped over uneven surfaces until he came to a stop.

Fight-or-flight instincts kicked in, and Derek chose the latter, sprinting down the path. He had no intention of leading the monster toward his friends by returning uphill.

After a minute, Derek skidded to a stop right before he ran into a crowd of children. He mentally kicked himself for forgetting about the Kid's Farm section and how he led the bear monster to a buffet.

He readied his power to protect everyone, but no monster had followed him.

Derek doubled back to catch the creature's attention, rather than rely on the noisy crowd to stave off an attack. Though he saw no more signs of it, he continued sprinting toward a less-crowded section of the zoo in case it was still hunting him. His throat burned with exertion as he forced his leaden legs to move faster. Faces blurred in his headlong dash.

Glancing over his shoulder to see if he was being chased, Derek ran into a man with his arms spread wide. Mr. Sprog caught Derek without being knocked backward.

"Causing trouble today, Mr. Fen?"

Derek gasped for air. It took a few tries to speak. Tossing caution aside, he said, "Did you see that giant polar bear?"

Mr. Sprog's voice was steady. "There are no polar bears in this zoo, giant or otherwise. I believe you are confusing it with the Maryland Zoo in Baltimore."

Derek couldn't say the words fast enough. "It's not part of the zoo. There was a polar bear running around outside." He specifically neglected to mention the fact this one had horns and blasted a force of light from its mouth.

"I don't appreciate your senior prank. Please go back to your student group or I'll take away your bonus credit for volunteering today."

Derek set a steady pace up the hill, his heart somersaulting. He joined Tracy and Louis at the Giant Panda Habitat. An adoring crowd took photos of the panda munching away on a carrot. The meal stained its white and black fur. When it finished, the panda tumbled down the hill, drawing plenty of "awws" from the spectators.

Rachel and John had yet to return from their walk, leaving a large group of students for Louis, Tracy, and Derek to handle.

"I saw the monster again," Derek whispered to Tracy. "It shot a beam of light from its mouth, but I blocked it with a shield."

Tracy studied the cuts along his knees and hands. Keeping her voice down, she asked, "How do we keep those around us safe?"

"I don't know. It nearly got me."

"Is it still nearby?"

"I haven't seen it since it attacked me and I haven't heard panicked running, so I think it's gone."

"What should we do?"

"Keep our eyes open and run if it shows up again. We need to be stronger if we're going to stop it."

"After school, we're getting one hell of a training workout. But first, we're patching things up between us and John. By next week, you can share your powers with our friends and they'll help with the monster."

Tracy's glare left no room for Derek to debate.

10

Paint

Tracy

Tracy decided on a slight detour to the Cold Snap on the way to Derek's house to gather her friends. Nestled in the neighborhood strip mall, the Cold Snap was a dream brought to life by Louis's parents. The gelato shop drew crowds from the small movie theater around the corner, classmates leaving school, and ironically, the gym Derek worked at. Maybe after a hard workout, people felt they deserved the treat. The store was a cozy size with a handful of small, square tables. Tracy and her four friends commandeered the corner seats.

She stewed over what to say to patch things up with John, who sat across from her. Instead, she watched Louis's parents, Nora and Frank, at their battle stations behind the counter. One served the long line while the other handled the cash register.

Louis's mom was tall, and her long, dark hair was trapped within a hairnet. She beamed at Tracy and her friends, calling above the din, "I got a new one. How do astronauts eat ice cream?"

Louis's face scrunched, his rumbling groan rising from inside. "Please, don't."

"In floats!"

A heavy sigh escaped Louis. "Why do we always end up at my shop?"

"Double scoop of pistachio and a single of dulce de leche," Louis's dad said to save Louis from his mom.

Louis's dad was shorter than his wife, an older version of Louis with their matching olive skin and light eyes. The biggest difference was Louis's dad's receding hairline. Hopefully, Louis wouldn't suffer the same fate given how his wavy hair was worthy of admiration.

Tracy slouched in the seat closest to the display case. There were fourteen flavors, from vanilla to the seasonal Halloween-themed, pumpkin-based specialty.

Hanging on the wall above the cash register rested a picture from a few years back of six stiffly smiling young teenagers, the Cold Snap's first customers. Nicole's smiling face in the picture dragged a weight down inside Tracy.

She missed spending every afternoon with Nicole. If Nicole was at Saturday's party, she would have charmed the cops to leave without writing any citations. She probably would have even got them to apologize for the interruption.

Tracy licked her Stracciatella gelato. Sugar danced across her taste buds from tiny chocolate chunks. "Your parents make a *fine* treat," she complimented Louis. "That's why I regularly post how this is the coolest place to go after a long school day."

Derek gestured in Tracy's general direction. "With free advertising, you get what you pay for."

"I like Tracy's comments," John snapped. His shirt bunched where Rachel's hand squeezed. "That came out harsher than I meant. I'm sorry." John spooned his plain vanilla with an expression like he was riding a bike with no seat.

Derek grabbed his backpack and stepped from the table. "I got work in an hour, so I'm heading home. Tracy, ready to head out for our assignment? If we hurry, we can make decent headway before I go to my shift at the gym's front desk."

"Sounds like a plan."

Rachel sat inches from the chair's back, maintaining excellent posture. She prodded John, "Well?"

John's knuckles braced on the table as he rose. "I was wrong to throw a punch at you earlier today. I let my emotions get the best of me."

Creases formed on Derek's sagging face, seeming to age him ten years. Tracy held her breath as he approached John.

Derek tapped his fist against John's, with the hint of a smile finally breaking. "It's fine. I caught the brunt of it without any harm."

John let loose a single, barking laugh. "Since when do you know how to fight? Your move took some skill, even if it wasn't the smartest one."

"I don't intend to have a rematch," Derek said. He made it halfway to the door before uttering, "Mind giving me some pointers in case I get stuck in another fight?"

"Anytime."

Tracy waved to Louis's parents as she and Derek left.

"See you tomorrow," Louis's mom called out.

Louis hurried out the door after Tracy and Derek, heading in the opposite direction to his newish car parked near the front of the store. "Feel like late night gelato after our shifts end?" Louis shouted at Derek.

"Sure," Derek said. "I'll meet you back here at ten."

"Why are you leaving to come back later?" Tracy asked Louis.

Louis made a show of smelling his shirt. "I need to shower after being outside all day, but I'll make it in time to help for the Cold Snap's post-dinner rush. I'm in a hurry, or I'd offer you a ride."

Louis drove away, leaving Tracy and Derek to walk along the pedestrian path of the nearby bridge, returning to school where their cars were parked.

The bridge spanned over nine highway lanes with multiple on and off ramps, a sea of rubbernecking vehicles idled below. Car horns blared as drivers struggled to make room for a motorcade of police escorting several unmarked vehicles for politicians leaving Capitol Hill.

Concrete barricades protected the pedestrian path from cars hurtling to slam their brakes at the other side of the bridge. From this spot, the bridge's rising curve appeared to lead nowhere, or drop directly onto traffic.

To her right, the chain-link fence stretched above her, curling inward at the top. The river running under the bridge cut a snaking, uneven trail through surrounding wetlands.

Derek picked up his pace. "Today, the evil monster moved a hundred yards faster than my eyes could follow. Think teleportation is one of our abilities, too?"

"Maybe. Are you sure it's evil? It's done nothing to us, yet, aside from destroying school property."

"The way it looks at me, it can't be anything less."

"That seems prejudiced against giant bears."

"It didn't look at me like I was a piece of meat to be devoured. There was intelligence behind those eyes. The creature held its ground, studying me, planning how to charge."

"You got all that from a look?"

Derek shook his head. "There was also the beam of light it fired at me. Without the mental shield, I would have been hurt or worse. It's more than that, though. I know bears don't have eyebrows, but I swear the space above this thing's eyes furrowed when it saw me. The monster looked at me like John did back at the Cold Snap."

Crossing the bridge, they walked around the progression of partially developed houses. Large yellow trucks dug into the ground, setting the foundation for more future homes. Farther over, people lay stone and mortar siding, finishing touches to model homes used to sell the neighborhood being built.

Tracy stared into the distance, their school grounds in sight. "We have to sharpen our skills. That's the best way to protect ourselves."

* * *

Tracy parked in front of Derek's house, coming to a smooth halt behind the disjointed shaking of Derek's car. Derek had yet to leave his car; instead, he swiveled his head about in every direction.

Recognizing her friend's worries, Tracy tapped his car's window. "I'll keep an eye out. At the first sign of any animal larger than a rabbit, we sprint for your house."

Her coaxing brought Derek out of his car, but he still refused to move toward the woods.

"Look, do you see this monster now?" she asked.

He shook his head.

"You want to get stronger to defend yourself against it, right?"

He nodded.

"It wasn't waiting for us at the Cold Snap and it's not here now, so come on. Between worrying about your dad catching us or blasting a chunk from your home, we can't train to our fullest so close to your house."

This time, Derek's feet moved.

Tracy placed her thick, quality headphones over her ears. She didn't intend to let Derek in on this inspirational mix. He never understood ambiance to set the right mood. It wasn't his fault. Most people failed to differentiate between Mozart, Beethoven, or Bach, whose influences hid in today's music. Classical orchestras sharpened her senses and let her gather power. Her eyes darted over every tree, checking for the monster's hulking frame.

Derek took out his phone and started blasting music, apparently following her example. Tracy heard little as her headphones dampened outside noises.

Red and golden leaves gave the forest the appearance of being ablaze as the isolation closed in. Brambles stretched to block her, scratching her exposed legs.

Derek moved erratically, ducking behind logs and peering around wide tree trunks.

Eventually, the shaded trees opened into a round meadow, their secret pocket in the woods. Tracy threw a hand over her eyes to shield them from the late afternoon haze.

Struck with the perfect distraction for Derek, Tracy ran into the meadow. She counted to three, then dove forward. Harnessing willpower into her palm, she slammed it into the ground, transmuting the small area around her.

Soil and rock sank into a shallow trench, and she formed a low wall extending up on all sides. She pulled in more material from the ground and created a bright rubber balloon filled with green paint.

Tracy leaped from behind her transmuted wall. "Think fast!"

Tracy threw the paint balloon, aiming for where she'd last seen Derek. Green exploded on the ground, instead of him.

"Come out and fight me with honor," she called to the encroaching woods, searching for the slightest signs of movement.

In reply, a rush of air battered the wall she formed. The force knocked Tracy onto her back and spattered her with dirt from thigh to arm.

"You're going to have to do better to win." Tracy transmuted the dirt around her into new walls. The surrounding earth awoke at her touch, sinking her hole a few more feet. The walls she formed on every side stretched to block the sun.

Using more dirt as raw material, Tracy transmuted a rainbow-colored arsenal of paint balloons. She strapped them around her belt and smeared dirt lines beneath her eyes.

Tracy lobbed two orange paint balloons over the walls. Two wet smacks were her reward. She hadn't expected to hit or even find Derek. She wanted to remind him she was here and armed.

Four gusts of wind struck her walls in quick succession. Derek's mental fists swept aside the hardened dirt. Standing waist-deep in the hole, she was exposed in the open field.

"Five points for eliminating your defenses," Derek shouted.

Tracy hurled paint balloons at the sound of his voice. "Minus ten for gloating."

Her first balloon collided with an invisible force. It spread to cover a semicircle dome in front of Derek, highlighting his tele-kinetic shield. Blue paint blocked his face from view. Her other balloon fell short, covering grass in more green. The trail of paint stretched farther than the first, reaching Derek's shoes. His mental shield dispersed, leaving the blue paint to drop to the ground.

"How do you expect me to block your telekinetic punches?" Tracy asked. "I can't see them clearly enough to dodge."

"Get better. Don't worry, I'm not firing those energy blasts since they rip my hands apart. Telekinesis may lack the 'oomph' of explod-ing energy, but it hurts me less to use. So, brace yourself." Derek sank into the forest, using his home-field advantage to blend into the surroundings.

Tracy bounded from the trench to sprint for the trees, having made a bad initial choice to be exposed in the meadow.

Gusts of wind in her wake clarified that Derek's attacks were a step behind.

She reached the tree line. Every crushed tree trunk reminded her of the power she faced. Derek had one glaring weakness: she knew how he thought. It wasn't much.

Tracy placed her hand on a fallen log to create a thin rope and long plank. She bent the plank and held it in place with the taut rope. Her transmuted mini-catapult was firmly set, but easily undone with a swift tug. She had no chance to practice without giving away her position, so she added a paint balloon and crept to the next spot.

She transmuted and set three more mini-catapults, then leaned against an elm tree to catch her breath.

Her legs gave under the taxing effort of too many creations, sending her falling back into the rigid nook. It took multiple tries to clamber upright by balancing against the tree, all while holding the ropes in her hand to launch the catapults.

"Derek!" Her voice bounced from one log to the next. "Plan on hiding all night?"

Underbrush crunched nearby. Tracy faced the sounds.

Derek's answer came from behind, close enough to hear through her headphones. "Not at all."

Sharp wind from the side narrowly missed Tracy, ruffling her clothes.

Derek radiated smug glee with his crooked smile and crossed arms. "You fell for my telekinetic distraction."

He deserved to have his ego trampled back down to normal, and he was standing right where she needed him.

"I win." She yanked the ropes in her hand and dove for cover.

Four twangs announced her assault. Paint balloons sailed at Derek. Two flew wide and splashed purple and blue across trees. The remaining shots hit early, breaking on his mental shield.

Of course, those were her decoys. Earth rumbled at her finger's touch. Loose ground shifted, transmuting its form according to her will. Tracy molded the raw material, condensing and pressing dirt forward into a rolling mound of earth aimed at Derek's defenseless back.

He turned at the last second and threw up his arms to form a mental shield. Striking beneath his defense, her pillar of hardened dirt slammed into his gut. Tracy never knew one of his abilities gave him the gift of flight—that was how hard she hit him.

Her headphones wrenched from her ears. Thoughts danced clumsily, colliding into one another. Grasping for reserves of power, she found a severed connection. Her powers were there, buzzing deep inside, but they ignored her pleas to come forth.

Tracy's vision darkened, threatening to fade to black. The haze made her lose balance.

She panted heavily. The urge to vomit raked through her as her body rejected the toll of pushing her abilities. She looked up to find Derek sitting there. He dropped the headphones in front of her.

Spite at her own limits formed words on Tracy's lips. "Why didn't you stop my music? At any point, you could have won."

Derek leaned back to stare at swelling clouds. "It's not a fair fight. I've had my powers for twice as long as you."

"Pretend to be someone you aren't and push me harder. Otherwise, why am I here?"

"You have a brand of creativity I lack, and today you've shown me how to fix my shortcomings. With practice, we'll be on even footing soon."

"Not that the gap in our powers needs to be narrowed." Tracy weakly threw her hands in the air to make a "V" for victory. "I got in the knockout hit to win."

"It seemed more like a stalemate."

Tracy pulled out her phone to show him what the word "stalemate" meant. Then she noticed the time. "It's a quarter to six. Don't you need to leave for work soon?"

Derek swore. "I needed to leave ten minutes ago." He was already in a headlong sprint as the words settled.

Tracy broke from the woods in time to watch Derek start his car. It immediately spun out, spraying gravel. She shouted slurs at him as he sent stones bouncing off her precious parked baby.

Derek disappeared around his winding driveway without a word of apology.

Once the quiet settled around her, Tracy played jazz songs discovered from class. Riding on the music's rhythm, she pulled in shreds of power to fix the damage to her car.

Stars seared across her vision. She had nothing left.

Tracy's arms moved too slow to catch herself.

She lay on the gravel, struggling to convince herself to move. Then she remembered Derek had a stocked kitchen and the world's most comfortable couch.

There were worse reasons to force her legs to stand.

11

Lies We Tell

Derek

Derek pressed the pedal to the floor, sending ragged coughs from the engine of his rust-coated trash-on-wheels.

Another late arrival and he'd be out of his minimum wage job, no matter the excuse. Stipends for his family, college savings, and a social life all evaporated without paychecks from the gym.

Like pushing a log, he applied a constant telekinetic force to the back of his car to go faster. The speedometer shook past eighty- five, the highest number shown. Clearly, the manufacturers assumed no one could get this piece of crap past that limit.

Under the steady force he applied with his powers, the car accelerated, vibrating so much it caused Derek's teeth to chatter. He expanded his mental force, causing a wedge to split the air ahead and reduce wind resistance.

He hugged around a tight corner. His telekinetic pushes kept him from losing traction and swerving over the grassy median into oncoming traffic. He brought his car under control before hitting the small guardrail protecting his car from falling off the road. Derek glanced nervously at the small hill beyond the guardrail leading to a cropped line of trees at the edge of a forest.

Whomp-whomp-whomp noises came from below when he drove over the rumble strips.

Straightening from the turn, he saw a slow sedan was blocking his lane.

He slammed on the brakes to avoid a collision, but was still going too fast. Derek sent telekinetic forces into the front of his car to push backward and stop in time. The initial impact of his mental fists dented the hell out of his hood but saved him from a crash.

The car ahead ignored his near impact and stayed below the speed limit, even with Derek tailgating it.

Mentally forming a fist, he aimed to push the terrible driver. Fracturing his attention in too many places, the shot went wide, missing the car ahead. He gathered more power and pressed a mental hand firmly against the side of the slow car ahead.

This connected, moving the other car none too gently onto the shoulder where it stopped. Though the driver had no reason to even think Derek shoved their car off the road, a rising guilt made him partially cover his face with his hand on the chance the driver was looking his way.

Derek turned his power against his own car and returned to well past its intended peak speed. All too soon, he slammed his brakes, stuck behind another slow driver. This gold BMW, however, at least traveled slightly above the speed limit.

He didn't want to send a second car off the road, although his alternatives were dwindling. Flashing his lights and honking had no impact on this road-hog.

An unsettling, but familiar, prodding nestled in the base of Derek's skull from the car ahead. He pushed the concern aside to focus on how unfair it was for his brick of a car to catch anything that so thoroughly outclassed it.

Giving the car in front of him a push with his mind, Derek coaxed the driver into speeding up or pulling over. When he removed his not-so-subtle psychic push, the driver dropped to their original speed, far too oblivious to know when to get off the road.

Today was the day for a valuable lesson from Professor Derek.

Anger built inside him, tying his stomach in knots. He was angry that he raced in traffic only to sit idly at a boring desk job, angry at his father's cancer for turning his world upside down, and more than anything, angry at the driver ahead, who, despite driving a vehicle Derek *knew* carried serious horsepower, refused to use it.

A tidal wave of energy unleashed into his telekinetic fist when he sought to use a small trickle. Derek's power struck the BMW, launching it to the side, its metal shell compressing on impact. The car continued rolling into a ditch as Derek drove past.

Derek screeched his car to a halt on the shoulder. He leaped from his seat and crossed the distance to the crash.

Step. Step. Seventy-three paces found him at the start of the wreck, all while he wanted to speed off and hide in shame.

The telekinetic impact spewed shrapnel over asphalt and grass. The pain in his chest made him want nothing more than to throw himself at speeding blurs of passing cars.

Traffic slowed, yet none of the miserable drivers stopped.

Derek bargained anything and everything he owned to remove the lump taking hold inside, making promises he knew he'd never keep, so long as the driver was alright.

I can fix this. I have to have an ability to undo this disaster.

No! These powers got me here.

Derek slid past the hole in the guardrail made by the car he'd hurled sideways.

At the bottom of the hill, the upside-down car's roof settled on the grass. Set against a tree, the start of the forest stopped the BMW from rolling farther. Its sides were crushed as though squeezed by a giant's hand. One tire spun lazily on a crooked axle.

Burned rubber mixed with oil stung Derek's nostrils. The metal was hot to the touch from the friction of scraping the road and patched dirt. Every inch was smashed, leaving little trace of the original shape. No matter how lightly he stepped, broken glass crunched underfoot. From behind the deployed airbag, the driver's wavy brown hair caught the fading rays of sunlight.

No.

Derek thought it wasn't possible to hate himself more; he was wrong. His legs tensed and locked. He'd sat in this car before. Not a similar model, this *exact* car.

Applying his full body weight, Derek pried the crumpled door open with a trembling hand and confirmed what he already knew. Louis hung by his seat belt. Louis turned toward the sudden change in light, unable to acknowledge Derek. Blood dripped from cuts hidden by Louis's hair, dropping onto the car's roof. He was in awful shape, but Derek needed to wait until the medics arrived to touch him.

Medics!

Derek's hands were shaking and it took more than a few tries to correctly hit 911. Giving vague details, the dispatcher's voice sounded dubious, but someone else had already reported the accident. Thank goodness paramedics were on their way. The operator told him to keep Louis awake by talking to him.

A fresh wave of nausea swept over Derek as he fell against the crushed car. That noise at least brought a groan from Louis. Derek shouted his friend's name and snapped clammy fingers to get his attention. Hanging by his seat belt, Louis remained mostly unresponsive.

In a futile attempt to undo the damage, Derek banged on the car. Louis slowly turned his head. For Louis, Derek forced himself into action. "Stay still. EMTs are on their way."

"Please," Louis called out in a cracking voice.

Derek needed to be like steel and give no indication he was the one responsible. "Don't move. You may have internal bleeding or a concussion."

"Please get me out of this chocolate fudge of a mess," Louis begged. His grip loosened on the fancy plastic door handle he'd ripped off, dropping it into the tiny pool of blood collecting on the car's interior roof lining.

"I should wait," Derek said, but a plea from the one he'd hurt was too much.

Against his better judgment, he unbuckled the seat belt and caught Louis, sliding him onto soft grass and free of the carnage. Lifting his friend's full weight to move him farther was more than Derek could handle. All he'd need was a little telekinetic push to get Louis away from the wreck.

No. I won't use these cursed abilities!

Louis's mouth moved, yet no words came out. "Thanks," he said, giving it another try.

That one word was enough for Derek's tears to fall.

Purple bruising on Louis's arms and legs made it too difficult for Derek to tell if anything was broken.

"Do I look that bad?"

Derek tried to smile to reassure his friend, but his quivering lips refused to work. "Can you remember what happened?"

Louis's eyes stared at the sky. "I was on my way to the Cold Snap for my evening shift... when someone behind me flashed their lights and honked." Louis breathed in and out, forming his words slowly. "I thought I forgot to close my gas tank or something, so I ignored them."

Derek rubbed the back of his neck. "That might have been me."

"So I guessed."

"What came next?"

"My car flipped over and over and over. At some point, I threw up in there, not that it matters."

There had to be some magic comforting words to say. Derek was at a loss for what they might be. "It wasn't your fault."

"Why say that? Of course, it wasn't my fault."

Louis pulled a piece of glass from his hair and let it fall. A splotch of blood smeared the sharp point. Derek ripped his shirt sleeve and pressed it to the small gash on Louis's head, saying nothing as Louis continued, "My parents are going to kill me."

Sticks snapped on the other side of the totaled pile of metal. Louis was too incoherent to recognize the sounds. His voice faded. The monster stepped out of the woods into broad daylight, claws digging into dry dirt. It crept forward as its pale eyes of Death and hulking frame made Derek forget how to think.

Red lights flashed from behind. The monster retreated from the wailing ambulance call.

An EMT hopped out of the ambulance and joined them near the crash. While the EMT shined her light in Louis's eyes and checked his breathing, Derek kept a vigilant watch on the woods. Staring between the trees, his eyes chased shadows, distracting him from Louis's cries of pain when the EMT lifted the wrong leg.

Another EMT brought a stretcher down to Louis, and together the medical professionals strapped him in place and carried him to the ambulance.

Blue and red lights joined the ambulance's red. A policewoman approached Louis and asked questions while she recorded the information on his driver's license. Derek's attention was split between straining his ears for the answers Louis gave and scanning the trees. When asked to describe the accident, Louis admitted what little he knew without mentioning the part about Derek antagonizing him.

As the details became sketchier, the policewoman faced Derek and collected his driver's license information. "Anything to add?"

Choking on his words, Derek shook his head.

She turned back to Louis and handed him a business card. "My name is Detective Patricia Kim. If you remember any omitted detail, no matter how minute, please call me. The ball's in your court."

Detective Kim towered over Derek. Her sharp nose gave her expression an intense glare, like she was Derek's mom catching him sneaking out at night. The Detective's thick biceps looked more than capable of pummeling him into oblivion.

Detective Kim walked along the path Louis's car had tumbled. Callused hands touched the deep impacts and recoiled. In a stern voice, the officer stated, "From what Louis stated, you were behind this vehicle. Did you see anything unusual?"

"See anything?" Derek struggled to remember his lies. "Nope."

Derek laid out the same story he'd told Louis: that he was driving behind him and saw Louis's car inexplicably roll off the road. His story concluded with the most promising piece of evidence.

"My car's not far. It's banged up, but nothing like his. Trust me when I say my scrap heap isn't capable of totaling a car like this."

Rather than averting suspicion, Derek's overly defensive stance caught the full attention of the investigator. "No one blamed you. The baffling part is how the vehicle was sent sideways. No tracks crossed the median and I can't, for the life of me, figure what might have caused this crash. Are you certain you saw nothing unusual?"

Derek knew she read through every lie he'd uttered. He shook his head, not trusting himself to speak. His phone vibrated.

Shit.

Even at arm's reach, his boss's pissed voice on the other end was deafening. "Where the hell are you?"

"I'm sorry. There was a car crash, and my friend was hurt."

"This is another tardy demerit on top of last week's complaint about you falling asleep at the counter."

The EMT interrupted to update Derek. "Louis has plenty of minor cuts and bruises, plus he's likely got several broken bones. We're taking him to the hospital to get X-rayed and monitor him overnight. He wanted you to ride in the ambulance, but we can't do that. You can meet him there."

Derek felt as though someone else nodded his head in response. "At least he's alive."

During the time it took the EMT to secure Louis in the ambulance cabin, Derek's boss's rant continued without a pause for air.

Metaphorical shackling weights fell from Derek's shoulders. Anyone this heartless didn't deserve his loyalty. "I quit," Derek uttered, and promptly ended the call.

He wanted to yell at his useless boss. He wanted to feel anything other than the rat gnawing through his sinking chest.

The ambulance left with its precious cargo, leaving Derek at the scene of his crime with an officer who must already suspect him. Derek ignored his vibrating phone as his boss called again.

"Is there anything else you need?"

The detective studied the guilty culprit one last time. "No, I have your information."

"Then I'm meeting my friend."

The detective raised her hand in front of Derek's face, leveling piercing eyes into the woods. "Shhhhh."

Derek followed the detective's example and held his breath. Beyond his pounding chest, the only other noises were the creaking branches of restless trees and rustling leaves. No pale eyes lingered beyond the forest's edge.

"I thought I sensed something," the Detective said, still scanning the woods. "Unless there was anything you failed to mention, that will be all."

"Nope."

"I'll be in touch if you need to make an official statement. You're good to go."

Not needing to be told twice, Derek ran, his mind blankly detached from his body. Each step was unsteady. After an eternity, he collapsed into his driver's seat.

He lay his head on the wheel, free to let the tears fall from his eyes. He felt a slight comfort at finally letting his emotions out.

When the tears dried, Derek fled.

12

Truth

Derek

By the time Derek arrived at the hospital, Louis was stabilized in bed. His left eye was swollen shut with purple bruises, and his limbs were wrapped to limit mobility. Acknowledging Derek's presence with a small nod seemed to sap the remains of Louis's strength.

Derek's legs shook with guilt. "I'm so sorry. This is all my fault."

"How? Your tailgating was obnoxious, sure, but you were behind me. I was launched from the side. I probably ran over a serious pothole and my tire exploded."

Derek's confession wanted to spill out, but it stuck at the tip of his tongue.

Louis's parents burst into the room and flanked their son, ignoring Derek. Dried tear streaks marked their faces. They were still wearing their Cold Snap smocks and looked ready to pounce on Louis and wrap him up in a hug. They settled for clutching his hands.

"Are you okay?" Louis's dad asked.

"I broke my arm and leg, not to mention a bunch of other inconveniences. They need to run some tests to gauge the total damage before they put me in casts."

"Thank you for watching over Louis after the accident," Louis's mom said to Derek without looking away from her son.

"It was the least I could do." After what he did, Derek hated himself for even speaking to Louis's family.

"You know," began Louis to his mom, "I'm feeling well enough to allow you one joke."

Louis's dad looked aghast. "Now isn't the time."

Louis patted his dad's hand. "It's okay. I'm not dying today."

"Where do sick boats go to get healthy?" Louis's mother put on her best smile. "To the dock!"

"Good thing we're in the hospital. Otherwise, I wouldn't be graced by your flavor of medical humor."

Louis's mom carried on. "Comedy is the best medicine. It's a shame my health-related puns feel out of place since I developed an irony deficiency."

"I said you get one," Louis muttered.

Derek made his way back to the waiting room, giving Louis's family privacy. He dropped onto a corner chair, unable to find a comfortable position even with exhaustion spread through every limb.

He stretched his hand to summon a plastic cup from across the room and fill it with water. Derek smacked his hand before so much as collecting a shred of power.

He got up to get water from the cooler, his shoes squeaking on linoleum tiles. Each step yelled to those in the room.

Guilty. Guilty. Guilty.

Automatic doors opened and John came running through. Red faced, he sprinted to Derek. "Do you know how to answer a text?" The others in the waiting room turned at John's raised voice.

Derek retrieved his phone to find new alert notifications. Had he responded to any of them, he knew he would have cracked and admitted to everything.

"Never mind. What room is Louis in?" John left no room for pleasantries.

"Through that hall, three doors down on the left. He might be getting more tests taken." Derek clutched John's arm as he walked past. *This burden is too much. I need to tell someone right now.* "What happened to Louis was my fault."

"Did you crash into Louis's car?"

"Not exactly." Derek lowered his voice so only John heard. "See, I have powers. Abilities. Ignore how crazy that sounds and trust me on this. I was running late. Louis was in front of me, driving slow and safe. I didn't know it was him and gave it a little mental push. Except everything went wrong and I... I... I don't know what to do."

"I know about your powers."

"You what?"

"I'm smarter than you think, and you aren't subtle. I've been replaying football game footage from when the Sunny Creek guy tripped over nothing. It never added up, until I saw you tie your shoes without using your hands. Then, you caught my punch like it was nothing. The signs were too obvious to ignore."

Derek stammered, "It's not what you thi—"

John pulled Derek by his collar. "Bullshit! I've been watching you when you think no one else is looking. You were bound to hurt someone."

"The crash was an acci—"

"This wasn't an accident. To call it that is a lie. *You* sent Louis here. I'm visiting *my* friend. Don't be here when I get back. If you ever, and I mean *ever*, use your powers again, I'll expose and destroy you."

John released his grip, letting Derek fall under the weight of his words.

13

Powerless

Derek

Derek lay in bed, his Monday morning alarm blaring after its third snooze cycle. Never in his life did an inanimate object deserve to be flung at the wall more than this plastic T-Rex with its electronic roars. Power welled within Derek, eager to smash the dinosaur into extinction.

Louis's wrecked car was etched in the back of Derek's mind, having taken up permanent residence over the weekend.

He released his power, reluctant to have it drain without using it; he turned the alarm off the old-fashioned way.

Burrowed within the mass of covers, warm comfort allowed him to hide from his mistakes. Except, he had been too cavalier about skipping school to train. Although his parents might be lenient on the first school day after Louis's crash, Derek was fast approaching the cutoff for being held back a grade.

He got in his car and drove to school, planning how to explain his screw up to Tracy. All he'd told her over the weekend was he'd stopped using his powers. It was a miracle she didn't drive over and protest on his front lawn. Either she was giving him space or obsessively discovering her own powers. He was too miserable to care.

He skipped breakfast and arrived at school a few minutes early. Derek settled in to talk to the one impartial listener about his plight. His guidance counselor made a decent sounding board.

Mr. Marshal's office smelled of roasted coffee, which explained why, unlike Derek, Mr. Marshal's eyes didn't droop.

Derek pointed to Mr. Marshal's steaming thermos. "Can I have some?"

"I shouldn't give caffeine to students, even to those who are so clearly sleep-deprived." Mr. Marshal reached into his desk and withdrew a piece of wrapped chocolate. "You can have this."

With the first bite, the urge to nap through the morning melted away. That alone emboldened Derek. Avoiding Louis's car crash, he chose the other source of his nightly terrors. "Ever see a monster?"

Derek expected many possible reactions, but Mr. Marshal's eyebrows jumping up his forehead was not one of them. "Like the monster you didn't see in your backyard?"

Derek saw no point in maintaining his previous lie. Worst case, he could claim this as a senior prank. "On Friday, I saw the same creature, twice." Under Mr. Marshal's piercing gaze, he added, "Does that mean anything to you?"

"Monsters are coming. Sooner than expected." Mr. Marshal clenched the stress ball on his desk until its shape turned into a shriveled worm.

Derek sat upright, his heart racing, craving to hear more. "What should I do about the monster that's stalking me, the one that's already here?"

"Do you have any means to protect yourself? Anything *unusual*?"

"I can do a few tricks. I made a shield that protected me from the beam of light it fired at me."

Mr. Marshal leaned back in his chair, sighing in relief. "I suspected you might be ready. You need experienced oversight. I'll start training you to improve those skills first thing tomorrow."

"Aren't you surprised to learn that I have powers?"

Derek almost fell out of his seat at Mr. Marshal's simple, "No."

"How can you possibly train me when I can throw you across the room with my mind?"

"Try it."

Images of his most recent and reckless use of telekinesis slipped through Derek's mind. "My abilities are dangerous. I promised I wouldn't use them."

Mr. Marshal rubbed his forehead. "Yes, they are! That doesn't change the fact your powers are a bastion against these monsters."

"One of my friends is in the hospital because I fucked up and abused my powers. I can't use them again."

"Countless others will die if you refuse."

"Tracy has powers too," Derek blurted out. "She can help."

Surprise was an understatement for Mr. Marshal's expression. "How?"

"I gave them to her."

Eyebrows arched, Mr. Marshal said, "Bring her here to train as well. More importantly, get over your hesitation to use your powers. Until tomorrow, keep your head down and focus on schoolwork."

Gritting his teeth, Derek resisted shouting. "What? How can I care about school when I know monsters are on their way? We need to tell everyone and evacuate."

"Assuming anyone believes you, the panic will cause more of them to arrive faster. Go about your day. I need a day to prepare and then I promise I'll help you tomorrow."

Mr. Marshal sent a stunned Derek drifting through the halls. Idle chatter and slamming lockers swelled from classmates and flooded the hallway. The noise made it difficult for Derek to focus on any one thought.

Derek was already seated in AP Chem when Tracy entered the room with the ringing of the bell. Her head swayed to whatever song blared in her ears. Derek caught hints of the thumping beat from halfway across the room. Under Mr. Sprog's gaze, she turned off her music and sank next to Derek.

Mr. Sprog addressed the class. "Assuming there are no further interruptions, start preparing for today's experiment."

John raised his hand and spoke without being called on. "Can I switch lab partners?"

Mr. Sprog stared at the three of them, his expression impossible to read. "I'm afraid not. It would be unfair to change the existing group dynamics. So, get to your assigned table with your assigned group."

John scowled at Derek. "If I have to."

"Good. Please complete the lab to measure magnesium's mass once burned."

Derek gathered slivers of magnesium and met John and Tracy at their table for the experiment.

John took the magnesium to the scale near the front of the room, leaving Derek and Tracy to prep their workstation. The equipment was already organized in the center of their black laminated lab table. Like a sword with nothing to strike, Derek didn't want to be left idle. His thoughts replayed Louis falling from the upside-down car and the pale eyes of the monster.

While Derek considered how to explain Mr. Marshal's prophecy about monsters, Tracy chided him. "By the way, you're an idiot.

Rushing to keep your job is a useless waste of time when I can make anything you ever wanted."

"It feels wrong to create something from nothing."

"It *feels* wrong that you sent Louis to the hospital."

Derek flinched. He scanned the room to ensure no heads turned his way. "You knew?"

"Of course, from the moment I heard about the crash. Thanks for hiding from me."

"It's not that simple."

"It never is. You've voluntarily taken your gifts out of commission, forcing me to step up my game. I went all out training by myself yesterday. I'm completely burned out."

"Don't worry. If your powers are like mine, they'll come back in a day or so." Derek reread the lab instructions. "Help me get the table ready to ignite the magnesium to add to its mass."

"That doesn't sound right."

"That's one of the few things I remember studying this week. There's a chemical reaction causing magnesium to bond with oxygen in the atmosphere. You of all people should pay attention as mass can't be created or destroyed. How do you think your trans-mutations work to make new objects?"

"Pure willpower."

John's curt voice interrupted their conversation. "So, you're a threat, like Derek. Neither of you are responsible enough to be trusted with any powers. By the way, the magnesium was fifteen point two three grams."

Derek lit the Bunsen burner. "John's right."

"I don't need you to back me up." John grabbed the magnesium strips with tongs and lowered them into the flame. He watched them turn blindingly white before he dropped them in the ceramic bowl. "The same agreement with Derek goes for you, Tracy. I'll be more lenient as you haven't harmed anyone, yet. If you screw up with your powers, I'll tell the world about you. There's no limit to what else the pair of you might destroy."

Tracy met John and Derek's eyes when she spoke. "I'll do whatever I damn well please and I won't cause a car crash or some other catastrophe. I'm glad shutting down my abilities is the one thing you two agree on."

"I'm not saying to give them up," Derek said. "I'm suggesting you use them with more care than I did. Tossing around power tends to hurt others."

She glanced over the printed instructions, aware they messed up the mass measurements by having this conversation.

"Are we done with this boring lab?"

"If this lab is not to your liking, perhaps try adding potassium nitrate, sugar, and food dye together," said Mr. Sprog, hovering behind them. "However, that experiment must be done off school grounds. Creating smoke bombs is dangerous and such a mixture is not in the curriculum."

Derek was at a loss for how to respond. "Why tell us to do an experiment that's unsafe for school?"

Mr. Sprog shrugged. "I am here to inspire your generation, by any means."

A fire burned behind Tracy's eyes. "Sounds like fun."

John's hands slammed against the lab table. The Bunsen burner's flame sparked. "Would you quit being so distracting? I'm trying to finish this assignment."

"I apologize for the interruption." Mr. Sprog pointed Derek and Tracy back to the table. "Need I remind you that lab partners are obligated to equally share the workload?"

John grunted orders at Derek as they completed the lab. Rather than work on the follow-up questions together, John returned to his seat, leaving Tracy and Derek to clean the equipment. The bell rang too soon. On the way out the door, Derek added his incomplete work to the pile right above John's sheet, which had every question answered.

* * *

Derek climbed the stairs to his bedroom, tossed his backpack to the floor, jumped on his bed, and screamed into his pillow.

I should have skipped school. I should have held my temper behind Louis's car. I should have kept my powers hidden. I should have. I should have. I should have.

Yelling into the cushion emptied his lungs. He gasped, inhaling a huge breath as though a sledgehammer hit him in his chest.

He opened his phone to text Nicole and stopped, deleting the vain attempt to reconnect with someone who'd moved on from him and his friends. Any response from Nicole would be a popcorn-like boost, the empty calories leaving him hollower than before, assuming she replied at all.

Derek stared at the wall, daydreaming about what it might be like to not exist. Louis would be better off without him and Tracy would find some way to shine, with or without powers. With no Derek, his parents would only have to put one kid through college. That would free up plenty of money for his dad's medical treatment and hospital bills.

Monsters may be on the horizon, but all Derek cared about was holding fast to his friends and the fact he failed to do so.

Three swift raps banged against his door. Derek's dad appeared. While not in any shape to run a marathon, he stood freely in the opening without leaning on the frame for support. Tiny sprouts of hair were showing on the top of his head. This was progress after his latest round of chemo.

"The door was closed for a reason," Derek said.

"I don't care." His dad moved the desk chair next to Derek's bed and sat.

Derek contemplated how long was an appropriate amount of time to wait before using homework as an excuse to kick his dad out of his room.

"Senior year can be a difficult one." His dad tilted back in the seat. "It's a lot to manage between standardized tests, college submissions, and planning your future, all while finding the time to have fun. The crushing pressure to excel in one field and perform well across the board has worsened since I was your age."

"You mean when dinosaurs roamed the Earth?"

His dad's head slanted sideways. "Don't feel obligated to devote the most carefree years of your life to schoolwork on the off-chance of curing my cancer. If you choose to study medicine, do so because you're passionate about the human body."

"I—"

Derek's dad held up his hand, waiting for Derek to fall silent before continuing. "Appreciate and live in the moment. Now, that isn't an excuse to do whatever you feel like. Revel in your senior year while keeping a solid head on your shoulders."

"That seems like one giant contradiction."

"It's a fine line."

"Your pep talk needs work."

"So, none of this helped break you from this slump?"

"Not really, but thanks for the effort."

His dad sighed and stood. "Life's too short to be miserable. Since your sister can't be here to expand on my advice, I had to find alternatives." Derek's dad glanced at the open door and bellowed, "Girls, he's all yours."

Tracy and Rachel leaned in from the doorway, sporting grins that made Derek shudder in fright.

Tracy winked at him. "We got this."

Rachel grabbed Derek by the wrist, leading him from the safety of his home. "Consider yourself kidnapped."

14

Leap Of Faith

Derek

Gray October wind blew through Derek's shirt the moment he stepped from Tracy's car. He looked up at the plaster icicles covering large blue letters of the Cold Snap sign.

"Plan to drown my sorrows in frozen sugar?" he asked.

Tracy clicked her tongue at him. "Have more faith in our ingenuity. We also bought movie tickets for later."

Rachel slammed the car door. "In the name of cheering you up, I can suffer through a B-movie zombie flick."

A small chime sounded as Derek entered the Cold Snap.

He was willing to go along with their scheming if it placed a gelato and a worthwhile movie in his future, until he saw John sitting at the corner table.

John sat facing away from the door with his chemistry book open to the section Derek should be studying. John's slouched form jerked in surprise as Rachel kissed the side of his head. His mouth met hers for a long embrace.

Derek leaned against the far wall, trying not to catch John's attention.

"Sorry," Tracy said. "John being here wasn't a part of the plan."

Derek kept his voice low. "It's fine. He has more right to be here than I do."

"Oh, no, you don't," she whispered, adding force to each word. "You are *not* falling into a Derek-sinkhole. We're getting gelato, then watching a passable movie until you stop wallowing in self-pity."

Tracy pinched Derek's lips into a smile and walked to Louis's mother, whose made-to-order smile was absent. Without the staple of a joke to greet him, the Cold Snap experience felt hollow.

Derek raised his hand to wave to her, but lowered it. *I deserve to be banned from this store for hurting Louis. He earned this night of mandatory fun, not me.*

Tracy ordered three gelatos and grabbed a cream soda. Louis's mother's eyes were downcast the entire time, moving through the motions as Tracy paid.

Tracy handed the birthday cake-flavored gelato to Derek and dropped a cream soda bottle in her purse. "This is to keep me awake through the movie. Since giving my all yesterday to hone my abilities without you, it's taken five cups of coffee to stay on my feet."

"Caffeine and sugar are terrible ways to survive the day," grumbled Derek.

"Hold that thought." Tracy approached Rachel and presented a pistachio gelato.

"Thanks. I owe you one," Rachel said.

John finally noticed Tracy and Derek. He nodded in Tracy's direction while she ate her cookie dough gelato. Derek offered a slight nod, bringing a dour expression to John's face.

No matter how I look at it, John is right about me. I am dangerous.

It hurt to admit the truth.

Derek finished his gelato. He might as well be eating flavorless shaved ice for all he tasted. He trudged outside on autopilot into the open air and freedom from being in the presence of Louis's mother. She didn't know what he'd done to Louis, but he couldn't stand there any longer without crying.

He walked past the panda statue in the middle of the open town center. The statue's smooth surface was painted with images of a dumbbell, a gelato cup, a basket of organic food, and a dozen others. It acted as a reminder of how local owners banded together to commission the D.C. staple and made him feel more alone.

He walked onto the raised bridge leading to school to get away from everyone else.

The sound of crickets chirping enveloped him. Derek got lost in the background noise of the river flowing under the bridge.

Plucking a red leaf from the tallest branch poking through the chain-link fence, he crushed it between his fingers. He needed to feel something.

The crumbled remains fluttered over the side of the bridge toward the wetlands beside the highway. An empty eighteen-wheeler truck rumbled along far below, spewing a cloud of smog toward him. Derek forced his eyes to look up at the under-construction neighborhood to distract his mind from the dizzying fall.

He paused at the middle of the bridge, turning around at the sound of Tracy's voice. "Tonight's activities were designed to cheer you up, and yet you're still moping."

Rachel joined in to rally against him. "As far as I knew, John got over that alcohol citation and you made up. I can't fix whatever's wrong with you two until you let me in on the real problem. His lips were sealed."

Tracy savored a spoonful of gelato, assuredly plotting Derek's demise. "I'm telling her. Considering your mistake, she has a right to know."

He didn't want to lose another friend. Derek was lucky Tracy understood totaling Louis's car was an accident. "Wait," he pleaded.

"John learned Derek has superpowers," Tracy said.

Rachel's head tilted. "What do you mean 'has superpowers'?"

Derek hid behind a half-lie. "Had."

Tracy refused to concede. "You still have them. You're choosing not to use them."

No one wanted to stand next to a bomb, which is what his powers had become. Maybe it was for the best if Rachel was never near him. Derek offered the knowledge for her to choose. "I can move things with my mind."

"Sure." Rachel rolled her eyes. "You two are hiding something, but not this. Tell me what's really going on."

Derek put his hands in his pockets. "It's true."

"This is a dumb joke. How'd you drag Tracy in?"

Tracy defended him. "That's what I said the first time he revealed his powers to me. Trust me, there's no trick."

Rachel encouraged Derek, "I have yet to see any so-called powers."

"Tracy can show you what she can do."

"Now I know you're lying. The day Tracy has powers is the day our world ends."

"Hey, now." Tracy paused, then shrugged. "You're probably right."

"I'm not lying," Derek said. "I wish I could get rid of them. In fact, I promised John I'd never use them again."

Rachel made exaggerated movements and looked in every direction. "Well, John's not here, so show me. Why does he care anyway?"

Rachel held out her phone with the movie receipt on display. "I won't give you the tickets until you admit you're lying."

Tracy nudged him. "This one's all you."

Derek gave in. "Fine! Watch closely."

After days of repressing his power, the world brightened as he opened his inner gate, allowing soothing power to course through fatigued limbs. The clouds shifted to reveal the last warming orange hues of sunlight on the horizon. Light winds carried scents of burned gasoline from commuters and the crunchy sweetness of Tracy's gelato cup.

Derek felt a twinge of arrogance as he unveiled his powers. He ripped Tracy's gelato from her clutches with his mental prod and dropped it on her head. Bits of cookie wedged into her hair.

"You moved that! Without touching it!" Rachel cleared her throat. "Tracy, let me see you move something too."

"Not what I was hoping for, Derek." Tracy's lip twitched. "My abilities are different from Derek's."

Tracy grabbed what remained of her half-melted mess and placed headphones over her ears. Milk, sugar, and cookie crumbs became a sloshing balloon. She lobbed it at Derek, drenching him.

Rachel blinked profusely, looking from Derek to Tracy.

With a telekinetic grip, Derek scooped a fistful of brackish river water from below. "I told you we have powers."

He was about to fling the water at Tracy when she fumbled for the railing support. He twisted his aim to slash a line of water in front of her.

"You ass." Tracy sucked in gulps of air. "Don't go easy on me."

"These powers are basically muscles. It's not healthy to over-exert them until they break, like you've done."

"Why not give Rachel a proper show?" Tracy asked.

Derek gestured at Rachel. "Look how much we've scared our closest friend."

"She'll get used to it once she realizes how amazing these gifts are."

"Like hell I will! How are you doing any of this?"

Rachel's voice faded for Derek as he looked past his friends to see the monster racing up the pedestrian path at them.

Larger than many cars on the highway, its white, fur-covered body rippled with the strength of its massive muscles. Each bound on its four stout legs were more than capable of crushing every bone in Derek's body.

Something worse than bile lodged in Derek's throat and refused to let him breathe. His hands, so flush with power, shook uncontrollably. Fear anchored him to the ground.

The monster's pale eyes leveled to meet his. Its snout tilted down, and nostrils flared. Sagging lips quivered back as it snarled and revealed four sharp canines. Curved horns pointed forward from behind its ears. This thing was a terrifying Beast.

Despite the urge to dig a hole and never crawl out, Derek uttered, "Run."

Tracy followed his gaze. She covered her mouth. "Oh, shit!"

"I said, run!" Derek's shout ruptured his tunnel vision, which had been locked on the Beast.

The three of them sprinted for the other side of the bridge.

Tracy glanced behind them. "The monster looks bigger than last time."

Rachel's voice was shrill. "What on Earth is that?"

"The Beast with a capital B," Derek huffed.

For each step forward, the gap separating them shrank as the Beast was overtaking them.

Claws dragged over concrete as though grating along Derek's spine.

"You both have powers," Rachel shouted, her voice reaching near hysteria. "Do something!"

Derek weighed time and distance. The bridge was too long, and they were exposed.

He stopped and faced the Beast, erecting a telekinetic wall. "Keep going! I'll hold it off."

Tracy and Rachel slowed to a halt. "No!"

The Beast unleashed a roar, and its deep bellow hit Derek with the force of an oncoming eight-car metro train.

Derek clenched his jaw. "I don't have time to argue."

The Beast paused to lick the water Derek had flung near Tracy. Then, it charged at them.

Tracy adjusted her headphones and touched the concrete lining the sides of the path, making a small piece of the solid surface ripple. She pitched forward, clutching her temples.

"My transmutation chops are busted from yesterday's training."

A pillar of concrete fired from the pedestrian path at the Beast. Tracy's stone structure fell short of hitting its target. She collapsed to the ground.

The Beast bashed into Derek's telekinetic wall. Derek's feet dragged over concrete as the Beast pushed him and his mental wall back.

Tiny cracks spread across Derek's wall from where the Beast pressed. Every inch the Beast moved closer added more interconnected, broken lines.

His barrier shattered.

A stray piece cut Derek's cheek. The rest of the telekinetic shrapnel pierced all over the bridge. The pieces dissolved a moment later, leaving gashes in concrete.

When it was within ten feet, the Beast leaped at him.

Drawing in power, Derek fired a mental punch. Luckily, the Beast's sheer size meant accuracy was largely a formality. It also meant he was about to be squashed by its bulk.

Derek rolled to the side and hit the lunging Beast's head.

His hit skewed the Beast's path. It collided with the barricade intended to stop cars. The Beast's shoulder slammed into Derek and sent him flying into the chain-link fence. The fence rattled, saving Derek from a fall.

The same couldn't be said of the concrete wall the Beast bashed into. It left a spiderweb impression. Chunks of mixed stone fell when it regained its footing.

Derek used the metal fence to pull himself upright.

A giant paw knocked him back down. The paw pinned him in place and smothered him. Derek's best efforts to lift it did little more than slow the life squeezing out of him.

He struggled to breathe and regretted it immediately. From the depths of the abomination rose the foul odor of, what could best be described as, years of exposed compost dipped in sulfur.

"Hey, ugly!" Tracy shouted. She pulled her hand from her purse and hurled a container of mints at the side of its head. The Beast didn't turn.

Rachel gripped Derek's arm and pulled. Five sharp claws dug into Derek's skin, holding him in place. For all Rachel's might, she was helpless to free him from beneath the Beast's paw.

The Beast's jaws clamped over Derek's ankle, sending fiery pains erupting within his leg.

Beyond his suffering lay an ocean of power, vastly surpassing the puddle he usually pulled from.

The Beast hurled Derek through the air. Sky and bridge spun, their colors blending. He groggily set a telekinetic shield as he collided with something solid.

Vaguely aware he was leaning against the railing, Derek sought trapped reserves of inner power. Waves of nausea hit him with each attempt. His vision darkened, fading as he dug deeper. A multi-sided star shifted into focus inside his head.

He drank from the fire hose of power, except instead of water, it used napalm. Derek tried to scream, he tried to inhale, he tried to do anything except feel his insides scorching in the face of power never meant to be contained.

Steering the power was a vain effort. It carved new channels inside him to escape. Released power collected in a pitch-black ball hovering above his hand. The ball expanded rapidly with the surges of power fleeing from him.

The Beast paced in a semicircle, no longer willing to approach him.

In attempting to wrest control from the growing mass in Derek's hand, he lost it entirely. The dark ball fell, carving a hole through the bridge, the concrete path, and the fence.

Even without physical contact, the sphere was still connected to Derek, sapping his strength. Try as he might, he was a useless child lifting a metric ton dumbbell. When the hovering dark pit swelled to the width of two people, its edge snapped and shrank.

The black sphere distorted the colors around it, turning the air into a pink hue of crackling energy.

The Beast huffed and shook its head from side-to-side. It covered its ears with its paws, avoiding the black opening.

Winds howled from inside the hovering sphere. The tear in space expanded impossibly within itself. Inside, the swallowed bits of bridge were suspended on nothing.

Desperation took hold as Derek tossed a broken bit of concrete into the tear in space. His experiment paid off. The concrete floated within the black sphere, unbroken, traveling further inside it.

Whatever this was, it led to another place. That was all he needed to know.

"It might be blood loss talking," Derek said, "but hop in this hole or get eaten."

"To the bitter end." Tracy leaped, her purse spilling pens and charging cables into the new space.

Derek's injured leg gave out when he jumped. He fell short of the bridge's new edge.

Rachel reached under his arm and dragged him upright. "See you on the other side."

Derek wished he shared her confidence. "Go. I'll make sure that thing doesn't follow."

Rachel hopped off the bridge and passed into the other place.

The Beast swiped at him, its quarry about to slip away. Derek plunged headfirst out of the Beast's range.

There was only a second to regret his hasty decision.

He crossed into the depths of darkness without so much as a sound.

15

Eternal Night

Derek

Derek floated on nothing. On some level, he recognized he should be falling. Darkness expanded in every conceivable direction, giving the impression he was floating in outer space, minus planets and stars. Muted half-light illuminated him in a dull hue.

He pushed aside severed metal chain-links and bits of concrete, consumed by the dark ball when it opened the way to this place. Spinning free, Tracy's purse sent a soda bottle tumbling out and added to the growing swarm of junk.

Through the shrinking opening, the large bridge he had fallen from appeared to be growing smaller.

Derek didn't have the urge to climb out to battle the Beast waiting on the other side. There, the Beast pawed the gash Derek accidentally cut from the bridge.

The rift's opening shut on its own. Limitless emptiness separated Derek from the Beast. The sealed opening left a crack where tiny amounts of light poured into this place of nothingness.

Heated knives stabbed at his leg, the bite punctures keeping him awake, for the moment. All of his other thoughts unraveled faster than they formed.

"Anyone else feel like shit?"

Tracy drifted toward Derek, her words sounding wrong, as if she stood on the opposite end of a hallway shouting through a spinning fan.

Rachel floated next to Derek. She ripped off her shirt's sleeves, using them to bind his leg and stem the flow of blood seeping from his wound.

"What is this place?" she yelled; her words also distorted.

"Who knows?" Derek said. "At least we're alive, I think."

He shifted his gaze in every direction, leaving him with a vague sense of blindly drifting across the ocean. His best reference points were the trash gobbled from his world by the doorway and the uneven crack where the opening had sealed.

Beyond the limits of his senses, something pulled at Derek, like an anchor wrapped around his ankles, dragging him to unknown depths. It made the skin on the back of his neck crawl. He propelled everyone in the opposite direction with his mind.

There was no sign they moved at all.

For all his efforts, he never lost the sensation of sinking.

Derek pushed harder, suppressing his gnawing exhaustion. The force pulling him strained, then snapped, shooting them free from its drowning embrace. Thoughts slipped. Even the pain in his leg sank to a dull throb. He grasped for any sense of clarity, but he lost yet another fight as he gave in to the void.

* * *

A sharp pain prodded Derek, bringing him back to his senses within the muted light of this place. It was impossible to know how much time had passed since they arrived.

"About time you woke up." Rachel drove her nails deeper into his shoulder blade. "You still here with us?"

Derek wiggled his toes on his injured leg, screaming in pain as sensation returned to his numbing limb. "Depends on your definition of 'us' and 'here.'"

Having lost their starting point and with no idea of how long they had been floating, he was at a loss for how to escape. He had to think of something. It was his powers that got them stranded, so those same powers had to lead to their salvation.

Sending random telekinetic blasts into the darkness, he probed for landmarks or some way to make sense of this place. He thought of everything he knew of his abilities, sifting through memories at random to find the gem explaining how to get out of this emptiness.

At each thought, they started moving in a different direction. As they did, he felt a hint of something familiar across the infinite expanse, much like driving by an old friend's house after they no longer lived in it.

Lacking any other bearings, Derek used his thoughts to guide the three of them toward the sensation. They drifted for an eternity. That feeling of familiarity grew closer until they were right on top of it.

He strained against a wall that didn't exist.

He summoned his energy and pushed it into a ball. The energy sizzled, dissolving into nothing as quickly as it formed.

He gathered power until his hand burned and punched the space in front of him. The fabric of reality shattered, revealing a shard of precious light in all its blinding radiance. Darkness fled in the wake of shining rays.

Too small to fit through, the light coming from the baseball-sized hole did nothing more than torment him.

He was too weak to expand it. They were stuck.

"Don't give in," Tracy said.

"We'll find a way out together!" Rachel's voice was clear, with no reverberation.

"Nice sentiments," Derek told them, "but I don't have enough power to get us out."

Tracy clutched Derek's shoulders. "Then take back all the power I can spare."

"You can do that?" Rachel said.

"Hopefully." Tracy gestured with her free arm into the void. "Otherwise, enjoy your new home."

Warmth spread from Tracy's touch, flowing right into his chest and filling his lungs with power.

Sacrificing all their remaining power, Derek forced it into a sphere, severing the barriers holding the void together. The breach he formed to lead them out of the darkness grew. The sphere above his hand stabilized as it swelled.

The sphere, now as large as Derek, revealed the most beautifully clear, pastel blue sky. Lush, green forestation ended at a cliff's edge. Turquoise water rippled, meeting a deep navy blue.

Derek had taken for granted all the colors within his world. After being trapped in a place devoid of life, the sight of miles of untamed coastline overwhelmed him.

The moment of tranquility was smothered. His body went rigid once his mind caught up to the view and realized exactly how high the exit had opened.

Gravity sent him plummeting toward water thousands of feet below.

16

From Somewhere Else

Aelaphus

Aelaphus cleaned rancid blood and staunched the deep bite wound on the young man's leg. He strove to save the unusual man and two women who'd fallen from the doorway in the sky.

Morning light entered Aelaphus's home, warming him. Seasons of disuse wrecked the single round room, and rain riddled the wood supports with rot until the roof collapsed. Still, it was home.

His hand brushed the bumpy table born from a single sapling stretched by his magic. He sat on a hard log, one of his few seats. Rows of clay pots lined the walls. They contained herbs and food, most of which had expired in his absence. He stoked flames within the cooking dome made of stacked stones and sealed by mud in preparation for their next meal.

Whoever they were, the frail forms who fell from the heavens possessed magic far beyond their seasons.

It's not the heavens, Aelaphus corrected himself. The opening appeared higher than birds flew, yet he refused to accept it as a path to the afterlife for those who were worthy.

The most damaged of the three was the young man who was broad-shouldered and large in his mid-section. The flames of his lifeblood dwindled, to be extinguished by the merest of breaths. He clung to existence through sheer steadfastness.

Aelaphus connected a gnarled thumb and pinky to the sleeping man's temples. Weak barriers of his mind peeled like a fruit revealing its seeds.

Much of the young man's memories, Aelaphus observed, existed outside reason. His past indicated a path far from the fields or the hunt. One which confounded the tongue: *scholar*. As a second-born, it was possible his life was devoted to study in support of his elder sister.

Aelaphus sank into memories within the young man's mind, each unlocking a new truth about the world and the odd red-bricked building of learning.

As Aelaphus dug into the fundamental building stones of life in something called "chemistry," the memories blurred. Like footprints in sand, the memories were washed clean by waves of other thoughts as though hiding their presence. Pushing further risked ending the wisp that was this one's life.

Done with the young man's memories, Aelaphus peered into the mind of the short woman who, through unknown magic, trapped the color of the sky in her hair. From where he sat, faint smells carried from her hair, reminding Aelaphus of a bee hive. That made him assume she was the one who prepared meals, until he inspected her hands. They were free of burns with no food residue beneath grass-colored nails.

Sturdy legs contradicted her round stomach, giving this woman the appearance of an adviser or messenger, ever moving. Too inexperienced to be a war leader, her memories showed her commanding others over trimmed fields.

The woman's magic, which saved their lives during the fall into Aelaphus's world, was growing. Akin to crabs found under the Great Sea, this one was ready to molt and reveal the strength of her magic in her first true shell.

The other woman was the tallest of the three and lacked the muscular definition of her companions. Her pale-colored skin looked smooth and untouched by the sun. Her glorified external appearance maintained a well-cared-for body with no marks of hard labor.

To her, memories within the house of learning carried the same sense of being washed clean as they had for the weakened man's memories, which made Aelaphus uneasy. Too much eluded his understanding. From her eyes, he glimpsed wonders. Carts crossed vast distances, drawn by no livestock. Every hand held a magic stone containing Worlds of Knowledge, clear evidence of nothing less than superior sorcery.

Aelaphus left her mind, tending to their wounds as he considered the day prior.

Yesterday had started on a low-hanging tree branch that bent beneath his weight as he waited for his next meal. He would feast in honor of the many seasons he had journeyed to dispose of the Great Weapon at land's end. Having returned, he was ready to live out the rest of his days in quiet solitude.

Faint sounds of crashing water lulled him closer to slumber's clutches. Coarse sand, a reminder that in all his travels he never strayed far from the sea, invaded his nostrils.

He let the thin hides covering the soles of his feet drop to the grass. Every step of his journey was etched on their rundown surfaces, which were now more burden than protection for his feet.

The sun's heat blazed, baking his skin despite the shade. He remained patient, passing on animals too young or thin. A four-legged deer flashed into view. It sniffed the air, failing to smell him hiding downwind.

Aelaphus crawled forward. No bird took flight in warning. The animal-hide bindings wrapped around his fingers muted any sounds of movement. They also covered his torso, reducing inner urges to savor the spilling of this creature's blood to dull whispers.

His quarry lifted its neck to munch on the leaves of a low branch with grace given to one born of nature. Its tan fur held a healthy sheen, and its pronged horn made the animal appear as though the single bone was split by a well-placed ax. It was not a mistake. Their entire herd grew such horns.

Aelaphus sprang from the bough, causing the faintest disturbance of rustling leaves. He twisted in the air and brushed through gaps in the branches.

He unwound the bindings around his arms. Lashing the flexible material to the nearest branch, he swung forward to gain speed. Aelaphus took great care to release only a small length to maintain his protective runes and not unleash his true magic.

The deer took flight through the underbrush along the coast.

Aelaphus was close enough to trip the creature, but such an action would snap its leg and be a much crueler death than a swift cut.

He drew his stone knife back, ready to deliver the killing blow and drink in the vitality of the animal's lifeblood.

Hairs of his sandy beard stood on end much like when a storm of flashing lights raged over open plains. He sensed the skin of this world ripping apart, sending a tremor through his bones.

He slid to a halt, gazing in the disturbance's direction, too far to see. His fingers grew numb, clenching too hard on the knife's handle.

Aelaphus tightened the bindings around his arms, resealing his power. Voices in his head cried in protest, to be silenced when he set the last seal.

The deer's nose flicked, testing the wind. It fled deeper into the woods, likely smelling the evil coming into their world.

Magic pushed Aelaphus's vision beyond its limits, piercing the forest for the source of the disturbance. He took off at a sprint and grabbed ingredients from his traveler's pouch to repair the hole to Somewhere Else. Other ingredients he allowed to lose potency, but these precious few he regularly replenished.

He would never forget witnessing the hole that was darker than a clouded night sky. Once again, he felt the twisting of the world like a knife being driven between his shoulder blades.

The forest ended along bluffs overlooking a surging coast. High-pitched squawks announced the flock of fleeing long-beaked birds.

Too high to seal, the splinter in the sky widened with a savage flash. Magic tore the air asunder, forming the hole to Somewhere Else. The power needed was beyond anything Aelaphus might muster without the aid of an untold number of deaths. Comparatively, he was a newborn in the path of a charging, hairy-tusked animal.

One body fell through the opening in the sky. Then, another two followed. Aelaphus assumed his aging eyes deceived him. Such a doorway was beyond the means of the three falling young ones. No other vanguards passed from the darkness of Somewhere Else. To Aelaphus's relief, the opening collapsed shut with a will of its own.

Whatever brought these three robbed them of wit as they dropped in the long fall to the sea. Their bodies spun like seedlings drifting where the wind willed them.

The brown-skinned woman steadied flailing arms to smooth her fall. She swung an arm into her closest companion. Magic flowed from her into the pale-skinned woman.

The man was well beyond the reach of the two women. Covering half the distance to the water below, they were falling faster.

The pale woman, who received her companion's magic, touched a flat stone in her hand which was connected to her ears by a thin rope. To Aelaphus's surprise, layers of her outer skin coverings were remade into an enclosed sash. She handed it to the one who fed her magic. New skin coverings appeared over the pale woman's feet.

Fire billowed from them, unnaturally speeding her toward the man now close to the sea. The other woman donned the sash and pulled a rope. A large sail appeared, spreading as it might when caught in a summer squall, slowing her fall.

Fire died from the pale woman's foot coverings. She collided with the man and held them together. At her touch, the outer skin coverings on the man melted into a second magical sash, which sprang into another large ship's sail. Catching the wind, the sail likewise slowed the pair's fall as their bodies jerked about.

The pale woman shoved the magic stone into inner folds of her created sash.

Dropping softly into the sea, the sails spared their lives from the fall only to become weighted with water and pull them under.

These three offered Aelaphus the chance to learn what lay beyond the opening to Somewhere Else. He unwound a binding over his wrist, using released magic to will the sea to carry them to shore. Sliding down the steep path, pebbles dragged in his wake. Aelaphus controlled rolling tides to deposit the three strangers onto the ashen sand shore.

Their waterlogged garments were fascinating. Aelaphus draped the life-saving sails over the two who wore thin strips of skin coverings. Knowledge of how to fashion this material and its colors were beyond Aelaphus.

The one closest to death bled from his leg. His lifeblood soaked through badly tied skin coverings. Aelaphus applied a fresh poultice over the bite wound to reduce swelling. He witnessed hunters survive similar injuries who died as their skin turned sick.

The size of the teeth marks left Aelaphus wary of what lived within the Somewhere Else.

Though not gifted in healing arts, Aelaphus possessed basic skills honed through experimentation. These were expended to their limit, given what few herbs he carried. Moving these three to his home, where his full stash of herbs hopefully still possessed potency, was their only chance at survival.

One of them groaned, but otherwise they made no sound as Aelaphus wrapped them together, folding the sashes and sails to cushion them. They were already struggling to survive, so he worked to cause them no further harm.

Aelaphus called for help. His former meal sprang from the woods. He lashed the sails to the stag and lifted the other end to support the weight of the three people.

As he passed deeper into the woods, the trek was not the most arduous of his life, but it was far from pleasant. Noises from his stomach were a reminder he'd failed to break his fast this morning. He hoped some unspoiled food remained in storage. Stockpiles of smoked meat and seeds should remain sealed and hidden, assuming his house had been left alone by wandering bandits.

Lush moss and vines covered the mound disguising Aelaphus's home. The roof was caved in from weather and nature. Scattered about his floor were clear indications several woodland creatures had sought refuge inside his home. As far as the forest was concerned, it gave its best effort to swallow his house whole.

Aelaphus checked his sealed pots of food. His magic extended their expiration significantly longer than the usual season or two. He ate a few pieces, testing their flavor. They were bland and stale but edible. Aelaphus dismissed the deer after presenting him with a handful of seeds.

He slid the table and log stumps against the wall and lay the three people who fell from the sky onto his floor. There was little room left for Aelaphus to move about.

He scooped mud from a nearby cool stream and placed it on their heads to reduce their fevers. They all showed signs that their bodies were fighting illnesses brought on by using too much magic.

Applying the mud caused the woman with sky-colored hair to awaken. She lifted her fist in weak challenge when she saw Aelaphus standing over her companion. With a grimace, the other hand dropped to sore ribs.

The woman drifted back into unconsciousness.

Aelaphus placed his hand over their foreheads and fed as much magic as he dared to spare into the resting bodies. Their breathing steadied, no longer shallow gasps.

That evening and the following morning, he dripped broth into their mouths and replaced their dressings.

As they improved, Aelaphus delved into their minds to learn their language and what lay beyond the portal to Somewhere Else.

Later, he removed clutter in the one room that was his home. It was no small task given the coating of dust, leaves, and moss, not to mention animal remains, accumulated in his absence. He left to set snares, staying within earshot of his defenseless guests.

17

The Flint That Will Strike The World And Turn It To Ash

Aelaphus

The night came and went before the woman with sky-colored hair opened her eyes once more. "Where the fortissimo are we?"

The first words to pass over her parched lips were incomprehensible, even to one whose magic granted him an understanding of languages. Aelaphus's magic manipulated words to share ideas in his travels over distant lands. Doing so proved to be useless here and left him guessing at her intentions.

The woman's eyes fell on her sleeping companions. Her gaze lingered, probably to count the rising and falling of their chests with each breath. She studied Aelaphus and his home. He remained still, presenting himself to be no threat.

She opened her mouth and strange, fast words continued to flow. "Fortissimo is too much at once. Bad marching bands misuse it to drown all nuance and skilled musicians. Point being, wherever we landed seems like an absolute mess. By the way, I'm Rachel."

Aelaphus discarded the tumble of words other than the woman's name. Magic flowed from him, infusing with his mind and mouth so his guest would understand him.

"My intonations may sound strange, but can you interpret my sayings?"

Rachel nodded. "You speak English?"

"I used my magic to speak in a language you know."

"That makes this easy." She clicked her tongue and mimicked knocking herself on the back of her skull. "Did I get hit in the head?"

"Not to my knowledge."

"Then why am I seeing music? Every word you've said looks like floating notes."

"Stop thinking at once and sleep. It is dangerous to use Aspects in your condition."

"What's that?"

"Something I clearly need to teach you to harness."

Rachel exhaled loudly. "In that case, who are you?"

Seeing no harm in disclosing his identity to these travelers, Aelaphus crossed his right arm over his chest and pounded it in formal salute.

"I am Aelaphus, the son of—" His voice faltered, the old honorific spilling too naturally. He continued speaking his title, skipping the part he rejected. "Former adviser to the elder chieftain, may he reign forever."

Upon hearing the word "chieftain," Rachel looked around the hut, as though seeking hidden meaning among his belongings. "Aelaphus. That's an unusual name."

"It means roughly 'The flint that will strike the world and turn it to ash.' My father sought high ambitions for me."

Rachel reached for a rectangular object within the inner folds of her leg coverings. Flint recognized the shiny stone as similar to the one the pale woman protected in her fall. "I need to step outside. Can you continue to watch over my friends?"

Though it was unlikely he would heal these three only to slay them, she was too quick to trust him. He replied with a simple, "Yes."

Using the table to steady herself, Rachel took her first steps since arriving. She limped toward the thatched tree branches covering the opening separating them from outside. It was nothing short of miraculous how the woman was walking after the passing of only two suns.

"Thanks for taking care of us." Rachel faced the woodlands and halted. She withdrew grass-colored strips and placed them in his hand. A man's face sat in the center. Strange markings littered its surface. "It's all I have on me."

The crinkling material felt unlike anything he'd ever touched. Still damp along the creases, it was both flexible and stiff. Aelaphus returned the scraps, unsure of the gesture's meaning.

"Instead of this, I prefer tales of what lies on the other side of the opening to my world. The one you fell out of."

Rachel glanced at her unconscious friends. "What are you talking about? We were sailing, and a storm crashed our ship against some rocks. It took us days of floating to reach shore."

"I am familiar with the doorway you used to enter this world. When I fought my master, I formed a similar doorway and bent it to my will, trapping him for what I believed to be an eternity in the Somewhere Else you arrived from."

She stared at him for a long moment, her brow furrowed in thought. Eventually, she said, "We saw no one in there with us. Just unending emptiness."

"Then count yourself lucky. Your arrival means that there may be a way for my Master to return."

The woman looked at her sleeping friends. Fear appeared in her eyes. "That place leads home. Do you think this person you sealed could get out there?"

"I do not know."

Rachel's lips pressed into a frown. "Crap."

She was not gone for long. Soon after she returned, Aelaphus left to check the snares surrounding his house. Their bounties were plentiful. More than half the vine nooses had captured hares. His magic soothed the furry animals to ease their transport. Fresher meat tasted better, and he intended to harvest their organs properly to replenish expired ingredients.

Aelaphus entered his home. He pressed fresh herbal leaves to the bite marks on the young man's leg. Seeing Rachel watching him, he spoke, "They recover well. Not as well as you. The one who built those magic sails will wake by tomorrow's sunset or the one following. The other will awake in twice that."

Relief flashed over Rachel's face. A twinge of guilt for lying passed through Aelaphus. False hope was needed for one still in the throes of recovery.

Rachel withdrew from her companions and sat on a log seat. "Who are you? Obviously, English isn't your native language and in a matter of hours your grasp of it has noticeably improved."

"Guests are the ones to offer stories of their past before asking their host to do likewise."

Uncertainty crept over her features. Rather than explain her past, she moved to the floor where she gave in to exhaustion.

* * *

The next morning, Rachel stood up, without needing to lean on the table, and wandered into the woods. Aelaphus stretched his spirit past the walls of his home while he sat motionless on the floor. He watched her long enough to know she was not drawing on her own magic by ending the life of another.

Taking her first steps into the realms of magic, she raced at speeds to match the deer Aelaphus hunted what seemed so many seasons ago. She used magic like a child learning to run before crawling, and her sprints lasted no more than a handful of paces. Untamed magic drained her spirit much too fast.

When the day's shadows grew long, a faint stirring carried the smell of earned sweat. His thatched house entrance swayed open. Rachel crossed the hut to sit on the dirt.

Aelaphus closed his eyes and rested his hands on his knees with his palms facing up. Clearing his mind of distractions, he let his thoughts become as gentle as the sea on a clear day. Not long after, Aelaphus heard Rachel sit opposite him.

Releasing his breath, Aelaphus spoke. "Is there something you care to ask?"

"Why are your arms wrapped in dirty leather?"

His eyes opened and narrowed to take in Rachel. Aelaphus was uncertain whether the question was by chance or held sinister intentions.

"Who among you opened the portal?"

She pointed to the one whose body and mind were the most battered. "He saved us by tapping into something I don't understand. Hell, I learned he had powers minutes before he fought some bear monster and opened the tear, which dropped us here."

Aelaphus lifted his arms. "In the battle against my former master, I sealed him on the other side of the doorway to Somewhere Else, the place you fell from into my world. I needed to gather a massive magical source into my body. These wraps trap that magic within me."

Rachel was about to speak when her companion stirred. She was beside the woman bundled in the sails before her words reached Aelaphus.

"Tracy!"

"I see we survived the fall," the pale woman croaked. She turned from the waning daylight shining through the collapsed roof. "Where are we?"

Aelaphus stepped forward. "You are in my home. Since your arrival into this world, I brought you back to relative health. Your other friend is resting. We're waiting for his fever to break, if he survives that long."

Rachel's eyes locked with his. "You said Derek would be good in a day or two."

"If he lives until then, yes, your Derek will heal," Aelaphus mused. "More than his outer shell suffered; his spirit is depleted. That he clings to life is proof of a powerful will."

The woman on the floor clenched her eyes shut. "Slow down. Derek is dying?"

"That depends on his desire to live," Aelaphus replied.

Rachel jumped in before Aelaphus had a chance. "He can't die. Aelaphus will fix Derek, like he did for us."

"Ale-what?"

Rachel patted her friend's hand. "Aelaphus. It means 'the flint to burn us,' or something."

"Why didn't you say so? I'm Tracy." Through half-closed eyes, she looked Aelaphus up and down. "The name Flint fits you better. Why don't we call you that for short?"

"My name is Ael—" Sighing, he stared at the headstrong, youthful woman. Arguing would get him nowhere, and a new identity might offer him the opportunity to earn redemption. "Flint can suffice, given how your tongues trip over my language."

He passed a bowl of herb-soaked broth to Rachel. "For now, recover your strength."

"There's no silverware, so open wide," Rachel explained as she angled the bowl to allow Tracy to slurp the warm broth. "By the way," Rachel's feet bounced as she fed her friend, "I have power. I can run very fast and more."

"That makes sense. I felt you send power into me as we were falling out of the hole from the void. How'd you know you could do that?"

"I didn't. Not really. When we were floating endlessly in the void, I thought I felt a spark inside. I watched you send power into Derek to get us out of there, so I tried to do the same thing out of desperation. We're lucky I was right. Derek must have shared his powers with me, and I sent them into you."

Flint excused himself to allow them a chance to talk without his presence.

Outside, he sat cross-legged on the ground and began chanting. His thoughts became a river of water without color. He swam within ebbs and flows until all sense of time was lost.

He sensed a diminishing magic within his home, ripping him from meditation. Aelaphus sprinted inside.

Derek's face was taut with a grimace as he drifted toward the shores of the afterlife. Sweat seeped from his boiling skin. He thrashed about on the floor, gasping for air.

Flint issued commands to Rachel, who hovered by her friend's side. "Bring all the caged hares you can carry. You will find them outside by walking to the setting sun."

Rachel stopped, her hands resting on her waist. "I'm starving too, but now isn't the time for a roast."

"Bring the animals. We need them to stay Death's grip on your companion."

"Why?" Rachel's facial features squeezed together, making her look like she might refuse Flint's order. She glanced at Derek and then hurried outside. "On it."

Flint moved his hand along Derek's forehead, bathing Derek in magic to replace what had been leeched from his lifeblood for days.

Tracy leaned on her elbows. "What can I do?"

"Sleep." Flint had no interest in guiding one, let alone two, untrained helpers.

She tried in vain to push from the floor. When it was obvious she could no more help Derek than stand, she propped her head to the side and watched.

Rachel returned with two wooden cages. The enclosed hares chittered in fright. Flint knew what needed to be done to save this man's life, yet he held his hands in place. His fingers flexed, eager to draw from his true magic. His vow to never again wield magic born of death weighed on him.

Derek's face stretched in agony, his voice too weak to shout.

But through these three, Flint might follow his master and hunt him in the world beyond.

Flint unwound the coverings along his arms. A slice of his knife sent warm hare blood dripping through clenched fingers. Flint traced a crimson circular inscription over Derek's exposed chest.

Death's icy breath surrounded them.

Flint held the hares against Derek, binding the young man's spirit to the world of the living and offering the animals in exchange for sailing from Death's shores. Fur melted off the hares, along with muscles and beating organs, until only skeletons and the odor of decay remained.

Such small creatures were too paltry an offering.

Grabbing Rachel's arm, Flint wrenched it over Derek's chest and held it above the skeletons. She squirmed to break free.

"He needs your blood," Flint yelled.

That was all it took. Rachel ceased the useless struggle.

She flinched at the sharp edge that opened her skin, sprinkling Derek in blood. Flint used the offering to send Rachel's magic into Derek. Her exhausted body faded into unconsciousness, the sacrifice too little to revive him. Flint bound her arm to prevent further blood loss. The pale woman was far too weak to have her lifeblood siphoned off. She had only recently triumphed in the same struggle against Death.

Flint made two small slices in his arms, dripping a steady blood flow onto Derek's body. Magic rushed from his inner lake into the drought within Derek.

The bindings over Flint's chest loosened on their own. He summoned more of his lifeblood.

Derek's eyes lifted. He took in the room with what appeared to be utter confusion. As quickly as he woke up, Derek returned to slumber.

Flint could hold out no longer. Setting no protection for their vulnerable bodies, sleep overtook him.

* * *

Light poured in from the hole in Flint's roof, warming exposed flesh during his silent meditation. A sputtering cough captured his attention. The sun had risen for the second time since Flint offered his own lifeblood, and the young man was somehow already awake.

Derek's hands failed to support the rest of him, dropping him back onto the bed of leaves. How he moved at all was an astounding feat.

"You're both alive!" Derek's voice was a harsh whisper.

Tracy and Rachel rushed to his side. Tracy patted his shoulder. "You had us worried."

"You are in my care," Flint said. "I am Aelaphus, though your friends chose to replace that with the name 'Flint.'"

"Aelaphus isn't so hard to say," Rachel replied. "Blame Tracy."

Flint considered returning to his birth name and the legacy of his master which it carried. "Flint sounds better in its simplicity."

"Where's the Beast?" Derek interrupted. His teeth clenched and his arms shook in the struggle to sit upright. "I feel like it's standing behind me."

Rachel offered a weak smile. "It's back home on the bridge, I think."

Flint compared intense images from Derek's mind with drawings etched in blood on his master's cave walls. "My master depicted beings of untold power, which he intended to release. Perhaps this Beast I saw haunting your memories is one of those."

"You saw our what?" Rachel shrieked.

Tracy ran a hand through her hair. "I hope you enjoyed the show, perv."

"Did this master mention how to stop the beings?" Derek asked.

"My master sought to summon them using Aspects and death. There was no method shown of stopping them."

Rachel suppressed her anger to ask, "That's the second time you mentioned these Aspects. What the hell are they?"

"They are what you refer to as powers, of which your grasp is meager."

Tracy lifted her chin, her eyes narrowing at Flint. "You're wrong. Did you not see the rocket boots I invented mid-fall? Our grasp of these abilities is flawless."

At a loss for understanding more than a handful of words, Flint gathered their overall meaning. "Each of you would have fallen into

Death's grasp without my skills. You had to sleep on my floor for days to heal from burning through too much magic."

Tracy stomped toward Flint, her words gathering volume until they consumed the enclosed space. "Again, I invented rocket boots while falling. What can you do that's so impressive?"

He unwound a single binding on his arm. A tree branch grew from the walls, spreading to seal the hole in his roof.

These three were now his Weapons, to be sharpened by his hands and aimed at his enemy.

"What can *I* do?" Air cracked at Flint's words, causing injured bodies to shrink from him. "I shall instruct you on the proper way to use Aspects. Rest today, for on the next sunrise you will—" Flint paused, reflecting on memories taken from the Weapons, then added, "—*study* magic."

18

Aspects

Flint

The murmur of swaying trees was interrupted by clumsy footfalls. Not that Flint needed another hint, but the silence of insects announced he was no longer alone.

"Batter up!" Tracy jumped from behind a tree and swung at Flint's head. She lost any semblance of surprise with her battle cry.

Flint leaned back to avoid the blow. Tracy's club brushed his loose sand-colored locks of hair.

Tracy's long club gleamed in the scattered sunlight penetrating the wooded canopy. Throughout their sparring match, Flint dodged all manner of sharp and blunt weapons, spawned from Tracy's twisted thoughts. Their home must be under constant threat to have invented so many devices.

The weapons she formed with magic littered the woods.

"My music is low on power. Cover me, Derek."

Tracy turned, no longer eyeing Flint. If he was an actual opponent, she would have been killed, not that these three Weapons possessed a semblance of battle awareness.

The woman in front of him pressed the magic stone she called a "phone." Doing so made songs spring from the ends of thin ropes placed in her ears.

Flint grabbed the ropes, bringing Tracy's head forward, and the sounds of her music along with it. "You rely too heavily on this crutch. I once needed to speak words to release magic. My power rose when I learned to harness magic without such a weakness."

He stepped back to check Derek's nonexistent threat. Sweat dripped with each exertion of Derek's dragging feet. His inner fire did not know when to stop, even when his body did. He collapsed two steps later. Flint wanted him to rest another day, but the man insisted on joining Tracy and Rachel in training.

Tracy's eyes shifted to the space behind Flint. Her bellow was incoherent and loud. She brought the club down in an overhead swing. Flint raised both his hands to absorb the obvious decoy's impact.

Their third member attacked. Flint lost Rachel in a blurred sprint as she used her magic to close the distance between them.

Rachel moved faster than he was able to block, getting around his raised leg. Her magic faltered the moment she struck his stomach, hitting him no faster than normal, a meaningless blow.

Flint countered with a kick to Rachel's hip, knocking her to the ground. Tracy leaped forward, her club swinging through the spot Flint previously stood. He chopped Tracy's back with the side of his hand, sending her face-first into the dirt, inches from being skewered by one of her many edged blade creations lying about.

"Why did you fail?" Flint asked.

Defiance burned in Tracy's eyes. "Because the three of us are recovering from nearly dying this week, and you're an asshole."

Derek grumbled a response mirroring such sentiments and swatted at bloodsucking bugs attracted to his sweat.

Rachel studied Flint. She was wise to not waste the effort of spewing insults.

Flint curled his fingers, bringing them against the bindings, which trapped his magic inside. "You are stronger than me, yet strength amounts to nothing when you lack the knowledge to wield it."

"None of us are in any condition for a fight," Derek said as he failed to sit upright. "Why not try teaching us like I assumed you would today?"

"Your enemies will not wait for you to be in perfect health. That is why your first lesson was to hit me when you were exhausted."

Tracy let out a ragged breath that might have been a laugh. "Believe me, I want to sock you right in the face. Wait until I'm back to one hundred percent."

A few of those words made Flint pause, his magic unable to recognize them. He understood enough. He passed around his freshwater pouch along with strips of smoked fish.

"Then it is in my best interest to continue to push you before, as you put it, you are 'back to one hundred percent.' For now, rest for a moment."

Derek licked his lips at the water dripping into Tracy's mouth. Rachel took a drink next and tossed the pouch to Derek. He inhaled the remaining water in a single gulp, then clapped his hands against the pouch to kill more buzzing bloodsuckers.

"Any idea where in the world we are?" Derek asked his companions, as though Flint were not present.

Rachel flicked her arm in a wide gesture. "We've explored for hours. Two nights ago, I climbed the tallest tree and there were no lights in any direction. It was the clearest night for stargazing I've ever seen in my life."

Tracy cleared her throat. "I have yet to get reception on my phone. I hate to say it, but think about the tools in Flint's shack. No stainless steel or plastic. Want to bet Flint has never seen a cast-iron pan?"

Rachel carried Tracy's thought. "Flint's clay pots are beyond outdated and show no signs of age. I don't think our eccentric rescuer stranded himself in the middle of nowhere. I think we left the present."

Tracy faced Flint. "Where are we and what year is it?"

"I know not what a 'year' is. As for where you are, we are on the western side of Minoota, the farthest island of my people's domain."

A small groan slipped from Tracy. "That doesn't tell us shit. Are we on a lost island or is this an alt-history on Pangaea where dinosaurs roam free? Nothing here matches what I studied in my ancient civilizations class."

"Shut up, Tracy," Derek hissed, inclining his head in Flint's direction. "Every word we say in front of Flint could change history if you're right."

"It doesn't matter," Rachel said. "Flint knows we aren't from here. What harm can there be in discussing candidly how we're from the future?"

"When the dominoes fall, we have no idea how they'll change our home," Derek said.

Hearing them admit they were from Tomorrow was not easily swallowed, even when Flint recalled such a truth held in their memories.

"My master depicted these openings to Somewhere Else on the walls in his stronghold, which told how to open the way again. We will use the lifeblood magic stored in the Great Weapon I hid to do so. No more lifeblood must be spilled to return you where you belong."

"Is your weapon hidden around here?" Rachel asked.

"No. It is many days of travel over land before arriving at the fastest ships to cross the sea. If we get a favorable wind, we may reach the mainland within half a moon's cycle. That is when our true journey begins."

"Hooray," Tracy added. "Days of hiking plus a sea voyage. What could be better?"

"There are many things more enjoyable than such a journey," Flint replied.

Rachel shook her head. "Not a fan of sarcasm, are you?"

"No." Flint peered through the shifting canopy to measure the sun's travel overhead. "Since you moved your mouths incessantly, we shall give your other muscles a chance."

Derek didn't bother to rise. "We won't. There's no reason to break our recovering bodies. Not while we get the crap kicked out of us to massage your ego."

"I am reinforcing your bodies and minds, teaching you to work past the point of pain. Until arriving here, you have been treated as babes, handled with care, and kept from a day of struggle."

Tracy patted Derek's shoulder. "I stand with my friend by sitting here."

Rachel sighed. "I don't say it often, but Derek's right. All I've learned from you is that you like brawling people a third your age, one of whom can't walk."

Refusing to let these three rile him, Flint prevented the angry heat rising in his ears from touching his words.

"Aspects are not idle playthings. It takes willpower and concentration to call upon such magic, none of which I have witnessed from you three. I am starting to believe someone opened the portal to Somewhere Else, and you fell in."

Rachel took a step toward Flint. "Instead of talking around them as grand concepts, why not explain Aspects while giving us the chance to rest?"

"Very well." He traced a circle in the dirt with his finger, adding a total of four and two hands' worth of dots evenly spread across it. "These are the Aspects through which magic is drawn. Much like a living creature, there is an outer skin filled with everything we see and touch. Then, there is an inner layer, filled with spirit, with life itself. In the case of our world, this inner layer contains magic. Aspects open the barrier between the layers. Pulling spirit from the living, particularly through blood, directly feeds Aspects, which can then be used."

Derek tilted his head to the side. "There's more. I know it. Where's the reason behind this?"

Tracy whistled. "So, all I needed to do was kill a furry little animal and I could have had these powers my entire life?"

"It can't be that simple," Rachel said. "Otherwise, mass murderers would be countless and unstoppable."

These three were smarter than their years. "Correct. Drawing water from the Aspect's well requires a steady mind and a missing piece I cannot explain. My master instilled the ability to use Aspects in me, which I have not replicated in others. I no longer try after causing a hand's worth of death in bodies unfit for magic."

Rachel's head angled to the side. "You killed ten people?"

"Those I bathed in magic succumbed, their red lifeblood spilling from their eyes, nose, and mouth." Flint's innards bristled at memories better left forgotten. "We lingered in rest for long enough." He shifted to a relaxed stance, with his legs spread to shoulder width and palms raised, waiting for them. "You will all attempt to strike me down."

Steadying himself with a stick, Derek stood. His legs buckled the moment he was upright. He added the contents of his latest meal to the forest floor.

Tracy took faltering steps to pat his back.

"Derek, return to my home and sleep. Tracy, too, will need to rest." Flint turned to the remaining woman. "While the three of you are untrained and undisciplined, Rachel, you are the most so. My failure was to assume otherwise. You and I will fix the erratic magic you call upon."

Tracy marched in front of Flint, looked down to meet his gaze. "Listen here, you ancient windbag. Rachel is awesome and discipline wishes it were more like her."

Rachel was at her friend's side before Flint retaliated. "My powers are new to me. I need more practice, and you should take Derek back."

"If that's what you want." Tracy lifted Derek's arm over her shoulder. He groaned under the strain of getting to his feet. They left to the sounds of crushed leaves and twigs.

Flint sat on the damp grass and gestured for Rachel to do the same. "Meditate to chip excess thoughts away until you are as a sharpened stone ax, ready to split wood for the fire."

Rachel sank to the ground in front of her. "Hold the metaphors and tell me how to improve."

"Using the Aspects is not simple to understand. When you can reliably pull in magic, then we may rejoin your friends."

While they sat together, Flint did his best to ignore the groans coming from the woman. Rachel's brow furrowed, her eyes starting to cross. "I've done this before. Why can't I do it now?"

"You are pushing, forcing Aspects to work for you. Such actions will poison the well you draw from. Stop thinking about doing and simply do."

Rachel punched the dirt with her fists. "Focus all your thoughts on a task, clear your mind, don't strain yourself. Am I the only one who sees these as mutually exclusive?!"

Perhaps, I place my hopes in shattered Weapons.

Without warning, Rachel scrambled from him and covered her eyes. "I assumed you were a burn victim. How are you alive? I can see shifting hands reaching for your heart from beneath those leather wrappings."

Feeling naked in front of this woman, Flint did not move as she saw what was not there, the remnants of his sin, forever fighting to control his body and spirit. Afraid to ask, Flint forced his words to take form.

"Do you see anything else?"

"No. Although I can hear musical notes from everywhere. That cricket is four tightly coupled sixteenth notes, repeating over and over. Each creaking tree is forming long whole notes. It should be overwhelming, yet there's a pattern to this forest's song." She raised an ear toward Flint. "You are both a melody entwined with this forest and one syncopated to butt heads against it."

Flint tensed. "Stop. Do not think, draw no more magic. Let it leave you, unused. You opened two Aspects at the same time."

I must stop her from plummeting deeper into danger.

"Plummeting into danger? I heard that, but your mouth didn't move."

"Stop," Flint instructed again. "Clear your mind."

"What can be so dangerous about feeling the world more fully? I get it now! I can see how to go faster using my powers."

With the speed of a leaping doe, she wove between trees. Flint was on his feet, trying to catch her and warn her. Even with magic-enhanced limbs, he was far too slow.

Rachel collapsed in mid-stride and released an ear-piercing cry. Twitching on the ground and gasping for air, she waved her hands in front of her face. "I can't see!"

"Our bodies reject opening more than one Aspect at the same time."

She turned to the sound of his voice, but went too far, staring at the space to Flint's side. "That seems like a critical piece of info to skip in this shitty attempt at training."

"It always felt wrong in my blood to even attempt to join Aspects. I believed you had some basic concept of the magic you flaunt."

"I'll show you a basic concept of magic." Her fists spun wildly, nowhere near him.

"I do not expect this loss of vision to linger, considering how you only opened the Aspects for a short moment." Flint extended his hand to guide her. "We will rejoin your friends."

She huffed. "Don't lead me off any cliffs."

They made slow progress. Rachel stumbled over every stick in the forest. She gripped his arm tightly, using it to remain upright.

She shifted to a steady march to avoid tripping, raising her knees above her waist before slamming her feet down, louder than a stampeding herd.

After crossing most of the distance to his home, Flint realized she no longer grasped him. Her eyes remained closed. She matched his pace, without walking headfirst into a tree. Flint amended his earlier judgments. This Weapon's ingenuity was a mistake to take lightly.

Rachel's back leg bent, bracing her weight. Flint considered restraining her from inflicting further self-harm. Curiosity got the better of him.

She sprinted in a straight line with magic-enhanced speed. With each footfall, she counted, "One. Two. Three. Four. Two. Two. Three. Four. Three. Two. Three. Four. Four. Two. Three. Four." Rachel halted, a hand's span in front of a tree. Her fingertips brushed the spiked seeds of its thick stalk.

A hearty cheer came from deep within her throat. "What now, old man? I used those same two Aspects from before in conjunction without using them simultaneously."

Flint offered his congratulations. "You are not as weak as I believed."

* * *

The next morning, Flint led them back into the woods. Rachel moved unaided; her eyesight restored overnight. Occasionally, she grasped branches and held them close to her face or stared up at the sky, ever muttering about beauty in nature.

For the second day in a row, they wore fresh skin coverings created by Tracy's magic. The grass and sun-colored material revealed most of their arms and legs. Flint remained in his same animal skins, one small fur draped over his shoulders and another fur tied about his waist for modesty. He'd left his animal skin foot coverings at home. His hairy toes wormed into soft soil.

Rachel stood rigid, an able warrior, comfortable holding such a position. Derek's shoulders hunched forward in a manner unfit for a warrior. His hands hid in the folds of his lower coverings. The last of the three, Tracy, fidgeted with the music-making stone at her waist.

Flint used his ax's handle to recreate the image from yesterday: a circle in the ground with four and two hands' worth of dots.

"Aspects allow magic to flow and be used, like drinking water from a stream." Flint connected two of the dots, making a line which crossed the circle. "Opening two Aspects greatly expands the amount of magic coursing within us and the strain on our bodies. Imagine drinking a waterfall and being unable to close your mouth, drowning in what would otherwise sustain us." He completed the three-sided shape. "Combining too many Aspects cost one of your own her sight for the evening."

Derek and Tracy glanced at Rachel, whose gaze stayed on Flint. "I won't do it again," she said.

Flint nodded, offering his best student encouragement. He continued drawing lines within the circle until he made a star with four and two hands' worth of points. Recreated from memory, his master's drawings represented the means to bring wreckage upon their world by opening the doorway to Somewhere Else. "Does this look familiar?"

"A triangle was the last thing I saw before my vision went blank," Rachel said.

Derek's face fell. "I saw one like it in my mind when I opened the portal to the void."

Flint let out a heavy sigh. "I, too, sacrificed a life to open each Aspect, along with the numerous lives spent to create the doorway to Somewhere Else."

"We never sacrificed anyone!" they shouted together, a mix of revulsion and fear crossing their features.

"Their deaths were the cost of ending a war and spared greater bloodshed. Your hands may be innocent in this, but another took those lives on your behalf to open the doorway."

"*No one* died for us to enter the void," Derek declared firmly.

Flint fought to keep the surprise from touching his face. If true, he must learn to open the doorway without killing. Doing so would allow him to pursue his master without being dragged by guilt's burdensome weight.

"You are almost correct. Even without the death of others, open-ing the doorway as you did would have sacrificed a life, your own."

Derek shook his head. "Not true! I fought the Beast, accidentally shared my powers with Rachel, and opened the way to the void. From my one experience, getting to the void shouldn't kill me."

Flint didn't care that his smile spread. Thanks to these Weapons, he would be hunting his master within the void soon, all without sacrificing a single person.

"That's where I saw another of those Aspect stars!" Derek shouted. "A star appeared in my head on the day I met the Beast, though it had fewer than fourteen points."

"Fun times. That was the day you almost crushed me with a tree." Tracy brushed her shoulder as though removing dirt. "Does that mean multiple Aspects summoned the Beast to us?"

"Perhaps you pulled it from the Somewhere Else." Flint pictured his master's last drawing; one he didn't understand. It depicted monstrous bird-like beings bathing his master in light, and the beings, in turn, basking in his master's light. "Or created it by combining Aspects."

Rachel remained focused on the star drawn on the ground. "What do these different Aspects do?"

"Between you and your friends, you should understand best. One Aspect you used to see me clearly, one you used to hear my thoughts, and one you used to sprint faster than a wild animal."

"What other Aspects are there?" Three voices stabbed him with the same question.

"Daylight is well underway. Your bodies are as weak as your minds. I choose to strengthen both. Today's training begins now. You have the option to sprint along this path until you reach the stream and then return, or to stay and defend against my attacks."

Without another uttered word, the three started. Rachel was out of sight. Tracy, too, was soon lost to the woods. Sounds of breaking underbrush echoed around Flint.

Derek limped with difficulty, using a stick to support his weight. He stopped to lean against each tree he passed.

Derek lifted his hand, a small amount of magic gathered within the young man. Unable to hold his arm steady, it dropped to his side, his magic remaining unused. The way his eyes narrowed; Derek appeared to consider chewing his arm off to teach it a lesson about obedience.

His entire body shook. When he did finally speak, his tone carried an iced edge.

"Sharing my powers was a mistake! That Beast would be no problem if I fought at full power. The portal wouldn't have opened, and we would be safe and sound back home. I wish Tracy and Rachel never took my pow—"

Derek's voice died when he realized they were not alone. The pair of women returned from their sprint. Tracy pressed the magic stone at her waist, bringing with it the faint sounds of music. At her touch, she used her magic to open the ground near her feet. She scooped and molded the dirt into a wooden container with sloshing liquid inside. She upended the contents over Derek's head, covering him in water.

Without the slightest hint of hesitation, Tracy's whip-like voice cracked over the forest. "Never talk like that again."

Rachel shook her head at Derek in disgust. "Your arrogance is the reason you flipped Louis's car."

"Did Tracy tell you?" Derek muttered.

"She didn't have to." Rachel stormed by Derek, leaving with Tracy.

Whether from shame over what he said or shock at the water soaking him, Derek refused to move, uttering one hand's worth of words. "Without my powers, we're stuck."

19

The Past Catches Up

Flint

A quarter of the moon's cycle passed, leaving Flint more drained by their bickering. The Weapons were making him lose his senses until madness descended over his thoughts. He once knew two jealous brothers who conspired to murder the other over land and stockpiled food. They were more respectful than his three guests who possessed far too much magic.

Tracy yelled at Derek for tripping over the dangling rope connecting her magic stone to another attached to Flint's roof. Tracy claimed the latter brought life to the magic stone using sunlight. Meanwhile, Derek shouted at her for slurping stew and stomping her feet too loud. Of course, neither side admitted their own faults, nor did Flint understand why these habits were worthy of such disdain. Flint freely slurped meals without quarrel.

Waking before rosy hues crept under his thatched doorway, Flint sat outside to watch the promise of a new day. An owl's hoot mingled with chirping bugs. He preferred these sounds to the verbal sparring matches. Flint had never longed to live in a larger home until he got stuck with these three.

He cleansed his mind like a flowing river sends clogging leaves downstream. Even so, the three Weapons invaded his thoughts, over-running mental walls.

As the sun climbed higher, Rachel appeared at his doorway, nodding once at Flint, then sprinting into the woods. She spent the past few days running wild, expanding her magical speed by mapping the movement of the deer who carried them from the beach. Whenever she caught him, she offered a handful of dried seeds from his stash.

"It's too hot to use our powers," Tracy said, stepping from Flint's home to sprawl in the shadows of a spiky plant's wide leaves. Using her thick hair to hide the ends of the thin ropes she placed over her ears, she listened to music and cast doubt over her words of conserving magic.

A loud thud from inside caused Flint to rise to face whatever mess the third Weapon had caused. Derek stepped outside. He leaned against a staff, his limp imperceptible to most.

"My powers are back!" Derek shouted. "I tossed a rock with my mind."

Derek made it halfway to Tracy and stopped, his cheers cut short.

Flint ground his teeth. "Are you both too wrapped in your squabble that you waste your lives like snails caught in a tide pool?"

Tracy nodded her head at Derek. "Tell that to him. He started it."

Whether the Weapons were ready for travel, Flint needed a change. If they didn't leave, he risked giving in to the temptation of ending their bickering, permanently. "Tomorrow we leave. A full season of training will do you no good and you seem well enough to travel."

"Good!" Tracy shouted. "I can't *wait* to explore more of this world."

"About time we got your weapon so we can go home," Derek said.

"Agreed," Flint said, leaving the pair to do as they pleased for the day.

* * *

In the morning, Flint emptied his perishable goods into a breakfast of flat bread and cooked bird eggs. He made ready to forcibly remove the three from his home. That proved unnecessary. The three guests felt the gnawing sensation to roam as well.

From the bundled sails that once slowed their fall to the ocean, Tracy reshaped the material into two packs to hang over their backs. She created a third pack from dirt and threw it at Derek.

They filled the packs with Flint's clay food jars and tools. Tracy and Derek hunched forward to avoid hitting their heads on Flint's roof, shouting and tripping over each other. The sprinter, shortest among them, moved comfortably as she prepared to leave.

By mid-morning, they crossed the threshold of Flint's home. These woods were free once more to reclaim what he had borrowed.

Rachel hefted the stuffed pack over her shoulders. "Given how far we are in the past, we need to limit our influence in this time. Which means: no powers, unless it's absolutely necessary."

Tracy patted the magic stone at her hip. "No arguments from me. My solar panel takes forever to recharge my phone."

Derek shifted his pack. Though he used a stick to brace his weight as he walked, he no longer relied on it. "Which way?"

Flint moved past the Weapons who acted before thinking. The three fell in line behind him. "We follow an animal trail leading to a clear stream. This will take us to the closest village, the first of many stops on the journey to the place I hid my Weapon."

Ancient, moss-covered trees surrounded them, muffling the sounds of their passing and limiting their line of sight. Flint's feet knew the way without the aid of his eyes.

"I've been wondering," Derek began, "why fourteen Aspects? Seems arbitrary to me."

Flint considered all he had learned of magic over the seasons. "That, I do not know. Perhaps it is a fundamental Truth, or maybe other Aspects have yet to be discovered."

"I'd hate to be caught anywhere near the blast radius of experiments to test for them," Rachel said.

"Think those undiscovered Aspects are like unstable super-heavy elements on the Periodic Table and require a lab to make?" Tracy asked.

Derek hobbled next to Tracy. "Mr. Sprog's class made one hell of an earworm, huh?"

Tracy's expression darkened. "My comment was for Rachel, not you."

Flint stepped between the two flexing their claws at the other. "Aspects exist in harmony with the Greater World. Working with an Aspect requires you to understand yourself. Otherwise, you burn more lifeblood to perform basic magic and risk your life to do more. When life expires, be it person, creature, or plant, it feeds our magic to mold Aspects."

Rachel took an extra step from Flint. "What kind of person can speak so callously of death?"

"The kind who acknowledges my actions and regrets them," he countered.

Water lapped against rocks, growing louder as they descended a steep incline. Flint showed his less sure-footed companions where to step. They ignored him, knocking stones loose with every stumble.

The stream's path fed into a wider current, carving around stubborn roots.

High hills hid the sun sooner than it was meant to set. Rather than risk twisted ankles from traveling at dusk, Flint halted for the day. Derek was asleep on uneven dirt before Flint's kindling lit larger logs. The other two ate their meals and likewise fell asleep early.

Flint curled into the nook of a tree, soothed by steady frog croaks until he too gave in to sleep's call.

An oppressive morning greeted them. Moisture hung in the air, carrying the taste of an oncoming storm.

"Now this feels like home." Derek extended his arm and the stick he used to support his weight lifted, unaided, from the ground. It shook, as did Derek's arm. Much like a bird fighting against a vicious wind, the staff jostled until it landed in Derek's outstretched fingers. His brow furrowed. "This used to be so easy."

"I thought we said no powers," Rachel's voice left no ground for Derek to stand on. She emerged from the thick, sealed blanket Tracy had formed with her magic, making Rachel appear to be a bug freeing itself from a cocoon.

Derek shoved his sleeping bundle into his pack. "No one else is nearby. Sorry. I wanted to stretch and test what I can do."

They broke camp, and Flint guided them all toward the village. Through the morning and afternoon, the sun hid behind dark clouds.

The stream they followed swelled, no longer a simple hop to cross to the other bank. Flint scouted for signs of rafts, preferring the villagers to remain unaware as they approached.

Derek scooped the water and dripped it onto his neck and forehead. "It's got to be cleaner than the Potomac River."

A loud boom echoed against swaying trees. Flint's chest lurched.

Frigid rain fell from clouds, eager to be rid of every drop. Water collected on leaves overhead until their contents filled and spilled on Flint.

Spears of white fire ripped the sky apart. Flint threw his hands over his face to ward evil spirits. Flashes struck near and far, each carved lines over his vision and forced his eyes to readjust in the otherwise dim light passing through the trees.

Tracy made a device she called an umbrella and placed the magic stone used to draw her power into a sealed pack to keep it dry. The umbrella's stretched grass-colored surface protected her from the water dropping on them. It amounted to little when the rain bounced off the ground so hard it seemed to be falling up.

Rachel's voice defied harsh winds. "Are we there yet?"

That regrettable question repeated two hands' worth of times from the three, until Flint's response matched the storm in veracity. "Soon."

Not as soon as he preferred, trees opened to flat land. This short sprint separated the forest from the wide hilltop which was surrounded on three sides by the river. Wooden stakes lined the bottom of the hill, a precaution against raiders.

Rising with the hill, mud and clay homes peeked above the stone wall inside the row of outer stakes, appearing as a giant, sharp turtle shell.

Flint's outer animal skin coverings were soaked, bringing a chill when he stopped moving. "Wait," he said, gazing at the village's entrance to see if anyone was standing about despite the storm.

"We're already wet enough," Derek said. "What's another dousing?"

In answer, Rachel ran from the forest, swaying and diving across the wide field. She used her magic to move with great speed, though her movements mimicked one who drank too much mead as she spun and flailed in a vain effort to avoid getting wet.

Derek and Tracy were next, their squishing steps lost beneath the pattering rainfall. Flint brought up the rear, forcing his legs and back against the wind's push and holding his skin coverings close.

They went through the open entrance into the village. A shout rang out, but Flint ignored it. No further challenges sounded. The village's guard must prefer to remain dry rather than chase four travelers.

Flint hiked to the village's center at the flat top of the hill. In his former life, he stood here and spoke to bolster his leader's army. He had done as he was told without knowing the ends only a madman might fathom. Too many lives of warriors, from this village and numerous others, were ended to bring his master's potent Weapon into existence.

Hurrying down several twisted, mud-covered paths, Flint's feet brought him to the familiar cube-shaped house. He knocked on the thatched door. Light and warmth emanated from inside.

A large shadow fell across the opening. The figure stooped to open the door. Taking one look at Flint's ragged group, the man slammed it shut.

Flint pushed the flimsy door inward. "Tell those in this village I beat you to gain entry."

The larger man recoiled. "My people remember. You are not welcome here."

"Give us shelter for one night, then I will be gone from your life."

"Not soon enough."

Flint offered a bundle containing his tools. "For your troubles."

Hands twice the size of his own carried Flint's worldly possessions with delicate care. The man nodded to Flint's companions.

"I am Oona. To my eternal shame, I served this man's family. You would do well to depart from him."

Flint translated the relevant parts to those otherwise lost, then added, "We're sleeping here tonight."

Flint stripped and laid his clothes by the fire to dry. His three Weapons averted their eyes, finding a sudden fascination with the floor.

"I don't suppose other rooms are hidden behind a wall?" Tracy asked.

"We're sleeping here tonight." Flint repeated. He pulled a less wet animal skin covering from his sash and wrapped it around himself to regain warmth.

Meanwhile, Tracy formed a large covering which absorbed water from her skin. Then, two of them stretched the material while the third changed into dry skin coverings on the other side. They rotated until all three wore new coverings, wasting considerable effort to prevent others from seeing bare skin.

Wrapped in thick bundles, the three were soon snoring gently on the floor.

Oona tended the fire.

"I am sorry for all my master inflicted on you," Flint uttered.

Oona turned away as if not facing Flint stopped him from being there.

* * *

Flint woke to noises outside of men and women repairing their homes from last night's deluge. He heard mud slapping on walls and the rustling of long leaves being woven into fresh, tight rooftop meshes.

As his companions got up, they complained of empty stomachs. Oona snored from the floor in an act reeking of deliberate ignorance. True to his word, Flint left with his three Weapons.

Flint guided them to the filling market, which sat on the hill's summit in the village's center.

Homes outlined the flat square around the hilltop. There had to be four or five hands' worth of people sitting around the sides of the open area, each with baskets in front of them. They sat under stretched animal hides at the ends of long sticks to protect them and their wares from the savages of warming daybreak.

The area could hold those in this village and those from smaller neighboring villages and everyone in between. Flint flinched at the memory of standing on a stump and beckoning to a full crowd to join him in defending their homes.

A fish hopped from a sealed wooden container, flopping on the grass. The thin man behind the container was hunched over from age and he scrambled to grab the slimy thing.

More so than any other feature, there were far too many wrinkles on those in the market. Flint could count the number of young men and women on a single hand.

Most were dressed in animal skin tunics similar to the one Flint wore. One of the few young adults wore coverings made from woven plants and animal hairs.

"This isn't what I expected of the past," Derek said. "It's a lot dirtier."

Tracy held her nose. "The town smells too. That's what happens when there's no indoor plumbing and baths are once-in-a-lifetime."

Flint was about to share what he thought about the smells coming from the pair, when a woman nudged him aside with the butt of a spear. Heavy lines around her eyes and mouth gave the impression of a diet consisting exclusively of sour berries.

She nestled the spear against her shoulder and adjusted the two hands' worth of animal pelts hanging over her back. She offered one pelt to a woman with a spread of fruits. The trader rubbed a pelt and nodded, giving the older woman a basket of figs.

Flint's three companions wandered, chasing sweet aromas of split fruit. They picked and prodded at a fuzzy outer shell, which revealed a bright red center oozing with juices.

Flint did not know why they bothered as they lacked the knowledge to speak the language or the means to barter. Tracy stuck something in her ear. She turned her head toward various speakers and nodded. Gesturing at a small vine of round green fruits the size of her fingernail, Tracy pulled circular discs the color of the sun from her clothing.

The trader stared closely at them, passing the unusual objects between his fingers. Even at his apparent age, the trader possessed powerfully built arms. He shook his head and returned the discs to Tracy, speaking the language of Flint's people.

"I have no need for shiny rocks."

"Who doesn't want gold?" Tracy asked, in her language.

Flint didn't bother to translate, instead he handed the trader a pot of sealed grains to barter for the fruit.

Seeing Flint, the trader's eyes widened. His hands shook so much that he dropped the pot. The trader hobbled down to retrieve the spilled food, sticking his wooden leg behind him for balance. Derek tried to help the wobbling man upright, but he smacked Derek's hand aside as he stood.

Derek flinched without saying a word. He moved to another stall with Tracy and Rachel.

Flint held eye contact with the trader for another moment and then left. He bartered the last two pots of stored grains for a thick broth of roasted vegetables and strips of roasted meat of question-able origin. The terrible exchange was enough to get them a meager meal. His first meal in a day tasted as though a fire on a cold night were captured in the bowl. It warmed him from the inside, satisfying his stomach.

While the four of them ate, the peg-legged trader approached. Sweat beaded his forehead and his eyes darted between the widest paths leading from the village's center. Drawing magic to enhance his hearing, Flint distinguished many footfalls rushing up the hill.

"We must leave," Flint commanded to the Weapons.

His companions groaned, sluggish to rise to their feet, unaware of what approached.

The peg-legged trader blocked the quickest means of escape. His burly arm flexed, and his thumb flicked the stone ax at his hip. "Did I tell you about my son? He fell in the battle that cost me my leg."

Flint cast his eyes about, trying to recall another way out of the village.

"My son would be a few seasons past those of your varied spawn," said the one-legged man while gesturing at Derek, Tracy, and Rachel.

Tracy turned in shock, somehow understanding this man's words. In her foreign language, she shouted, "One of his? Not a chance." Tracy's indignation was lost on the trader who likely took her tone as an insult.

Flint heard the footfalls of those running up the hill.

He kept his tongue civil, seeking a way to spare the three Weap-ons from battle. Their exhaustion was like cracks in a stone knife, threatening to break into fragments the moment they were struck. "Your suffering brings me great sorrow. I am certain your son was a courageous man worthy of honor."

"Not a day passes when I do not see the man's face who killed my son by convincing him to serve in battle: Yours." The trader's arm shook with rage as he pointed at Flint.

Men and women sprinted into the market brandishing axes, wooden spears, and slings. Flint should have been impressed that his appearance rallied such devotion. Those fools were being used as much now as they were in the past.

Oona's tall form stood aside from the crowd. His eyes met Flint's gaze and fell, exposing dark bruises, which covered half the man's face.

The trader hopped back a few paces. His arm raised and dropped in a chopping motion. Whistling stones streamed through the air at Flint. These bounced aside, colliding with an unseen wall. Derek swayed, his magic protecting them from the first volley.

The trader yelled and drew his ax, swinging at Flint. Magic bubbled from inside, covering Flint's hand as if it had turned to stone. He caught the chiseled ax, its impact little more than a dull, child's punch. Flint kicked the man in his chest, toppling him into a puddle of mud.

When Derek repelled a second volley, the stone-slingers charged with sharpened farming tools. The villagers surrounded Flint and the three Weapons, using their advantage of superior numbers.

Tracy touched the magic stone at her waist and formed a blunt club from the earth. Her eyes moved between the multiple paths leading from the open square. She knocked villagers aside, leading Flint and the rest toward the path with the fewest enemies.

Good. One of them is keeping a level head.

Tracy slammed her fists into the ground. Magic took root to spread into a wall of soil, separating them from those villagers rushing to take Flint's head.

"Remember: don't hurt anyone," Derek stated. "Our lives depend on the past not changing."

Villagers ran through the wall Tracy formed, brushing aside dirt clinging to them. A few unlucky ones were too slow. They collided with the wall after Tracy's magic reinforced the material into something stronger than earth. The slow villagers bounced against the surface, stunning them, and halting their advances.

From the crowd, the faster villagers gave words to their hatred.

"Kill them!"

"They are *all* sorcerers!"

"Burn them!"

Flint unwrapped the outer bindings along his arms. Intoxicating magic filled his mouth with a bitter taste. The uncoiled bindings slithered about his feet.

Four and two hands. With such a small sacrifice, I could open the doorway.

Far more than four and two hands of villagers attacked him, so willing to toss aside their lives. It was his right to spill their lifeblood to open the doorway to Somewhere Else. Flint stayed his desires to hunt his master and smothered vile thoughts of slaying those weaker than him.

The muscular ax-wielding trader muttered several choice curses, which slid into incoherent shouts as he became more creature than man. He threw his weight at Flint with no thought or awareness.

Flint's whipping bindings rebuked the man's ax, then bound his wrists. A gnawing desire urged Flint to rip the trader in half. Instead, he used one of the bindings to slap the man's face in the hopes the trader regained his senses.

The other binding held surrounding enemies at bay by striking exposed skin and snatching weapons from anyone who got too close. The front-runners stopped short, to avoid being hit. Pushed from behind, there was nowhere to move except right into Flint's defenses.

Flint checked on his three Weapons.

Rachel used her magic-enhanced speed to dodge beneath stabs and swings. Tracy swung her club in any direction, nearly smacking Derek's head.

Spinning arms in a wide arc, Derek commanded the wind, sending villager's bodies and weapons hurling backward. One villager jumped at Derek's unprotected side. Rachel caught the man's arm and slammed him into another man past his prime, who should have been far from this fight.

"Thanks for saving me," Derek shouted, his eyes drooping for a moment before snapping open.

The old woman who had traded pelts slid under Tracy's lacking defenses. The woman's experience compensated for aged limbs, and she stabbed Tracy in the hip. The sharp point failed to penetrate Tracy's skin coverings, giving Flint a moment to pause in admiration at her quick thinking. Her flexible skin coverings hardened into armor. Still, the impact knocked Tracy to the ground.

The woman pulled the spear back for a killing blow. A blur bashed into the old hunter, sending her falling to the side.

Tracy hopped to her feet, a fire alight in her eyes. "Thanks, Rachel!"

Rachel moved between villagers, tripping them as she went. "Don't get distracted."

Above the fray, Derek shouted, "Come together. I'll make an alley to rush through." His blast of air parted a channel in the sea of bodies.

Flint and his companions sprinted into the shrinking gap of villagers.

Out of nowhere, a wooden spear glanced off Derek's shoulder. Blood trailed down the side of his arm. He pressed into his outer skin covering to staunch the flow.

Tracy and Rachel rushed to Derek's side.

Regardless of their unusual reasoning, his Weapons showed restraint by not delivering death. They deflected spears and axes, pushing villagers aside, rather than maim their foes.

The path to freedom closed as more villagers surrounded them. Flint directed Tracy and Rachel to form three points around Derek to protect him. Shouting above other battle cries, Flint called to Derek, "Open a doorway to Somewhere Else. We cannot escape without killing. There are too many to subdue."

Derek unleashed a yell from deep inside. A great swell of wind flung from him. Flint and the two women struggled to remain in place. This magical outburst halted the closest villagers. Derek sank, and the storm he unleashed died. His body doubled over.

Everywhere Flint turned, sharp weapons approached to end his life. Tracy and Rachel were losing ground. One of them was bound to make a mistake soon.

Flint jumped sideways to avoid a stab from a man's spear and countered by wrapping his arm binding around the villager's neck. A deafening yell from inside Flint shouted to sacrifice those who wished to end Flint's life. That way, he might create the hole to Somewhere Else himself.

The thick hide the villager wore as armor was meant for one of a smaller frame, while his cap was meant for one larger. Bulging eyes and purple-faced, he clawed at Flint's tightening binding around his neck. Other villagers hacked at Flint's binding to free the suffocating man.

Flint released his hold to keep the old man alive. Coughing and sputtering, the villager fled through the crowd, his spot replaced by two more.

Tracy's yell sounded. "To the bitter end!"

Derek called back to her. "A bit morbid, you think?"

Walls of earth sprung in front of Flint, spreading outward. It gave a momentary respite, though sharp sticks were already puncturing Tracy's magical shield.

Tracy punched her magic stone. She placed her hands on Derek. "Have the rest of my power." A flash of magic passed between them, and she fell to the ground.

Rachel followed Tracy's example. More magic drifted into Derek before she, too, collapsed.

The wall of dirt broke apart, showering Flint and the other three.

Magic gathered in Derek, one which dwarfed Flint's natural abilities.

Derek pulled in more magic from the trees, grass, and dirt beneath his feet. Like countless stars in the night sky, tiny bright lights swirled, spinning and falling into him. Frost tinged the muddy footprints left by countless people moving about. Villagers halted their advance, glancing fearfully about at the sudden chill which settled over the battle.

Awestruck, Flint stared at the Weapons he was preparing to aim at his former master.

Derek opened his hand. Sparks erupted from the dark ball he held. Wisps of magic blinked to life and disappeared as quickly. Wind whipped in all directions.

The most steadfast among the villagers fell to their knees.

Regardless of Flint's dredged up memories of the expanding darkness, he refused to turn from the opening doorway and cower behind the villagers.

The hole dropped from Derek's fingers, continuing to grow and shatter the world. Tall enough for a full-grown adult, the edges around the hole flickered, shrinking as soon as Derek brought it into existence. Flint flinched at the terrifying magical feat performed by one so young.

He unceremoniously tossed Tracy, Rachel, and Derek into the emptiness of the hole to Somewhere Else.

Villagers stood frozen by what lay before them. They must have assumed Flint and the others could do no more than summon fire from their hands, or at worst, call down streaks of light from the sky. Opening the doorway went far beyond rational magic and frightened the sane. The sour tinge of urine came from more than a few villagers who had been so ready to toss aside their lives to stop Flint.

Had he not once witnessed his master disappear into a similar void, Flint's courage to follow the three Weapons would have fled.

Flint stepped into the opening.

In crossing the threshold, his body pressed together, and his muscles constricted into nothing as though made of kneaded clay. Worse than a drug-induced frenzy, he lost all sense of awareness. Up was down, and down was left.

On the other side of the collapsing hole, the villagers lay flat with their faces pressed to the ground, some gesturing in prayer to whichever spirits they worshiped. From the kneeling crowd, a lone man hobbled to the entrance. The brash trader was emboldened to cast his life aside in a meaningless gesture.

Flint slammed the opening shut before the trader entered Somewhere Else. Though the trader might never find peace, the fact that, from his point of view, an evil like Flint was removed from the world had to suffice.

All light from his world dwindled as the doorway shut, leaving only the twilight glow from some unknown corner of this world.

He shuddered at an itch under his fingertips until it spread beneath his entire skin. Discomfort overpowered other thoughts. Pushing past the mental fog, Flint grabbed Derek.

Stretching his mind outward, Flint sought signs of his former master even as the void swallowed all other senses.

20

So Close

Derek

Derek studied the void, which was much more familiar in his second pass. Invisible to the eye, he sensed the lingering thread from his last frantic journey slowly unraveling into the empty fabric of this reality. Using it as a guide, he hoped it didn't disappear before he brought them home.

Memories were the beacon he used to guide them, the link keeping them alive. The house Derek grew up in, the family he lived there with, and friends that visited propelled them onward. He couldn't see any changes within the void, yet he sensed himself being pulled, a feeling similar to being trapped in a moving elevator. Recalling movie nights in Tracy's basement sent them in one direction, while memories of staying up all night on John's couch to conquer an action-RPG video game sent them elsewhere.

Thoughts overran one another and spun them about in the void. Like the last cart on a roller coaster halfway over the peak, his legs were sinking, dragging the rest of him into the depths of the void.

Floundering around in his mind, Derek found a memory to clutch onto, one from years ago, when Louis's parents opened the ice cream shop. He and his five closest friends sat at a table, the day before the Cold Something officially opened. *The Cold Snap!* He forced his brain to remember, lest he lose his mind to the void.

Louis's parents propped the six of them on one side of the table for a spontaneously planned picture, long before distance wrenched Nicole from their lives and differing interests stretched the group to the point of fracturing.

His thoughts fit into a 10,000-piece puzzle. Images of his life coalesced, and in doing so, they kept Derek and those holding onto him from sinking deeper. His memories guided them, carving a trail leading home; he felt close enough to smell the hot apple cider wafting from the town center's shops.

Derek fought swelling currents to not sail past his goal. For all the good it did, he was an ant floating on a twig as it fell down a waterfall. He slammed into someone he wasn't traveling with who was moving in the opposite direction. Too fast for him to see who they were, the vacuum in their wake sucked Derek along. With nothing left to slow the spiraling motion, the pressure hurled them out an exit from the void.

Derek found footing on the smooth, tiled surface. Through blurred vision, four walls in the dimly lit room encroached on them, the opposite of the open bridge he expected to land on. Underneath the trapped musty smell of the room, he was made bluntly aware of the last time he'd bathed.

A figure lunged, engulfing him in an embrace that forced precious air from his lungs. Derek's weakened legs faltered, and together, they toppled to the floor.

"Deeeeeeer!" shouted an oddly familiar female voice. Clearing her throat, the woman released the tight hug. "Two hours and fifty-one minutes. Welcome back."

He clung to the knowledge of that nickname, a shortened form of his first name. No one had called him that in months, not since Nicole Felcos moved thousands of miles. Now, she sat in front of him. Nicole's curly red locks were gone, replaced with free-flowing hair past her shoulders. There was no way around it. In their time apart, her face had become radiant, lighting the room.

"Nicole?" Derek was at a loss for words. "How on earth have you been? There's so much to tell you. I'm sorry for crashing in like this. What are we doing in your old house's cluttered basement?"

Polished drills and saws rested on a clean, wooden shelf above blue tool chests. Next to the tools, thick dust clung to a bright yellow kayak in the corner of the unfinished basement.

"Electricity!" Tracy shouted as she went on her hands and knees to all but kiss the socket. "Thank you, modern life. Hiya, Nicole. Mind if I borrow a charger?"

Rachel's hands were constantly in motion, punctuating her words as she spoke, "You will never believe where we were, or when, not that I know the answer to either."

Flint's head swiveled. He warily studied the room as though everything in it might bite him if he turned his back.

"Anyone else getting SIM card errors?" Tracy smacked the side of her phone.

Derek grabbed the dead brick that was his phone. "Mine's been busted since our unexpected swim when we landed in Flint's time. Not all of us can create waterproof bags on the fly, like you."

Nicole's thin smile spread to the edges of her round face. Narrow magenta eyeglass frames highlighted eager eyes shifting between Derek and his friends.

She raised her hands to counter their verbal bombardment. "One question at a time."

"Since when did you go back to wearing glasses?" Derek asked. "I thought you loved those contacts."

Tracy coughed loudly, her head jerking to the side to get his attention.

"Since always. Are you feeling okay?" Nicole inspected the gashes along his arm and cheek. "Were you attacked by an army of rabid raccoons?"

"Something like that," Rachel grumbled.

Nicole held a hand to his forehead. Derek winced, feeling a good-sized bruise from when a villager clubbed him. Flint escaped without a scratch. The rest of them had a fair share of torn clothes, scrapes, and open wounds.

No more words formed on Derek's bone-dry mouth. He pantomimed eating.

"Do you all want something to drink?" Nicole asked.

He could do little more than nod.

Nicole climbed the stairs to oblige. She ducked back into the basement, pointing at the opening to the void. "You should close that. It's worse than an overactive AC unit."

Her footsteps grew fainter. Derek had minutes to rally. "Why isn't she surprised to see us? Why was the portal here and how is it still open?"

Icy currents blew from the sphere as though it knew he was looking at it. Derek held his torn and stretched shirt closer.

Unlike two of the portals he'd created previously, this one held its shape without collapsing. It had taken every ounce of his power to keep the prior doorways open for more than a few seconds, yet this one stayed open.

Flint crushed herbs from his pack and waved his arms. The fabric of reality stitched together, sealing the hole.

"You were right to worry about changing the past," Tracy said. "That isn't our friend."

Nicole is finally back in our lives.

"You're wrong," he insisted.

Rachel let her backpack drop. "Think we're now ruled by robot overlords?"

"Doubtful." Derek searched the basement for an old newspaper or magazine and found nothing to tell him about the present. "I hope we didn't erase my sister. We were getting along now that she left for college."

Flint tapped the washing machine in the corner, making loud metallic clangs.

From the corner of Tracy's lips, words formed as she restrained herself from shouting. "Did you hear what I said? That's not the Nicole I grew to love."

The staircase creaked, announcing their host's return. Derek had missed their chance to plan how to gauge their corruption of the past without Nicole knowing.

Nicole lowered the carefully balanced tray of food onto the tabletop. Derek reached for a glass of water and a fistful of carrot sticks. Nicole lobbed two rolls of gauze at Tracy and Rachel. "Please don't bleed on my floor. I brought my medical sewing kit to patch you up."

She handed out ibuprofen pills like candies to dull their pains. Derek took two and gulped his glass of water down to the last drop. He flinched at the ice pack Nicole pressed to his shoulder.

His free hand went to work on consuming the handful of fixings, not caring that sweet sugar cookies and bitter broccoli clashed on his tongue.

Using a butane lighter intended to start a charcoal grill, Nicole ran the flame along a narrow needle.

Derek leaned away from the reach of the wannabe doctor. "What do you think you are doing with that?"

"I'd prefer to not go to the ER. There's too much we don't want to explain." She handed him a couple of tongue depressors taped in a bundle. "Bite this."

Nicole went to work sealing his split skin. Biting into the wood, Derek did his best to act tough. Instead, he winced with every puncture Nicole made as she tied his skin together. Glancing down was a mistake. He coughed to cover the full body shudder at the sight of blood gushing from his shoulder.

"Quit being a baby." Nicole held his arm steady and pressed the wound together to help with the suture. "This is long, not deep. I've watched our coach patch worse after a muddy field hockey game."

To distract himself from the pain, Derek set his attention on Flint. The man from the past inspected his glassware, then drained it. He crumbled a cookie in his palm. Flint's dirt-crusted fingers placed a small piece in his mouth. The next second, the cookie was gone, along with all those remaining on the tray.

Nicole finished with Derek's shoulder and applied bandages to the smaller cuts on his face, chest, and legs. Tracy and Rachel finished wrapping their own cuts. With a sigh of relief, Tracy applied ice packs to her multitude of bruises. The armored clothing she'd made protected her, but each impact had left a good-sized purple welt.

With his wounds closed or covered, Derek found his voice. "For the benefit of everyone else, can you remind me why the void was open?"

"You always leave the doorway open to find your way home," Nicole explained.

"Always?" Flint asked. "I was led to believe our encounter was your first passage through the Somewhere Else."

Nicole moved on without catching the silencing glare Derek sent at Flint. "After the second hour, I was worried you wouldn't get back before my parents come home in a few days. We never had a plan to explain the portal." Looking them over for the first real time, she asked, "How did you get Rachel and Tracy in there? For that matter, why get them? We don't know them well enough to trust with this secret." Tracy winced but let Nicole continue unimpeded. "Who's that old guy dressed in animal carcasses? More importantly, what *is* that peach fuzz monstrosity sprouting from your chin?"

"His soul patch *is* getting unwieldy." Rachel flicked Derek's chin.

Nicole's voice cracked as she asked, "Why leave me behind if you planned on bringing two people you barely know?"

"Haven't we all been friends since we were kids?" Derek mentally kicked himself. He might as well be holding a neon sign telling her the past shifted without him.

Her small, nervous laugh rang out. "Not even a little. What happened to you on the other side of the gateway?"

Wheels spun slowly in Derek's head. He'd collided with someone in the void, someone from this place.

Tracy was right. This isn't our Nicole.

Fearing an attack from every direction, his heightened senses darted over the room, casting everything in arm's reach as either a weapon to be used on him or by him.

Lines stretched over Nicole's face. "Where did you go after leaving here?"

Derek kept his answer vague. "Into the past."

"That's incredible! I told you there was something beyond the nothingness."

"I'm losing count. How often have I slipped in and out of the void?"

Nicole chewed over her words, speaking with care. "You've been inside five times over the past three weeks, but never for more than an hour."

As strange as it was to wrap his head around, the person he collided with inside the void must have been another version of himself from this place. A warning alarm went off inside his head. "What's today?"

"November eleventh."

Three weeks from the day I tore open the hole on the bridge.

"You're acting weirder than usual." Nicole leaned forward, planting a kiss on his lips. The instant she made contact, she recoiled. "Who are you?"

Her unsteady whisper cut into Derek as though this were his friend, Nicole, who he'd gravely hurt. He held his hands open to convey he wasn't a threat.

"I'm me." He tried the truth. "I'm Derek, just not the one who left here."

Dashing toward a kayak, Nicole threw open a metal box. Derek stared into the barrel of a quivering orange gun. "Where is he?" she sobbed.

"Is that a flare gun?" Tracy asked. "Seriously?"

Unsure who to aim it at, Nicole's hand, ever at risk of firing, moved between them. "This is enough to mess you up unless you return my Derek."

Derek's throat caught and his mind reeled, unable to separate this Nicole from the one he'd known for over a decade.

"Hey, now," Rachel began, holding her hands up as though conducting them to be quieter, "why don't we *poco meno mosso* this situation?"

If anything, Nicole looked more terrified and confused.

"She means we all need to relax," Tracy said slowly, holding her hands out in a calming gesture like she was lowering the volume of the room.

Derek reached for his powers and found nothing. He was too spent from opening the void to leave Flint's time. Yet, more than anything, he knew his friend. Stepping forward, he covered the gun barrel with his bare palm, angling it to the floor.

"An accident threw us here. I want to go home, to my real home, as surely as your Derek wants to return here. I promise I'll find him and bring him back to this world."

Wrapping his head around those weird words, Derek struggled to imagine another Derek who was, but wasn't, the one he saw in the mirror. He steadied shaking legs and took a seat on the couch, folding into its worn cushions. "We can go home tomorrow after finding the version of me that went into the void."

Derek's head sank forward, his body feeling all the heavier.

Tracy snickered. "Maybe a little longer. You need your beauty sleep after a..."

The world faded. Derek greeted his old friend: weariness.

21

Dessert and Desert

Derek

Loud knocks against the bedroom door jolted Derek awake. He rose from the soft bed as fast as his aching muscles allowed. Teal bed sheets dropped to the floor.

Band posters from pop garbage to punk rock to bands he didn't recognize covered the room. A collage of pictures included some with his face at places he had never been, reminding Derek of the alien room he occupied.

It might have been his imagination, but even breathing in the air seemed different on this Earth.

Knocks sounded against the door again. Nicole's head poked around the corner.

"Consider these clean clothes a peace offering for threatening to shoot you. These belonged to my Derek. I'm assuming they fit you too."

"Do I even want to know what you're doing with his clothes?"

Nicole ignored him. "I gave my spare clothes to Tracy and Rachel, and Flint took some of my dad's old stuff. Who is he? I've never met someone who needed a rundown on how to zip a fly. Not to mention those bunny slippers tied to his feet were made from real bunnies, I think."

Imagining that man struggling to put on a pair of pants made Derek smile. "He's from the past and hitched a ride with us to hunt down someone who pissed him off. Are you going to watch while I change?"

Nicole's cheeks flushed scarlet. She spun so her back faced him.

Derek dressed in the softest clothes to ever grace his skin. Regular cotton blends felt wonderful compared to the rough clothing Tracy had used her powers to transmute for them. The other Derek's long sleeve shirt had last year's Turkey Trot race logo emblazoned on the front, reminding him of his annual Thanksgiving 5K tradition with his sister. His hair stood on end at yet another blaring reminder of how similar this world was to his own.

"You're good to turn around."

Nicole prodded his face. "You look so much like him," she mused.

"Well, we are the same person. More or less."

"I'll never get used to that." She paused, staring right at him. "Are we even dating in your world?"

"We're dating?" he cried out.

"I'll take that as a no. I don't know if that makes this better or worse. Aside from giving you clothes, I came here to apologize. Sorry is an understatement for aiming a flare gun at you."

Derek bundled his dirty clothes on the floor. Hopefully, they'd be dropped down an incinerator shaft to prevent contamination. "It caught me off guard. I wasn't aware you owned any kind of gun, much less knew how to use one."

Rubbing the back of her neck, Nicole let out a dark laugh. "I don't. I was scared and didn't know what to do."

"I have no idea what I'd have done if you arrived from the void into my basement."

"So where do you think Derek..." Her voice faltered. "Where do you think my Derek went?"

"Anywhere. The void spit us on some ancient island where we met Flint. Help me narrow the possibilities and tell me what your Derek experienced while inside."

"He never went far. He told me he stayed within eyesight of the opening. What do you think the place is?"

"My running theory is it's a space between places where the universe, or apparently multiple ones, overlap and intersect."

"What the lost Derek did was dangerous," Flint's gruff tones carried from the hall. "Reaching into the open jaws of a great hairy cat to flick its fangs would be safer."

Derek sighed in disgust. "You're in our present time, and here we have a thing called privacy. Stop listening in on our conversations."

Flint entered the room without a hint of remorse. He no longer appeared like the wilderness hermit who saved Derek's life. That version of Flint was one step above a caveman with scraggy, twig-infested hair, full beard, and animal pelts for makeshift clothes.

Having ditched his biohazard loincloth and animal-hide vest, Flint replaced them with yellow and black flannel. He looked like a human-sized honeybee. Instead of pelts tied to his ankles, he wore proper tennis shoes.

His dripping hair was pulled behind his head, and he didn't carry a hint of coated mud or grime. Flint had hacked his thick beard to a short length, revealing the man beneath. Derek didn't want to imagine the muck clogging the shower drain.

"Failing to observe niceties does not make me any less correct," Flint uttered. "In leaving the portal open, the Derek who left placed you and this world in grave danger. My former master might have used it to worm his way here and destroy your village."

Nicole hugged her arms to her chest. "We didn't know. He left it open to always have a link back to here. With it closed, how will he find his way home?"

For once, Derek had the answer. "The void reacted with my memories. We seemed close to leaving safely when we veered here. If your Derek honed in on thoughts of this world, he should have returned if he were able—" Derek stopped, but the damage was done.

Without feeling the moment, Flint charged into it. "I did not intend to listen to your conversation. I heard you wake, Derek, and wished to have words with you."

Derek patted Nicole's arm. "Give me a few minutes with the eavesdropper, then we can plan how to find your Derek."

Flint led him into the narrow hall. Unlike his Nicole's house, bookshelves which belonged in the guest bedroom lined the walls.

Derek longed to know how the Nicole he grew up with was spending her morning. It was probably more mundane than risking time itself by bringing someone from the past into the present.

Flint played with the light switch, toggling the recessed lighting until it felt like a rave. "We should form a team."

"What?"

"Is that not the right word? I am still unfamiliar with the specifics of your tongue."

"What are you talking about?"

Flint fidgeted with his jean pockets. "This is not where we intended to arrive. Another accidental stop may occur when we return to the void. Enlarging our party bolsters our combined magic to defend us against the unknown, and I have a perfect choice selected."

"No." Derek massaged his forehead. "Another jump gets us home."

"What happened to bringing this world's Derek home?"

"Fine. We find this other me, then go immediately back to where we belong."

"I taught you to use magic in order to search for my former master within the Somewhere Else."

Derek ignored the implication of assumed debt. "That reminds me, how have you acclimated to our present so well? We're what, thousands of years into your future?"

Flint smirked to the point Derek thought he wouldn't answer. "Magic, remember? To know whether you and your friends served my former master, I searched into your minds. Glimpses from your world revealed the unimaginable machines in this house." His hands plucked a snow globe sitting on the shelf, nearly dropping it when the white plastic bits fell and settled on the Washington Capitals' hockey logo. "That said, touching these now common items is fascinating."

Poking through fragmented memories from his first days of meeting Flint, Derek recalled why he selectively forgot Flint had read his mind.

"Right. You mentioned the Beast, and I pushed aside your invasion of our privacy."

"I assumed you were my replacements serving my former master, possibly even my siblings. How I discovered you were neither is not important. What is important is we need to stop my former master."

Derek held up his hand to stop Flint from talking, though the gesture had to be lost on him. "I'll talk with the others, and we'll decide together. We owe you that much for saving our lives. Maybe there's some compromise to search for both this master of yours and the other me at the same time."

Nicole flung open her bedroom door to brush past them, having remade the guest bed. Derek followed her and joined his friends outside.

Tracy sat on the porch, transmuting new jeans and a long-sleeved shirt until they fit.

Slowing to a normal walk, Rachel stopped her power and swerved to avoid crashing into Nicole. "Feels good to stretch my legs," Rachel said, after making sure Nicole was okay.

Nicole's mouth dropped. "How do you have my Derek's ability?" Nicole asked Rachel.

"I gave it to her," Derek said. "I'm not sure how. A few times during my fight with that Beast I felt drained without doing anything. Maybe I gave you powers in a desperate attempt to protect us, kind of like how I opened the way to the void."

Rachel blocked Nicole's fingers from poking her thighs. "Do you have any powers, Nicole?"

"Nope," Nicole sulked. "That's the reason Derek foraged in what you call the void without me. If I had shown the slightest hint of abilities, I'd be with him."

Tracy leaned forward. Her gaze focused solely on Nicole. "What powers did the other Derek have?"

Nicole's brow wrinkled. "Quite a few, actually. Why don't we go to his training site and compare notes? Maybe using your powers will draw my Derek here. How about in exchange for my help, you transfer some of your power, like you did with your friends?"

Derek shook his head. "No. I'm much weaker after sharing my power with these two, and I need all my remaining power to open the portal to the void." Feeling his insides wrench apart as Nicole's face fell, he added, "I'll do what I can to share a minuscule amount before saying goodbye."

Her eyes lit at the promise. "Mind if we visit Derek's house? With you here, we can calm his parents and buy us a day or two."

"I don't want to offer false hope to my almost-parents." That was too much for Derek to process. Thinking best with food in his belly, he went back inside to scrounge for a snack in the kitchen. He had one hand buried in the cookie jar when Nicole appeared.

"When you leave, you're taking me," Nicole said.

Peering into those eyes, Derek couldn't help but mistake this woman for one of his oldest friends. "That makes no sense. What if your world's Derek returns tomorrow? I won't take you from your home, from your life, to throw you into danger."

"It's *my* life and *my* choice. You're my best chance at finding Derek." Nicole stared at Derek, her gaze unwavering. "I'm leaving with you."

Such unbending willpower meant the only way to jump into the void without Nicole was to abandon her while she slept. Derek grumbled a half-promise until Nicole left him alone.

With his head resting in his hands, Derek was stirred from troubled thoughts by someone opening the refrigerator.

Flint stared at stacks of fruits, vegetables, and leftover pizza. He clicked his tongue. "This is a season's worth of food. I understand why your humanity gave up the hunt. Also, your thoughts were valid. There is no way of knowing what we will find when searching for this lost you."

"How long were you listening to our private conversation again?" Derek was wasting his breath berating Flint.

"Private? Your voices carried to all rooms of this house." Flint halted the insult on Derek's tongue by continuing. "Have you given thought to how you intend to track the other you?"

Derek considered what little he knew of the place between worlds. "The void reacted to my thoughts. I had almost gotten us safely back to our real home before I collided with the other Derek, and we were thrown off course. If I had a picture of him, I might be able to use that to track him like a scent." Derek rubbed his head, seeking any other alternative to the simplest solution, the one he didn't want to use. "Nicole's memories may be the best chance we have to find the other me."

"How do you know we won't get lost? We must gather one from my time to reinforce our strength."

Cookie crumbs fell from Derek's open mouth. "And who are you suggesting we kidnap?"

"The Blood Dancer."

Letting out a long sigh, Derek said, "I don't know what that is."

"A wielder of immense magic. They evaded numerous guards to end their intended targets' lives. In forgotten villages, I found former guards of those victims. Of them, one spoke of a warrior who danced in blood. For fear of their lives, none of the other surviving guards offered any descriptions."

"We're not breaking the timeline by removing some assassin from the past," Derek said.

"They were more than a killer. To find those the Blood Dancer hunted required a tracker of great skill. Warriors in their path were removed, not killed. Walls in the Blood Dancer's way were evaded, not knocked down. Those are the skills we desire when traveling the unknown."

"How do you intend to find this person?"

"My memories can lead us through the void the same as yours did."

"Sure, why don't we kidnap history's greatest to join our cause?" Derek sighed and threw up his hands. "Fine. *Fine.* If everyone else agrees, then we will delay the search for the other me to get one more person, and *only* one. Once we find the other me, you, Nicole, and everyone else gets put back in their rightful time and dimension. After that, I shut the void and never look back."

Flint grasped Derek's hand and shook it. "Agreed. I believe this to be the customary sign among your people when a deal is struck."

Derek coaxed his friends into the kitchen with melting cheese wafting from the pizza in the oven. Weary companions took seats around the table.

He cleared his throat to get his friend's attention. "Flint wants us to capture some killer from his time to help us find the other Derek. Care to fill us in on more details, Flint?"

Flint's eyes lit up at the first gooey slice of pepperoni. Chewing quick, he spoke around his meal. "Long ago, my master used my magic to forge the Weapon of all weapons at the cost of considerable death. This opened the way to what you call the 'void.' I trapped him inside, though in seasons since, I sought and studied unusual deaths in near and far lands. I traveled, investigating them on the chance they were signs of my master's return. This led me to discover a ruling duo and their family benefited from the deeds of a single killer. We will travel to their home and anger those in power to draw out the one who dances in blood. Then, we convince this warrior to join us."

"Why would they come with us?" Nicole asked.

"I can offer knowledge of magic and Tracy can offer anything else if they are motivated by trinkets."

Tracy's wicked smile spread across her face. "Sounds like your plan means we get to annoy some people in charge. I know there are concerns about altering the past, so we won't do lasting harm. What do you say to being a band of traveling magicians who insult our hosts until they want to kill us with this Blood Dancer?"

There was a semblance of logic behind Tracy's idea, and Derek had to admit it offered a well-earned chance to unwind.

Flint traced imaginary spots along the wall with his finger. "The family lives in a village of villages some claim rose from the sand. Rumors of the village are unreliable as they spoke of splendors beyond imagination. I once journeyed near it, but was chased away before setting eyes on the village. That memory will guide us through the void and bring us within a day's travel."

Tracy pumped her fist in the air. "I'm in for any plan that has us making a ruckus the likes of which these stuck-up prehistoric slobs have never seen."

"Is Flint prehistoric?" Rachel asked. "I never pinned down when he lived."

"I can't tell. He definitely seemed to live before anything my history class covered. Anyway, our next move should be to restock on supplies." Tracy placed a brick on the table. "I found this outside. You're welcome." The red material sloshed as though made of liquid and reshaped into slips of dollar bills. "Check these against a twenty-dollar bill that Nicole has to make sure it's passable in this dimension."

Seeing Nicole's mouth drop open, Tracy explained, "I can transmute things. In this case, I'm a portable ATM." Tracy slid the cash to Derek and Rachel. "Buy camping equipment and food for us. I'm too tired to run around all day and there are some TV shows to catch up on, assuming my favorites exist in this world."

Rachel nodded. "Tracy and I will stay to plan our supplies and figure out how to ration them. We'll watch Flint, too. We can't have him wandering around learning more about our present than he has from our memories. If he knows too much, then he could alter our timeline when we drop him off in the past, assuming he's from our past and not a parallel Earth's past."

22

Cookie Debate

Tracy

While Derek and Nicole crisscrossed across town to shop for supplies, Tracy helped Rachel pack. Tracy counted energy bars and added them to their backpacks, checking items off Rachel's list.

Tracy turned her nose up at the jar of flax seeds in Nicole's cabinet. "Bleh. In our world, Nicole had this same setup. Protein bars on the left and health junk on the right." She paused. "In our world... Now, that's a phrase I'll never get used to."

Rachel hung her head, for once agreeing with Tracy. "There isn't a bag of processed chips in sight. Does Nicole not know the immeasurable value of snack food?"

Tracy added an unopened box of chocolate chip cookies to her backpack, cramming it inside a cooking pot. "This time around, we're having fun in the past."

Rachel lacked the same enthusiasm. She swiped the cookies from Tracy's backpack and replaced them with another water bottle. "This trip needs to be taken seriously. I want to avoid hurricane Tracy."

"It won't be easy getting these all-powerful rulers to want to kill us. We need a creative idea or two."

Rachel waved her written supply list one more time. "I'm having enough issues reconciling with the decision to get this killer to join us. So please stick to this list of essentials so we don't run out of food or drinking water."

Tracy snorted. "We'll put Flint's killer warrior right back where they belong in a day or two, once we find the other Derek. So tomorrow, I'll make sure we have one helluva party with the ancient rulers. Who knows? The day after we may explore outer space, but only if we stop this nonsense of being superheroes."

Rachel rested her hands on her hips. "You're acting like every freshman at the start of summer marching band training. You're overly confident and assuming someone will cover for you when you mess up. We need to rely on each other, and it *will* be hard work."

Tracy hated to admit Rachel was right. Regretting her decision to skip the supply run with Derek and Nicole, Tracy applied a new tactic.

"How long do you think it will take for us to find Flint's killer warrior? With how little we know about this person, do you think she's a towering woman swinging a two-handed battle ax or a robed, old man able to call down a hailstorm? Maybe something in between?"

Rachel grunted in the struggle to zip another overstuffed pack shut. "No idea. Ideally, this is a quick snatch and grab. Within twenty-four hours relative to us, I'd like to be eating dinner in our present time and that accounts for finding the other Derek."

"Entire worlds are opening for us, and you want to go home to our boring lives?" Tracy scoffed. "I don't want to be like Flint. He's still in the living room, forced to read through a boring dictionary to isolate him from most of our pop-culture and history. Think about how much his mind would explode if he watched a single movie."

"I like my life," Rachel said quietly. "I'm all about using our abilities, but we have to be more careful on this next trip to the past. What if we unmake all we know? What if we unravel time itself?"

"What if this? What if that?" Tracy mocked. "With our power and Flint's knowledge, we can stop whatever paradox you think may be rushing at us and still make it home for precious dinner."

"You can't honestly believe that," Rachel shook her head.

"Our powers are growing exponentially by the day."

"Think about if the world discovered we existed. Do you care about your family and how that would affect them?"

"We're going back into the past to kidnap someone. We're in the present. Anything we do next should logically have already happened."

Deep red flushed Rachel's cheeks. "By your logic, we can't kill our grandparents from the mere fact we exist. For all we know, tomorrow we could set events in motion to prevent our ancestors from being born, and time is merely playing catch-up. Don't forget, we're on a parallel Earth. Who can say whether ours is still there?"

Tracy stalked out of the kitchen to check on Flint. "We'll find out tomorrow."

23

Returning To The Void

Derek

Nausea and cold sweats took turns assaulting Derek through the early morning hours. He tossed and turned, ready to leave this dimension where he didn't belong. Since he and the other Derek were able to break into other worlds, perhaps neither of them belonged anywhere.

Tracy was already cooking a hearty breakfast for the team when Derek wandered into the kitchen, attracted by savory smells of frying bacon. Usually a late riser, Tracy appeared to have been awake for hours. Her head bobbed along to steady beats coming from the headphones resting around her neck. She clicked the metal kitchen tongs in time with her music while rotating strips of bacon.

"Enjoy your last civilized meal." Tracy scooped two sunny side up eggs onto a plate and handed it to Derek. "I added my special ingredients to rouse your spirits. Spoiler alert, they're a dash of Sriracha and a sprinkle of paprika."

Derek rubbed sleep from his eyes. "Since when do you know your way around breakfast, aside from a bowl of cereal?"

Tracy wiggled her fingers. "These babies are for more than filling your earholes with the best drum solos. As for breakfast, I've always been a pro. You've never thought to ask."

Pans of sizzling breakfast drew everyone else into the kitchen.

Rachel piled her plate high with bacon and eggs, lingering in front of Tracy. "I'm sorry for what I said yesterday about hurricane Tracy."

Tracy offered a smile and more bacon. "I'll get over it. For what it's worth, I don't want our past to be undone either."

"I know."

"When we make it back to our world tomorrow, do you mind showing me some new tricks on drums? I'll also teach you what I've learned despite my lack of your classical Symphonic Band."

"Sounds like a plan," Rachel smiled, taking a seat at the table.

Nicole filled half her plate and stared at it, obviously too stressed to eat.

Flint prodded the bacon on his plate and sniffed it. He tore off a piece with the side of his mouth, gnashing it like a goat. Ignoring the fork and knife, he shoveled the egg and meat directly into his mouth with grubby hands. Flint licked his plate clean and leaned back in the chair. Bits of egg sprinkled in his beard.

Derek tried to savor the mouthwatering fried bacon dripping with grease. Yet every bite brought him one moment closer to leaving and turned the gooey center of his eggs into flavorless sustenance.

Tracy served herself a full plate and joined them.

His stomach turned in knots. Derek began his poorly rehearsed apology. It seemed so easy in his head, yet his tongue tripped over the words.

"Tracy and Rachel, I'm sorry I took out my frustrations on you over how weak I am. Every time I close my eyes, I still see that Beast mauling me on the bridge. We were lucky to survive. Still, that's no excuse for what I said. I don't consider your powers to be stolen from me."

Rachel angled her fork at Derek. "You'll lose every fight when you underestimate your opponent and overestimate yourself. An entire orchestra is needed to create a symphony, so we'll fight it together when we get home."

"Wow, everyone's apologizing to me this morning," Tracy said. "It's not like we're going to unmake ourselves today, right?"

Derek gulped, not daring to respond.

Tracy waved her hand in the air. "Anyway, took you long enough to say sorry, Derek. We're good. We've always been good."

"Assuming no one else has any confessions," Rachel said, "once we make it to Flint's time, we need to blend in as well as possible. Watching all those movies is going to finally pay off."

"What are you talking about?" Tracy asked. "I'm the best pre-pared one, given my class on ancient civilizations."

"Didn't you brag about sleeping through it?" Rachel straight-ened her back and waved her hand in some misguided honorific. She spoke in a horrid accent. "Greetings, yon fair lord or maiden. We be traveled knights seeking to partake in ye oldey fun."

Tracy's short-lived laugh seemed more like an insult rather than a genuine response. "We already know Flint's people don't sound like that. Even if we were going to the Renaissance period, which Flint likely predates by a few thousand years, you'd still be lost with whatever *that* was. Not to mention, the 'e' in olde is silent."

"I'm with Tracy," Nicole said. "That's plain bad."

Rachel looked down, glumly. "We had a small sample size of Flint's time. There's still a chance my phrases were passable."

"I'm betting all the money in the world your fake accent is woefully inaccurate," Nicole said.

Tracy turned to her. "I can create those riches, and it still wouldn't be enough to bribe Rachel to never use it again."

"Ouch, my pride." Rachel clutched her heart.

Tracy pushed her chair from the table. She was on her way out of the kitchen when Nicole said, "Feel like taking care of your plate?"

"Are you serious?"

Nicole pointed at the used plates and utensils. "I'm not leaving that mess for my parents."

"This isn't our world," Tracy replied. "A few dirty dishes shouldn't matter."

"Please."

Tracy set a level gaze on Nicole. "I have to keep remembering you aren't our Nicole."

Nicole glanced around the table. "I do the same with all of you."

"I got it." Derek collected everyone's dishes and started hand-washing them, needing to keep himself busy. Plunging the dishes beneath the steaming faucet distracted his turbulent thoughts. He felt like he was about to jump off a bridge, hoping that the bungee cord wrapped around his ankles didn't snap.

One by one, everyone left except Nicole. Stuck at the kitchen table with blank pieces of paper and a pen, she kept crumpling her work and throwing it away.

After finishing with the dishes, Derek ignored his better judgment and investigated. Opening a note, he got as far as, "Dear Mom and Dad, I'm sorry I need to leave," before clenching the private message shut.

Stepping over the balled-up papers, Derek sat across from Nicole. "Not a fan of texting in this dimension?"

"This way my parents won't get the message until they're back home and I won't ruin their vacation," Nicole said. "Who knows? We may get back with Derek before they come home and all my worries would have been for nothing. I have to find Derek, but how can I explain it? Telling the truth means my parents will send every Army, Navy, Air Force, and Marine member looking for their crazy daughter."

"You're not crazy. We'll find him. As for your parents, tell them Derek disappeared and you need to bring him home."

"It's not that easy."

"You're right, and nothing you leave in a note will stop your parents from worrying or getting the police involved. All the more reason for you to stay."

"Drop it." Her eyes met his. "I won't be sidelined. You're searching for Derek, so I'm coming with you. There. That's what I'll say. I may not always be safe, but I'm with people I trust to find Derek. I'll end by asking them to deliver another message to Derek in the event he shows up." Penning a separate note, she muttered, "Now, if the Derek of this world makes his way home, he'll have a reference for when I began to track him."

Derek left her for his own final preparations. Once he was convinced his stuffed backpack held everything he needed, he gathered the small crowd in the basement.

Hiding behind a false mask of confidence, Derek described the plan one last time, untying a long length of rope for everyone to hold.

"I'm going to open the portal and then we're going back to the opening we made leaving Flint's time. From there, Flint will move us through the void using his memories of traveling to, what he believes is, the Blood Dancer's village. If that doesn't work, then we use the same exit from last time and go the long way, starting at Flint's island. This is your last chance to opt out. Tracy can make money for anyone not joining us, and we'll pick you up when we get back."

Tracy raised her hand and tapped her headphones resting around her neck. "I'd like to put my vote in for an alternative plan. Nicole's world isn't our home, but who cares? An island paradise on this parallel world is still an island paradise. We can make a new home here."

Derek didn't even consider it, and no one else took her up on the offer.

Tracy shook her head. "Can't say I didn't try. Let's go through hell, then."

From the inner well of power, a cyclone of pressure built around Derek. The heavy weight of the opening portal dragged his arm down. The space between his hands bent, folding over a part of reality. This gap solidified, enlarging into a dark ball. Light from the basement did little to penetrate the depths of the pit. The opening grew enough to fit one person at a time.

Tracy held the front end of the rope and crossed into the void in an ungainly swan dive.

Nicole approached the doorway as if it were a giant mouth about to gobble her whole. She pushed her forearm into the sphere and pulled it back, her arm shaking, rejecting the void itself. Derek gave her shoulder a reassuring squeeze; all the while sweat formed across his body from maintaining the opening. Nicole stepped through the opening, her hand resting on the rope. Flint went next, followed by Rachel.

Derek didn't delay in leaving this false home. He picked up the end of the rope and crossed into the void.

The void's dim light reminded him of walking along the road on a cloudy night, where vague light pollution from D.C. carried from the horizon.

Everyone was still holding onto the rope, staying together. Derek floated next to Flint. Derek pictured the aromas of seaweed and mild salt of the sea near Flint's home. The memories moved them forward over the void.

Tracy yelled at him, fear plastered across her face. Her finger frantically gestured into the distance, but her voice arrived as a jumbled mess.

The doorway to Nicole's world shut on its own, no longer fed by his power.

Too tired to open the way back to Nicole's world, Derek spoke through heavy breaths, "We go forward."

24

Crash Landing

Tracy

Passing from the real world into the void was like no other experience. Thoughts squeezed from Tracy's mind as she tried to make sense of them.

She hovered by the spherical opening, clutching her end of the rope and waiting for the rest to leave Nicole's basement. There was a vague notion of lines connecting her to places across the void. The harder she looked, the more a drill burrowed deeper into her mind, nagging her.

Light from Nicole's world stopped short when spreading into the endless void. Its lone ray of light was swallowed whole.

A massive shadow flew toward her from the void's inner depths. Its arms lengthened, reaching for Tracy. Eyes covered its body, and all of them were open. They looked at the light escaping from Nicole's basement.

As it approached, its size continued to swell. Whenever Tracy thought it had arrived, it was still some distance away and the shadow had only became larger.

Her friends entered, unaware of the shadow within the void.

"Go back!" she shouted in warning. She pulled on the rope to climb from this place. Hiding in Nicole's world wasn't a terrible option.

The portal sealed, trapping them in and muting Tracy's senses. Without the light from Nicole's world, she lost sight of the monster made of shadow. She hoped whatever was out there was as equally lost as she was in the limited eerie half-light. Tracy held her breath, straining her ears for the sounds of anything moving.

Flint seemed less certain as he guided them back to his time. Stutter-stop motions disoriented Tracy's senses, leaving her stomach roiling from moving across the void.

In a place where distance meant nothing and there were no landmarks, Tracy was at a loss for how far they had gone from Nicole's world.

In here, her powers were useless. That thought caused Tracy's chest to clench, making it hard to breathe. She gripped Nicole's arm, wary that the shadow thing might be close.

Their speed, if it could be called that, slowed. They had to be close to creating an opening. But no, they arrived at a spot resembling splintered glass superglued together.

Light seeped in from the crack in the void.

Flint and Derek floated without a care in the world. Tracy knew better. She held her tongue rather than risk yelling at them and drawing the shadow's attention.

They moved again. Flint or Derek sent them away from the fractured light. Tracy no longer cared where or when they arrived, so long as they left the void.

She pulled the rope until she was next to Derek. "We need to get out of the void now. There's something in here with us."

Derek nodded. He opened his hands, and the ball formed, blinking out of existence before reaching its full size. Tracy forced herself to remain calm as her heart raced.

She put her headphones on and pressed play, feeling refreshing power gather inside her at the sounds of music. She placed her hand on Derek's shoulder and sent him all her spare power.

This time, the portal Derek formed sustained itself. Tracy fed him more power, anything to speed up their escape. Fresh air singed her lungs ever so sweetly as the gateway grew large enough to fit through.

She pushed her friends out of the opening and then plunged to freedom.

Wind caught her hair and lifted it straight up.

Her eyes adjusted. Verdant shades of a distant green forest guided her eyes to the horizon. Far, *far* below, the trees ended at mounds of tan sand that spread out like a strange, textured shower mat.

Below. Crap.

Tracy fought the air currents to keep her headphones over her ears. She needed more power to create parachutes for everyone and slow their deadly plummet.

Coarse grains of sand rose to meet her falling body. Judging by Flint's hand motions, his magic was saving their lives by forming a solid sand surface angled to the ground, which climbed hundreds of feet into the air. Wide enough for everyone, the sand became the world's largest, grittiest spiral slide.

Her feet hit hard and held none of her weight. Her butt slammed into compact sand and a jolt of pain shot up her back. Her backpack threw her off balance. Sky and sand blurred as she rolled and rolled and rolled. Backpack. Forearms. Backpack. Forearms. The cycle repeated in the uncontrolled tumble down the sand slide.

The world was spinning so much she didn't recognize it when she came to a stop. She felt like an awkward turtle stuck on its sides as she swung her arms to adjust the heavy backpack keeping her down.

Had she thought to bring lotion their fall might have been the start of the best spa day of her life. "I guess I don't need to exfoliate for the next year."

Rachel whooped nearby. "We're alive!"

Tracy tried to shake her spiraling vision. Above, the portal they'd used to enter this world spun along with the rest of the sky. A long, black shape merged with the swirling blue.

What might be considered a hand breached this world from the portal Derek had formed to leave the void. Seven fingers made of shadow, each ending in claws as long as a person, curled and extended, testing their flexibility.

Small bits of smoke evaporated from the shadow arm like steam in a pot of water boiling into vapor. The arm retracted into the void.

Tracy clamored to her feet on shaking legs. Lurching at Derek, she pointed at the portal. "Derek, close it! Now!"

Derek hardly noticed her; his attention never left Flint. Rachel was inspecting the damage to her backpack. Nicole lay on the ground, laughing.

Flint was the only other one looking up.

The hand made of shadow pressed into the world again. What passed for its skin began turning into smoke.

Derek raised an arm and collapsed the portal without looking. The wave of worry consuming Tracy fluttered away as the void slammed shut. Except, the hand still hung high above them in midair, severed from the rest of its body. With nothing holding it aloft, the shadow's hand fell toward her and her friends.

"That drop almost killed us!" Derek shouted at Flint, clearly unaware of the shadow approaching. "Your selfish detour to gather some warrior was a terrible idea. Executive decision: this fool's errand is over, having broken apart in record time. Once I regain my strength, we're going home."

Winding his fist back, Derek slammed it into Flint's face.

Tracy barely registered the loud crack as she watched the sky. With Flint stunned, his slide was in free fall, burying them in sand. Above that, the shadow hand continued its fall, losing some size as it turned into smoke.

Someone's harsh shriek pierced Tracy's ear.

Tracy worked what little power she clung to in order to protect everyone. She formed a bubble of sand overhead, pulling in more sand as material to transmute her barrier into metal.

Derek followed her example without asking questions. He erected a telekinetic shield as an additional brace.

Crouching into a curled ball, Tracy sought to be as small as possible while hiding with her friends beneath her wall of sand and metal. Seconds ticked by. She lifted her head, counting herself lucky to be alive.

The next instant, blackened spires cut through their defenses, one of which sliced her forearm. Tracy screamed in pain from the razor-edged fingers, which narrowly avoided splitting her in half. Its outer layer smoked, the fumes burning her nostrils. Buried halfway into sand, the shadow dissolved steadily into the air.

Her skin burned and blistered where that thing had cut her. Blood dripped from her arm.

Tracy's senses could endure no more. She fell onto a bed of sand.

* * *

Sandpaper dragged across the top of Tracy's mouth. Opening and closing her jaw, she realized her dried tongue was the source. She heaved a sigh of relief to see no lasting evidence of the shadow hand from the void.

Derek was beside her within a moment. "You're alive. I was worried we needed to drain another water bottle to soothe your fever."

"How much have you given me? I'd swear it's been years since I had a drop."

"You inhaled a full five days of drinking water since yesterday and we used a little more to lower your temperature."

Tracy glanced through one of many openings in the dome she'd formed out of desperation with her powers. They sat in the base of a frozen sand wave about to crash. The harsh angle shielded them from most of the elements.

Their backpacks were gathered in the center of the makeshift tent. Each bottle and energy bar sat to the side in a pile along with an accompanying paper marked with what appeared to be a schedule. There were a lot of Xs on the water column.

Tracy turned on her music, pulling in power to replenish their fresh water by transmuting a fistful of sand. A stabbing itch deep within Tracy's forearm refused to be satisfied by scratching. Dried blood flaked off to reveal not so much as a scar from where the shadow had cut her. She let the power leave rather than work through the discomfort beneath her skin.

Derek glanced up, staring through the sand ceiling to where the portal was sealed.

"I know that look." Tracy shuddered. "You can't be considering going back through the void. Not now, not ever."

"Our choices are running out," Derek stated. "We've no clue where we landed. The void may be our only way to escape a slow death from heat exhaustion and dehydration."

"It's not up for debate. Something exists within the void, and it nearly killed us. It's big and powerful. Mind-numbingly so."

"I'm with Tracy on this one," Nicole added, glancing at the empty dunes. "I want a hundred percent less shadow monster in my life."

Derek chewed on his lip. "You're right, but that doesn't change the fact that we're lost."

"Then I'll create a drone to gain some altitude and find us an oasis," Tracy said.

Rachel piped up from her seat. "That's a risky gamble. Our supplies are dwindling and using abilities spends them faster."

Nicole's voice rose above their bickering. "Flint knows the way. He stayed to lead us to the village he told us about."

Derek chewed through his retort. "Flint is choosing not to speak to me right now." He glanced at the man idly sitting as far from Derek as possible.

Rachel's chilling glare toward Derek made Tracy shiver by association. "That's what you get for hitting him in the face."

"I'm not apologizing. Flint's dumb plan nearly killed us all." Derek fidgeted, looking outside. "Besides, how can he know where we are? We almost landed on a forest, which Flint said nothing about. We could be hundreds of miles away from where we planned to exit the void."

Flint's gruff voice carried, drowning all others. "I am waiting for us to regain our centers before continuing. This will be dangerous, and we need to act like adults and not brash children."

Derek let out an exasperated sigh. "Then what's your master plan, O Great Leader? Wind covers our tracks and changes the horizon.

We'll be walking in circles and each moment wasted depletes our limited reserves."

Flint gazed through the opening cut from Tracy's sand bubble. "I sense a great swell of lives close together in what must be the village of villages. We are near where we intended to land. Once rested, we will walk there. Within those walls which embrace the heavens, we shall announce ourselves with the abrasive style you men and women are so fond of." Flint's lips twisted into a mischievous smile. "My understanding is we intend to, as you called it, make a ruckus."

25

Breaking Glass

Tracy

Days of trudging across unending sands brought them to the city. They snuck inside the city walls under the cover of night. Standing on the highest tower, the illuminated homes appeared to be a fire pit filled with cooling embers. Block-shaped houses spread before Tracy in a full 360 degrees atop her perch. Flickering lights spilled from windows, halted by the monstrous city walls.

Archaic and simple compared to modern standards, Tracy failed to fathom this city's existence. "How on earth did they build this tower without it collapsing? We have to be at least a hundred feet above the ground."

Mouth agape beside her, Flint took in the surroundings.

From the top of any skyscraper in her time, honking cars or people watching videos on their phones interrupted these moments. Here, stars dotted the darkening sky in a beautiful black and blue tapestry.

Against the cool evening, Tracy felt how beet-red her face was after the long days under an unforgiving sun.

Two heads peeked over the tower's rim by her boots. Rachel and Derek rose unsteadily. Rachel studied the view. Derek kept his eyes hidden behind his hand. He had no problems using telekinesis on others to lift them to the rooftop, but when Derek's turn came to leave the ground, he refused to lift himself, his annoying fear of heights kicking in. That is, until Rachel grabbed his hand and guided him.

Rachel spoke, disturbing the peace. "Wow, there's no way ancient people built this city." Her head tilted to the side. "It's too... structured and uniform."

"We're not on a sightseeing vacation," Derek hissed, unwilling to look. "How much farther?"

Flint grasped Derek and pulled him to the flat part of the roof. Rachel came along for the ride, her hand still caught in Derek's white-knuckled grip.

When his foot touched down on the flat roof, Derek collapsed to his knees.

Rachel rubbed her hand, crushed by Derek. She checked her green fingernail polish. It was scratched beyond repair thanks to days of blowing sands.

Nicole patted Derek's back while studying the centerpiece of the roof.

The multifaceted dome took up most of the space on the roof, reminding Tracy of the eye of some gigantic bug. Whoever built it clearly wanted to impress birds of prey who roosted in this tower's nooks as few others could ever view it properly.

Flint used his knife to remove panes of the glass from within the metal supports of the dome without cracking the fine material. Warm air flowed out of the opening from the dinner below.

Tracy stared through the glass into the full chamber. A hundred feet below, armed guards lined the outer rim of the circular hall. Their lean muscles were taut and not an ounce of body fat clung to the hundreds of men and women.

They wore uniform leather vests and ankle length pants. Some had sheathed swords at their waist and others carried spears strapped to their backs. Their posture reminded Tracy of the scorpion she narrowly avoided stepping on yesterday. With its tail pulled back, it had been ready to strike had she come an inch closer.

Above every fifth guard, lit torches leaned into the center of the room. Their flames swayed, casting long shadows across the smooth walls. Tracy's breath caught. Each moving shadow was a reminder of the creature from the void and the claw which burned her flesh, yet left no mark.

Three full tables that were twenty people long formed a large U-shape. Each of those seated around the tables were like peacocks on display, dressed in vibrant rainbow fabrics to catch the eye. Their skin tones were likewise difficult to single out, ranging from onyx to pearl and every shade in between. Their hairstyles were as unique as their clothing choices with a few managing gravity-defying wraps. Several opted out of this fashion display by shaving their heads.

Guests sat on the outer side of the tables facing both an open area and the raised platform beyond.

Tracy's eyes followed the stairs to a woman and a man lounging on twin carved wood chairs. Built for giants, neither ruler occupied much of their seat. The woman, who looked old enough to be Tracy's mom, wore a green dress with an impressive neckline that plummeted to her navel.

She's pulling it off, though.

Extra fabric spread from her wrist to her shoulder, which fluttered like wings as she waved her hand idly. Gem-encrusted blades lay on either side of her waist.

The middle-aged man on the matching throne was equally decorated. He wore a vest without a clasp to expose his well-formed abs to the elements. Silver streaked his pointed beard. Puffy yellow clothes gave him the appearance of a melting golden statue.

Tracy licked her cracked lips, enviously staring at the full cup he waved about without a care.

Flint turned from the spectacle. "The man on the throne is known as the Tak and the woman is the Tol. Titles that translate roughly to 'God's Chosen.' Making them feel like children will be the quickest way to draw out our intended warrior. Ready to grab some attention?"

Derek's legs shook. "Give me a minute. It wasn't easy getting everyone up here using my powers."

Rachel kept her voice low. "Okay everyone, we need to be careful to not upset the past. We make one huge exception tonight, and then we're going back into the void to limit any further impact. Tracy, remember the plan. You're our frontwoman. We need you to be our obnoxious and bold voice. Really ramp it up."

Despite her usual bravado, fear tinged Tracy's voice. "Considering the shadow in the void, we can't go back in without the best fighter this time period can offer."

Easing his eyes over the glass dome, Derek pulled back the instant he looked down. His face scrunched, sweat appearing on his forehead.

"Sadly, instigating a fight to kidnap some warrior is our best and worst idea among a sea of terrible options."

Tracy put her headphones over her ears and turned on music from her phone. A rotten knife twisted in her stomach the moment she drew in power. She clutched the cut on her arm she knew wasn't there. Pushing past the discomfort, she molded plastic buckets from the strange material of the roof.

At first, it appeared to be a smooth yellow surface, yet upon closer investigation, the gritty texture was like concrete. Even without knowing this exact year, such a complex material shouldn't exist for thousands of years.

Reining wandering thoughts, she formed cubes of dry ice and buckets to hold them. Wisps of smoke rose over the plastic lips, awaiting the chance to show these past people the superior intellect of her present.

With an effort, Derek lifted his head to glance down at their targets. "Give me another minute and I'll be ready. I got this."

Nicole piped up. "Why not close your eyes and I'll shout when to catch us?"

"I'd rather not risk our lives so recklessly," Derek panted.

Tracy offered her phone. "Take it to steady your nerves. I have a 'We're about to kick some ass' playlist all picked out."

Derek shook his head. "Thanks, but that noise is too distracting."

"Suit yourself."

Tracy distributed the translator earpieces she'd transmuted on the long walk to this city. Flint proved useful in troubleshooting the devices she made using her powers. She had fine-tuned these since the first translator she'd transmuted when visiting the market near Flint's home.

Rachel raised her hand, waiting a moment to speak. "This. This is the exact moment someone from our present, or especially the future, must be on their way back to prevent."

Tracy stashed their backpacks in a pile. "We'll try not to disrupt time, but we *need* Flint's warrior if we want to brave the void again. That's assuming they're as powerful as he claims."

She transmuted the clothes they wore into new ones to fit their party-crashing personas while her friends downed the last swigs of bottled water to prepare for tonight.

For herself, Tracy went with an elaborate style based on what she saw below. Her blue shorts extended into loose pants. She filled concealed pockets with backup material chipped from the roof to transmute in an emergency. As it was a warm evening, she formed a yellow tank top from the shirt she had been wearing.

Derek fidgeted beneath his plain brown robe. It hid his face to give an allure of danger and mystery, or so Tracy hoped when she'd designed it. She handed him several flashlights to accessorize the dangerous wizard costume.

Hiding behind a grin, Tracy gave Rachel a bright green hat that stretched into four elongated points, each ending in tiny bells. These clanged at every turn of her hapless friend's head. The full body covering had a colored pattern divided down the middle, with one side colored orange and the other electric yellow. It was debatable whether dinner guests would see or hear her first.

"Is this really necessary?" Rachel glanced sideways at Derek for help.

"Absolutely." Derek coughed to hide his smirk. "I can't think of a better disguise while we risk altering the past and fading into nonexistence."

Turning a critical eye on Nicole, Tracy studied her as one of the primitive people might. Green sequins on her knee-length dress caught the eye.

It wasn't until Tracy formed her a freshly made guitar that Nicole spoke. "What am I supposed to do with that?"

If they took any longer, the evening's festivities would finish. "You play it." Tracy mimicked plucking strings.

"I don't know how."

"Our Nicole did." Tracy wracked her brain for an alternative. "Do you know any simple chords?"

"No. I'm not your flawless friend you keep comparing me to, but I'm a damn good singer."

"In that case, sing, and if someone gets rowdy, break the guitar over the head."

This left their last member. Flint was still dressed in Nicole's dad's yellow-and-black-striped flannel shirt, jeans, and tennis shoes. He shook his head, displaying a menacing old-man glare.

"Do not change this. I prefer this soft shirt and proper foot protection to my usual stiff skin coverings."

Arguing with Flint was futile. "Fine." Tracy gestured at the opening Flint made in the glass-windowed dome. "Shall we start this game?"

"I still don't like how we're risking changing the past," Rachel said.

"Me neither," Derek said, "but I can't think of anything better. Let's get this over with."

They all dove from the fresh evening air into the torch-lit chamber.

Blood thundered in Tracy's veins. Seconds ticked. The unmoving ground expanded in her vision as its distance closed in on her. Guards pointed up at them.

"Derek!" Nicole shouted. "Catch us!"

Derek let out a yell, which was matched by cries from startled guests.

Tracy and the rest stopped in midair several feet above the stone floor. With a sigh of relief, she surveyed the room.

Large drops of sweat leaked from Derek's forehead, chest, and arms. "I can't hold it."

They dropped the remaining distance. Tracy landed on her stomach, the buckets in her hands spilling dry ice.

Guards rushed from every side. Though none of them stood above her shoulders in height, every one of them carried deadly grimaces and looked intent on making Tracy much shorter. Metal scraped against leather as they drew swords. Spears leveled at Tracy and her friends, forming an inescapable sharp wall.

Tracy bounded upright. "Shit. Those weapons seem much more deadly up close."

The dry ice she scattered over the floor sent gas billowing about their feet. As though Tracy's modern science experiment were the spirits of the dead come to life, sounds of awe and horror came from the stunned, ancient faces filling the room.

Derek used his power to wave hovering flashlights through the air, turning the dinner into a strange rave. Most of the people who had the lights shined in their eyes fled screaming into the hall. Well-dressed dinner guests rushed to the lower stairs and formed a defensive line, brandishing their weapons to further protect the Tak and Tol. Rather than being filled with fear, the rulers looked on in curiosity at Tracy and her friends rude interruption of their meal.

While some guards slashed the floating flashlights, the rest advanced, encircling Tracy and her friends.

This is like any other band gig. Take a deep breath and make them believe in us.

Using the stone floor as material, Tracy transmuted a loudspeaker, which included a translator. Combined with her earpiece, she could now hear and speak with these people. While practicing with Flint during the trek across the desert, the hardest part was shrinking the conical shape to a size which fit her mouth. Each attempt at a translator looked like a party hat strapped over her face until she was struck with the idea to add it into a loudspeaker.

"I am Tracy, the *most* powerful alchemist in the world." Her mechanical words echoed, unrecognizable to her ears and devoid of the flourish she poured into what she said.

Rachel used her power to move fast and grab weapons from the nearest guards, tossing them aside before they had time to react. Derek raised his fists, standing back-to-back with Nicole.

That was all Tracy spared as the closest guards took another step closer. She formed and threw two potassium nitrate pellets at the guard's feet for crowd control. Her chemistry experiment reacted, making a loud flash and spewing purple smoke.

Seeing grown warriors dive to the floor was laughable, were it not for the fresh warriors who filled in the gaps. "Thank Mr. Sprog for the assist," she shouted at her friends. "Dangerous is fun."

Rachel made another pass and removed a handful of weapons from guards. "Then you must be having the night of your life."

They haven't booed me off the stage yet. This is better than my worst show. Of course, that crowd never wanted to kill me.

She gestured at Derek and spoke into the loudspeaker. "Next up, we have Derek, my wizarding companion and master of his trade."

Derek lifted a goblet from the ruler's table with his mind. It floated into Tracy's outstretched grasp. She took a victory gulp, then immediately regretted it. The stuff had a consistency of orange juice with too much pulp and a taste of stale bread. It took her most menacing grimace to cover the gag reflex.

Derek collapsed. Flashlights clattered against the ground as his power expired.

"Told you we should have waited another day to rest," Nicole hissed.

Serves Derek right.

It was his decision to push them all, claiming the sooner they antagonized the rulers, the sooner they could leave. Now they might be gone permanently from every time. Then again, they used up their supplies. They needed to act fast or integrate into this society. Both had inherent risks to the timeline.

To cover Derek's weakness, Tracy pointed at Rachel who grabbed another sword from a guard and tossed it aside. "This is our traveling jester. Her antics brought great mirth to all on our perilous journey."

Rachel went through the drum major routine while her hat's bells jangled. As far as everyone in the room knew, Tracy's band might kill them, but first, they entertained.

Rachel wove through a gap in the circle of guards, knocking weapons from a few of their hands. Little more than a blur of movement, she slowed long enough to make a show of yawning.

Pointing to Nicole, Tracy announced, "Here is our musician. Her legendary voice has marveled queens and kings and brought oceans of common people to tears."

A single note rang from Nicole's mouth, fizzling to nothing without pacifying the terrified audience. Her jaw slammed shut as her eyes pleaded to end the misery.

Tracy moved on. "Finally, allow me to introduce Aelaphus." She let the audible gasps settle. At the mention of Aelaphus's name, every unarmed person still in the room scrambled to run away. "Be still and I promise no one will come to harm."

Red coloring flushed the Tol's forehead, then it turned purple. It took a moment for calm to return her flesh to its normal shade. She addressed the room, her voice carrying to every corner.

"Welcome, *esteemed* guests. I see you felt the need to destroy our illustrious sky view. Is there anything else you care to ruin before your lives are forfeit?"

A hot iron burned somewhere inside Tracy. Here, this woman ruled in her safe and contained bird feeder of a city. Tracy imagined herself as a metaphorical wasp inside the tower, stirring up trouble.

"We were in the area and knew you would wish to dine with us. Let me make one thing clear: we are the closest thing to gods you will meet."

Sharp swords moved closer to Tracy, cutting off any route to retreat.

"Wait!" the Tak shouted. "What if we spare them to see if they possess the potential to serve?"

The Tol sighed. "That would be prudent. Imprison them."

Guards grabbed Tracy, pulling her arms behind her and binding them with thick ropes. They dragged her to the foot of the raised platform leading to the twin thrones. Though quite muscular, the people Tracy fought were normal. There was no sign of the warrior they risked their lives to find.

Too tired to fight free of the restraints, she lifted her head to gaze at the seats of power. The Tol and Tak looked down at her, dismissing Tracy as they surveyed the room, settling on Flint.

An unconscious Derek provided no resistance when a guard tossed him by Tracy's side.

The sound of a shrieking guard ripped through the room. Nicole bit down on the hand of the woman binding her in ropes. Thanks to her earpiece translator, Tracy understood the swears spat from the guard's mouth. Tracy winced at the kick Nicole received in retribution before she, too, was dropped at the foot of the stairs.

Rachel was wheezing, slowing in the wake of her fleeing powers. A guard tackled her and three more jumped on the pile to keep her still.

Flint's yell enveloped the hall. Along the wall, torched lights climbed higher, emitting red sparks. Cries of commotion rang.

Stalwart guards, seemingly carved from boulders, threw down their blades to run. In their flight, they shoved aside more regal guests.

What guards remained surrounded Flint. No one volunteered to be the first to cast their life aside and advance. Spears flew, deflected by Flint swinging his arm bindings.

Bluffing was their last means of escape. Tracy listened to her music and ignored the skin-crawling sensation writhing beneath her arm as she gathered her power. She transmuted the rope around her wrists into a loudspeaker with a translator inside to replace the one she'd dropped.

"STOP!" Tracy shouted at the warriors on the verge of adding extra holes in Flint. "I order you to hold."

A portion of the group advancing on Flint broke apart to circle Tracy.

This is like any other band gig. This is like any other band gig.

Gambling her life on a lie, Tracy addressed the Tol and Tak. "Tell your soldiers to stand down or I'll change the walls to air. Your impressive dome above will crush us together."

She forced control into her knees and arms, pushing beyond exhaustion. Tracy refused to wipe her forehead. The slightest hesitation meant death.

"However," she continued, "if you feed us and allow for safe passage, I shall reward you beyond your wildest dreams."

Grabbing a flashlight from the ground, she transmuted it into gold. For effect, she tossed it into the air. Tracy held her forearm to ease the itching sensation creeping beneath her flesh.

The woman on the throne spoke, her words lashing Tracy. "Who are you to make demands of the divine Tol and Tak, rulers of the vastest empire in the world, caretakers for the lone paradise among the ever-shifting desert, and bringers of the lush, migrating forest?

Were either of us to utter the word, our guards would flay you until no flesh remained on your broken bodies for wild beasts to pick at."

Tracy's lie failed. Lacking the energy to kill them as promised, she devoted all her effort to standing without leaning. She had to try a new tactic.

"Oh, gracious rulers," she began, adopting a saccharine tone, "your fame has spread across the world. Though powerful, we have reached our limits during our travels and seek refuge. I beseech you, spare our lives and grant us our freedom. For your generosity, I'll create weapons made of stronger material than you can imagine." Tracy held her breath. "We can even repair your gorgeous sky view."

The Tak rubbed his oily beard from base to tip. When he looked at the Tol, she flicked her wrist, rippling her winged dress.

Casting his arms wide, the Tak's voice swelled. "Great Savior be praised! These strangers are hereafter under our protection, so long as they do as promised and act with honor. Cut their bindings and revive them. Clean our hall and punish those who scurried away like mice hiding in their holes."

"Yes, my lord," came the unified response. Dozens of guards, servants, and well-dressed guests set about to perform their tasks.

The pile who wrestled Rachel to the ground released her.

Rachel was immediately at Tracy's side. "We're still alive?"

"For now."

"Care to explain how?"

"I think we got lucky."

Guards waved wooden fans to blow the colored gas from Tracy's smoke bombs into adjacent halls. They carried in fresh chairs and tables to replace those damaged in the scuffle.

The Tol raised her hand, palm facing up, gesturing to the now empty table near the base of the dais. "Please, honored guests, would you care to join our meal?"

Looking at Flint for guidance, Tracy waited for someone else to take the lead as her heart rate returned to normal. "Eat," he said. "I will watch for betrayal."

Tracy sank into the nearest seat.

Men paraded a roasted pig on a skewer, moving about the table to serve slivers of meat. The smells alone pulled Tracy closer to the meal. Flint sniffed their food before he let them eat, eventually nodding in satisfaction.

Tracy graciously snatched her share. A long, sharp stone strung to a wooden handle was left at the seat in what must be a crude dinner knife. She used this and her fingers to pull tough meat apart as though ripping a shirt. Stabbing with a two-pronged fork, the meat bits slipped from the utensil before reaching her mouth.

After her third failed attempt, Tracy grabbed the clamshell she assumed to be a spoon to eat what remained on her plate. Where these people found clamshells in a desert was of little concern compared to how it was used to get food to her face. She took no mind of the looks of disgust from the Tol or Tak while licking her fingers. Proper manners be damned.

Of course, there was water too. She emptied whole pitchers without coming up for air. The water was warm for her preferences and tasted nothing like water from the tap, but it quenched her thirst.

Nicole attempted to be dainty until hunger got the better of her. Grease dripped down her chin as she drowned the already-inhaled first course with a huge gulp of water. Rachel was in the middle of her own feeding frenzy.

Their bodies hadn't forgiven them for the starved, dehydrated days marching over the desert.

Guards trickled water into Derek's throat, stirring him awake. They spoon-fed Derek like a newborn until he drifted back to sleep.

Flint refrained from joining the meal, standing to the side as though he were Tracy's hired guard.

Tracy's eyelids drooped. Each bite was reviving, making her more formidable even as it brought her closer to a food coma.

A solid helping from some part of a pig rested on her plate. Though it made her mouth water for its savory taste, she couldn't take another bite. Her head was too heavy. She slumped forward.

Guards moved in. They took greater care this time as they lifted her face from the table.

A twinge of fear ran through Tracy at the thought of a knife slipping into her back. She made an attempt to stand and fight, though it was too much. Her eyelids closed. Within a body littered with aches, she succumbed to dulling sensations.

26

Supply Run

Tracy

Sunlight smacked Tracy awake, causing her throbbing headache to worsen. Feathers from the pillow prodded her face and the blanket irritated her skin.

Last night's dinner hung on her breath. Meat from a spit never tasted so delicious, nor had she ever eaten so much in a single sitting. It was worth the sluggish morning to have filled the empty sinkhole of her stomach. Her body still hadn't forgiven her for the strenuous trek over the desert as their supplies ran out, but last night she had made a valiant attempt to make up for the skipped meals.

She squeezed tighter beneath covers that amounted to ropes tied together. The mat was a crude cushion, though it was more comfortable than the sand she'd been sleeping on.

The room's walls sported the same solid yellow material of the tower. For all she knew, she was still there. An unglazed rectangle window let in fresh air along with the bright sun which had rudely woken her. The view offered an overlook from several floors above ground.

"About time you're awake, sleepyhead," Nicole called out.

Lounging on a lofty chair across the room, Nicole looked like a new person. What had been a curly mess of hair from days in the arid desert was tamed in a tight, red bun. Her skin was washed, leaving no trace of sandy grit. Vibrant blues and greens of her dress seemed ready to jump off her clothes. She handled the unusual attire well and looked beautiful.

Two women stood by the opening to the hallway. Tracy noted with annoyance that no door separated her room from the rest of the building. Between Flint and these people, no one in the past held a modicum of privacy.

Dressed in dull, yellow garbs, the women stared ahead. Were it not for their occasional blinks, Tracy might have mistaken them for lifelike statues.

Under a labored breath, Tracy groaned. "You're way too awake this morning."

Nicole gestured at an empty tray on top of a wooden table. "*Morning* is mostly gone. I'll order your brunch to be prepared." Nicole clapped her hands and pantomimed gestures of eating.

"As you command, my lady," said the attendants. They bowed and hustled from the room.

"I could get used to these people catering to our whims." Tracy rose from the bed of itch. "How long have I been out?"

"Half a day. Rachel is watching over Derek while he's recovering. When I got up at sunrise, Flint finally went to sleep."

"Good for him. At least I didn't sleep for too long. Last time we overextended ourselves, it took days to wake up and Derek should have died." Tracy rotated her arms, stretching sore limbs. "With last night's exertion, I feel like I went another round with the Beast."

"Is that what you call that shadow in the void?"

"As much as I wish we only had one monster to worry about, they're different. The Beast is a giant bear-looking monster that first chased us into the void."

One of the brown-eyed attendants returned with an overflowing platter. "My lady, these are dates, grapes, honey-dipped nuts, and choice flank from the finest bull."

Sugary scents lifted Tracy by her nose.

"Thank you," Nicole said. The attendants did not react to her words but left out the open doorway. Nicole nudged Tracy. "Care to make me a voice translator? Thanks to your earpiece, I understand these people, but I'm terrible at charades to get them to understand me."

Two muscular men entered carrying a copper tub. They were the largest men she encountered in this time, yet they reached no higher than her eye level.

An assembly line followed, each person wielding steaming buckets, which they dumped into the tub until it filled. One of the women who brought in the food returned, placing fine clothes at the foot of the bed.

"The Tak will arrive soon. Make yourself presentable." The woman's nose wrinkled. "Might I suggest bathing before eating?"

Tracy glanced at the hot bath. "Here, I thought the past lacked any decent comforts." She turned back to offer a retort to the woman only to find her gone.

Nicole picked at the tray of food. "It's much better than whatever torture the Tol and Tak originally planned for us party crashers."

All the attendants had left the room, giving them the impression of being alone. Tracy dropped her dirty clothing to the stone floor on the way to the tub.

Nicole turned toward a blank wall and inched to the open doorway, her face red. "Did you usually take a bath with the Nicole of your world?"

Heat rushed to Tracy's cheeks. "Not since we were toddlers, but I knew my Nicole long enough not to care. Let me get under the water and we can brainstorm how to find this warrior. The past has been oh so much fun, but we need a way to safely go back into the void. Plans A and B collapsed last night when our team passed out."

Tracy added a flowery, fragrant oil to cloud the water that was a touch too hot.

Only when the water turned murky did Nicole get comfortable on the chair. She hummed a soft song, nothing more than a series of notes from some forgotten melody. Yet with each passing tone, Tracy thought of a home to return to. The first thing she'd do when she got there was apply a clay face mask to clear her pores and watch her favorite movies back-to-back. Hot water bore into her unyielding muscles, their tension releasing.

Grasping what looked like an expensive pumice stone, she scrubbed her feet with fervor to undo damage from days of walking. "Any ideas on how to upset the Tol and Tak into sending the warrior after us?"

Nicole paused her singing to shrug.

Built-up soreness in Tracy's limbs struck, and she remembered why she'd dreaded waking.

Rachel stomped into the room, bellowing at Tracy, "Have you lost your mind?"

"Good morning to you too," Tracy replied, lowering her eyes so she didn't have to see the growing number of people in the room while she bathed.

Rachel held no such reservations about Tracy in her birthday suit. "Flint told me you promised to make shit tons of gold."

"I also promised to transmute weapons for these people." Tracy found it difficult to take a definitive stance when she was exposed in the tub. "I followed the plan to be abrasive to the Tak and Tol so they'd send an assassin after us."

"I'm missing how giving them gold and weapons will piss them off. Unless you're lying from the start and intend to cancel the deal."

"I'm not sure I can. No unstoppable warrior appeared when we attacked. We need to bide our time and gather info. That means playing the long game."

"In case the forced desert march was unclear, we need to stay in this time for as little as possible."

"You wanted to limit our interactions in the past. That's what I'm trying to do. Our first attempt almost got us killed. That was the wrong move."

"You're only saying that so you can live it up like a selfish party girl."

"Stop it." Nicole's quiet voice settled the still room.

Rachel sank onto the bed and rubbed her face. "I want to go home."

"I do too," Tracy said, her conviction in those words surprising her. She grabbed a towel to cover herself.

The same attendant appeared in the doorway. "The Tak approaches. Make haste to be ready." Finding Tracy in a towel, the woman rushed to the bed and thrust clothes into Tracy's hands.

Using a surprising influx of power following her bath, Tracy transmuted the towel's corner into a small box translator. Having learned from the previous design, this was more advanced than the speaker she'd made the night before. She applied it to her neck.

"What's your name?" Tracy asked.

The translator repeated the words in a different language.

The woman's face was a mask of confusion. "I am the Ri Ur Tol."

"Ree or toll sounds like a name."

"It is a title. Like the Tol and Tak, mine marks me as the first maid of the fifth daughter of our glorious rulers." The woman pointed to the clean clothes. "Dress quickly."

The presented robe was snug around Tracy's shoulders and cinched at her waist.

The Ri Ur Tol clicked her tongue, eyeing the full-bodied robe which stopped above Tracy's knees. "You are quite tall. This was the most suitable outfit I found."

"Not a problem." Tracy smiled. "I'll make it fit."

She spent her remaining power to transmute the robe into comforts of her modern era: thigh-length shorts, a shirt, and sandals. Not that it mattered to these people, but she wore her band's tee shirt. *Former band*, Tracy mentally corrected herself.

Trails of steam rose from droplets along her arm, carrying an itch she couldn't scratch.

The Tak's voice invaded from the hall, "Come, Alchemist. I hoped to discuss our arrangement. Is everyone decent? I am not accustomed to waiting but will offer a few more moments."

The Ri Ur Tol's eyes pleaded at Tracy, whose hair remained a sopping mess. With another hour it might be passably dry. Tracy shrugged.

"They are presentable, Your Grace," the Ri Ur Tol announced.

The man Tracy met last night entered. A pointed crown guarded the top of his head. Inscriptions and tiny gems wound about its silver surface. His wide smile covered much of his face and revealed pearly white teeth, which must glow in the dark.

She was unable to pinpoint the Tak's age based on his wrinkle-free face, but his sunken and sagging eyes led her to believe he was much older than forty.

"How soon until you do as you promised?" The Tak spoke like Tracy was a crash cymbal and he was counting the seconds until he used her to make bronze encrusted music.

Tracy looked at her two friends for inspiration in how to stall for time until their whole team was well-rested. "I require precise calculations to be certain, um... um... your highness?"

Before Tracy elaborated, the Ri Ur Tol whispered to her and gestured at the Tak, "Your Grace."

Tracy bowed deeply. "Your Grace, I must gather the ingredients and... and... and..." Tracy waved her hand above her head in a broad gesture. "I must await for the proper alignment of the full moon to fill the night's sky."

"Why do you need supplies? You turned the flying metal light into gold last night."

"Forming a sparkly stone is trivial. I can make another now, if that's all you want." Tracy added, with a performative flair, "On the other hand, if you want a significant transmutation before your eyes, then I must prepare."

"You have until this evening."

"That's too soon."

"More can be done with less. You already benefited from my hospitality. Tonight, you will join me at my banquet to fulfill your promise." The Tak's words carried barbs, each an unspoken threat to her life.

"I also need a pile of raw material to change into gold," Tracy called out.

The man turned to leave, before he added over his shoulder, "You shall have it. For your lofty claims of being better than human, I expected more. The magic you have shown is but paltry imitations of the Great Savior, may the stars guide his return."

Tracy's breath caught. "Who is this Great Savior?" she asked the Tak, but he didn't answer. "What of the ingredients, um, Your Grace?"

This time, the Tak responded. "My daughter shall take you soon."

A snapping sound reached Tracy's ears. The walls played tricks to make her believe it came from within the room and not the Tak. She was about to ask the Ri Ur Tol if the Tak was always this full of himself but found only Nicole and Rachel.

* * *

In less than an hour, Tracy regrouped with her friends. Nicole and Rachel watched over a sleeping Derek. Preferring someone born in this era join her, Tracy woke Flint. He agreed to join her without complaint.

Attendants approached Tracy's room, where she and Flint waited. A stunning woman led the ensemble. Her hair was darker than a raven and held together by a band of emerald beads, which cascaded down her back. She kept her left arm bare, while her right was fully concealed beneath the large fanning sleeve of a navy-blue dress.

She pointed at the remains of Tracy's lunch. Men and women leaped to do her bidding, removing the trays of leftovers from sight. While the Tol and Tak felt like actors wearing costumes, the woman in front of Tracy carried the weight of the room with her presence.

Her green-painted lips pressed to a flat line. "Greetings. I am the Ur Tol, the fifth eldest daughter of the mighty Tol and Tak. Where do you wish to go within our city?" Her words were smooth and pleasing to Tracy's ear, even as the Ur Tol regarded Tracy as one might evaluate livestock.

Tracy shuddered, more exposed than when she was naked in front of Nicole and Rachel. "Your Grace, we require herbs so that I can create what I promised."

"Follow me." The Ur Tol spun on her heels in one fluid motion.

Attendants followed in the Ur Tol's shadow with the Ri Ur Tol being the last of the entourage. As she hurried by, the Ri Ur Tol uttered in a single breath, "Keep up. The Ur Tol does not tolerate stragglers."

Tracy bit her lip to stop from voicing her thoughts and followed the trail of the Ur Tol's attendants. Flint followed Tracy wordlessly, his eyes regarding each person while his expression betrayed none of his thoughts.

Rectangular window openings offered glimpses of the city at regular intervals along the corridor. High outer walls loomed from every vantage point. Small, block-shaped buildings occupied the space between here and the walls. Tracy guessed they were this time's equivalent of row houses. They appeared to be dug into the earth, rather than raised above it.

Larger blocks, likely warehouses used to stockpile food or weapons, scattered about the city in uniform patterns. Much like Washington, D.C., Tracy saw no high rises. Unlike D.C., this city lacked architectural beauty and personality in the form of museums or monuments.

Descending to the entrance, guards strained and pulled open the first doors Tracy saw in this palace. At over ten feet, the wooden doors slid open to flood the dim entrance hall in light, silhouetting the Ur Tol as she left.

Tracy followed the Ur Tol outside, raising a hand to shield her eyes from the scalding sun. Although the thermometer-topping temperature sapped liquid from Tracy's mouth, the dry heat was more comfortable than the soupy humid summers of home.

From the small plateau where she stood, the long avenue stretched to the solid gate embedded into the city walls. The prized tower with the glass ball on top sparkled above the building behind her.

"How could these people have made this with such simple tools?"

"Explain," commanded Tracy's guide.

Tracy put on her most charming personality to learn more about this city. "What I meant to say, Your Grace, is I wasn't aware sand could hold its form like your marvelous tower."

The Ur Tol sniffed. "Prior to my birth our Great Savior raised this home from the desert as a gift to my worthy parents. Our people had nothing to do with its formation."

Tracy salivated. Capturing this Great Savior meant they could leave the past. Last night's celebration was fun, but she missed running water and the Internet.

"Where is the Great Savior?"

The Ur Tol's face remained neutral, but Tracy sensed the woman's desire to roll her eyes. "He who was chosen by the gods has continued his wandering journey."

The Ur Tol moved them past highways of wooden planks connected to the main road by way of the rooftops. Rope ladders led to lowered entrances of basement homes, which were cut to be slightly larger than those resting on top of them. These solid cubes cut into the ground were no larger than Tracy's kitchen.

Two women left the nearest lower house, climbing a rope ladder to join street traffic. They moved hand-in-hand, whispering too closely to notice Tracy and the rest. Their blueberry-colored loose pants and vests seemed more accommodating in the heat than Tracy's cotton shirt.

Bronzed skin was in abundance across those she passed, yet there were too many other varieties to track. Men and women with brown skin moved alongside those with pale complexions or painful lobster-red sunburns. They all followed an invisible maestro. Personal space was wishful thinking thanks to the sheer number of people, but no one bumped into anyone.

Those they passed lowered their heads in reverence for the Ur Tol. Once she passed, all eyes lifted to take in Tracy, the giant in their midst. They stared as if they wanted to pet her like she was a damn dog. Guards and attendants formed a buffer to keep the crowd at bay.

Swelling voices rushed from the earpiece until individual words were lost amid the cacophony.

Flint fumbled with the bindings wrapped around his hands and looked around nervously. "Why do so many live so close together?"

"Seems like a city to me," Tracy said, taking in the sights. "Nicole lives in the outskirts of a city and you were fine there."

Flint's stiff body resembled Tracy at her band's first performance. "Over seasons upon seasons, people advanced to achieve your world. This is my time, and this place... defies all I know."

Repeated clanging sounds caught Tracy's ears. Though the day's heat was getting to her, she got closer to the open flames to study the blacksmith's work. A large vat of orange molten metal was poured into a triangular mold. Stocky male and female bodybuilders swung hammers into the cooling metal wedge.

Flint's eyebrows raised at the formation of a farmer's plow; his speechless mouth hung open.

The Ur Tol was not one to let him admire the smithy in peace. "Ah. You see what my family has bestowed. My mother, the Tol, was the one who first shared the method of forging metal into all manner of shapes to add to the conveniences of life. My eldest sister has a nose for discovering buried stone deposits in the earth to use in the forging."

Tracy pushed Flint on lest she pass out from the radiating heat of the fires.

She hid from the brunt of the sun's wrath beneath stretched cloths of all colors that were held together by a network of poles. The setup reminded her of the market Flint's people used. Merchants sat in the shade next to woven baskets overflowing with more foods than Tracy could recognize.

Pungent smoking meats caused her stomach to grumble. At the same time, the stale odor of bodies permeating the air made her gag. They smelled as desperate for showers as Flint's people. Maybe she should alter the Tak's deal to make deodorant instead of gold and weapons. Her height, a head above most in the market, mercifully offered a breath of fresh air.

They passed a stall with water buckets containing sea snails, crabs, and fish. Tracy steered clear, having little faith in seafood found in a desert, especially in an age without refrigeration. The locals didn't share her opinion.

Small seashells switched hands with merchants as often as any other. Tracy glimpsed the shells used for payment. Their surfaces were round and smooth on the top with a slit opening on the bottom which looked like a narrow, toothy smile.

Glancing around the streets, one thing was missing compared to every other city she visited. "Where are your beggars," she asked the Ur Tol, adding, "Your Grace?"

"I do not know this word, beggar."

"Someone asking for food or money who may not have means of their own."

The Ur Tol's lip curled as though biting into a rotten apple. "We take care of all our people no matter the hardship in their lives."

"Try our fresh pomegranates," a skinny kid shouted at Tracy. There wasn't a hint of facial hair on him and he wore only loose-fitting pants. "They traveled across the sea to delight your every taste!"

The hunched woman at the next basket pinched her nose. "He grows that garbage on the other side of the wall. Now, if my lady cares for a treat, I suggest these luscious plums."

"Find what you must to perform your magic," the Ur Tol said, jangling her metal bracelets. "We did not journey to this market for you to gaze at our offerings."

Moving with fake purpose, Tracy walked to a merchant's basket overflowing with spices. The woman, who had to be Tracy's age, stopped fanning herself and smiled. Tracy pointed to objects at random to purchase based on how their smells tickled her nose. The merchant dumped everything into clay cups.

Tracy grabbed the cups and stepped back to leave. The woman cleared her throat and kept her solid grip on the cups. "Five," she barked, the first words she said to Tracy.

Thinking fast, Tracy turned on her music from her phone. The headphones caught the merchant's attention, yet she said nothing. Tracy transmuted seashells from the inner lining of her shorts to match what money she glimpsed. The merchant accepted them with a nod.

Seeing no alarm raised, Tracy assumed she paid the right amount and left. On the way to her next random purchase, Flint tapped her shoulder. "What is the purpose of the shells you gave to the trader?"

The Ur Tol clicked her tongue. "I forget how simple people are outside these walls."

Tracy clanked more created shells in her hand together. "We give money for goods. How do you buy food you need?"

"You were there when we bartered for food." Flint craned his neck, his eyes following a merchant shuffling shells in a bag tied to his hip. The red-faced merchant patted his damp forehead with a cloth.

"Seems confusing to keep track of debts over a long time," said Tracy.

Flint shook his head. "Exchanging trinkets is equally confusing. I prefer a direct approach. Why does no one make their own shells to use or harvest more?"

Tracy held an index finger over her lips. "I did. Plus, I assume these are rare animals, so the number of shells is limited."

She returned to making an assortment of useless buys with Flint in tow. As the sun dropped to rest on the city walls, Tracy approached her guide. "Your Grace, where do these goods come from?"

"Many lush gardens are within sight from our walls," said the Ur Tol. "Normally, those gardens use water from a nearby lake. As it is the dry season, we pull water from deep underground until the lake refills. Our fleet is also docked in the port a day's travel from here which bring goods from the sea."

Wiping sweat from her face, Tracy noticed the Ur Tol's hair was not pressed to her forehead from sweat and no stains seeped through her clothes.

"Aren't you hot?"

The Ur Tol gazed above them, as if considering the sun for the first time. "Yes."

"Then how are you not dripping with sweat?"

"By the will of our stars, this day is like the prior day. I tolerated it then and do so now."

Tracy waved a merchant away. Since the Ur Tol was speaking, albeit with an arrogant air, this was the opportunity to wring her for information.

"Truly, this city is incredible. Care to tell me more about the one who made it? Will the Great Savior end his wandering to join us tonight?"

The Ur Tol placed her hands on her hips. "If you are willing to ask about our history, I can safely assume you have prepared for your task. The palace and your magic beckon."

The Ur Tol's voice stirred the attendants around them to walk back to the palace.

"Wait," Tracy pleaded. "You never answered my question."

The Ur Tol sighed. "Ask your sorcerer to know more of his father's handiwork."

Flint stopped walking. Blood dropped from between his clenched fists, his fingernails digging into palms. "Aesbraack built this city?"

A nudge at the back of her thoughts called to Tracy. From its depth came a sense of familiarity at the name. It was going to bug her all day.

"Our *Great Savior*," hissed the Ri Ur Tol. "Carry his name with the respect it deserves."

The Ur Tol and her guards were halfway up the hill, leaving Tracy and Flint.

Tracy needed to act fast. "Any chance your father was the warrior we've been after?"

"No," Flint spat. "My father, my master, is the one I intended the warrior to kill."

The brave face Tracy put on for the benefit of everyone else fell. She slumped in the middle of the street. People walked around her, giving her a wide berth.

In her mind, she saw the shadow monster waiting beyond the thin veil leading to the void. She was never returning home. "This Great Savior was a bust, and we're no closer to finding your warrior."

Flint collected himself, anger receding into some crevice inside. "Do not discourage. Magic gathered at the banquet last night. In the commotion, I could not tell where it came from, but I have faith the one I seek was present."

"Why didn't they show up to stop us?"

"I would not have. We were no threat, despite our boasts. Our numbers dwindled too fast, and we hamstrung ourselves by creating a deception with no substance."

"Now you tell me. Thanks."

"Come. There will be plenty of time this evening to renew our search once you purchase our lives with shiny rocks and pointy sticks."

* * *

After a day of walking to the far end of the city and back, Tracy expected her friends to be as productive. What she found was one shirtless Derek doing push-ups, one Nicole passed out in a chair, and one Rachel missing.

"What the hell?" Tracy shouted at her friends. "How can Nicole be sleeping? We have too much strategizing to do."

"She was singing," Derek said, not stopping his push-ups. "That woke me up, and I felt *alive*. Then, she curled into that ball and went to sleep."

"Think it's related to powers stuff? What if she revived you, which made her pass out?"

Derek scrunched his face in thought. "Anything's possible."

A day spent in the heat left its mark on Tracy's skin and muscles. She sat on the bed and rubbed her feet. "My best lead on Flint's warrior turned out to be Flint's dad. According to Flint, he doesn't fit the build, so I'm out of ideas."

Holding the push-up position, the scar on Derek's shoulder stretched. The stitches had fallen out days ago in their long walk over the desert, which Rachel collected and stored so they left nothing behind.

"We'll think of something," he said. "We have time while Rachel is performing recon and finding stairs to retrieve our backpacks on the tower's roof."

"Good to know someone was useful while I was out. The strange thing is Flint's dad's name is Aesbraack. I swear it sounds familiar. Do you recognize it from a history book?"

"I guess so." Derek hopped to his feet, careful to avoid the many empty bowls of food scattered over the floor. "Look on the bright side: my power has rekindled. I'll be ready to cut a hole in the universe once we find Flint's warrior."

About that. Water pressure welled up behind Tracy's eyes while telling him the deal she made with the Tak.

Derek's voice wasn't tinged with anger or annoyance. "You did what you had to, and your desperate ploy bought us another day."

"Thanks. Tell that to Rachel. Do I need to be next-level obnoxious again tonight?"

"It seems the fastest way to get the assassin to attack us."

Tracy palmed her forehead, and then lightly nudged the unconscious Nicole awake. "Wake up, sleepyhead."

With a stiffness of muscles long unused, Nicole stretched her arms and legs. A yawn emerged. She wobbled and grabbed the seat for support.

"When did I run a marathon?"

Tracy paced about the room, dreading what was to come. "I could use a nap, too, after walking halfway across the city and back. Too bad I can't rest because I have to prepare for tonight. You both get ready. This will be the most important show of our lives."

27

Honored Guests

Tracy

Tracy met her friends in the hallway outside their rooms wearing the newest style of the Wayfield Clothing Line, trademark pending. The short dress she created was in a color these primitives dreamed of: purple. Thanks to the modern marvel of pockets she added to her dress, the other dinner guests were about to get a jump-start on their fashion sense. She topped her attire off with a golden hairband.

Tracy formed full translators for her friends and attached them to their necks.

Men and women in flowing robes rushed them along torch-lit hallways. Shadows writhed between the lights set along the walls. Tracy stopped below each torch to spend as much time in the light and far from the shadows. Even normal shadows reminded her of the monster in the void.

Lavish rugs hung on the walls. They depicted glorious battles of the Tol and Tak leading small bands against significantly larger armies. Each decoration must have taken skilled hands months, or even years, to weave.

Thirty seconds tops for me to transmute copies of these.

Flint brushed the fabric with his fingertips, feeling the intricacies of the woven decorations.

"Come on," Tracy said, to return Flint's attentions to the important evening. She raced into the bright main chamber, outpacing their guides, and bursting into the open dining hall.

She stood exposed to a room full of judgmental stares. There were no offers of greeting or the slightest of head nods.

Thousands of miles and years of travel and I'm back in a high school lunchroom.

Many of those already seated had large brown eyes, prominent cheekbones, and damn near flawless amber skin, marking them as branches of the Tol and Tak family tree.

Unlike the village they'd visited with Flint, no warts marred the dinner guest's faces. They looked like touched up images without the benefit of a makeup kit.

Those who didn't resemble the rulers dressed in finely spun clothes and carried sheathed short swords. Some were short, some tall. However, they shared one common trait: muscles. Uncovered arms and legs, even on older men and women, displayed honed muscles. They weren't ballooned bodies sported by those at the beach; these people's muscles carried strength from years of labor.

Her friends appeared at her side, finally catching up after Tracy's eager sprint to start the evening. She helped herself to the empty table closest to the door. Her friends followed her example. Two long, filled tables separated them from the dais upon which the Tol and Tak lorded over those present, leaving an empty space in the middle of the room.

Trailing in a line, more people filed in, each carrying a stone that looked like compressed sand and was the rough size and shape of an average brick. Building level upon level, they laid these between the tables and the dais.

Any consideration for the bricks was gone the moment platters of food entered. Attendants set roasted birds at the ends of each table, their carcasses surrounded by honey-dipped nuts.

No longer the starving excuse of a human from last night, Tracy refused to use her hands as shovels, and instead displayed her best attempt at table manners. Precise movements kept the meat on her two-pronged wooden fork. The predecessor to chicken tasted familiar enough.

With each bite, more attendants entered, putting down new stones, building a narrower level upon the base set in the room's center. A worming suspicion crept inside her, detracting flavor from an otherwise enjoyable meal.

General table manners and hand-eye coordination varied among her friends. Rachel and Nicole managed to eat without making a scene. Derek broke his second clamshell spoon. A woman draped in a thin cloth brought a replacement while shaking her head at him.

Flint was hopeless. He was clumsy with his spoon and splashed broth onto the table. Somehow, he was worse with the fork he clenched in his fist. He used it to stab food as though he meant to kill his meal again. Figs and meat flew from his plate, landing on the floor. Thankfully, he had the decency not to eat those morsels.

An attendant in the center of the room stretched to place the last stone on the outer edge of the top level. This stone assembly reached a head taller and twice as wide as a person.

Horns blared in deafening tones. Tracy dropped her fork in surprise. "Can't I get one solid meal in peace today?"

The Tol raised her clay cup above her head and addressed all within the hall. "Welcome, family, friends, and other guests. Praise our Great Savior for our bountiful meal."

She took a long swig and extended the cup to arm's-length. Spilling what remained of her deep reddish drink onto her raised platform, she called out, "For Aesbraack's return."

Everyone else in attendance, except Tracy and her friends, mirrored their host by taking a drink and shouting with a single voice, "For Aesbraack's return."

Flint scowled, muttering curses at the worship of his father.

The Tol lifted her hand and the audience fell into silence as she gestured to the Tak.

The Tak stood, unleashing his booming voice. "Behold, as our guests from afar turn these stone blocks into gold and weapons, or they are put to death."

Rising from the table nearest the dais, the Ur Tol and an equally fantastic male specimen approached Tracy in her seat. He wore a red threaded vest which opened in the front to reveal his bare chest and stomach. Calling it a six-pack did little justice to the taut muscles Tracy wanted to flick. She assumed the man must never eat since his juicy biceps held form without flexing.

The man bowed to Tracy. "I am the Ba Tak, eldest of my father's sons."

Next to him, the Ur Tol brandished two long blades at her hip. She was no longer the poised royal escorting Tracy through the city but a potential executioner. "We are here to ensure you do not run."

Tracy glided between the Ur Tol and Ba Tak toward the amassed stones. Up close, the Ba Tak was impressive as he was the one man in the room who was close to matching her height.

He spoke from the side of his mouth. "I heard you spent the day with my little sister. I apologize. She tends to be grains of wet sand stuck in one's ears."

"I enjoyed her company."

The Ba Tak halted in front of the stones. "I'm disappointed to have missed your entrance last evening. My life-mate tells me it was impressive how you held my father and our guards at bay. Show us your magic." The Ba Tak tapped the stones and then stepped away to give Tracy space.

More than a few guards drew their swords, staring at her across the still hall.

"Very well." Tracy faked a yawn, hoping no one noticed her voice quake.

Tracy placed her headphones over her ears and let music flow. Classic rock steadied her fluttering heart, and her attention jumped solely to the literal rocks that metaphorically crushed her future.

She lightly touched the plain stones. She transmuted them into a single, solid block. As a byproduct of her powers, this was smaller than its original size. Mild, yellowish hues appeared close to golden on the outer surface, and she transmuted the inner layers of stone into a different substance. Uncertain claps arose from her captive audience.

Tracy swallowed, feeling the press of blood moving in her ears. Holding her breath, she hoped the deception of creating a pile of fake gold went unnoticed. Her life back home and this place's future were too precious to risk giving this ruling family a mountain of gold.

"There," Tracy said, too nervous to breathe. She scratched at her itching forearm and took a seat on the open floor.

The Tak smiled genuinely, his eyes alight. He clapped his hands together and raced down the steps, outpacing guards. "Excellent. Most excellent. This exceeds every expectation and then some."

The Tak withdrew a shiny knife from his inner robes and scraped it against the corner of Tracy's creation. Greenish-black powder of fool's gold sprinkled the floor.

Well, shit.

The Tak sighed. His smile wide enough for two people instantly faded. "This is not the gold we agreed upon. Kill them."

In a last-ditch hope, Tracy looked around for some hidden warrior to rush in and kill her. That would have made this act worth the risk. She saw only guards closing in.

Stall for time. Stall for time.

"Wait." Tracy threw up her hands. "I wanted to ensure I didn't waste my gifts. You passed my test. I will uphold the bargain."

Before anyone moved, Tracy slapped the mound of gilded stones. For a split second, the material transformed into what seemed like chocolate on a bright summer day, a shimmering liquid ready to be sculpted by her masterful hands. The liquid rippled over her feet, rising into a shining mass of pure gold. She snatched the knife from the Tak's fingers and rubbed it against the side of the table-sized block. Yellowish gold powder fell.

"Now's a good opportunity for applause!" Tracy let the knife drop and clatter to the floor. Everyone in the room was too stunned to speak.

The Tak patted the golden block. "How do I know this isn't a thin outer layer to cover more deception?"

Tracy appeased the suspicious man, transmuting the single cube into thousands of smaller bars no longer than her hand. "Cut these open, if you want. I've done my part."

The Tak faced the Tol seated above on her throne. "What do you think?"

The Tol's eyes shifted from Tracy to the mound of gold bars. "We are still owed weapons."

Tracy's heart beat at a feverish tempo, yet she refused to breathe, lest it shatter the moment and doom her and her friends.

The entire kingdom fell silent as the Tol passed judgment. "Yet for tonight, your offering will suffice. You and your companions shall have freedom to go where you want in our kingdom."

Tracy sank against the bars of gold she transmuted, using them to hold herself somewhat upright as feeling returned to her legs.

The Tak's face split into a wide smile. He grabbed a gold bar as though he was a bird of prey and it was his next meal. "When will you create my weapons?"

"Tonight, I'm celebrating our deal. Your weapons can wait for tomorrow."

The Tak flicked his hand, allowing Tracy to take her seat. "I noticed you used no supplies obtained from the market. Do not lie to me again when you uphold your full side of the bargain."

He sauntered up the stairs to his cushioned throne, handing the golden block to the Tol for her to inspect.

An attendant poured what smelled like wine into each of the clay cups at Tracy's table. She snatched the large jug from the attendant's hands. The body-builder-type resisted but gave in under her stern glare. She drank in her victory.

The sweet wine lacked obvious fruit flavorings, though she was no connoisseur. It had little in common with the $2, or on the rare occasion $5, bottles she usually got her hands on. There was a bitter aftertaste she couldn't describe as anything other than gross.

The attendant's legs shook as he sprinted to the kitchen to replace the drink before a noble gained so much as a parched throat.

Flint eyed his dark red drink, dabbing a finger in it. He raised the clay cup to his eye and swallowed a sip. His eyebrows jumped. "What is this?"

"A decent drink," Tracy said.

"I see it is a drink. What is it?"

"Have you never had wine before?"

Flint shook his head.

"Drink up then."

He eyed the liquid and shook his head, pushing the cup aside.

Between bites, Tracy looked for anyone to challenge to a drinking game like Flip Cup. No one seemed ready for modern era fun. They were content to eat, talking around Tracy and her friends. Everyone was enjoying the meal except the Ba Tak, who rapped his sword against the gold blocks.

Derek leaned in close to Tracy's ear. "I didn't see anyone except the guards react to your stunt with the fake gold."

Tracy took another bite of meat and whispered, "Are we sure the warrior is here?"

"According to Flint, considerable power gathered in this room when you lied. You bought us another day. We'll come up with a plan tomorrow. Plus, now we need a separate one to destroy all that gold you made."

Tracy stared at the Ba Tak over her cup. "Those are problems for tomorrow."

Derek nudged Tracy. "Fine. Are you about to make a move on the Tak's heir? If it helps, you'll be getting us back on the bad side of the Tak and Tol."

"He is delicious looking. Don't you want to maintain the space-time continuum crap?"

"I do, but my bigger concern is surviving a return trip into the void, which means annoying these rulers. Besides, your mouth is hanging open at the sight of him."

"I'm not a homewrecker and he has a partner or life-mate or whatever they call it." Peeling her eyes from the Ba Tak, Tracy stole a glance at a more interesting challenge. "Although, have you seen the Ur Tol? She qualifies as a princess, right?"

"That will get us on the Tak's and Tol's bad side."

Tracy glared at Derek. "Not everyone is so heteronormative."

Derek rubbed his forehead. "That's not what I meant. I've watched you flirt, and I'm already cringing for what's about to take place."

"You wish you could flirt like me."

Tracy gulped what remained of her drink, shuddering at the bitter hints coating her mouth. Through swishing vision in the tilting room, she admired her handiwork, the golden transmutations she had paid in exchange for her and her friends' lives.

The room's golden centerpiece was lifted bar by bar onto a cart. It would take hours to move every piece. Someone more sober than her better be tracking where the gold was being moved to, so she could destroy it when they left. Otherwise, her past was bound to shift like the wobbly floor.

Tracy walked past the guards loading the blocks, heading for the Ur Tol with her ornate robes.

Derek fell in step at Tracy's side. He didn't have to say it. He was there to ensure Tracy left this meal alive.

Tracy checked her other friends. Nicole found the courage in inebriation to get over her stage fright and showcase her singing talents with the top hits. Even without the aid of background music, she turned the room into the best karaoke bar for the next millennia.

Rachel dragged people in to sing and dance along with the refrains. Flint tracked the members of their group as they split up.

Tracy squished into a seat between the Ur Tol and some other member of the Tol's litter. "Come here often?" Tracy asked the Ur Tol.

"I live here. I thought that was obvious."

Tracy bristled and swallowed the lump in her throat. "Where I'm from, that's a conversation starter. Excuse me for wanting to know more about you."

The Ur Tol nodded. "You are excused."

Tracy used every ounce of strength to not chew out this stuck-up Ur Tol. "Care to show me more of your city tomorrow?"

The Ur Tol frowned at Tracy. The woman locked eyes with those on the thrones where an invisible conversation passed between mother, father, and daughter. After a minute, she spoke.

"You earned praise this evening for creating the gold."

Tracy waved for more wine, pouring a cup for the Ur Tol and then herself. It tasted sweeter than the wine served at the rejects table where her friends sat.

Derek remained standing next to the Ur Tol's attendant, the Ri Ur Tol, and struck up a conversation with her. Perhaps there was hope for him, though the Ri Ur Tol's eyes never strayed from Tracy's direction, or more specifically, the Ur Tol.

Tracy let more words fall from her mouth. "What are the impressive sights to explore in this city if we were to leave the following day?"

Peering down the length of her pointed nose, the Ur Tol gestured behind her. "Perhaps you will be better entertained by another guide."

Four stunning bodies stepped forward, two men and two women. Thinly woven fabric draped over them, providing a bare minimum amount of cover. They were each inviting. Such obvious ploys held little sway over Tracy.

"Y'know, we survived countless near-death experiences in finding your illustrious city. Only a ruler knows it well enough to make our sacrifice worthwhile."

"Then I shall do as asked." Each syllable from the Ur Tol's lips was like pulling teeth without anesthesia. Meager responses required monumental effort to twist and yank.

Tracy sought inspiration from the people at her table to crack the Ur Tol's shell. Like their matriarchal ruler, no drops of wine spilled outside these people's lips. Disgust curdled in Tracy's stomach when she glanced back at her sloppy friends. Flint slurped vegetable soup, and the sound grated against her ears.

The Ur Tol offered a filled cup. "Here, my lady. Have a drink."

Mind reeling against the spins, Tracy accepted. It tasted different from the good wine she'd already tried at this table, more bitter than sweet.

They must know someone snuck up from the cheap seats to join the Ur Tol.

Some story Tracy told about her home made the Ur Tol smile and then blush. Obviously, Tracy's charms didn't take full effect until she lost all sense of sobriety. Damned if she knew what words she used once they left her lips.

Tracy glanced around the hall and was shocked to find how few people were left.

Dessert arrived. Squishy grapes introduced new tastes that enlivened her dulled tongue. In the background, an ensemble sung of the Tol and Tak's splendor. The tune sounded broken, blaring in and out of her eardrums.

A shadow appeared over Tracy. *The void monster followed me here!* Her veins froze, halting all the blood they carried.

"Father!" exclaimed the Ur Tol.

Tracy released her breath. *I'm safe.* "Ello ore mabestry." Her mouth gave up on forming correct words, forcing the translator to overwork itself.

Too far gone to listen, she stared at the Tak's moving lips. His voice drilled into Tracy's skull without bothering her mind over its meaning. Until shrouded thoughts caught two words: *family alliance.*

Tracy's mouthful of wine sprayed across the table. "That sounds like marriage to me."

Smiling, the Tak clasped one of his muscled hands on Tracy's shoulder. For a split moment, the room stopped rotating. It collapsed on her with the building's full weight.

The Tak's face was lit with an unquenchable enjoyment. "Aesbraack be praised. What better way to reward you for improving our city with magic than by offering my son? Ca Tak will make a fine choice and you cannot be his elder by more than three harvests."

For all she knew, Tracy stumbled into becoming her own great-great-and-a-few-more-greats-grandmother. The only son of the Tak she cared about was otherwise unavailable. Not to mention she had no interest in marrying anyone, let alone some kid who was a freshman's age. Tracy met the Ur Tol's eyes.

In a voice equal parts wine and sarcasm, Tracy asked, "What about one of your daughters?"

The Tak's smile didn't lessen by a hair. He looked to the Tol sitting on her throne. She offered a slight nod. The Tak's voice echoed between Tracy's ears.

"If you wish. Your gift this evening will forever provide drinking water to all our people."

"Don't get too excited," came the subtle voice of reason that was the Tol. "We know nothing of her people's customs." Her regal face turned from the Tak to Tracy. "Be sure to let us know of your culture so we may accommodate you as befits your future place in our society."

The infernal room wouldn't stop its off-kilter spin. Rather, it moved faster.

She'd intended to insult the rulers, not become their daughter-in-law.

Maybe if I break off the engagement, we'll piss off the Tol and Tak to earn a shortcut to finding the warrior.

Unable to hold herself together, Tracy dumped the contents of her personal wine jug on the floor and threw up into it. A deep, bellowing laugh filled her ears.

Someone clapped her on the back, then lifted her by the under-arms. Her feet floated above the ground. She was being carried to sleep it off and think over her poor decisions like a child sent to her room.

In the darkening hallway, shadows swirled about the men carrying her. She tried to study their faces. The rotating room wouldn't let her.

From nowhere, the Ri Ur Tol appeared, snapping her fingers without moving her hands. "Place her with the others for their last night together."

28

Snapping

Tracy

The room shifted. Moonlight filtered in from the open window revealing Tracy's palace bedroom. She struggled to lift her head. Her fingers refused to wiggle and weak stomach muscles failed to pull her upright. Only her eyes moved.

Her mouth tasted like regret. This was no normal hangover. Drugs prevented her limbs from working.

Other forms littered the floor. Four bodies, most likely her friends, had been deposited on the stone floor. Someone stood and moved to the corner, grabbing food from a leftover tray. She heard soft snaps that brought her attention to the other side of the bedroom.

A cloaked figure stood where none had been before.

Rachel's unmistakable curse carried across the room as she tripped over a stool while foraging for a snack.

Tracy struggled to scream in warning. Nothing left her throat.

Quicker than her eyes followed, the figure appeared behind Rachel and struck her in the back of the head. The cloaked figure caught Rachel's falling body before she hit the ground, lowering her silently.

The figure was difficult to track. They moved erratically, disappearing and reappearing, each time accompanied by a snapping noise.

Snap. They were in the shadows along the wall. *Snap.* They were at the foot of Tracy's bed. *Snap.* They stood at Tracy's side; face hidden in the dim light.

Chilling sweat formed along Tracy's arms.

Her body wanted to shiver. She needed to move.

Quickening, shallow breaths sucked in air.

The figure leaned over Tracy. Hushed breath warmed over Tracy's cheek.

"My Ur Tol's father ordered me to make you the lone survivor. He wants you to magic away our problems. I shall ignore him this once and suffer his wrath. You must die for dishonoring my mistress. One such as yourself should have asked for the honor to sit beside her. Instead, you pushed into a seat you did not deserve. Every word after that moment was a blight. My mistress wishes no lover and forcing one on her is a corruption of her will."

The figure held a blade clenched in a quivering hand over Tracy's motionless body. "I know you hear me," the figure said. "The effects of my drug were chosen to leave you in this condition. Your disrespect is unforgivable."

Tracy mentally screamed at her rigid limbs, but she failed to utter real sounds. In trying to gather power, nothing formed. This was a front-row seat to her own death.

The figure swung a blade at Tracy's throat. They were about to sever her neck when the blade struck an invisible wall.

The ricocheting blade rang out. The would-be assassin's head darted from side-to-side, seeking the unknown presence protecting Tracy.

The figure made a wild stab for Tracy's flesh, yet the invisible wall held. Their arm jerked at an uncomfortable angle and pinned to their back without a whimper. The figure's free hand reached toward their belt. A knife appeared from hidden folds of cloth and flew at Tracy's heart. The blade rebounded across the room. The failed assassin's free arm was pulled tight against their covered body.

Much like a flashlight with loose batteries, the thrashing body flickered, held in place by their wrists and accompanied by snapping sounds. A high-pitched growl escaped from the failed assassin's lips. In a desperate attempt, they flailed their legs to kick Tracy. These likewise struck a hard, invisible surface. The figure slumped to the ground, accepting defeat.

Torches flared to reveal Tracy's friends slumbering forms and the assassin. Flint was the first one up on his feet, staring down at the slim, cloaked figure. Desperate to break free, the cloaked figure squirmed.

"Thanks for the lights, Flint," Derek said.

Beneath the assassin's cloth mask, a woman's voice shouted, "Release me from your star-spurned magic!"

Rachel stumbled to her feet, rubbing the back of her head.

"Are you okay?" Derek asked Rachel, combing through her hair to inspect the damage. "What happened to pretending to sleep until Flint's warrior made his move."

"I got tired of waiting for them to attack. Besides, I wanted a snack. I think I'm fine."

Flint placed a hand over Tracy's eyes, and her vision cleared. "I have purified your blood of the poison and removed much of the wine muddling your thoughts."

Derek was at Tracy's side before she had adjusted to being able to move again. "You doing okay, Tracy?"

Sensation returned to Tracy's limbs from Flint's powers like tiny needles pressed into her flesh. She wiggled her toes and slowly moved about until the pain subsided.

"Thanks for waiting until the last millisecond to save me, jerk face."

"You were bait to spring the trap," Derek replied. "Flint warned us they drugged our drinks and revived me before I joined you at the Tak's family table. I faked collapsing when you did so they would take us together."

Tracy hid none of her malice. "Now I know how a worm dangling on a fishing hook feels."

Derek shrugged. "I couldn't let Flint use his magic on you without being obvious, so we resolved to watch and protect you."

"What if they didn't throw us all in this room?"

Offering his hand, Derek supported Tracy's weight. "The same thing we always do, improvise a new poorly constructed plan."

Nicole wiped dried grease from her cheek. "I played the part best, falling face-first into my meal."

"Let's find out who joined the growing list of those wanting to kill me." Dizziness subsiding, Tracy removed the mask of the assassin held in place by Derek's power.

The Ri Ur Tol's hair flowed freely, no longer trapped beneath the tight cloth.

Even held in place, the woman's furious expression made Tracy shudder.

"Is she the one we crossed time to find?" Tracy held her breath.

Derek angled his head sideways and squinted at Tracy. "No. This is some *other* person with abilities. Apparently, in the past everyone has powers."

"She is not the one I sought," Flint said. "Her magic will allow us safe passage through the void, though she lacks true power."

The Ri Ur Tol lashed against the forces holding her. "You are nothing more than a band of filthy scavengers." Redoubling her efforts, the Ri Ur Tol contorted into remarkable pretzel shapes to break free. "Where do you hail from to possess so much magic?"

This woman's ability to move in an instant was their ticket to safe travel home. Tracy saw no point in lying. "We come from tomorrow."

"How can you be from tomorrow? That makes no sense." The Ri Ur Tol stopped struggling.

Nicole held her face level with their prisoner. "Will you join our group? We won't hurt you, either way."

Hearing her life was being spared, the Ri Ur Tol looked at them to gauge their intentions. "Join?"

Nicole spoke calmly yet definitively. "We need your skills for our journey to return safely to tomorrow's tomorrow. Will you help us go into a place between places where we lost my friend?"

An arrow sailed through the window, driving into the wooden bedpost with a thunk.

The Ri Ur Tol barked a laugh of defiance. It carried no joy in its hollow sounds. "You are mad. That is good. For I have taken too long. My people's army has been unleashed to kill us."

29

To Unmake Mistakes

Derek

Derek stared at the arrow for a fraction of a second. Its metal tip was buried in the chair, and the arrow's feathered tail vibrated like a string being plucked.

He raised a telekinetic shield over the window. A second volley of arrows plinked against it.

Derek's shift in attention allowed the Ri Ur Tol to break free of his telekinetic grip. She grabbed a blade, pointing it at her own heart. Flint leaped at her, bending her wrist backward.

"Death already thrives!" Flint twisted her wrist farther until the dagger fell from her hand.

The Ri Ur Tol's voice came out as a whisper. "I failed. Allow me to end with honor."

"There is no honor in taking your life!" spat a red-faced Flint.

Nicole approached their subdued captive. "You may have tried to kill us, but we need your help. *I* need your help to find someone I care about. Anything you want, I'll make it happen. Please."

The Ri Ur Tol looked down. "It matters not. I hope you made peace with your life. My people's warriors will soon end it for us all."

Nicole's demeanor softened. "Why would they come after you?"

The Ri Ur Tol's face was hard steel. "In failure, I become no more than a faulty tool. It is easier to kill us all than worry about me being used against those I serve."

Nicole did not give up. "What if escape was an option? Then would you help us?"

The Ri Ur Tol avoided Nicole's gaze. "My life is forfeit. I will do as you command, so long as no harm comes to the Ur Tol."

"We can't trust her," Tracy said. "A few minutes ago she was about to slit my throat. We can stay in this time and never deal with that void monster again. Better that than rely on her to get us safely through the void."

Nicole shook her head. "She's perfect. I had no idea she was here until Flint lit the torches."

"So, we're risking our lives on the off chance this killer can hide us?"

Rachel stepped into the middle of the debate. "If we don't move fast, it won't matter. Tracy, we won't bring her if you don't want to."

Derek peeked over the window ledge, glancing outside. Arrows hit his shield in a steady stream. "Can you decide quickly? There's a lot of people with sharp, pointy things headed our way."

Tracy looked the Ri Ur Tol up and down. "I can't trust you, but we need you. How far can you teleport?"

The Ri Ur Tol opened her mouth and paused. "I do not understand this word: teleport."

Tracy hopped in random directions. "Move from one place to another in the blink of an eye like what you did to get close to kill me."

"Ah. I can move as far as I see or to places I have been. Though I no longer know my limits. I have escaped from other bindings before, but your magic was able to hold me."

"Maybe you weren't able to break free because I caught you in a telekinetic bubble and held your hands in place?" Derek suggested. "We can experiment later when we aren't about to die."

"Speaking of experimenting with powers," Rachel interrupted, "we'll have to put our powers to the test. My speed versus your teleportation. Assuming we survive the night."

The Ri Ur Tol made a noncommittal grunt.

Tracy moved until she was face to face with the Ri Ur Tol. "None of us have a power like yours. If we open a door to tomorrow's tomorrow, you need to teleport us as far as you can see inside. Can you do that?"

"You speak in riddles. I will tire fast when traveling with such a large company. I will do as you ask." The Ri Ur Tol locked her gaze with Tracy, before flicking her wrists at Rachel. "Though can you not use your short, fast friend to move you all around?"

Rachel's head sank, her gaze falling to the floor. "Speed only gets me so far, and I'm limited in the void with nothing to run on. You move instantaneously."

Seeing the Ri Ur Tol's confusion, Nicole added, "She means your magic works differently."

Tracy lifted her forearm in front of the Ri Ur Tol. "There's a monster that cut me on the other side of a doorway. Once we open it, you need to get us past it. Can you do that without killing me?"

"Doors. Tomorrow. Monsters. You are strange ones. As I said, I will do as you ask."

Tracy nodded at Rachel. "She passed my test. I'll keep her in front of me at all times so she can't stab me in the back."

The Ri Ur Tol's lip curled. "I was in front of you when I went to end your life."

"That hardly counts. I was drugged." Tracy looked ready to lunge at the Ri Ur Tol.

Rachel held Tracy back. "I'm not asking you to like or trust this Ri Ur Tol. I am demanding we not fight amongst ourselves until we get home."

"Remember, soldiers are racing here to kill us." Derek let his words soak in. He drew in power, surprised at how much he held. Somehow he recovered more from this afternoon's nap than from a full night of sleep. "Grab everything we brought. We can't leave any traces of our presence. Let's destroy the gold and leave the past."

"I'll buy us some time." Tracy put on her headphones. The stone archway over the window dripped, then hardened, sealing the opening. "I'm transmuting a stone wall at the stairway, trapping us on this floor. That gives us time to make a new exit."

Derek lowered his telekinetic shield outside a window which no longer existed. "Can someone clean my room of anything from our present and grab my backpack? I want to plan our next move." He faced the Ri Ur Tol as everyone except Tracy left the room to pack. "Where would the gold be stored?"

"In a vault at the base of this palace."

"Can you teleport us there?"

"I have never visited it. I know it is in the lowest levels, though nothing more. It is unwise for me to send us to a place unknown."

Tracy stopped packing to stretch her arms in exaggerated motions. "Since the Ri Ur Tol can't perform yet, I guess I'm the opening act."

"I do not understand your meaning," said the Ri Ur Tol.

Tracy flexed her arm muscles. "I'll get us to the gold. Save your magic to move us through the void later. We'll drop floor by floor until we reach the vault."

"Works for me," Derek said.

One by one they gathered, shouldering stuffed backpacks. Rachel, having collected Derek's belongings, tallied a full inventory. "Nothing from our time remains, except Tracy's golden bribe for our lives. That's where we head to."

The Ri Ur Tol shook her head. "Though impressive, your magic will not matter. You cannot evade their vast numbers, or the woman I serve."

Tracy's smirk gained a razor edge like barbed wire ready to ensnare the unprepared. "Watch us, Ri uh... You're one of us now. Do you have a name other than your title?"

"Star-spurned night! I was born nameless and have served my mistress for all nineteen harvests of my life. It is an honor to be granted the name Ri Ur Tol."

There were enough problems to go around without riling each other.

"She wants to be called Ri Ur Tol. We call her Ri Ur Tol," Derek said.

"Fine," Tracy replied. "Time to escape this hellhole."

"Hellhole? This city is wonderful," Rachel countered.

Tracy's harsh laugh echoed across the room. "Did you forget the Tol and Tak are actively trying to kill us?"

"The rulers are eccentric, but we antagonized them for this exact purpose. That doesn't change the freedoms these people share. Regardless of race, the culture approves of people living their lives. The Tak didn't bat an eye when you brazenly asked to marry his daughter. Think about how well that'd go over in our time."

"Okay. Okay. This place is awesome." Tracy sprinted through her words. "Mind if we flee before the ideal society murders us?" Stones in the floor changed to air, opening a hole at Tracy's bidding. No one was below. "We go down to get out."

Derek sat on the edge of the ten-foot drop, unwilling to jump. He counted to three. Then, didn't move. He counted to three again.

A well-placed boot sent him careening onto a stone slide, which suddenly formed beneath him. "You're welcome," Tracy said. "Now, hurry."

Tracy and Rachel slid down the transmuted slide while Derek lifted the rest of the team individually and brought them to the lower floor.

As soon as his telekinetic grip touched Ri Ur Tol, a snap echoed off the stones. She appeared next to him, teleporting on her own to the lower floor.

"Do not carry me unless I tell you."

"Fine."

Footsteps echoed in all directions, impossible to place. Tracy sealed the ceiling and opened a new hole to the floor below them. The lower hall was filled with warriors clad in leather armor, racing in the same direction.

One woman below pointed up at Derek. Her shout had not yet left her lips when she threw a spear at him. He formed a hasty telekinetic shield. The spear clattered against it. The rest of the army spun on their heels to attack.

Derek expanded the shield into an empty tunnel connecting Tracy's opening in the floor to the level below. Those on the outside stabbed at his invisible barrier while being pushed back by it.

Derek looked up as he lowered himself to the next floor, pretending he wasn't floating in midair. He brought everyone else to him, minus Ri Ur Tol, who teleported herself. On the next floor down, soldiers ran at them from both ends of the hallway, striking Derek's erected shield. Those on the floor above threw spears that didn't reach them thanks to Tracy closing the hole in the ceiling.

They descended two more floors, each overflowing with warriors racing upstairs. Derek pushed them aside using his power to form telekinetic tunnels to connect each floor until Tracy resealed the ceiling.

Unafraid, the warriors hacked and slashed, seeking to breach Derek's mental protection.

Finally, Tracy opened a new hole and found no light. The torches in the hall and those held by attacking soldiers illuminated little of what lay below. Damp air rushed to escape. Stone blocks as tall as Derek extended past the limited light without hinting at a bottom to the hole.

Rachel looked over their faces. "Who's going first?"

Nicole peered into its depths. "It's no portal to the void, but I vote for someone else."

Tracy created a cocoon from the stone above them, protecting Derek and the rest from the wave of oncoming warriors. With the more permanent wall in place, he removed his telekinetic shield and stared into the gaping pit.

He tossed a flashlight from his backpack into the hole. Several seconds passed, then a colliding smack sounded, followed by a dozen or so bouncing impacts.

Derek stilled his frayed nerves. "I'm not levitating myself or anyone else into a hole I can't see the bottom of and I-I-I can't."

Tracy rubbed his shoulder. She transmuted a piece of the nearby floor into a rope, which she wrapped around Derek's chest.

"I got you covered. We'll lower you, then you can carry us to you with your powers."

With no rebuttal, they lowered him into the tight hole wide enough for one. He clutched the spare flashlight and struggled not to tremble. Hanging in midair, his friends moved him one painstaking inch at a time.

Stone blocks of the foundation gave way to orange bedrock underneath. He counted over one hundred rows of various thin orange hues in the rock. He imagined each as a year, much like lines in a tree.

Minutes of cramped darkness dragged on. His foot touched a solid surface, sending him toppling. He threw an arm wide and caught himself on the smooth wall cut from the same orange sandstone as the building's bedrock.

The limited beam of his flashlight revealed a passageway fit for three average-sized people of this time to move side by side. Derek needed to stoop as he moved along the carved stairs.

Rhythmic patting sounds carried from farther up the stairway, and a faint light flickered at the bottom of the steps.

Lowering the rest of his friends was a process. The distance was difficult to judge, so Ri Ur Tol decided not to teleport anyone. Those above were brought down using the rope, allowing Derek to conserve his power. Grunts and strains echoed as fewer people remained above to hold the weight of the person being lowered. When only Flint was left, Derek carried him down with his powers.

Rachel retrieved the broken flashlight pieces and stowed them in her pack.

They proceeded deeper into the palace bowels.

The stairs opened into a wide cavern. Lights from their flashlights failed to reach the other side of the underground lake, which brushed up to a path carved from the rocks. Lengthy natural columns connected the ground with the cave ceiling.

Torches highlighted the straight path leading to the opposite end of the cavern. There, built into the stone of the cavern wall, rested a twenty-foot tall wooden door. Metal reinforced the dark wood at the corners and edges.

Derek sprinted across the cavern and pulled the metal rung to open it.

The door didn't budge.

Derek drew in power to punch through the door and wound back his arm, ready to strike with his full mental force.

Rachel grabbed him. "This cavern is probably supporting the weight of the entire palace. Instead of going superhero and smashing through a load-bearing structure, let Tracy transmute a hole in the door."

Derek backed away, listening to patting sounds coming from the stairway they used to reach the cavern. The noise grew louder like a light drizzle gathering into a downpour.

Tracy touched the door, and a large hole spread in its center as the wood changed into sand, sprinkling the ground.

Torchlight reflected off an enviable stash of all things shiny, hoarded from the world above. Several carved statues of green rock captured the Tak and Tol's likeness.

Ignoring piles of other riches, he saw the gold!

It's right in front of us. It's—

A lone woman barred their path. The Ur Tol held a sword in each hand. Her presence was menacing, but there was little her sharp metal could do against the might of the future and power at Derek's disposal. He stepped forward to push her aside, as he had every other warrior.

The Ur Tol flicked the blades over her palms, drawing blood. Red liquid oozed and stretched in tendrils to coat her swords, forming teeth along the edges of both blades. From the open cuts on her palms, the blood slithered into intricate patterns covering the Ur Tol's arms and legs.

"I knew you would nullify your deal." The Ur Tol's words came out like a whip lashing the air.

"At last, I found the one I seek," Flint uttered.

Tracy let out a small groan. "You could have saved me a lot of anguish if you'd figured out the same Ur Tol who guided us across this city was the one we intended to bring into the void with us."

"I did not know," replied Flint. "She hid her magic well until now."

Steady patting sounds from the stairwell transitioned into the distinct clattering of many footfalls racing down the stone stairs, blocking their escape.

Derek swung a telekinetic fist at the woman. Her swords flashed and his blast split around her, doing nothing more than stirring the air.

The Ur Tol's blood-soaked swords pointed at Derek and his friends. All thoughts of gold, returning to the future, hell, even the ability to think, were washed clean under the terrifying sight of her approach.

30

Dancing With Blood

Derek

The Ur Tol stepped warily, measuring Derek. Blood infused her weapons, outlining them in red, yet no drops fell.

That can't be sanitary.

Instinctively, he took a step back.

Footsteps echoed from the tunnel behind them.

Though his first attack proved useless, Derek formed a telekinetic bubble, trapping the blood-covered Ur Tol inside. "Tracy, unmake the gold and do it fast while I have the Ur Tol contained."

Tracy stood at the entrance to the vault with the others, apparently mesmerized by the riches or terrified by their defender.

Ri Ur Tol dropped to her knees and lowered her head until it touched the carved stone ground. "I lost to them and failed you, my Ur Tol."

Ri Ur Tol's gesture made the Ur Tol falter. Cold eyes regarded Derek from within his bubble. "My Ri Ur Tol, there is no fault in your defeat. You performed admirably against powerful foes. Once

I dispose of those who captured you, you will be free to live at my side again."

The Ur Tol lunged with a sword, hitting Derek's bubble. Cracks formed where it struck. The blood surrounding the blade extended forward, puncturing the bubble and spearing forward at Derek.

He dove for the ground, knocking around heaps of shiny gems. Though the Ur Tol remained in place, the bloody tip of her lengthening blade curved to follow Derek. He raised his hand and formed a telekinetic shield at his palms. The Ur Tol's sharp blood hit his shield, sending vibrations coursing through his arms.

Derek scrambled on the ground to distance himself from the Ur Tol. The bloody points of her swords slid around the edge of his shield.

An inch from gutting his heart, the blood dropped to the vault's stone floor.

Flint now stood between Derek and the Ur Tol. His leather bindings wrapped around the Ur Tol's weapons. All the Ur Tol's blood on Derek's side of Flint's bindings fell to the ground, returning to liquid after being severed from her power. Everything on the other side retained its rigid, deadly form.

Her second sword stabbed at Flint, forcing him to break his hold.

Spinning from the slashes, Flint landed next to Derek.

Fallen pools of blood crawled back to the Ur Tol's weapons and left trails on the ground. She swung renewed blades and split the bubble Derek contained her in. With nowhere to go, stored energy in his telekinetic shield fired outward, cutting his skin as though from tiny shards of glass.

Rachel dove in front of Nicole, protecting the one person among them without powers.

Unable to turn from his fight, Derek yelled at Tracy. "Unmake your gold. I'll keep the Ur Tol distracted."

The Ur Tol leaped in front of Tracy's path to the gold, but Derek did something stupid and charged at the woman holding two magic swords, forming a telekinetic shield in front of his hands. Bloodsword thrusts met the shield.

Tracy sprinted around small piles of jewels to where the stack of gold bars waited, their existence a threat to Derek's past. She heaved a huge sigh. "I promise to make a mountain of gold twice as big when we get home."

"Do what you want when we're home! Fix the gold problem now," Derek said.

He fell into a loose rhythm of blocking and dodging, unable to counter or gain an advantage. Flint rejoined Rachel, Nicole, and Ri Ur Tol, using the bindings along his arms to protect them from the expanding crossfire.

A war cry sounded from the narrow stone stairs.

Waves of armed warriors funneled into the cavern. Led by the Ba Tak, they trapped Derek and his friends in this tomb.

Derek deflected the Ur Tol's renewed attack. Her sword stirred the hairs on his chin as it passed by. Gems in all colors shifted under Derek's weight, risking his footing.

"They are mine to slay, brother," the Ur Tol snarled to the advancing army.

The Ur Tol's repeated hits bent Derek's telekinetic shield.

The unarmed Ba Tak raced at them, flanked by hundreds of warriors carrying swords, spears, and lit torches. "They are yours. I merely wish to preserve our fortune."

"One step closer and I unmake your fortune." Tracy's voice rang over the vault.

The Ba Tak and his warriors came to a halt outside the vault's entrance.

"The tall woman can make more gold and she still owes us the weapons she promised," said the Ur Tol. "Kill the others."

"Agreed," the Tol said, appearing from the wave of armed warriors. "Bring me the alchemist alive." Covered in intricate metal armor designed to topple a weaker woman, the Tol conveyed a haughty air of magnificence.

Beside her, the equally adorned Tak held a madman's smile as he boomed across the cavern at Tracy.

"I wished to call you daughter. In you, I finally had one not of my blood who gave more than they took. Too many of the others welcomed into our family depleted these stores." His hands spread in an open gesture. "I am nothing more than a caring father who wants the best for his offspring and his people."

"I already have my dad, and Derek's dad is a close second. Three seems like overkill." Tracy pressed her hand against the golden stones and transmuted them. Spreading like a disease, the surface of the gold bars dulled into a common red shade. A slab of bricks and mortar stood in place of what was once more wealth than Derek had dreamed of.

The vault grew slightly darker without the gold to reflect the torchlight.

Tracy heaved deeply, sinking to the ground while the Tak yelled, reaching a level of incoherence.

Their job was done. Tracy saved the past from her desperate bribe.

Derek pictured a large hammer in his mind. He swung the mental force at the Ur Tol's unprotected side, hitting her. The impact sent her sailing into her brother and the advancing warriors. Her blood swords flew in opposite directions.

The Tak let loose a battle cry, pressing the army forward to slay those who spoiled his prize.

To Derek, the army faded into a haze of sharp points and edges. Fear coiled in his chest, as though a vice squeezed his insides.

Rachel sprinted for the first line of warriors.

What was solid ground around their feet sank, the fluid wave of earth rising into an eight-foot-high wall to slow the army's rush. Tracy's sweaty face faded to a paler shade from all the power she used. Massaging her arm, she groaned. "This is worse than the last time I got food poisoning from that shady breakfast sandwich."

Unable to stop, Rachel ran headfirst into the wall Tracy transmuted. She scowled at Tracy. "We need a team effort to live through the night."

"Then work with me," Tracy called back, forming stairs along her wall and filling the hole Rachel had made.

Rachel sprinted to the top of the wall as a warrior vaulted up to land beside her, spear in hand. The warrior showed no fear, possibly emboldened by her height advantage over Rachel. In a blur, Rachel moved beneath the spear thrust to kick the woman over the wall into the waves of oncoming warriors.

Flint jumped on top of the wall. His bindings whipped about like they were consumed by a mind of their own. They toppled anyone who climbed over.

Tracy placed a long wooden stick in Nicole's hands. "I made this staff for you. In case anyone gets too close, bash them with it."

Nicole nodded several times too many. She swayed on the balls of her feet and cradled the weapon far from the fight.

From the other side of Tracy's wall, two giant muscular arms enlarged to the size of his rusted car. These raised high into the air, smashing into Tracy's construction as Flint grabbed Rachel and dove off the wall.

The impact from the giant arms toppled most of the wall and covered Derek in a layer of dirt. He coughed, but couldn't escape the terrible taste.

The Ba Tak stood at the destroyed section of wall. His swollen arms returned to their regularly scheduled size. A man and woman with matching straight, shoulder-length dark hair and strong jaw-lines stood on either side of the Ba Tak, holding each of his shrinking arms.

"Thank you, Ar Tak. Thank you, Ar Tol," the Ba Tak said.

The brother and sister pair collapsed, drifting off to sleep.

The Ba Tak paused to allow warriors to carry his siblings from the front line. They must have worked some magic to alter the size of the Ba Tak's arms and make him into a human battering ram.

Then he strutted toward Derek. "We defend our home!"

The Ur Tol was at the Ba Tak's side, wielding one of her blood-infused swords. "We defend our home!"

Cheers carried across the swell of soldiers closing in. The time it would take to count their number was far more than Derek had left in this world.

Prolonging this fight risked killing someone. Already, their existence in the past had likely created too many changes. Derek hated to think of all the time he wasted studying historic facts that may no longer be true.

Derek rallied his friends. "Hold them off and I'll rip a hole to the void."

"I'll grab our assassin," Nicole said.

"Wait." Tracy pointed to the Ur Tol. "She's the warrior we're looking for. Take her instead. We need the strongest one here to stand a chance against that thing in the void."

Flint's response was gruff. "Take them both."

Rachel ran forward to trip a soldier who broke rank. When she returned, her tone carried an iron will. "Now isn't the time for debate. We need an exit."

Derek shook his head to clear it. "No. Kidnapping one person already risks the entire timeline. I'm already worried about the ripples this fight will cause. I won't take more than one person from here."

Tracy's hawk eyes glanced between the two women. "In that case, making peace with Ri Ur Tol sounds easier than spending another day with Miss High-and-Mighty." Tracy yanked Ri Ur Tol to her feet. "When the doorway opens, teleport as far as you can inside."

Rachel tripped another line of warriors, which caused those behind them to trip. "I agree with Tracy. I support any plan where we don't steal a ruler's daughter. Taking anyone else instead would likely have less impact on our present."

Overwhelming power tore the universe open between Derek's fingertips.

Swords and spears held by warriors slowed along with their feet as the gateway came into existence. Those nearest to Derek dropped their weapons. A current of frightened bodies pressed against the tide of the crowd, trying to flee. Even the Tak stopped yelling, unable to move except to quiver in fear.

Across the still vault, a wailing, stiff wind hurled from the void.

Most of the army prostrated themselves on the ground at the sight of the void. Those who didn't made signs in the air to ward off evil.

An arm made of shadow sprung into the world through the opening. Razor fingers became scythes to cull the rows of warriors, harvesting them by splitting the men and women in half. Dozens of warriors fell, convulsing as smoke rose from the opened wounds.

In Derek's efforts to avoid having his internal organs litter the vault floor, he fell backward, dragging Nicole with him, lest she be killed by the shadow arm.

His hands fumbled, grasping for anything, until he came across a smooth, leather-bound handle lying by someone's dismembered foot. His fingers curled over the blade. Though difficult to recognize without the blood coating, this was one of the Ur Tol's blades which she had used in the attempt to end his life.

The hand of shadow wrapped around a grown man as though he were an action figure, pulling him toward the void.

Derek cursed his stupidity at opening the portal. He refused to let the shadow monster kill everyone here and, in doing so, destroy his present.

Derek slashed at the shadow arm, a faint blue shimmer appearing around the blade's edge. His sword bit into shadow while hundreds of daggers and spears passed harmlessly through it, clattering against the floor. Derek held his ground, steadily cutting deeper into the shadowy arm.

The Ur Tol leaped to his side, using her blood-drenched blade to cleave beneath the shadow's outer layers.

Derek stood shoulder-to-shoulder with the Ur Tol. Blood on her blade bubbled where it came in contact with the shadow arm.

A mind-rending howl carried from the void. The shadow arm withdrew, dropping its captured warrior and leaving him in the realm of the living. Though his skin looked burned, the man remained whole. He crawled on all fours from the shrinking portal. The Tol pulled him to safety, gazing at the horror within the void.

"Ri Ur Tol, get us as far into the void as you can," commanded Nicole. "No pressure, but if it's not beyond that shadow thing, we all die."

Ri Ur Tol glanced at the Ur Tol. "I must go. I swore to follow them."

The Ur Tol held Derek in her gaze and offered the subtlest of nods. Derek clenched the handle of the blade he recovered.

The Ur Tol hurried to Ri Ur Tol, and they gripped forearms. It might have been a trick of the lighting, but tears appeared to form in the Ur Tol's eyes.

"You have been more than a sister for all nineteen harvests of your life. Leave and hunt with honor."

"Hunt with honor." Ri Ur Tol released the embrace. She grabbed Derek's arm and started a chain of his friends using her other hand.

With the sound of a snap, Derek's body was pulled by his stomach, then compressed and stretched as he passed into the void.

Arms of shadow closed in from every direction; the skyscraper-sized mass of darkness sealed their escape.

Derek slammed the closing portal shut, sparing the people of the past and trapping himself and his closest friends with the monster made of shadow.

31

Living Shadow

Flint

Bathed in the void's pale half-light, Flint stared at the shadow of impossible size. Surely this was a summoning of his father's. The enormous creature had the faintest hint of a human's shape, one which possessed far too many arms.

Its wail sliced Flint's thoughts like one skilled in carving choice animal meat from fur, sinew, and bone.

The living shadow cupped two of its hands together, their size more than enough to trap Flint and everyone else inside. Flint had watched the devastating might as those clawed hands cleaved honorable warriors. Wisps of black smoke rose from their skin where they had been touched by this unnatural being. Flint unwound his arm bindings, lashing at the shadow, desperate to not suffer the fate of the warriors in the vault.

Snap.

Ri Ur Tol moved Flint. He watched the creature close its hands from afar, no longer floating between them. Ri Ur Tol released

Flint's arm and disappeared. In a breath's span, she returned carrying Rachel, then Derek, Nicole, and Tracy.

Though not his intended warrior, Ri Ur Tol was proving her usefulness. Still, not having the Ur Tol's raw power was bound to hurt in the hunt of Flint's former master.

The living shadow cried out. Its shrieks enveloped Flint, pecking at his mind like a bird seeking bugs in the sand. Eyes spread across the shadow's arms and head spun to track Flint and his companions. Long arms sprang from its torso, which were aimed at Flint and the others.

Snap.

The living shadow fell into the distance as though such a word held meaning in the void. Ri Ur Tol sent them farther, each snap barely audible over the creature's wails. Eventually, the creature's cries faded into the darkness of this realm.

Flint did not stretch his magic to gaze behind at the creature of shadow. Should his life pass at the hands of such an evil, he preferred not to watch it bear down on him.

Over and under, Flint was aware of tumbling and moving across the void. Ri Ur Tol shifted them about under Derek's direction, skewing their trail to confuse the living shadow.

Even while Ri Ur Tol jumped them about, Derek propelled them all in a steady direction from the sealed entrance they had used to enter the void. Flint stared into the endlessness, feeling like a fisherman lured to the deep sea with no land in sight.

What little there was to study of his master's drawings did not prepare him to navigate this Somewhere Else. His prior two journeys proved inadequate to make sense of its size or observe anything recognizable aside from the sealed entrances he still vaguely sensed.

Light seeped through the hole Derek had opened. Though not strong, it was a blinding beacon compared to the darkness, which illuminated strange objects floating nearby. Tracy grabbed one object that resembled her water containers, except the liquid inside was the color of dried dirt.

Flint pushed fragments of rigid nets out of the way in his approach to the doorway.

Beyond the opening stood the underside of a large bridge. The closer they floated to the gateway, the larger the bridge grew until it occupied all Flint's vision. They gathered speed. Derek sent them sailing from the void up and over wooden boards onto the bridge.

Flint caught himself and stood. Fighting for his first breath was like inhaling a smoldering fire.

The others did not react as quickly. A jumble of bodies bounced and rolled.

Ri Ur Tol's hands flailed, yet she regained her balance without collapsing into the heap of bodies.

The portal sealed shut on its own.

Derek lay on the bridge and closed his eyes. Eventually, his panting breaths slowed to normal.

Rigid mud-colored netting on the outside of the bridge kept them from falling over the side. They were the same nets he had found in the void. Blocks on wheels traveled on a passage beneath Flint's feet. Each filled the air with unique rumbling roars. A longer one carried multiple blocks upon its back, spewing gray clouds from a reed attached to its top. It made a blaring sound like an animal's challenge.

Sparse forestation spread to the edge of the road. Water carried sticks and debris downstream as it moved in a wide path between trees,

"Home!" Rachel cheered.

32

Decisions

Derek

Crisp brown leaves crunched under Derek's tattered shoes, which had enough holes to qualify as sandals. He pulled himself upright using the cold metal bars along the pedestrian path.

The six of them stood alone on the bridge. Red and golden trees stretched to the rusted chain-link fence. The bear-like Beast who haunted his dreams wasn't here waiting to rip out his throat. Relief escaped Derek in a sigh, and his tense muscles relaxed. Though, he refused to give up looking for the Beast until he was certain it had fled.

New wood panels filled the gap missing from the concrete and metal fence, Band-Aids on the wound he caused when he left this world.

A car revved its engine and inched forward in a long line.

Ri Ur Tol clutched her ears. "By the stars," she muttered nonsensically.

Flint stood behind her, his eyes in constant motion. He spoke through clenched teeth. "Your memories I witnessed did nothing to prepare me for this."

Despite nausea-inducing heights, Derek leaned over the side of the wood barricade for a better look under the bridge. No monster was waiting there. A gaggle of Canadian geese pecked at the riverbank for food. His home was in for a bitter winter if the geese migrated south this early through the Northeast Corridor.

Derek basked in warm sunlight, which was much cooler than expected. He was so happy to be home, he even found the muddy aromas from the river to be damn near savory.

He pulled old clothes from his backpack to wrap around his sword, the prize won from surviving his fight against the ancient warrior. He fit the bundle in the gap between his back and the backpack to hold the weapon in place.

Wind ruffled his hair, sprinkling it with golden flower petals. Grasping a few of them, Derek ran his hand through the bird's nest of hair on top of his head. When he last stepped on this bridge, he was on the verge of needing a haircut. Now, it was well overdue.

The railings had a bouquet of wilted green flowers woven along its length, spanning from some art project wreaths on display.

"I don't get how our world is still here, but I'll accept it." Rachel jumped excitedly.

"Nice Earth you have." Nicole leaned against the chain-link fence.

Tracy inclined the top of a cream soda toward Nicole. Popping it open, she chugged the bottle. "Here, here."

It took a moment for Derek to recognize where the bottle came from. "Please tell me you didn't take that from the crap at the void's entrance. Ever hear of botulism?"

"I'll take my chances for this victory sip."

Rachel cupped a hand around her ear. "Listen to that north-bound, rush-hour slog. Given the disaster we left in the past, I thought I'd never hear it again."

"It *is* a nice pat on the back for surviving," Tracy said.

Derek hugged the closest lamppost.

"The past may not have changed, but our present sure has." Tracy pointed at the row of three wreaths Derek mistook for art. Each waist-high easel supported a ring of pine with tiny green and gold flowers. A picture of Derek, Tracy, and Rachel sat in the center of each. Handwritten notes from classmates encircled their images.

Derek read the messages. "There's a lot more people than I'd expect hoping for our safe return. Think that's a sign that we changed the past?"

"No idea," Tracy said, retrieving her phone from her backpack. Rachel snatched it.

"What the hell?" Tracy shouted.

"I can type and read faster using my power. I need answers now." Rachel skimmed the results. "Look at this: 'Though no bodies were found, one driver claimed to have seen a large animal along with three teenagers... DNA evidence from blood at the scene confirmed the identity of one of the missing persons as Derek Fen.' There are plenty of comments debating our chances of survival after forty-eight hours."

"That's pretty grim," Derek said. "I can't imagine how our families feel."

"A DNA test takes what? Days? Weeks?" Tracy began. "How much time has passed?"

"About a month, assuming your phone's clock synced correctly." Rachel's finger flicked over several screens, scrolling past loading images. "We missed Homecoming!"

"No loss there." Derek chuckled. "I can't handle another trip into the void at the moment, but when I regain my strength I'll take us back to the moment immediately after we left. My aim was off before, but I'll fix the past so our families don't need to worry."

"We can't go back," Rachel cut in. "That might create a paradox now."

Nicole stepped in front of him. "Is this where the Derek from my world landed?"

Derek rubbed the back of his neck, debating how to tell her the truth. "Not exactly. We needed to recover from our fights."

Nicole pointed at the wide-eyed woman from the past. "We escaped the void-shadow thanks to her. We could have searched instead of taking another detour."

Derek didn't back down. "Dying in the void means no one's left to save the other me. I returned to a known safe place rather than face unknown dangers."

"Fine."

"How about this? We rest tonight, then we search tomorrow. After that, we'll go back to the day I first opened the void."

"Fine."

Looking over Rachel's shoulder at her phone, Tracy's grin hadn't faded. "We're here. English reads like the same mash-up language I remember. Our families will be relieved to have us back. Why not drop this quest to save a Derek and thrive in the now?"

"Why don't I drop you off the side of this bridge?" Nicole's menacing smile left Derek uncomfortably uncertain if she would follow through on that suggestion.

Rachel tapped the phone. "Our past few presidents were the same. Here I was, worried our adventures caused them to be replaced by lizard people. Also, John texted me back on your phone. He's thrilled we're alive and..." Rachel paused, her cheeks flushed with a darker tone, "John sent a message I immediately deleted about wanting to meet up tonight."

Nicole looked at the town center and smiled. "Have you considered the past did change and we're too caught inside the puzzle to understand the overall picture?"

"By the stars." Ri Ur Tol closed her eyes and then forced them open. She rubbed the concrete path holding them well above the highway, unwilling to look over the barricade. "I shall wake when this nightmare ends."

Derek, likewise, preferred not to look down over the side, focusing on Ri Ur Tol and not the traffic below. "Our lives are in your debt."

Ri Ur Tol exhaled a long breath. "I agreed to accompany you, regardless of this strange hunting ground." She straightened herself, returning to the emotionless mask she regularly donned. "Where are we? Is this your promised Tomorrow?"

Derek pointed toward the setting sun. "I live a couple miles that way."

Tracy applied a translator on the back of Ri Ur Tol's neck. "This will help you live in our time."

Flint cut in. "I wish to discuss the real matter at hand. You may not be the warrior I sought, but will you join my cause to defeat my former master?"

Frost bit into each of Ri Ur Tol's words. "Already this day I left my home and, so far, the two of you seek to use me to further your own ends."

"I..." Derek clenched his eyes shut. "You're right. We took you to save ourselves. I'm sorry. I'll work to earn your trust. Would you please stay with us until then?"

Ri Ur Tol stared at the place where the opening to the void had sealed. "Though I do not have a choice, thank you for at least asking. I shall stay without causing trouble."

Flint addressed Ri Ur Tol while wrapping the bindings around his arms. "My master ended many lives to grant me magic. He must have done the same to bestow magic in you and the Tak's family. I will make him suffer. Would you join me?"

Ri Ur Tol raised a finger at Flint. "I shall consider it."

Flint's eyes fell on the space over Derek's shoulder. "What manner of weapon have you taken from Ri Ur Tol's people?"

Derek stretched his arm behind him. "It's the Ur Tol's magic sword, which I'm *borrowing* for now. When we return Ri Ur Tol to her people, I'll give it back."

"What is it made of to hold such a sharp edge and capture light like a clear stream?"

"You saw metal knives and spoons in my house," Nicole said. "It's more or less made of the same stuff."

Flint had the grace to look at his feet. "Everything in your home was so far beyond what I know. You took this sword from my time. During the war between our people, I was never given the chance to ask how their weapons were shaped."

Shaking his head, Derek lifted his sword. "There's more in this weapon than mere metal. Regular swords and spears passed through the shadow monster. This allowed me to cut it and that doesn't take into account the weird moving blood that appeared when the Ur Tol wielded this sword."

Daggers appeared in Ri Ur Tol's hands as seamlessly as breathing.

Derek braced himself to fight Ri Ur Tol for callously mentioning how he stole her mistress's weapon. Instead, her gaze was fixed down the slope of the bridge where a white-haired man waved in greeting.

His other arm had a shirt sleeve tied in a knot to keep it close to the base of his missing arm.

Derek tensed, his joints locked in place. He considered hiding Flint and Ri Ur Tol from his guidance counselor or pretending they were strangers.

"Welcome back," Mr. Marshal said.

Derek was certain his jaw creaked when it dropped open.

Ri Ur Tol threw a dagger. It struck the concrete in front of Mr. Marshal's foot. "Come no closer."

"Interesting." Mr. Marshal's face showed no signs of shock from the near miss. Rather, he made a smug half-smile and stepped forward.

Derek tried to shout a warning, but he was too slow to stop Ri Ur Tol from throwing her dagger at him again.

Before Derek could gather the power to grab the weapon with telekinesis, it halted in front of Mr. Marshal, hovering in place. Mr. Marshal held out his hand and tapped the stopped dagger. His voice lacked any hint of anger at the attempted maiming.

"There is much for you to learn, both in terms of manners and, apparently, powers."

Mr. Marshal tapped the blade again, and it dropped, clanging against the bridge. Ri Ur Tol stepped back, pointing her other dagger at Mr. Marshal.

"Friend or foe?" Ri Ur Tol called out to Derek and the rest.

"Friend! Friend!" Rachel shouted, using her power to cover the distance and stand in front of Mr. Marshal. "He's absolutely a friend."

Ri Ur Tol lowered her weapon and bowed forward. "I am sorry."

Derek shook his head to clear it from witnessing someone else displaying mental abilities. "Shit, Mr. Marshal, you have powers too?"

Flicking his wrist, Mr. Marshal returned the dagger into Ri Ur Tol's hands without touching it. "Indeed, and it's well overdue for me to teach you how to wield yours properly."

Tracy's hand fluttered back and forth. "We're experts in the subject of using powers."

"I find that difficult to believe, considering I was the one who gave Derek his powers," said Mr. Marshal, tallying those present with his fingers. "I assume he then shared them with at least two of you. In the mere months you've had your abilities, there's no way you've reached your true potential."

"That was you!" Rachel karate chopped the air. "Thanks for giving us the means to kick ass."

Gears turned in Derek's head. "Wait, have you been drugging me with those chocolates?"

Mr. Marshal looked at the attentive crowd with what Derek took to be a twinge of shame behind sagging eyes. "Close enough."

Derek's teeth ground together. Emotions swirled, each fighting for dominance over him. "Why choose me?"

"It's a long story. I acted as I saw fit at the time, and you all are now Earth's last hope."

Derek's voice caught in his throat. "That can't be right," he stammered. "There has to be someone better."

"Earth's last hope against what?" Tracy asked. "We could've taken over any of the places we visited, if we tried. We got your unknown threat handled."

Mr. Marshal's voice was tinged with bitterness. "You won't be fighting empires, but monsters."

"Like the Beast hunting me?" Derek asked. Seeing Mr. Marshal's confusion, he added, "The thing we fought here on this bridge already."

"Yes."

Rachel sank to the ground. "We're the wrong ensemble to save the world. There has to be someone else."

Mr. Marshal rubbed his hands together. "Your training begins tomorrow. Meet here at seven in the morning so we can go together to my facility where I'll begin your lessons in magic. Derek, Tracy, and Rachel, say any goodbyes to your friends and family tonight. Give them peace of mind that you're alive."

Rachel refused to give an inch. "Why say goodbye? Can't we go to school and train by night?"

Mr. Marshal shook his head. "That would be a cruel joke to live half a life and your training will suffer if you don't dedicate yourself entirely to it."

Tracy raised her fists. "What if we're done with training altogether? What if we want to enjoy our powers?"

Faster than Derek's eyes tracked, Mr. Marshal tripped Tracy. He pinched her forehead and a faint light traveled up his arm.

As Derek rushed forward to help Tracy, a force pushed him back. He shouted in frustration, throwing himself against the near invisible wall without a shred of power behind his blows.

He'd spent all his power traveling across the void, leaving him with nothing but flesh and muscle. He grasped the sword handle over his shoulder, desperate for anything to sever the gap separating him from Tracy and ready to swing it at Mr. Marshal.

"If you fail to arrive tomorrow," came Mr. Marshal's gruff tone, "I'll take back what I generously granted. The extracted power won't be as strong as what I started with, yet I'll make do."

When Rachel spoke, her words were shaky. "What about our families? They're wondering if we're alive or not. We can't leave them so soon."

The look Mr. Marshal threw at Rachel made Derek glad he hadn't opened his mouth to mirror those sentiments.

Mr. Marshal descended the bridge's pedestrian path back the way he came. "Tonight is a gift. Use it. The three of you who are not of this world's present will come with me."

Flint obeyed in silence.

Ri Ur Tol addressed Derek, Tracy, and Rachel as she started down the bridge to join Mr. Marshal and Flint. "If you do not show tomorrow, I will learn from this odd man and protect you."

"Well, there's really nowhere else in your world for me to go," Nicole said as she followed those leaving. "Come train tomorrow. Derek, I'm expecting you to uphold your promise and help me rescue my Derek."

Derek was stunned into stillness, weighing the hefty decisions unraveling in front of him.

"Any opinions on how to decide our future?" Rachel asked.

"Nope," Tracy replied, her typical confidence absent from her face.

Mr. Marshal, Flint, Ri Ur Tol, and Nicole were halfway to the shopping center. None of them looked back. Derek's frail voice sounded like another person spoke for him.

"We may as well say hi and bye to everyone else we care about. Got any ideas on a believable lie to explain where we've been?"

Rachel shook her head. "Not without a full demonstration of our powers, so that's a bad idea. My parents would never let me leave the house again if they had half an idea of the danger we've been in. Still, they deserve to know we're alive, and it's been too long since our last home-cooked meal."

Tracy's ears perked at that thought. "Your mind's in the right place. Want to get our crew together tonight, after dinner, for old time's sake?"

"Sure, if I can sneak out." Rachel's flash of excitement turned into a frown. "Although, how do I explain to John what we've been through? I'm sure he led every search party looking for us. This can't be our last night together."

The thought of all his friends sank Derek's insides, reminding him of a different cost for using his powers. "Rather than a night filled with nostalgia, why not give it some meaning by undoing the damage I caused?"

"I think the timeline's okay," Rachel said. "Tomorrow, I'll re-search history and look for inconsistencies to what I remember."

"We should do that too. For tonight, I'm talking about Louis," Derek said, louder than intended. "Tracy, can your abilities fix him?"

"How should I know?"

Derek considered their fight in the underground cavern. "The Tak's kids transformed their brother's arms into giant battering rams and then shrank them back to normal."

"Do you want my first attempt at human transmutation to be healing our friend?"

"Fair point," he agreed. "Use me as a guinea pig for practice and we'll sneak away from training to fix Louis's body when you're ready."

Rachel looked side-to-side. "Anyone consider how we're getting home?"

"Think our cars are still at school?" Tracy asked.

"Probably not," Derek said. "Besides, the four-mile run home will clear my head."

Adrenaline from the run would keep him going, but he was headed for a major crash. He craved to crawl beneath his bed's covers and sleep for days.

"It's so far," Tracy groaned.

Derek hefted his backpack onto his shoulders and took off. "Our clothes can't get any dirtier. My house is the farthest. Get home however you like, then."

* * *

He turned onto his home street thirty minutes later. It appeared as it always had. No matter how he turned the details over, their actions in the past should have triggered chain reactions which compounded over millennia.

His neighbor's house proudly showcased its same off-pink coating. Mrs. Weatherborn's yellow Labradoodle yipped and chased him from within the boundary of the fence. Chew toys were torn to shreds across the yard, more or less as he remembered.

Derek reached his arm over the fence to scratch behind the dog's ears. She sniffed the air, recognizing his scent. Bounding from the porch, her brother snarled. Derek leaped back, lest he lose the hand. Long parallel streaks of missing fur stretched along the bristling dog's back as it launched against the fence.

Derek backed away slowly, unnerved by the violent welcome. He looked over his shoulder and found nothing, then hurried down his driveway for the shelter of his home.

Derek's breath caught at the last bend. Thick tree trunks opened to reveal his home. It paled compared to the Tak and Tol's palace, yet was absolutely perfect for him.

Parked beside the house, his car looked no worse than expected. His family must have paid to haul this piece of junk here. Ditching it in a scrap heap would have saved everyone the trouble.

Seeping from an open window, the smell of spiced seasoning congratulated him on a safe return. Assuming his nose wasn't lying, his mother had made slow cooked pot roast. That meant there was a side of duck fat-roasted potatoes or maybe buttered broccoli.

He thought hard to recall his last enjoyable meal and couldn't picture it. The finest dishes of the ancient kingdom were too difficult to savor when he was worried about unmaking his past with each bite.

He banged his hand against his home's front door with a booming knock that shook the frame.

33

Home

Derek

From the other side of his front door, Derek heard chairs scraping wooden floorboards. The door swung inward to reveal his mom. Derek's chest squeezed air from his lungs and tears formed.

His eye level went over the top of his mom's head as it always had. Her highlighted hair hung in a loose style with more volume, but that couldn't really be counted as a difference to the timeline. He knew better than to wish home remained an ever present constant, as though isolated in a glass ball.

She wrapped her arms around him in a bone-crushing embrace. "We knew you were alive!" She ushered him through the front door. "Come in, come in. It's about to get dark, and you never can be too careful."

His mother closed and twisted the deadbolt. The clicking of metal surprised Derek. This was a house that never locked its doors.

Propelled into the dining room, Derek lay his backpack and wrapped sword in the corner. His father and sister eyed his belongings from the dinner table, their faces a mixture of confusion and fascination.

"Where on Earth have you been?" his father asked from the opposite side of the table.

What had been Derek's frail, skeletal father now had meat attached to his bones. A flush pinkish skin tone had replaced his former ghostly, pale complexion. His features had de-aged ten years, carrying the presence of a flourishing tree, instead of a twig blown over by a light breeze.

Before Derek could answer, his mother cleared her throat loudly at his father and held a finger over her lips. "Don't you think your father is recovering well?" she asked Derek.

"You're looking good, Dad."

"I've put on the five pounds you seem to have lost this past month," he rubbed his stomach, still too narrow to be considered a healthy size. He ran a finger through his short silver hair. "I grew this out too, while you were missing."

I didn't change history. Dad recovered in the time I lost.

Derek's sister pointed her fork at him and grinned broadly. "Of course you come home during dinner."

Dining room lights accentuated freckles on Olivia's nose. Derek found no noticeable differences between his sister and the one from his memories.

Hunger took over. He drooled at the sight of gravy-drenched pot roast accompanied by steamed vegetables brushed in butter. Though not as extravagant as Tak and Tol's elaborate feast, this was better. What mom's plain meal lacked in colorful presentation, it made up for in nostalgia. Right now, he wanted nothing more than ordinary and usual.

Choking up, his mom gestured to his empty seat at the table. Whether from hope or habit, his spot was already set.

Cushioned chairs never felt so comfortable beneath him. Such a small addition was nonexistent on the hard benches of the past. Padded seats were the real treasure the Tak and Tol should wish for.

His mom placed an overflowing plate of tuna mac and cheese in front of him. "I've cooked your favorite meal every week on the off chance you might come home. I wanted to have it ready."

"Thanks," he managed between bites.

She took her seat at the table, smiling and staring at Derek as he ate. "Wherever you were, did you have a nice birthday?"

A pang roiled inside Derek. He'd lost track of time so thoroughly that he forgot the day he was born. Given his track record, he was probably unconscious on October 31 and missed his chance to celebrate Halloween as well. Not that it mattered, since he had been stumbling around in a time before calendars.

"Nope. I was busy."

Derek doused his tuna mac and cheese in hot sauce. It pleasantly burned his nostrils and gave him an excuse to let his eyes water.

Crinkles formed around the edges of Olivia's warm, brown eyes. "Happy belated eighteenth birthday. I'm glad you're home. Welcome to adulthood, little bro."

"Shouldn't you be at college?" Derek asked.

"I've been driving back every weekend to help around the house and search for clues to find you. I'll leave tomorrow morning to get to my first class around noon."

Though the cheese of his tuna mac and cheese was as creamy as ever, his sister's words turned the bites into molten lead. Swallowing left a burning sensation down his throat.

"You shouldn't have put your academics in jeopardy for me."

"I absolutely should. Besides, I *am* a genius still pulling top grades. You have big shoes to fill next year when you leave this nest for college."

Derek winced, remembering his duty to be training with Mr. Marshal for, presumably, the rest of his life. Compared to the hell storm of near-death experiences, college looked like a beach vacation with calm skies and soothing waves. It would take no more than sleeping in tomorrow to have a normal future. That, and giving up his powers.

Come to think of it, what good have my powers done? I almost killed two of my closest friends, and the verdict is still out on whether I unraveled history. Without these abilities, I'd be free to fix the friendships I ruined and pursue college and beyond.

His mom's face scrunched. "You smell awful."

Derek leaned back to check his reflection in the dining room mirror. His dirt-caked face had the makings of a patchy, chinstrap goatee. Sniffing what remained of the ripped cloth he wore, which was barely recognizable as a shirt, he recoiled.

"I didn't get many chances to bathe."

"Where the hell did you disappear to?" his father interrupted.

"Look at our son!" His mom reached across the table to scoop another spoonful of tuna mac and cheese onto Derek's plate. "He's wearing rags. We decided weeks ago not to ask him the specifics of where he went until he was ready to tell us. Remember?"

Derek's father rested his head on his hand. "They found your fingerprints and blood along the bridge. Not to mention the unexplained pieces missing from the otherwise solid structure. We combed the area every day for a body. Tell me, *now*, where did you go?"

Unwilling to submit, Derek met his father's gaze. "There's no way to explain it so you'd believe me."

"The only way to get me to understand is to tell me."

"I trained to fight in a forest and enjoyed dinner with what amounts to royalty."

His father bristled. "I won't be lied to in my house."

Olivia offered Derek a chance to breathe by drawing their dad's attention. "When you, Tracy, and Rachel went missing, we thought you were dead."

It would be so easy to show his abilities. Except then he'd be stuck here explaining, in excruciating detail, everything he knew about them. All while his last few hours of freedom dwindled.

I earned one night off before being shackled to Mr. Marshal's training. Assuming I decide to opt into the hero business, I'm not spending my last night like this. All I need to do is sneak out.

His friends were waiting to watch a movie or play video games. Perfect activities to take his mind off the number of times he narrowly escaped death.

Derek gnashed his food, speaking firmly and forcefully, trying not to spit out his dinner. "I'd like to eat this meal in peace. I need to leave again in the morning."

"You're not going anywhere besides school." His mother stressed each syllable, as though trying to beat sense into him with words.

"You've already missed too many classes," his father said, shaking in anger. "Don't you care about graduating?"

"This is more important than graduating." Derek kept his voice flat, struggling to contain the boiling pressure cooker of his stomach.

With speed to rival Rachel, his mom tried to distract Derek and his father. "What's so important you'd give your poor mother a heart attack?"

"It's too difficult to explain."

His father slammed his fist on the table, toppling glasses. "I won't let you run off to who-knows-where and we still don't know where you've been for the past month!"

Derek squashed the urge to fire a warning shot with his powers. "I *am* leaving tomorrow morning, so say any worthwhile goodbyes tonight."

"No, you're not! You're grounded, *and*—" his father stressed his word to ensure it was absolute "—you'll be at school tomorrow after we stop at the police station. There, you can explain where you went. Secrets are a malignant tumor. It's better to rip them out right away, then you can recover."

Lest he erupt molten power and destroy the first floor, Derek grabbed his plate and bolted from the table. He picked up his sword and his backpack as he raced to his room.

"It's so good to be home."

Taking two steps at a time, he slammed his bedroom door so hard it cracked along the outer frame. He tore off his grimy clothes and dropped them in the trash, replacing them with fresh clothes from his closet.

He turned on his desktop, hoping for a distraction in one of his favorite video game runs, then turned off the machine. "What's the use?"

Derek gathered all his clean clothes, which included everything from a thick winter jacket and mittens to shorts and breathable running shirts. Never again would he underestimate the value of soft fabric against his skin. He emptied his backpack and shoved the pile of clothes inside.

He charged his dead phone and didn't bother turning it on. He didn't want to be around anyone, including his friends.

Derek stabbed the air with his sword. A stray hit clipped the ceiling, dropping bits of drywall onto his floor. Ripples of power coursed along his arm and down his spine, as it had when he battled alongside the sword's original owner. He felt unstoppable like he could tear down any tree in his backyard and carry it for miles on his shoulders.

A knock at the door interrupted any further musing. Olivia wrenched the door open without waiting for an answer. "That was intense. Want to talk about it?"

"Not particularly."

"How about telling me why you're carrying around a sword?"

He leaned on the sword, using it as a pointy cane. "I won it in a fight."

"Care to elaborate?"

Derek rubbed his face, feeling the creases in his forehead. "Not really."

"Do I need to quote Dad's rhetoric?"

"Don't." Derek responded flatly. "It was his way of making us confess as kids when we did something wrong."

"You need to be nicer to him."

"We've walked on eggshells around him for the past six months. He looks better, so maybe we act normal and call him out when he's an asshole."

"No, you didn't see things firsthand. He took your disappearance the hardest. Mom told me how he hobbled around the bridge every day looking for you."

"I had no idea."

"Kind of like how he never told us he was skipping his doctor check-ups."

Derek slid off his sword's handle, catching himself on his desk. "What?"

"After his latest round of chemo a few months ago, he chose to be done with treatments. In his words, 'Either I'm cured, or I'm not.'"

"That's messed up."

"Some good came from your disappearing act. Dad decided he needed to be here when you came home and set an overdue check-up to make sure his pancreas was clean. Ignoring a problem doesn't make it go away. So tell me what you're keeping inside that head of yours."

The floor fell out from under Derek like he was dropping thousands of feet toward the sea all over again. Returning home was fast becoming a horrible mistake.

Against such an indomitable will as his sister's, he was helpless. Derek made a show of waving his hands and forming intricate signs. "Abra Kadabra."

His dirty, discarded shirt flew into his waiting hands.

Olivia jumped high into the air. "What the hell was that?"

Derek sent the headphones on his desk to land over her ears. "Levitation."

"How... How... did you do that?"

"We're still fuzzy on the details."

"We?"

"We: Me, Tracy, Rachel, Nicole, and some others." Seeing his sister's face light up at the mention of Nicole's name, Derek added, "She's not my old friend. This Nicole is... from out of town. Anyway, most of us have abilities."

"This is incredible! Screw being well-rested for college classes tomorrow. We're staying up all night until you tell me everything about your abilities."

"Not now. I need to decide whether I deserve to keep them. I need some space."

He lifted her with his mind and deposited her gently in the hallway. His sister's eager expression deflated like helium leaving a balloon.

Derek offered her one last secret. "As for where I was, I went to the past."

"Really? What? How?"

"I'll let you know when I figure that out." Derek shut his door. Too weary to think, he sank into the soft pillow on his bed.

* * *

Loud knocking on his bedroom door made Derek leap to his feet with his fists raised. Predawn light filtered in through the windows, and the sun struggled to rise above the tree line.

"Time for school," his father called through the door.

Derek let his racing heart rate slow. He rubbed sleep from his eyes and opened the door, intending to remind his father he was leaving home, permanently.

Dressed in a business casual shirt and slacks, his father was already returning to his bedroom.

"Good morning. Take a shower. I'm driving you to the police station to complete any paperwork for your missing person's case and then to school. Now that I'm healthy and you're home, I'm going to talk to my boss about returning to the JHU Applied Physics Lab after taking you to school."

"Can't I have breakfast first?" Derek slammed the door. His power manifested outside his control, flinging books about his room. Ideas were already forming on how to leave home.

His father's gruff voice penetrated through the walls. "I raised you better than to throw a tantrum when you don't get your way."

Derek's nose twitched. Before he realized it, his fist was mid-swing at the door.

Metal hinges ripped free, sending his bedroom door flying through the wall across the hall.

Derek wiped his torn and bleeding knuckles on his shirt as he craned his neck into the hallway, checking whether his dad witnessed his outburst. The coast was clear.

He sent his broken door crashing through the wall of his sister's room where it landed on the middle of her bedroom rug. Thankfully, her room was empty. A thin curl of smoke rose from the scorch mark where his fist struck. He needed to move the door quickly before anyone ran to investigate the loud noise.

From beneath the door, an arm rolled weakly into view trying to lift it. With little thought, Derek gathered his power and tossed the door to the other side of the room. It splintered against the wooden dresser and scattered his sister's array of running medals.

Derek helped his dad sit up. Blood dripped from a forehead gash and spilled onto the carpet. His father's eyes moved in an unfocused daze. When he settled on Derek, his father's expression formed one Derek had never witnessed. It was half disbelief, half anger, and one hundred percent unadulterated fear.

Derek purged every ounce of power from his body, the weight of his guilt sending tremors through his legs.

His mother raced in and stopped. "What was that racket?" All life drained from her voice, and it came out in a hushed whisper. "What happened?"

Derek's knees buckled under her glare. "He wasn't supposed to be there."

I hurt everyone around me with my powers.

The fresh thought burrowed deep, unwilling to dislodge from the base of his skull. Isolating himself from the world for training was the best way to protect those he cared about.

Before his parents could stop him, Derek fled back into his room. He wrapped his sword in spare clothes and strapped it to his back with belts tied together. Grabbing his backpack, he leaped from the second-story window. Derek slowed some of the drop with the smallest amount of power, wanting to feel the sharp impact coursing up his legs.

Olivia stared at him from the dining room window, her open mouth wide enough to catch a fly.

He waved once and mouthed two words, which were the understatement of the century, "Sorry. Bye."

Tears streaked down her cheek as she nodded and returned to her breakfast, not fully aware of the damage he'd caused above. Greasy bacon wafted into Derek's nose, calling him to walk inside and forget about abandoning his family.

He started running, making it as far as the first bend when he stopped to take in his entire home. His father appeared from Derek's open bedroom window, shouting at him. The specific words he used were lost in the space between them. He held a small towel to his head to stanch the flow of blood.

Booming thumps sounded from the woods. Tree after tree collapsed with thunder-like crashes, cutting a path through the woods like an arrow aimed at his home.

Each resounding thump locked Derek's legs. Fear trapped him in place.

The Beast broke from the tree line as a mass of white fur much bigger than it had been on the bridge and taller than any land predator had a right to be. The Beast belonged in the times of prehistoric megafauna. Its sharp claws dug into soil and left deep imprints due to its massive size. The Beast sniffed the air, giving Derek precious seconds.

His mother emerged from the den's side door, having run through the house. "Get inside, Derek!"

Derek's father appeared next to his mother. "Hide in the house," he beckoned, holding the door open for Derek to sprint inside.

The Beast had knocked over trees. A few wooden boards and drywall wouldn't hold it back.

"I can stop that thing," Derek shouted, though a waver in his voice cut through the lie.

Derek's dad grabbed gravel stones and threw them at the Beast, for all the good it might do as a distraction. "What? No! Come into the basement. That thing's too big to get us there."

"It'll bring the house down on us." Derek gathered power, firing a small energy blast at a tree to get the Beast's attention. "That's where I disappeared to. I learned how to fight, to wield powers."

The Beast's eyes tracked the energy blast. It licked the burned bark where Derek had struck. When it finished, the Beast lumbered toward Derek's house.

The tremendous Beast's hind legs stuck out from around the corner of his house, giving Derek a partial view of it rearing up and smashing against his sister's room. Sounds of splintering wood mixed in with its crunching jaws.

Derek started working on a plan. "I need more time," he told his father. "Can you stall that Beast somehow so I can get my friends together and fight it?"

His father's wide eyes stared down at Derek. "You can't possibly take that thing on."

"We don't have time to debate! Please, trust me and keep Mom and Olivia safe."

"I'll give you a few minutes." His father's expression hardened. "Now go."

Derek ran to the end of his driveway and on.

His ears caught the sound of a car crash and the dying cry of his decrepit car's horn. The Beast's raging howl carried on the wind, scraping over trees.

Derek raced for the spot he knew his friends would be: the bridge where he had opened the portal to the void. Condensation formed from his heaving breaths, making him think he was exhaling smoke.

Occasional crashing noises from behind him mixed with the sound of his own footsteps as he hurried on. Police cars sped past, going in the direction he had fled from, their sirens a deafening wail.

His brick school building came into view. Classmates funneled from the school's parking lot to class, oblivious of the Beast somewhere behind him. He gave the school a wide berth in his race to the bridge.

Rachel was waiting there with her arms crossed. Her foot tapped out a rhythm as she pressed the grass into a groove. She had tied a large cast-iron pot and sleeping bag to the top of her overstuffed backpack.

"You're late," Rachel said. "Luckily, Mr. Marshal runs on Derek, or worse, Tracy time."

Derek's oxygen-deprived lungs fought for air, and his voice was too raspy to be understood. "Help! I need help. Beast."

Tracy pulled up beside them on a bicycle, sweat soaking through her shirt along her spine.

Rachel made tut-tut noises with her teeth. "Why can't either of you ever be on time?"

Tracy checked her phone. "I'm barely ten minutes late." It vibrated in her hand, and she swore. "Allerie is back to sending me patronizing texts. I don't know how she knew I was alive and home, but it's yet another reminder of why I'm glad to say goodbye to this place."

Derek pushed down wells of pity for his friend as he sucked in air. "The Beast's heading this way. I need your help to fight it."

A roar sounded. Derek's heart clenched under unimaginable pressure. He couldn't inhale. The Earth spun as he alone remained still.

A whimper escaped from his lips. "The Beast is here."

34

Thunder And Lightning

Tracy

"HHHHRRRROOOOOOOOOAAAAAARRRRRR!"

Somewhere a few blocks away, the creature that sounded like a T-Rex said hello to Tracy.

"What do we do?" Rachel asked.

"I-I-I don't know." Derek hurried the words, wrestling with whatever ideas bounced inside his head. He unclipped his backpack and removed the leather dress belts holding the sword against his shoulder. He stared at the sword for a few seconds, then placed it, and his backpack, on the ground. "I don't know how to use this sword, so I'm fighting the Beast with my fists and powers. Otherwise, it will stalk me forever."

Rachel's backpack hit the ground with a loud clang. She leaned forward, stretching her calf muscles. "Battle a monster? Count me in."

"You might die."

"You definitely will if you go alone."

"Am I the only sane one here?" Tracy asked. They looked at her as though it was their first time hearing her speak. "Why fight at all?"

Derek stared in the direction of the monster's roar. "Who else can stop it besides us? It's too big now to survive on small animals. That likely means people will be next."

Rachel tapped her phone's screen. "I need to warn everyone that a giant bear is on the loose. They probably won't believe me if I mention the monster part. I'll let the other Earth's Nicole know too. She can tell Flint and Ri Ur Tol to get their asses back here."

"Escaping to the void is by far our best option," Tracy said, hoping her friends would listen.

"You're suggesting fleeing a monster by running at a bigger monster?" Derek replied.

Tracy squinted. "OK, bad idea."

"I'm done running away." Derek raced for the roar coming from the other side of the half-finished homes.

Rachel matched his pace.

Tracy stood still, noting every tree to use as cover.

A blue minivan arced over the line of houses, tossed with strength Tracy didn't want to think about. It crashed into an unfinished roof, breaking into the lower floor. She glimpsed the top of the Beast, in all its two-story-sized glory, as it passed in the space between half-finished houses.

Men and women in hard hats and yellow vests sprinted past her, screaming and pointing behind them at the half-built neighborhood.

"This is going to suck." Tracy took one step in Derek's direction. Then another. Soon she was cutting across a yard and climbing over a six-foot wooden fence.

Stilling her bladder took effort at the sight of what awaited her.

She recognized little of the monster from their brief encounter on the bridge. The Beast had clearly eaten its vegetables. It was a perfectly normal size for a bear, if normal bears were the better part of thirty feet on their hind legs.

The creature's white coat was splashed with dark maroon splotches. The most distressing part was its original skin hadn't grown as much as the rest of it. Instead, bulging muscles stretched its skin taut, displaying every contraction to the world. Its horns no longer pointed forward. They had lengthened and spiraled outward in vain attempts to leap to freedom. In the time since it attacked them on the bridge, the monster's pale eyes had changed to a crimson color that gave the appearance of fires blazing within its eye sockets.

Where the Beast had been too bulky to run around skeleton houses, it plowed through them leaving a trail of wood, mortar, and glass.

The Beast paced on the grassy cul-de-sac island, sizing up the comparatively small Derek standing in front of it.

"How have you gotten bigger in half an hour?" Derek shouted.

Derek's fist punched air, and the Beast swayed, struck by a faint telekinetic outline Tracy couldn't fully see.

The thing swung its paw down on top of Derek. A blur moved him beyond the Beast's reach by less than an inch. In the space where it struck, there were now long grooves carved into the concrete.

The Beast snapped its jaws at Derek who was again moved back by a blur in motion. Tracy was grateful Rachel fought alongside Derek.

Tracy watched a third person crawl across the ground, filming the fight. Allerie raised her phone to get both her face and the monster in the same shot. She made it to the Beast's shadow next to where Derek was holding his own.

The Beast lunged at Derek who raised his hand, deflecting the brunt of the attack using his telekinetic shield. The Beast's weight pushed him back while he shielded Rachel and, unfortunately, Allerie.

Movement at Tracy's side ruffled her shirt. Rachel slowed from a blur, holding Allerie, having extracted her from the fight. "This wannabe influencer was filming her supposed alien invasion," said a winded Rachel. "Get Allerie to safety."

Thinking of every hurtful word Allerie had spat at Tracy, she asked, "Do we have to save her? I'd be okay with a casualty or two."

"Allerie may be reckless, but that doesn't mean she deserves to get hurt."

Tracy clicked her tongue. "Fine, but if she's reckless, what does that make us?"

"Crazy." Rachel flashed a quick grin at Tracy, then took a step to rejoin Derek, only for her legs to give out. "I need a few measures of rest. That monster isn't as slow as it seems and I got clipped."

A snapping sound announced Ri Ur Tol's arrival. She pushed Rachel and Allerie to the ground and then tackled Tracy.

Wayward pale light fired from the Beast's mouth, narrowly missing them. Its crushing back-draft stole Tracy's senses.

Tracy shoved a finger in her ear to clear the ringing.

Ri Ur Tol lifted Tracy and Rachel and brushed pebbles off their clothes. "This is no time for distractions. One hit removes you from more than the fight."

Ri Ur Tol wore sheathed daggers strapped to her sides and back. Tracy counted eight daggers she could see, knowing Ri Ur Tol likely had more hidden on her. Yoga pants looked more out of place on her than the Kevlar body armor she wore over a light shirt.

Popping her ears to ease pressure, Tracy said, "Thanks for the lucky save."

"We were observing. I stepped in. Don't die until the others join us on this hunt."

"I'd prefer not to die at all. Who's with you?"

"Flint, Nicole, and Mr. Marshal."

"That's not enough to bring down a monster this big."

The Beast lunged for Derek.

Ri Ur Tol disappeared, her powers snapping the air. She reappeared instantaneously next to Derek, then they both vanished. The confused Beast's momentum spun it past where Derek was no longer standing.

Still on the ground beside Tracy, Allerie stretched a shaking hand to the burned channel carved from the Beast's blast. She withdrew the moment she touched the smoldering ground, shoving her singed fingers in her mouth.

"This place is too dangerous for normal people," Tracy muttered.

The Beast faced her. Tracy cursed herself for being one of the few targets still in its sight as she, Rachel, and Allerie clumped together.

The Beast opened its mouth.

A white light of pure energy started to rise from its stomach.

Tracy pressed play on her phone. No sooner did music reach her ears than she shifted the surface beneath them according to her will. She transmuted the ground into air. They dropped into an angled hole, coming to a stop behind a solid barricade of soil she'd formed. Scorching heat of the Beast's white light passed inches above her. When it was over, the cool air returned. Tracy was afraid to touch her cheek for fear scalding scars marred it.

She lifted her head from the trench she had formed. Derek was back in the fight from wherever Ri Ur Tol had sent them. His comparatively tiny fist rose to meet the Beast's giant paw, fitting in the gap between claws longer than his arm. Claws dug into Derek's chest and drew blood in the stalemate.

Tracy shook Allerie who huddled by Tracy's feet, "Derek has that thing distracted. Now's your chance. Run and don't stop."

Using her newfound ability to move, Allerie climbed from the hole and ran with the speed of a track All-Star. She sprinted around a house without uttering a single word of thanks.

Snap. Ri Ur Tol appeared next to Tracy. "Are you content to watch the hunt, or will you join so we can die together?"

Tracy moved to the next song on her playlist. Boring and slow, her full power refused to flow. *Next.*

Snap. Ri Ur Tol was gone, stabbing the Beast and teleporting away before it could touch her.

Rachel rejoined the fray. She ran from behind Tracy's makeshift wall to leap at the Beast's claws as they pressed into Derek. Looking like a mouse pushing an elephant, she hit with enough speed to break the Beast's contact with Derek. In retaliation, the Beast lunged for Rachel, but it only caught air. She was already on its other side. Rachel grabbed fistfuls of fur. The Beast made a sound that was equal parts dog yelp and rocket launch.

An unsteady car lifted into the air and hurled at the Beast's back. Sweat dripped from Derek's strained face with the effort. The car collapsed on impact, crushing into itself. The massive Beast sank to the ground, growling and snapping its jaws as it stood. Derek followed through with another telekinetic punch.

Winds picked up around them thanks to the opposing forces clashing between Derek and his enemy. The Beast's deflected slashes sent bursts of air flowing rampant into the street. Each telekinetic punch Derek fired did the same in the opposite direction.

What started as a clear day became overcast under fast-moving clouds.

Tracy rubbed her arms, massaging her long-sleeved shirt to stave off the November chill. She considered creating a jacket but needed all her power to turn the tide of battle. Her shaking fingers searched the music on her phone.

Come on. Give me a song I can work with.

Flint, Nicole, and Mr. Marshal sprinted from behind a house and joined Tracy. Flint sported a dad look. Today's clothing rotation included a plaid blue and black shirt along with a pair of jeans, making him look better suited for hand-washing a car rather than fighting a monster.

Mr. Marshal stood tall against the distant chaos from the Beast and Derek blows. He never flinched at the collisions of claw and mental shield. Oddly, the guidance counselor didn't look out of place on the broken down street. Even the winds surging through the neighborhood had little effect on the man, aside from stirring his empty, tied shirt sleeve. His grim expression made one thing clear: this was not his first battle.

Strong winds ripped through the neighborhood, forcing Nicole to drive Derek's sword into the soil to anchor herself in place. The woman appeared to be plucked from a heavy metal album cover. She seemed ready to charge into a fight against overwhelming odds with her hair swaying about.

"Derek dropped this. Maybe it can help."

At her words, liquid power flushed inside Tracy, every muscle cheering her on to make new transmutations.

"Does he know how to use a blade?" Flint hollered over rising gales. "If untrained, it will hinder him."

Nicole raised her arm in front of her face, protecting her eyes from flinging debris. Though powerless, she stood tall against the wind threatening to scatter them.

"We need every advantage. Unless your expert hands want to claim this, I'm giving the sword to Derek."

With a snap, Ri Ur Tol teleported to where Mr. Marshal and Flint stood. She dropped two broken daggers and drew two more from her arsenal. As her heaving breaths returned to normal, she managed to say, "That thing's skin is too star-spurned tough."

Tracy stepped in front of Nicole, acting as a human shield for the rising winds. "I get Ri Ur Tol and Flint being here, and though I'm not quite used to it, Mr. Marshal now makes sense. They have powers, but why are you here, Nicole?"

"Without Derek, I'm stuck in this world. I'll find a way to help."

Ri Ur Tol put her hand on Nicole's shoulder. "Tracy's brash words carry weight. We obeyed your wishes to bring you to the battle. This is a place for warriors, not you, yet. When next we hunt, I swear you will be ready to fight alongside us."

Nicole refused to be thrown from the fight by the wind. "No. I'm staying as long as I can."

Finally, Mr. Marshal spoke. "I'll protect her and anyone else caught in the crossfire."

The Beast spat another blast of white light. It split around Derek's telekinetic shield, spraying to either side and setting the grass it touched on fire.

Mr. Marshal raised a telekinetic shield, protecting those removed from the battle from being burned. "I thought I saw Mr. Sprog in the perimeter sweep." To Flint and Ri Ur Tol, he added, "He's another teacher at their school."

Tracy couldn't wrap her head around anyone else willingly being this close to the Beast. "Was he trying to do what Allerie did and sneak in close to film the monster?"

"Is he a threat?" Ri Ur Tol asked.

"I don't know. They were too fast and far away for me to see clearly. More importantly, I need to keep you all alive by protecting you and striking when I have an opening. I can't wander away to search for whoever it was."

Tracy didn't care whether it was or wasn't their teacher. The Beast was their biggest concern. "We can debate who's watching this later. Derek's fighting that thing to a standstill. With all of us together, we can bend this fight in our favor."

"Derek and the Beast are not on even footing," Flint stated. "Your wishes cloud your judgment and the advantage is swaying in our opponent's favor. You have not critically wounded that creature as long as the fire it breathes will kill us when we tire."

Ri Ur Tol's eyes were in constant motion, studying every angle of the battlefield. "We will find its weakness."

Snap. Ri Ur Tol stood on the Beast's muzzle, driving her daggers at its face. The creature shot light from its eyes, melting the metal weapons. Ri Ur Tol teleported back to Tracy's side; quick reflexes saved her limbs.

Tracy's finger stopped above the next button on her phone. One of her favorites emerged from the headphones. A good chill coursed through her, turning her mind into a tightly tuned snare drum, ready to keep her friends in time.

Tracy transmuted the concrete below her feet into liquid metal, sending it crawling along her shins to attach at her knees. Her power moved the metal higher, reinforcing her spine, then extending it down both arms and over her head as a series of rods. The heavy exoskeleton hardened. She formed spinning motors to support the rods at her joints. These compressed and released to propel her at the damage-absorbing monster.

She formed a metal encasing over her fist. Mechanized arms drew back, releasing a hammering blow on the unsuspecting Beast.

Her metal fist collapsed on impact like a fan folding in on itself. The Beast stumbled. Tracy leaped sideways and ran for cover, not giving the Beast a chance to retaliate.

"There. I did a thing."

"You OK?" Rachel used her powers to move about, steadily closing in for a strike.

Cupping her hands, Tracy shouted, "For now."

"Back me up?"

"Any time," Tracy replied.

As the Beast brought its paw down on Rachel in her headlong sprint, Tracy transmuted the ground into spikes angled toward the Beast's paw. *Rachel's counting on me.* Tracy pulled more power. Her knees knocked together under the strain of transmuting the dirt into iron from a distance.

The spikes hindered the Beast for a precious second, allowing Rachel a clear shot. She punched its underbelly and kept running.

The Beast roared, rattling Tracy's brain long after it fell silent.

Ri Ur Tol appeared on the solid grass patch of what remained of the cul-de-sac's island, close enough to touch the Beast. Glints of metal flashed. Her daggers rebounded from the monster's skin, giving it a nice shave without drawing much blood.

That close, she was exposed. The Beast's claws grazed Ri Ur Tol as she teleported from the brunt of its counter.

Red droplets colored the grass next to Tracy. Ri Ur Tol clutched her shoulder, blood seeping from beneath the long gash in her body armor. Ri Ur Tol removed the armor altogether, taking a shambling step back to the fight.

Tracy surprised herself by restraining Ri Ur Tol. "Stay here."

Teeth clenched, Ri Ur Tol refused to give in. "This mesh protection caught much of the claw. Remove your hand, else I remove it from your body."

"You know I'm right. There's no excuse to discard your life so hastily."

"Fair." Ri Ur Tol bound her flesh using fabric torn from her shirt. "This injury slows me."

Sirens shrieked. Police cars from ten counties over, and everywhere in between, screeched to a halt at the bottom of the street. Trained police formed a perimeter barricade with their cars.

Nothing prepared those first responders for the thing bulldozing this neighborhood.

A megaphone enhanced voice ordered them from a safe distance, "Run, kids! Get out of there!"

Tracy gathered raw material from the street to transmute long stone spires, which she stabbed at the Beast. "What the hell do they think is happening? We're the ones holding it at bay."

One spire after the next fell apart on impact, doing nothing more than obscuring the monster's view of Derek as he pressed in to attack with mental punches.

Rachel slid to a halt at Tracy's side. "The police don't know what to do. If we stop, we're dead."

The Beast opened its mouth, spreading a miasma of white light aimed at the police.

Tracy transmuted the ground in front of the parked cop cars. The street sank, becoming material she used to raise a solid ten-foot wall of stone. She reinforced her creation with metal braces to protect the police.

Her wall sagged under the light fired from the Beast before collapsing on itself. Fractured shards spewed at the police she struggled to save from the blast.

Flint used his leather bindings to pull the police out of the fray. Flint lowered the terrified men and women, depositing them far from the hazards of battle.

"Stay out of my way," Flint yelled above Tracy's commotion.

"We're on the same side," Tracy shouted. "I was saving—"

The Beast rammed Tracy with the force of a bomb.

Hurled through the air, her senses reeled. Her exoskeleton ground against concrete. Sparks flew. The friction emitted an ear-splitting screech. She came to on a bed of twisted scraps. Her creation had held together about as well as Derek's car on a highway.

Colors solidified. White fur above her. *The Beast is within arm's reach!*

In a last-ditch effort at self-preservation, she touched the Beast, hoping the physical contact increased her ability to transmute it. She hardened the monster's fur as she pictured it becoming a giant chocolate bear. She penetrated no deeper than a patch of its skin and made only a small piece of chocolate at that.

The Beast's low growl brought Tracy's blood to an abrupt halt.

Rot assaulted her from the creature's recent meals, which still clung to its breath.

Pearly canines longer than her arm stretched wide to impale her. Staring into the mouth of her demise, all she thought of was how its teeth had no yellow stains or signs of plaque. This might be the cleanest mauling on record.

Chaos of this fight gave way to a quiet serenity, her last moment in this world.

A snap sounded and air rushed over Tracy. From fifty feet back, Tracy watched the Beast crush her metal skeleton machination between its jaws, with her no longer inside. She squeezed Ri Ur Tol's hand in thanks for teleporting her to safety.

While the Beast freed itself from her metal brace it had chomped through, Derek landed a skull-shattering punch right across the top of its head.

The Beast shook and huffed, kicking up a cloud of dust, then hurled a wave of white light that struck Derek at point-blank range. Instead of blocking it, he deflected the blast into the atmosphere. White light split clouds in a tower piercing the sky. Even at this distance, the heat warmed Tracy's skin.

"Can anyone help me?" Derek shouted above the crackling release he sent into space.

A blur ran into the cul-de-sac. Rachel reached Derek's side.

The Beast opened its mouth to fire vibrant white light that tore open the street in a wide arc.

Light from the blast faded, burning an afterimage into Tracy's eyes. There was no sign of either Derek or Rachel in the trail cut from the street. A lump formed in Tracy's throat.

A near invisible fist hit the Beast's face from above.

Derek, Rachel, and Ri Ur Tol were falling from the sky. Tracy exhaled in relief that the Beast's light hadn't disintegrated them.

Derek let loose, raining telekinetic punches on the Beast's head and shoulders.

Ri Ur Tol teleported the duo to the ground, landing hard from their built momentum. Derek recovered in time to erect a shield and block the Beast's next blast.

The deflected energy split a multi-story family home like it was no more than a dollhouse opening on its hinges. Outlying police officers dove behind the pitiful remains of Tracy's earthen barrier. Apparently, the stunned servants of the people lacked protocols to handle giant monsters clashing with super-powered humans.

Clouds rolled in and darkened the mild day.

Derek's fist met the Beast's paw.

Static in the air raised the hairs at the base of Tracy's neck.

Krk-Aaaah-Krakoom!

Silver-blue jagged lightning struck the ground close enough to make Tracy's teeth chatter. More lightning flashed, scar tissue formed by a planet recoiling as titans danced on its surface. Under the repeated flashes, Derek and the Beast appeared trapped in a series of stop-motion images, locked in their deadly struggle. Swelling winds swirled clouds into a wide spiral.

The clouds unleashed their burdens, dropping heavy, frigid rain. Goosebumps spread up and down her arms. She clutched her drenched shirt closer.

Tracy regrouped next to men and women in navy blue hunched behind broken cars. What remained of her manifested wall provided the barest defense.

Wind tore her skin, so strong it turned trees sideways and tossed trash about at hazardous speeds.

Tracy's toes curled inside her shoes in a useless attempt to remain in place. It took all her willpower to not be sent flying. That, and the metal, knee-high boots she created to anchor her to the ground. The boots dropped her mobility to zero, yet kept her in the fight. The cop next to her wasn't as lucky. A gust caught his jacket, and he flew across the street like a hawk in an updraft.

Under the onslaught of senses, she lost sight of her friends, except Derek and the Beast.

Its muzzle was no longer the color of pure snow, having mixed with rain, mud, and concrete each time Derek knocked it down.

The Beast brought its full two-story weight against her friend. Derek countered with his powers, losing ground with every blow. He alternated between telekinetic punches and outright defense of an erected mental shield. Tracy cringed at each collision and the winds they unleashed.

Clouds spun and twisted overhead. A wide funnel sank toward them from above to meet turbulent vapors rising in a circle not far behind Tracy. This rotating vortex trapped her and Derek with the Beast in the tiny eye of the storm. They were within the one place where the sun now reached. Outside the cul-de-sac, angry skies brought forth their wrath in a deluge of water and hail, pelting the neighborhood. Forked lightning struck houses and trees again and again. Overloaded electric circuits fired sparks, imitating Fourth of July fireworks.

For all the explosions and noise outside the wall of rain and ice, absolute quiet settled over the still air.

In the absence of other sounds, neither foe advanced, locked in the deadliest staring contest Tracy had ever witnessed. Derek bled from gashes all over his body and his enemy limped, keeping weight off one of its front paws.

With an inhuman sound of ribbed steel grating over etched glass, the Beast breathed in. It appeared to swell. That wasn't an illusion. Sinew expanded under sparse, matted fur.

Across the calm eye of the storm, Derek's voice carried. "Why are you haunting me?"

The Beast focused wholly on Derek, the one person standing in defiance against it. Steam billowed from the sides of its mouth.

"Get out of there now, Derek!" Tracy shouted.

Rearing to its towering height, the Beast crashed down on him. Although removed from the fight, the impact reverberated up Tracy's legs. Broken concrete lines expanded from where the Beast struck Derek's shield, hammering him deeper into the ground.

Outside the eye and still in the storm, shifting Earth from the attack swallowed a police car behind Tracy. Those stuck inside banged against glass windows, trying to escape before the ground moved and crushed them.

Flint appeared through the downpour. Using his leather bindings to wrap around the car, he prevented it from sinking deeper.

Tracy gathered power and shifted the ground to push the car out. Ri Ur Tol was faster, saving the police by teleporting into the vehicle and disappearing with its occupants to wherever she was hiding to survive.

Unwilling to give Derek the chance to escape, the Beast pounced on his telekinetic shield like a polar bear breaking a sheet of ice.

Although it held, the force of the blow rocked Derek against the wall of his sphere. His protection reduced him to a mouse trapped in a ball being jostled by a ravenous tiger.

From the distance, Tracy spent more power to protect Derek. Spires of stone stretched from the concrete, reinforcing the outside of Derek's shield. These crumbled beneath the weight of the Beast. Unaccustomed to making large transmutations back-to-back-to-back, Tracy's dwindling abilities weren't cutting it so late in the fight.

She took a step to get to Derek, but fell. Flint helped her up, the two of them supporting each other as they retreated.

"Can your makeshift whips do anything against that monster?" said Tracy.

"Doubtful. I need to draw on inner magic with care," began Flint, "or risk becoming another monster to battle. I've spent most of my power saving the lives of those too close to this, though I may be able to hold the Beast's attention."

Together, they reached Mr. Marshal as he overlooked the fight from the safety of his telekinetic shield.

Tracy howled at him, "I'm helping my friend fight for his life. Please, feel free to not lift a finger."

Mr. Marshal didn't even bother to face her. His attention was captured by the Beast throwing its weight against Derek's shield. "Which is your friend, and how can you tell? This looks like a fight between two sides of the same coin."

"What bullshit are you going on about?" Tracy shouted. "I'll give you a hint. My friend is the one who isn't the growing monster."

The Beast slammed into Derek's bubble with a thud. His telekinetic shield flickered in a sputtering, final breath. The force of the blow to his shield sank Derek to his waist into a crater. Dust showered Tracy.

Again, the Beast pounced. Derek's shield exploded on impact, deflecting the Beast but leaving Derek defenseless. Lashing energy from the shield burned patches of grass and sent up thin lines of smoke.

Unable to control herself, Tracy yelled at Mr. Marshal. "Help him!"

Mr. Marshal's body tensed. "I had hoped Derek would do more."

The Beast's last hit knocked Derek senseless, leaving him cradled in the concrete pocket. The Beast rose on stout hind legs. At its full height, it blocked the sun from view. It dove forward, bringing down what had to be multiple trucks' worth of weight and stealing Tracy's breath.

She transmuted a wall of rock over Derek. Her cracker-thin structure broke before it fully solidified.

The monster was falling, falling to crush her friend.

Raging lightning flowed from the storm and into Mr. Marshal's missing arm. He raised his other hand as the light passed into and through him. Blinding spears fired from his fingers.

The energy emitted created a deafening crack, sending high-pitched waves undulating within Tracy's eardrums.

The lightning ripped the Beast's head apart, leaving it charred and sizzling. Instead of pancaking Derek, the Beast slunk sideways and crashed to the ground with a massive thud.

35

Stolen Breaths

Tracy

Mr. Marshal collapsed in exhaustion next to Tracy. The lightning burned his clothing, leaving shredded pieces trailing from his arm like ribbons. No longer hidden beneath thin layers of his shirt, a patchwork of old scars covered his chest and back. Blisters formed on his fingertips where the lightning had exited.

Tracy was afraid to touch Mr. Marshal, lest the contact shock her and kill them both.

The Beast lay still. Its nose had been burned off to reveal its mouth's musculature structure and teeth. Tracy clenched her stomach and turned from the horror, preferring not to throw up.

With no more powerful attacks fired by Derek and the Beast, the tornado and harsh winds had ceased. The rain and hail outside the eye of the storm dissipated. Mist rose from the ground, billowing and thickening to obscure the unfinished homes as though nature was cleansing the blemish of the fight from view.

Unwilling to question a miracle, Tracy sank to the ground. She could check on Derek in a minute or two, once she took a nap in the middle of the street. Wishing to be far from the Beast's carcass, she lacked all motivation to force herself to move.

Ri Ur Tol trudged toward Derek at a snail's pace. After watching her flit about during the fight with a snap, it seemed odd to see her walk. She stepped over the trails of scorched grass from where the Beast's toxic breath had burned all it touched.

Police who had been tossed about by the gales were getting to their feet and reconvening in the street. Two or three raced to the incapacitated monster with guns raised.

Supported by Ri Ur Tol, Derek limped to Tracy. Tracy doubted if there was a square inch of Derek not openly bleeding or purple with bruises.

Rachel dropped next to a barely conscious Mr. Marshal. "Anyone bring a gallon of coffee?"

Nicole rushed from behind the meager cover offered by the line of cop cars with that stupid sword in hand. "Sorry, I'm all out."

"Why was that monster here in the first place?" Rachel asked.

Tracy didn't want to admit what she observed in the fight. She faced Derek with a sense of fear at her words. "It was hunting *you*, Derek. It only attacked someone else when it couldn't find you or when we prevented it from hurting you."

Derek's shoulders slumped; his brow furrowed. "What did I ever do to that Beast?"

Before Tracy could answer, purple lights emitted from the Beast's mass of thick skin, muscles, and claws. The lights combined into a solid oblong shape surrounding it. Before the Beast disappeared behind the purple covering, a quivering twitch ran along its paw.

Sucking in air, Tracy gasped, "I thought we killed it."

Ri Ur Tol ran to the oblong shape surrounding the Beast and stabbed it with a dagger. Liquid spurted out. Ri Ur Tol dodged to the side to avoid the spray. Meanwhile, grass and concrete touched by the liquid dissolved as though burned by acid.

Derek sat on the ground with a sigh. "Tracy, are you sure the Beast was after me?"

All eyes turned toward her. Blood flushed Tracy's cheeks. She prided herself on how well she handled extra attention when playing on stage, but now their lives rested on her words.

"I wasn't studying it for hours, but I'm pretty certain."

Derek attempted a smile. The result was a grimace, making him appear nauseous.

"We've been lucky so far. This in-progress housing development looks empty, but we aren't far from major roads and lots of people. When that Beast attacks again, I'll lead it from this populated area and figure out how to stop it for good along the way."

"Not alone you won't," Rachel's words flowed with ease.

Tracy followed her example a heartbeat later. "We go together or not at all."

Mr. Marshal's face was a grim mask. "We might have gained a few minutes before that thing continues the fight."

Derek glanced over his shoulder at the Beast. "What? That soon?"

Mr. Marshal nodded. "I've seen this before. We can't risk that monster running free and hurting others."

"Back up," Tracy started. "You've seen another monster?"

Mr. Marshal's legs buckled under his weight. "Yes, and this one's waking up now, so hurry. I'll stay and fight as you run. If this monster chases you, I'll hold it here as long as I can. If it doesn't follow you, then you need to get back."

Ri Ur Tol shifted her feet. "In desperation, you act as a cornered animal. Your magic is spent, and that thing will snack on what little remains of you."

Mr. Marshal pulled himself fully upright. "I'll survive. Assuming Tracy's correct, then I won't need to do more than slow it."

Flint held Mr. Marshal upright. "We fight it together. The rest of you need to run."

Light pulsated from deep within the purple shell surrounding the Beast.

An itch stirred inside Tracy's arm where she was unable to scratch. "We need to go where that thing won't enter. Care for an escape into the void?"

Derek violently shook his head. "As drained as I am, I couldn't open the portal. Even assuming I run to another time or dimension, that leaves our home unprotected like a platter of food to be devoured."

Tracy needed to rally them. No one else offered useful suggestions. They were too busy licking their wounds. "Why don't we plan later and run now?"

Anyone else concerned about the Beast popping from its bubble to kill us?

A deep, rumbling voice followed, flooding her mind and overpowering her sanity.

That is so much more than a bubble. It is a cocoon. Inside, it grows.

The deep inner voice left Tracy shuddering, wanting to never be alone in the dark with its sound. "Stop dawdling and run," she said out loud.

"My magic can get us far," Ri Ur Tol said, "but I need more rest to use it."

The cocoon emitted a hum. Flashing strobe lights inside the cocoon quickened.

Derek clenched his jaw. "Tracy's right. We need to move. I'm going on foot so this Beast won't lose my scent."

"Before I forget, take this." Nicole returned Derek's sword. "I'll wait with the rest of the cops and get people to safety."

Derek flourished the sword with no skill. "Thanks. I need all the help I can get."

Tracy formed a strap for him to latch to his back. That way, he wouldn't trip over it while running and would hopefully decide against using it altogether.

Light burst from the cocoon, skylights announcing another round in a fight no one was ready for. New odors stung Tracy's nostrils, a combination of burning tires and overflowing sewage on a hot day. She gagged, managing not to lose the contents of an already swishing breakfast.

She hurried deeper into the thickening fog, followed closely by Rachel with Derek and Ri Ur Tol trailing. Tracy never ran so fast in her life.

36

Five Minutes

Derek

Derek's feet clopped on damp pavement. Mist thickened around him, the lingering effect of the violent storm created during his brawl with the Beast.

Vague house shapes became looming, cubed shadows. Fog swirled about their sharp corners like tendrils unfurling to ensnare walkers on a morning stroll.

For the first time since obtaining these abilities, he had held nothing in reserve. Unlike his battles in the past, he didn't have to worry about rewriting this present or accidentally killing a person. All he had focused on were the countless reasons to end the Beast.

The sky had opened in retribution from his lack of restraint. With the battle on hold, the rain subsided into heavy mist. The mist blanketed the reeling neighborhood, dropping visibility to a few paces in any direction.

Labored breaths drew water-saturated air into his lungs. Derek's leaden feet dragged longer with each step. The sword attached to his back added weight, slowing him. Derek had no intention of ditching it. The weapon he won from Ur Tol's fight carried a jolt of electricity when he reached over his shoulder to grasp its hilt, offering intoxicating power.

He moved closer to Ri Ur Tol and Rachel to not lose them within the mist. Tracy wheezed worse than him. Her burst of speed at the start expired in the first stretch. She struggled to keep up.

Derek had nothing inspirational to say except the truth, which he gasped out as they ran. "Given the thunder during our fight, it's safe to say the Beast got over its fear of noise once it grew big enough to eat me in a single bite. There went our one advantage."

The crack of a gunshot bounced off recently built, and more recently demolished, freestanding houses. The echoes accosted Derek from all sides until he no longer knew which direction they came from.

Struggling to pierce the fog, he sought to make sense of the suburban labyrinth, passing another curving street identical to the last. He guided them in the direction he thought opened into a park.

No genius strategy shook loose in his head on how to defeat the Beast.

They sprinted up a hill and rose above the mist. Its thickening clouds drifted among empty houses on the lower side of the development as they climbed above it, hiding the Beast and everyone he left behind to fight.

Early morning sunlight baked Derek's skin, removing some of the cold blanket which had settled over him after being caught in the initial downpour. Soaked clothes clung to his skin, adding friction with each swing of his arms.

A second shot rang out, much closer than the first. In quick succession, the sounds of two more shots bounced against the neighborhood houses.

Then silence.

Derek raised his arms above his head to ease the cramping stitch in his side. "I hope Nicole and the police got away. Ready to turn back and check that Flint and Mr. Marshal survived?"

Boom.

Vibrations traveled from the ground up Derek's legs, sending a shudder coursing through his veins.

Ri Ur Tol grabbed his shoulder and urged him on. "No. We keep going."

Boom.

No lightning ripped apart the sky. No thunder clapped from above.

Boom.

Derek fired a gust of wind at their backs to push the four of them a bit faster.

BOOM.

Derek looked over his shoulder.

Two red, glowing pinpricks shone through the fog a mere hundred feet back.

The Beast's open maw lifted above shifting fog. Whatever its cocoon did had fully restored it, sealing the hole in its head and returning it to the same general shape, though at a significantly larger size. Its mouth had reached cavernous proportions and its body was now as wide as the street.

The Beast stepped forward until its entire form emerged from the mist.

"I can't defeat the Beast alone, but we need to split up." Between ragged pants, Derek laid the groundwork of his improvised plan as they ran. "I'll distract it while you three regain strength. Then feed me your power so I can open the way to the void. We lock the Beast inside with the shadow monster and they'll cancel each other out."

Tracy massaged her forearm and flexed her fingers. "Like I said, we should have opened the void already."

Derek shook his head. "This is different from using the void to escape."

Rachel raised her thumb in approval. "I'm in to send the Beast to defeat that shadow monster or vice versa."

"How much time do you need to get that much power to spare?" Derek asked.

Rachel frowned, likely calculating how quickly the Beast would catch him. "Ten minutes. More would be better."

He made his own estimates. "I might hold it for five."

Ri Ur Tol squeezed his shoulder. "I am not familiar with 'minutes.' We will stay near."

Seeing the looming Beast gave him a second wind. "Meet me in five minutes to end this."

The three women turned onto a side street. The Beast sped after Derek without shifting its focus to the women leaving. Tracy was right: it sought him and him alone.

Five minutes. Three hundred seconds. I can do this.

Too slow to lose the Beast, he knew he couldn't hide from it either. Derek drew the blade hanging from his back.

The sword fed him a steady IV drip of energy. Power swelled in taut muscular fibers, igniting his limbs from where he held the sword hilt.

He raced at the Beast. It lifted a paw to squash him.

Derek swung his sword, catching the blow.

Concrete ate his feet as the Beast's weight forced Derek down. The outpouring of his telekinesis supported the sword and prevented him from being crushed.

Globules of warm liquid dripped onto his shoulders. A frothing mouth above revealed a full set of teeth anxiously waiting to rip him apart.

Derek fell to one knee.

He focused solely on the point of contact where his sword held the Beast's paw at bay. All else grew hazy.

He pushed against countless tons of monster all while it assaulted his sense of smell with the strong odor of a wet dog.

A hairline fracture appeared along the length of the blade.

Lest he ruin his best weapon, Derek fired a telekinetic wave sideways at himself. It hit harder than intended, sending him sailing free of the Beast. Derek barrel-rolled, skinning arms and legs over the cracked street.

Getting to his feet, he saw sharp claws swiping to rend his flesh. He dropped flat, narrowly avoiding the razor claws. The Beast's momentum brought its underbelly passing overhead.

Derek sprang. Lost beneath snow-colored fur, he stabbed the sword through skin tougher than solid stone.

The Beast's furious bellows surrounded Derek on all sides. He forced the sword deeper into the Beast. It squirmed, leaking putrid red blood onto him.

The Beast drove its car-sized paw into Derek. He formed a telekinetic shield just before the Beast's paw collided with him. The impact carried through his mental shield and hit his embedded sword.

With a crunch that resonated within his bones, Derek's weapon shattered as both he and the pieces of his broken sword flew. Splinters of his weapon looked like stars in the reflected sunlight as they fell.

Derek bounced and rolled over the concrete. His vision took precious seconds to clear. Blood dripped from scores of wounds all over his body. He released a half-grunt, half-groan in the effort of sitting up.

Shards of his blade littered the street. He reached for his weapon's hilt. One last spark of stored energy traveled into him, a pitiful offering compared to the might of the full sword.

Derek tossed the useless hilt, wondering if he looked as broken as the sword. Derek gathered raw power into his hand, making it glow blue much like if his flesh were on fire. He melded the power into a basketball of spinning energy.

"I haven't seen you since I almost killed Tracy," muttered Derek to the orb in his hand.

Holding the glowing ball to the gashes on his arm and back, he cauterized his wounds.

Derek grimaced at the pain, burying it deep inside. There were bigger problems to occupy his thoughts.

He threw the ball at the Beast's head.

A brilliant light display erupted where it struck. It glanced off the Beast's nose and slid along one side of its face, scalding its fur and skin. Its ear-splitting wail made Derek cringe and cover his ears.

The Beast's eye sealed shut from the wound. Missing swaths of fur revealed tough, wrinkled skin.

How did I ever think I could hold my own against this monster? "I'm so stupid."

"Yes," uttered the Beast.

Throughout his life, Derek heard countless voices, from a baby's squeak to a singer's deep bass. None of them sounded like this. The single uttered syllable was a rusty cemetery gate swinging shut. It was the screeching tires of a twentieth car in a pileup. Not even raging winds from a thousand-foot plummet carried such a sense of dread.

This was inevitable death.

Derek applied every shred of self-control to keep from curling into a ball and crying. A guttural cry escaped his throat. "What do you want?"

The Beast's snarl did nothing to resolve the unanswered question. "Answer me!"

Whether Derek touched some inner working or it was frustrated by their fight, the Beast grabbed him. Sandpaper foot pads scratched across his face.

The Beast tossed Derek into the air and stretched its mouth wide. He arced above the Beast's mouth, falling with nothing to stop him from being eaten. Nothing, except his power.

Derek fired pure telekinetic force from his hands. The steady force held the Beast's teeth from snapping shut like a mental stick stuck in its mouth. Its clenching jaws inched closer together.

The steady telekinetic blasts flickered. Derek's arms shook as his power waned. To give in meant dropping down the Beast's throat. If it came to that, he intended to die by causing the Beast a terrible case of indigestion.

Its slick tongue lobbed over Derek's shoe, sneaking a taste of the main dish.

Derek angled the energy firing from his hands down slightly and expelled more power. The force rocketed him up and out of the Beast's mouth a fraction of a second before its jaws clamped shut.

Derek formed a shield bubble, though the impact with the ground jarred his senses. He dragged himself onto his knees, ignoring aching muscles.

Clinging to life, Derek trusted in his abilities even as his body refused to work. Power sprang from his mind. He raised his head and opened his mouth, emitting a yell so primal it shook the ground.

His vision went in and out of focus. Red sparks flew from his fingertips, ripping his skin apart. Stones by Derek's feet shot to the four corners of the Earth. He was losing control of these powers, of his very being. It was glorious to give in. He fell ever deeper into the river of hate surging at the Beast.

The Beast lowered its face to a foot above Derek. Its charcoal black nose sniffed Derek, in all his sweaty musk. If the Beast had any sense of smell, Derek did more harm now than with his sword.

Derek gave a ferocious roar and smashed his fists into the concrete street. Pounding the ground once more, he used the force to propel himself at the Beast.

Behind quivering lips, a snarl brushed over its teeth.

Derek's clenched fists smacked the side of the Beast's muzzle. He hardly registered the nerve-rending agony shooting throughout his arms. He was too focused on how he deserved to live and, by association, how the Beast deserved to die. Sharp edges of energy formed from his fingertips. He raked them over the Beast's face.

The Beast swatted at him, surrounding Derek with teeth and claws. The Beast caught him squarely in the chest with the backside of its paw. Flying and spinning, Derek bounced and eventually came to a stop.

When his rattled head cleared, Derek studied the Beast. What a sight it was. The already gigantic Beast hit another growth spurt. Shaggy fur dropped in thick patches and clumps. In its place, leathery skin stretched, breaking apart in places to form crimson scales across its arms. The Beast's flesh bubbled, swelling in size.

It was unfair. Derek would have sacrificed anything in his possession to be granted such awe-inspiring might. He regretted ever believing he had the means to protect his home and friends.

Adrenaline drained from his veins and was replaced by unending fatigue. His shoulders sagged and his eyes drooped while more power gathered inside the Beast.

More power. More power.

All the power I'm hitting the Beast with makes it stronger.
I'm feeding the Beast.

Derek's insides writhed as though the Beast's claw speared his gut.

With a single step closer to Derek, the Beast sent an earthquake tearing through the community. Having surpassed the limitations of muscle, sinew, and skeleton, the giant was shattering under its bulk even as it shattered their surroundings. Audible snaps of the creature's bones breaking due to its increasing size brought Derek the faintest sign of hope.

Skin dripped from the Beast's face, drastically changing from the face he first saw in his backyard. Its nose elongated and its fangs jutted at new angles, cutting holes in the side of its mouth. Its remaining eye burned red with no less intensity.

Faster than a thought, the Beast knocked Derek onto his back. It stood on him, pressing into his chest.

He thought he understood pain. Pain was the body's warning to stop to prevent serious injury. Fire burning your hand? Move farther from the heat. Break your leg in a fall? Don't climb a tree until its branches break. Those were simple to comprehend. Never in his life had Derek experienced this flavor of pain. It kneaded his insides and squeezed life from him.

What little air remained in his lungs escaped as a hoarse scream.

He spat rising bile.

Colors danced over his vision.

Pressure fled as suddenly as it started. Relief flooded Derek's trembling limbs, allowing him to breathe again. The Beast no longer used his chest as a stepping stone.

The Beast's lips flexed, giving it the impression of smiling in the same way a cat smiled at a mouse who had its tail caught in a trap.

Derek pushed past stabbing pains from every muscle and joint, commanding his useless legs to stand.

White light spilled from the Beast's mouth in an attack meant to burn Derek to cinders.

Derek couldn't roll clear of the flowing energy. Summoning all his power, he fired his own blast in the false hope of taking the Beast with him.

He let loose one last hearty laugh of defiance.

37

Falling

Derek

Snap. In the space between himself and oncoming death, a figure appeared and came into focus as the perfect silhouette of long, swaying hair.

Derek didn't know whether to be furious at Ri Ur Tol for choosing to die with him or grateful.

Snap.

The beam of white light emitting from the Beast's gaping jaws cut into the street, raising a mountain of dust. Derek watched from a safe distance. Melted concrete was all that remained of where he had been standing.

Rachel slowed from a blur with Tracy at her side. The four of them lined up to die together. Rachel showed him the stopwatch on her phone's screen.

"You held out for two hundred and forty-seven seconds. What happened to five minutes?"

Derek's words cracked under the strain of using his voice for more than screaming. "I got too arrogant."

Tracy snorted. "Arrogant? You?"

The Beast nudged the smoking ground, looking for Derek's remains.

Rachel leaned forward, stretching her toes like a champion athlete warming up. She made it as far as her ankles.

"Considering all the commotion you caused a block over from us, you didn't make our job of resting to regain our powers easy."

"When we watched the Beast swell above the rooftops, we hurried here," Ri Ur Tol explained. "We *ran* to conserve my magic, but when we found you in dire trouble, I acted."

The Beast's head swung from side-to-side, stopping when it saw him standing with the others. "The Beast absorbs my power," Derek admitted.

"No wonder it's attracted to you," Tracy said.

Derek considered what little he knew of the creature. "There's more to the Beast than attraction. It hasn't eaten all the power I threw at it."

Ri Ur Tol stuck her hand out, gesturing to everyone to add their hands to the pile. "No time to talk. Derek, form a bubble around us. We'll steal the time needed to give our power to you."

He obeyed, creating a psychic ball to hold the four of them. Rachel and Tracy placed their hands on top of Ri Ur Tol's. Derek added his hand on top, and said, "This is going to—" *Snap.* Ri Ur Tol shifted them to another place before his thoughts finished with, "—suck, right?"

Gray vapor obscured everything outside his barrier. Condensation streaked up from the bottom of his shield. There was a twinge in the back of Derek's mind as he puzzled over whirling motions outside.

"Where are we? Do I want to know?"

Ri Ur Tol was the only one not looking outward. Her gaze was locked on their pile of touching hands. "A safe place."

Derek's arm tingled. His scrapes and bruises didn't fade, but their discomfort lessened. Soothing warmth spread from their hands into his, then up his forearm and throughout his body.

Rachel's bell-like voice rang out, sending more of her energy into Derek. "Here's your power-up."

While he had lacked the will to stand, his limbs regained their strength thanks to donated power from Ri Ur Tol, Rachel, and Tracy.

Tracy's eyes carried a hunger Derek failed to recognize. "Open the void when you see the Beast."

With the rising power, Derek thought more about this Beast. Ripping open a portal to the void wide enough for two people had been a strain. He couldn't imagine opening one to fit the Beast. Even opening a smaller portal to tear off one of the Beast's legs was beyond his current power.

His stomach rolled in knots from more than just the thought of facing the Beast. He vaguely recognized the sensation.

It's almost as if we—

Bright daylight drowned his senses. They dropped from the clouds into open air.

Derek got out, "You didn't," before realizing the futility of saying more.

They were falling and had been since arriving. His palpitating heart reminded him how much longer they still had to go before being stopped by the ground. Trees and houses weren't the size of a child's playset, yet, but they approached quickly.

Physics equations for dropped objects and terminal velocities ran through Derek's head. Anything to distract his mind from the fall itself.

From their vantage height, he understood the neighborhood's design was centered around the park and shopping center. One lucky home was about to win a free sky roof and paint job when the sudden conclusion to this fall pulverized their bodies.

With nerves of steel, Rachel stared at their hometown. "What a view."

Derek traced familiar routes, both of pavement and water. He looked down and moved his foot ever so slightly, covering the bridge to pretend he wasn't falling. Hiding it from sight did nothing to abate what felt like an invisible hand clutching his throat.

"Ow," Tracy shouted to him. "You're holding too tight."

Derek loosened his grip, looking into the distance and trying to do anything but glance directly below. "Whose idea was it to do the Beast's work for it by killing us?"

Consumed by fear, both from the falling and the inevitable end to their fall, Derek hurled telekinetic force upward to meet them. For a split second, they slowed.

Ri Ur Tol smacked his hand. "No. Our offered strength is for you to defeat the creature."

This woman had no clue about gravity. Derek watched the surface of the Earth hurtling at them. "We're going to die if I don't levitate us and stop our fall."

"Worry not," she said. "Combine our magic and burn no more of your own."

As they continued falling, Ri Ur Tol looked up and inhaled sharply. She shoved him and Rachel to opposite sides of his bubble.

"What the—" Derek started, landing flush against his telekinetic wall.

Roughly six-foot long upper and lower canines pierced the bubble. Ri Ur Tol saved him from the Beast that appeared above them. Derek did all he could to hold his mental shield together against the tons of pressure applied by the Beast's jaws. Its warm breath fogged his telekinetic shield.

Together they spiraled in a plummet to their deaths. Derek's face pressed against the wall of his shield as they spun.

Rachel punched the giant tooth. She winced and shook her hand.

Tracy flattened against the telekinetic shield wall to be as far from the nearest tooth in the limited space. "What do we do?"

Ri Ur Tol reached around the tooth, grasping Derek's ankle. "Brace yourselves."

"With what?" Derek asked.

Snap.

A few feet above Derek's head was a river. His feet faced the blue sky. Up became down and down became up. Rather than smashing into the body of water, the speed built while plummeting flipped when Ri Ur Tol's abilities spit them out and moved them in the opposite direction.

Ri Ur Tol is a genius!

Flying up, his shirt flapped and bunched at his neck. Gravity slowed them until it pulled them back down toward the river. Derek's feet went from pointing up to aiming at the horizon.

Ri Ur Tol lost her grip on him, sending Derek twisting about as he fell.

His back skidded over the river's surface. A frigid clutch took hold of his spine at the touch of the water. It made him gasp, filling his mouth with cold water and chilling him from the inside out.

Waterlogged clothing dragged him under. Kicking his legs, he guessed at the way to fresh air. Murky silt clouded his vision.

Numbness spread to his extremities, and he kicked in a new direction. Derek's head broke the surface of the slow current.

Tracy sputtered water next to him. "There had to be better places to land."

They swam to shore. "I didn't want a bath either," Derek said. "Ri Ur Tol did save us from being eaten or turned into pancakes."

Rachel flopped from the water a little upstream, throwing Ri Ur Tol onto the embankment. Derek and Tracy collapsed next to them.

A gigantic impact exploded nearby, spraying them with water and muck with the force of a bomb.

The newly formed crater diverted the river's flow. The Beast was sprawled in the center of the deep depression. Steadily filling water and fading fog caressed the mass of leathery flesh and white fur. Much like a pie splitting in the oven, red and black inner fillings spilled over and soaked into the mud. Cracked bones punctured its hide. One paw dangled by a thread of muscle.

For a perfect moment, the Beast's immense form lay still.

Then, its leg stirred, unleashing a cracking noise, which carried the subtlety of a tree falling in his backyard. With the creaks and groans of a dilapidated house lashing itself together, the Beast's tendons stretched between broken bones, dragging innards back inside and reconnecting nerves in flaccid limbs.

Air left the Beast's lungs, whistling over holes in its jaw like grunts from Death itself stuck in an echo chamber.

Derek turned to his friends. "I can't do it. I can't open a portal to the void large enough to swallow this Beast, and that was our last chance."

Tracy slammed her fist into a puddle, flinging mud about. "What do you mean you aren't opening the void?"

Rachel heaved herself upright to stand. "We didn't come this far to give up."

"I'm not," Derek said. "We need a new plan."

"One that'll work, meaning not your typical Derek mess." Tracy grabbed him, power flowing from her hands into him. "I have just the thing."

An unquenchable shudder spread over Derek's arm from her touch. Seams on his right shirt sleeve ripped open. His arm grew.

Bones crunched, resisting their change. Derek let air slowly in and out to soothe the sensation of millions of ants burrowing inside his arm. He flexed a hand that was disturbingly baseball mitt-sized. His knuckles popped at the motion.

Tracy's work made his arm three times its original size. The added weight pulled him off balance. He fell to one side, propping himself up by his enlarged arm.

Through a grimace, Tracy spoke. "This worked when that Tak's son toppled the wall I created."

Derek steadied the heavy arm. Its larger size allowed a greater reservoir of power to be contained within. Wringing every ounce of his power to the singular cause, his organs felt like they were corroding.

His chest threatened to burst, making breathing next to impossible.

Hold it together, body, just for a little longer.

Derek swung his arm, getting a feel for its heft, easily a match for the rest of his weight. A cart pulled by turtles might have moved faster.

Skin on his enlarged hand ruptured, spurting a ribbon of blood. "It's a good start, but I'll need more to stop this Beast."

Rachel placed her hand over Tracy's, sending more power into him. "Don't let this be our end."

Their power ascended, three spirits melding together. Derek's back straightened, his burdens leaving, floating free to harass someone else.

The ground shook.

The Beast's one working paw lifted and dropped again, dragging itself closer to them.

Long chords from inside the Beast bound its mostly severed paw back in place. Flesh folded, stretched, and melded together at the joint until Derek could no longer tell that its limb was ever on the verge of detaching.

Derek swung his arm as a test. To him, it appeared to move as slowly as before. Yet, he watched the wind catch Rachel's individual hairs with the urgency of a lazy Sunday afternoon. Her eyes followed the motion well after he stopped. Relative to them, his arm would have been moving as a speeding blur.

"Thanks."

The Beast rolled onto its stomach. Its paws reformed to support the horror brought to flesh. It took a step closer. Its sickle claws sliced hapless saplings in the way.

The three women stood beside him. Derek had never been flushed with so much pride for those he called his friends.

"I will get you close," Ri Ur Tol uttered, adding her hand and strength to the mix.

Energy pumped alongside blood in Derek's veins, injecting raw power into every cell. Although it ripped him apart from the inside, he had never been so alive.

Within his head, Derek found the strange circle Flint once described. He plucked the strands one at a time, rather than strum multiple Aspects.

Snap. The Beast was at arm's length.

Ri Ur Tol held his normal-sized shoulder, offering her power until the last second.

The gargantuan form in front of Derek was too large to see in its entirety. He leaned back, but still most of it remained out of view.

Wet, mud-covered claws flashed. The Beast pounced, throwing its full weight onto Derek to end him with the single hit.

Power sparked from Derek's lungs to heart to stomach. The world outside his thoughts slowed. The creature's crawling movement gave him time to think before it reached him.

Throughout the battle, the Beast had feasted on Derek's attacks when he let his hate and fear infuse his punches. That was when the Beast grew. Derek resolved to not repeat his same mistakes and continue feeding it any longer.

Unburdened by stewing anger, Derek took a deep, full breath on a sea of calm.

He wound his Tracy-enhanced arm back, stumbling with the shift in weight he used small telekinetic bursts to keep his balance.

Shining metal caught his eye. Part of his broken sword protruded from the Beast's skin. He adjusted, aiming for the lodestone already stuck inside this creature.

Moving at a normal speed, the wounded creature's rasps beckoned while its claws sought Derek's flesh. "End. Pain."

Derek struck, not with uncontrolled rage as before, but with a clear mind and purpose. Their fight was wrecking his hometown and threatened those caught too close. It needed to stop.

His punch drove the blade deeper until his fist collided with the rigid coating of the Beast's skin, *his* Beast.

Arm buckling, Derek didn't allow a minor detail like pain to slow his driving force. The summation of his power, and that of his three friends, channeled through the embedded blade, traveling deeper inside his Beast.

Lines of his fired energy illuminated its skeleton.

Three bodies recoiled under the blast.

His Beast hit the ground with a thunderous slam a moment before Derek and Ri Ur Tol did.

Straining his neck, Derek watched his impressive foe in the empty aftermath of the destruction they caused. Its body expanded and deformed as energy he shoved into it sought means of escape along internal highways.

His Beast thrashed, coating Derek in dirty water.

Its breathing grew shallow. His Beast settled into stillness, the sounds leaving its mouth closer to whimpers than savage growls. Even the horns and hideous protrusions receded.

The creature's coughing fit splashed red flecks from the back of its throat. Its one eye stayed on Derek. Any fury once held in that large, burning sphere mellowed as its color returned to the original pale shade.

Neither Derek nor his Beast spoke. No words needed to be said.

His head sank with an exhaustion which made it too heavy to move. Darkness flooded his senses until he succumbed to the serene sounds of the babbling river.

Thoughts faded. Each breath took in less air than the last. Someone's hand held his, though Derek was too far gone to know who it belonged to.

38

Through

Derek

A blistering burn of fire and ice wracked Derek from the inside out, spreading through every extremity. He wore his pain closer than the rags he'd used as his clothes. A building-sized spike seemingly bore through his temple, pressing deep into a broken mind.

He tried to wiggle his fingers. One hand responded. The other made him scream. It was as though he awoke after falling asleep on his arm, and frozen shards stabbed him when feeling returned. He couldn't bear to look at his arm.

He licked cracked lips, tasting blood.

Time slid as he wrestled for control of fleeting thoughts. He must have lost consciousness.

Opening his eyes was a struggle worse than any past torture. As soon as he managed the feat, he regretted it. Spears of sunlight stabbed through clouds. The brightness scraped the back of his skull.

Light-brown eyes fringed with red streaks stared down at him. Chestnut hair hovered loosely over Derek's face. It was too difficult to tell where Tracy's falling salted tears ended and the cool mud caked to his cheeks began.

"Everyone okay?" Derek attempted to speak, though he had no idea what he really said.

"Shhhhh," Tracy whispered, glancing down.

Derek followed her gaze to find two white rods protruding from his arm, which had returned to its regular size. The snapped bone pierced through his skin. Red seeped from his wound, soaking the mud.

"I'm not a doctor," Tracy said. "I used my power to shrink your arm back to normal but didn't dare try to fix it."

Careful to not shift his body, Derek took stock of what little was in sight. They lay on the slanted edge of a massive crater he had formed when he fired all his power. Water pooled into a small pond at the bottom, fed by the river's changed flow.

Then he saw his Beast.

It lay by his feet, having shrunk back to a polar bear's size, albeit a large one. Though faint, its sides rose and fell in a steady pattern. Clumps of brown mud fell from gray-white fur like honey dripping from a beehive. If its horns remained, they were hidden beneath fur. His Beast huffed, exposing its canines, now no longer than a human finger.

There was little left of the terrifying Beast who tore this neighborhood apart. Rather, the creature appeared as it had on the day he revealed his powers to Tracy.

Resting on its belly, his Beast's ghostly pale eyes watched him. Its paw delicately rested on Derek's foot, sending power into him, which steadied his breathing.

Tracy's hand slid from Derek's chest. "I thought we lost you. You had no pulse."

Tiny shreds of laughter welled inside Derek. Each shake hurt, but he couldn't help it. After fearing his Beast for so long and sacrificing himself to stop it, his Beast was the reason he was alive.

"Did you give me mouth to mouth?"

"Don't make me hit you. In your condition, that's a death blow, and I'd feel bad about ending Derek the Magnificent."

"We aren't dead yet?" Ri Ur Tol groaned, crawling toward them.

Shrugging hurt Derek's ribs as much as his meager laughs.

Ri Ur Tol ripped the remains of his shirt into two long pieces. Her graceful hands bundled his arm against his chest and tied the cloth around his neck to support it.

"This needs a more capable hand than mine to fix."

Rachel appeared over the rim of the crater, pulling the rest of them up on their feet. "I like the Beast much better at this fun size."

Derek stared at the living creature. "Back when I first showed my powers to Tracy, I created my Beast or made it my own. My anger has fed it since. I guess that last hit reset it." Derek wiped rainwater from his face. "At least that's the first explanation to make sense. Then again, I probably have a concussion, so my thinking's shot."

Derek found no desire to slay his weakened Beast. He hoped the moment of mercy meant something to the great being.

His Beast stood, no longer emitting any earth-shattering footsteps to rattle through Derek's legs. A winding yawn escaped it; the kind Derek let loose on weekends when his mom woke him before noon. His Beast stared at him for a moment longer, then wandered out of the marsh, its paws making sloshing noises in thick mud. Soon, those sounds were lost.

Derek inclined his head in the direction the creature left. "Whether it returns as friend or foe, we'll be ready."

Rachel stepped under Derek's arm, carrying most of his weight. "We need a doctor to patch us up and the nearest hospital is three miles."

Tracy smacked her phone, water spilling from the headphone jack. "Anyone have a working phone? I don't suppose Ri Ur Tol can teleport us?"

Ri Ur Tol wobbled on her feet and shook her head.

Rachel started toward the highway. "Then I guess we're walking."

"I have a better idea," Tracy cheered. "We hitch a ride on an ambulance after we get Cold Snap gelatos."

* * *

Derek awoke in a hospital bed. As if by magic, he had been treated overnight. He was thankful he had been mostly unconscious when the ambulance arrived at the Cold Snap. From there, they were taken to the hospital without too many questions.

The police were awestruck by the teenagers who saved their lives and stopped the Beast rampaging through the otherwise peaceful suburbs. With enough favors called in by those same police, including a few to frantic parents to smooth over hospital consent forms, they hurtled through the emergency room in record time.

Derek was the unlucky one who needed surgery. The rest had their wounds sewn shut and patched before he was fully prepped.

When he woke up in the hospital bed, the rising sun peeked through his window. His arm felt tender beneath the hard cast and he had a month of recovery to look forward to. The encyclopedia of other injuries to his legs, neck, and chest risked tearing open as he sat up.

Tracy and Rachel waited at his bedside, along with his mom. Tracy handed him a handwritten note.

"It's from Mr. Marshal, and I quote, 'Those not of this time or dimension have returned to my training grounds. Meet at the same designated time and location as before. This time, don't get sidetracked.'"

The words sank Derek's heart, but he saw reason in the need to get stronger.

He hugged his mom goodbye and promised this wouldn't be the last time. He changed his clothes and stopped in a nearby room to say bye to his dad. The brave man had fought against the Beast armed with only Derek's car, and he needed a good number of stitches. His dad was asleep, so Derek left the hospital, vowing to visit him soon.

No one seemed willing to stop the supposed monster-slayers on their way out.

After a short drive, he sat with Rachel and Tracy on a bench, waiting to be picked up. Behind them stood the bridge leading to the Cold Snap.

Derek tugged at the gauze and plastic brace wrapped around his arm. It yanked another hair every time he moved. He imagined how much removing the cast was going to hurt.

A carful of students stopped for a coffee breakfast at the expense of arriving late to school.

Derek pointed to them, nudging Tracy. "It's a shame they didn't even receive a two-hour delay for yesterday's tornado."

He checked Tracy's newly created phone. Their guidance counselor was late to his own invite. Taking advantage of the lack of punctuality, Derek practiced the speech he intended for Mr. Marshal.

"I've decided I'll be a good soldier and train, but I'm doing it on my terms. This life is worth fighting for and living in. Starting tomorrow, I'm going back to school while we train."

Tracy's eyes shifted in the direction of Highland View High School. "Are you sure you want to contain all our power in what we used to be? I mean, why learn about history when we experienced it?"

Scattered memories of bathing in anger while battling his Beast replayed in his mind. Like a movie on his computer with a questionable Internet connection, parts skipped, others blurred, and a few seemed to make time stop.

"My ego came close to costing us everything. I need to stay here to remain grounded instead of living in some ivory tower."

Rachel nodded. "I agree. I like my life, and dammit, I put a lot of work into the here and now."

"Of course you would," Tracy muttered. "I guess I'll stick with you two and make sure you learn the *best* ways to use our powers."

A few minutes later, Ri Ur Tol teleported in front of them, appearing without a care whether regular people saw her. Discretion was one of many things to discuss about their present world.

Bandages dotted her body, making her look worse than Flint with his leather bindings. A sickening guilt flooded Derek's gut. Unleashing the decisive punch into his Beast decimated not only himself and his Beast, but Ri Ur Tol, who was caught too close.

Though not one to normally smile, her eyes carried a brightness Derek and his friends lacked at this early hour. "I'm glad your injuries have not left you immobile," said Ri Ur Tol. "It is my duty to collect you three stragglers. Flint and Nicole are already there."

Tracy raised her hand. "Is anyone else impressed that my translators survived that battle?"

"I'm too tired to care," Derek answered. "Although, I owe you big for saving all our lives at the end of the fight."

Tracy nodded. "None of you respect true talent." She hopped up and grabbed Ri Ur Tol's hand. "Get us out of here then."

Rachel stuck her hand on top and added, "Training montage, here we come."

Derek heaved a throaty grunt as he stood, sounding like his grandfather trudging about during a snowstorm. Putting his hand on the pile of the three others, he said, "Next time, I'll be better. Together, we'll keep my Beast from attacking our home again, and we'll find the version of me lost in the void."

A tug pulled from his navel, sending Derek through space with a snap.

ACKNOWLEDGMENTS ▌

This novel has been a labor of love. For everyone in my life, I cannot possibly thank you enough or adequately express what you mean to me.

First and foremost, thank you to my loving wife and alpha reader. Adriana, you encouraged me everyday and refined my words so they're coherent.

Thank you to my supportive family. To my parents: Mom and Steve, thank you for providing an embracing home for my creativity to flourish and allowing me the freedom to chase after my writing dreams. To my siblings: Dan, Joe, Emily, and Jon, I love you all, even when we fought as kids. If the love shown by the siblings in this story seems to strike a chord, then you may be remembering the moments that inspired my writing. To our growing family: Yael, Jackie, Ryan, and Alexis, thank you for sharing your varied and incredibly creative interests. To all of my aunts, uncles, and cousins who made your houses feel like my home, thank you Essie, Mike, Carol, Ruthie, Harry, Roni, Jeff, Jim, Geoffrey, Alex Gunter, Josh, Jeremy, Matthew, Zachary, Michelle, and Alex Gurbein. To my loving grandmothers, Wilma and Hedy, you indulged my love of books when I visited and fostered a love of exploring the worlds within them. Thank you to my in-laws: Kendra, Dave, Kaiden, and Connor, who welcomed me into your home and always treated me like a member of the family. Thank you to Leandra and Phil, mom and dad, you believed in me through this entire journey, and were stalwart supporters of the stories I wanted to tell.

To everyone in my Discord writing group, thank you! Brennan Bishop and Marc DeGeorge, you found me when I lost hope in meeting helpful writing partners to improve my rough manuscript. We inspired one another with our endeavors and I'm always excited to read your latest manuscripts.

For everyone in the AuthorTube community, thank you for pushing me to publish this novel. It has been a loooooong journey and each of you has moved me closer to my dreams. Shanon (S.D.) Huston, Morgan Lee, Barrett Laurie, Richard Holliday, Martin Lejeune, Author JM Celi, Margaret Pinard, Author Lauren Adele, Nicole The Blind Mage, Books by Adrian, Amy Rosenfeldt, Natalie Locke, Nia the Vixen of Fiction, Mr. Vlandus, and too many more to name, I would never have had the courage to publish this novel without you.

To my friends in real life who I tricked into reading this novel, thank you Jordan Effron, Max Saperstone, Joshua Chapman, Brian Posner, Greg Roberts, Todd Koren, Michael Schwartz, Joseph Lewis, Greg Taylor, Kim Taylor, and Andrew Huber. Thank you for putting up with my ramblings about a vague story I wanted to eventually write.

Thank you Josh Angell and TJ Braley for procrastinating with me and talking about all things storytelling when we should have been working.

There are far too many additional people in my life to thank as it truly took hundreds of people to bring this work to you. If we know each other in real life, know that you matter to me.

ABOUT THE AUTHOR

Ben Pick is an avid runner and application security analyst who enjoys writing character-focused stories in his spare time. He also posts weekly videos on YouTube about the writing process on his channel, Running2Write, where he compares writing to the struggles of running. He loves getting lost in worlds, from the books and games he enjoys to the stories he creates. When not writing, running, or gaming, he takes care of the laziest Plott hound in the world.

Did you enjoy the adventures of Derek, Tracy, and Rachel? Sign up for the Running2Write newsletter via the link or QR code to get updates on future books and the first two chapters of book two!

https://eepurl.com/hv7755

CPSIA information can be obtained
at www.ICGtesting.com
Printed in the USA
BVHW041211290722
643329BV00003B/45